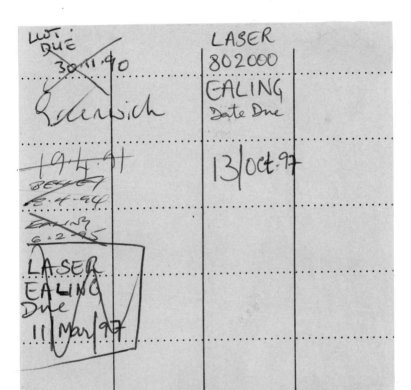

Wandsworth

FICTION RESERVE

Battersea Park Library
Battersea Park Road
LONDON SW11 4NF
01-622 7483

THIS BOOK SHOULD BE RETURNED OR RENEWED BY THE LATEST
DATE SHOWN ON THIS LABEL, UNLESS RECALLED SOONER

L.121

THE PLUTONIUM FACTOR

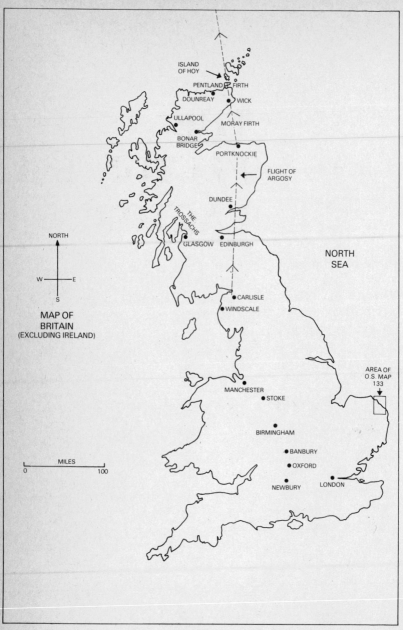

ISLAND
OF HOY

PENTLAND FIRTH

DOUNREAY

WICK

ULLAPOOL

MORAY FIRTH

BONAR
BRIDGE

PORTKNOCKIE

FLIGHT OF
ARGOSY

DUNDEE

THE
TROSSACHS

GLASGOW

EDINBURGH

NORTH
SEA

NORTH

W—E

S

MAP OF
BRITAIN
(EXCLUDING IRELAND)

CARLISLE

WINDSCALE

AREA OF
O.S. MAP
133

MANCHESTER

STOKE

BIRMINGHAM

BANBURY

MILES

0   100

OXFORD

NEWBURY

LONDON

THE PLUTONIUM FACTOR

Michael Bagley

Allison & Busby
London

First published in Great Britain 1982 by
Allison and Busby Limited,
6a Noel Street, London W1V 3RB.

British Library Cataloguing in Publication Data:
Bagley, Michael
  The plutonium factor.
  I. Title
  823^1.914[F]   PR6052.A/

ISBN 0-85031-485-2

Set in 10/11 Times by Top Type Phototypesetting Co. Ltd., London, W1.
and printed in Great Britain by The Camelot Press, Southampton.

Contents

FAUST: Go bear these tidings to great Lucifer:
Seeing Faustus hath incurr'd eternal death
By desperate thoughts against Jove's deity,
Say, he surrenders up to him his soul,
So he will spare him four-and-twenty years,
Letting him live in all voluptuousness;
Having thee ever to attend on me,
To give me whatsoever I shall ask,
To tell me whatsoever I demand,
To slay mine enemies, and aid my friends,
And always be obedient to my will.
Go and return to mighty Lucifer.

Christopher Marlowe, *The Tragical History of Doctor Faustus* (1604)

Plutonium has a half-life of 24,000 years.

MEPHISTOPHELES: A task that gives me little cause to shrink,
I'll readily oblige you with such treasures.
But now, my friend, the time is ripe, I think,
For relishing in peace some tasty pleasures.
FAUST: If I be quieted with a bed of ease,
Then let that moment be the end of me!
If ever flattering lies of yours can please
And soothe my soul to self-sufficiency,
And make me one of pleasure's devotees,
Then take my soul, for I desire to die:
And that's a wager!
MEPHISTOPHELES: Done!

Goethe, *Faust* (1805)

————

For my wife

Author's Note

There are four main types of nuclear reactor in operation in Britain, or in process of construction: the Magnox Reactor, the Advanced Gas-Cooled Reactor (AGR), the Pressurized Water Reactor (PWR) and the Fast Breeder Reactor. The first three are thermal or "conventional" reactors — that is they use *uranium* as their fuel. The Fast Breeder, on the other hand, uses *plutonium*, or, rather, reprocessed plutonium oxide.

The Department of Energy says: "The case for the fast (breeder) reactor rests on its ability to make use of the plutonium and depleted uranium which are by-products of thermal reactors. Without the fast reactor, shortages of natural uranium could begin to constrain nuclear power station ordering beyond the end of the next decade" (21 December 1979).

The Fast Breeder has been in development in Britain since the 1950s and the experience gained has given the country an international position as world leaders in Fast Reactor technology. It is seen by many as *the* energy development of the future. At the moment we have one experimental Fast Breeder at Dounreay on the north coast of Scotland and a reprocessing plant, which supplies the plutonium fuel, at Windscale in Cumberland.

The author is convinced that what follows is possible. Indeed, it is that conviction which led him to write this book. But it is not his intention to provide a blueprint for any criminal mind so inclined. He has therefore not only deleted one or two key facts (the word "deleted" will appear in the text), but also deliberately changed others, because he does not wish to precipitate the events he is trying to avoid by writing the book.

However, the places and statements of fact are real and accurate. The people, though, are a product of the author's imagination and any reference to individuals, alive or dead, is purely coincidental.

PROLOGUE

Thursday, 8 May

THE TOWN had about three dozen small houses and four or five larger buildings. They formed two rows on either side of a dusty road, ending in a square, in the centre of which stood the church and, beside it, a well. The buildings were all made of white stone, with black holes for windows and doors, all shutters closed against the heat of the day.

The cantina, like all the dwellings, was flat-topped and flat-sided. The owner had rigged a large canvas awning outside, that had faded a dull, yellow-green colour, with several battered tables and chairs scattered around underneath. At this time of the day it was seldom used, his customers preferring the cooler air inside. But yesterday the two strangers had arrived by helicopter — an Englishman and an American.

As he stopped at the door the owner saw them, out there sipping their beer and watching the road. They had shown everyone the photograph, but no one had seen the man. They had been insistent that he might have passed through. But no one passes through San Claro. There is nowhere to go. No one ever comes to San Claro. There is nothing to do. Yet, there they were, waiting and looking down the road, dressed in stupid clothes, the sweat pouring off them. Still, who was he to complain? They had paid handsomely for the room, they drank beer (which was expensive) continuously, and they provided a ready topic of conversation inside, which kept people drinking.

He continued his journey with the two beers and put them gently on the table beside the two men. As he did so, one of them stiffened. It was so out of character with the general malaise that had overcome them that the innkeeper was momentarily captivated by the slight movement. Then the blond American kicked his companion awake and they both stared down the road. The Mexican turned his head and there, just entering the gap between the houses, was a man on horseback. The rider was wearing a white and brown patterned poncho and a straw hat left the face in shadow.

As he approached, the Englishman withdrew the photograph.

"What do you think?" he asked.

"It's gotta be him," answered the blond man. "Too much of a coincidence. Anyway, you heard Slim," flicking his thumb at the owner. "No one ever comes here — only mad dogs and Englishmen."

The other smiled. The rider dismounted from his sweating horse at the well and removed his hat.

"The beard changes his whole appearance," said the Englishman.

There was still some water in the bucket from the last time someone had drawn water. The rider poured it into an old trough nearby and allowed his horse to drink. When he considered that she had taken enough, he tethered her to one of the well stanchions and stroked her head for some time. Then he walked over to the cantina.

By now most of the inhabitants had come out to watch. The man stopped in the shade of the awning and eyed the onlookers. He seemed unsurprised by the interest shown in him. No one spoke.

What they saw was a tanned Caucasian, in his late twenties, with brown hair bleached by the sun in streaks. He had a nose that was a little too flat, a generous mouth and a wide jaw. The latter was covered by a thick, but trimmed, black beard. He was about six feet tall, must have weighed about thirteen stone and, Striker thought, in that get-up he looked the image of a nineteenth-century Mexican bandit. The only thing missing was a crossbelt of bullets.

The rider's gaze lingered on the two strangers as they found themselves unable to speak. Then he looked at the owner of the cantina — his position in the group obvious from his apron and rotund figure. Only the innkeepers could afford to eat well in that part of the world.

"*Dos cervezas blanca, por favor, Señor,*" said the rider.

This time it was the owner's turn to jump, as if being awoken from a dream. "*Si, Señor,*" and he hurried inside.

The rider walked slowly to a table and sat down. Then he eyed the onlookers again. Most averted their faces as his gaze alighted upon them and some went inside. As his look took in the two obvious strangers for the second time, Striker began to feel distinctly uncomfortable. The rider looked away to his horse.

"Mr Calder?" ventured the American.

The rider's expression didn't alter. Then he laughed. It was a full deep-throated laugh.

"This has got to go down in my memoirs," he said, and threw his head back and roared again.

The other two men looked at each other, got up and walked over.

"My name is Peter Striker," said the American. "This is Tony Fox."

Calder looked up at them and, now that they were standing, took them in quickly. They were both in their mid twenties and very fit, especially the fair-haired American, although, judging by the way their shirts were plastered to their bodies, they weren't prepared for this sort of temperature. By the colour of their skin they hadn't been in Mexico more than a day or two.

"Sit down, and bring your beer — it's precious out here."

Fox walked back for it, and the owner arrived with Calder's two bottled lagers and a glass. With a sigh and a quick "*gracias*" he

9

reached out and started to pour one, very slowly.

"I'm intrigued to hear what's brought you all the way out here to find me, but just at this moment even that must take second place to this beer, even if it is American."

With the froth at the top of the glass, he raised it to his lips and, with eyes closed, drained it. He filled it again with the remainder of the bottle and drained that too. A low sigh emerged from his throat and between slitted eyes he stared at the empty glass.

"There are some moments in life," he said, "some pleasures, that must be savoured above most others. And that was one of them."

For a few moments more he gazed at the glass, then swivelled his eyes to look at Striker. They were grey, the latter decided, and the most piercing he had ever seen.

"You had us fooled for a moment," said Fox. "The beard...."

"I've got rather fond of it," said Calder, stroking the result of two months in Central America.

"General Stoddard," said Striker. "He wants to see you urgently."

The eyes swung back again, boring into him this time.

"Why?" asked Calder in a low voice, still glaring at Striker. The blond man was determined not to look away, but blinked instead under the steady gaze.

"We don't know exactly," said Striker, glancing at Fox. "But the General did say to tell you that something you told him would happen, has."

Calder looked away for several seconds. He then filled his glass from the second bottle and drank it slowly.

"Have you made transport arrangements?" he asked.

"We've got a helicopter just outside the village," answered Striker. "We picked it up from Mexico City, but it's probably better to head north, across the US-Mexican border and catch a direct flight back. We could be in London by tomorrow morning."

Calder grimaced. "Then we don't have time to waste," he said. "If I were you, while you're settling up with the owner, I'd buy some food and beer for the journey. How much money do you have?"

Striker was a little taken aback. "Enough."

"Good. Then when I've found an honest man to look after my horse until I return, you can pay him what he asks."

He drained his glass and stood up.

"There is one other thing. Do you think I could see your IDs?"

Striker had asked Stoddard what they should do if Calder refused to come. The General had just smiled and said that the question would not arise. It had struck him at the time that the Old Man must really have something going with this guy. Now, with Calder smiling at him, he thought he understood.

I: HIJACK

Monday, 5 May (three days earlier)

Chapter 1

IT CAN BE very cold at dawn in early May at Carlisle Airport. The sun had not yet risen but a delicate glistening of frost could be seen in the slowly gathering light. It was also very quiet, so when the curlew called across the flats, a stark and eerie sound, the man in the thicket, on the west border of the airfield, came fully awake.

Not that he had been sleeping. The biting cold had seen to that. But he had become drowsy as the heat from his body had slowly dissipated into the night. He began to beat his arms across the front of his body, trying to be as silent as possible. As the blood started to circulate he began to shiver. He was still some way from dying of exposure, he thought, but pneumonia was a distinct possibility. Gradually, he explored the sensations of his body. They weren't many. He had spent the night standing against a sapling, clothed in fur-lined anorak, hands in pockets. His hands were not too cold but his feet weren't there at all. He wanted to walk, to get some life back into them, but knew he couldn't. So he began to stretch on to his toes, breathing deeply, his breath visible in the chill, still air. After a few minutes he stopped, conscious of how his back ached. He still couldn't feel his feet. God, he was cold.

Carefully, he stalked forward and, crouching down, emerged from the copse behind some low bushes. From anywhere but the air, he reasoned, he was totally invisible, even if you could see in the near-dark.

Looking to the east, as he was, the man could dimly discern a control tower against the lightening horizon. Behind it were two large hangars and beside these, across the entrance road, were the various ancillary buildings, stretching in line about a hundred yards or so along the perimeter. Electric light shone through some of the windows. There was a large concrete space outside the two hangars, which came towards him in two tarmac roads. These led to the east-west runway, stretching into the distance to his right, and the north-south runway, which ran across in front of him. Neither could have been more than half a mile long.

Carlisle Airport, the man thought, was not a major international air terminal. Indeed, now that the sharply rising hills were coming into focus against the brighter sky to the east and with the first beams of light touching the still snow-capped mountains to the south, glistening spectre-like against the darker sky, the airport looked more like an almost forgotten Andes staging post in some South American dictatorship. This impression was added to when the fence which surrounded part of the field was taken into account. It could not have been designed to keep out people, being the sort of obstruction you normally see around a field to retain cattle. But even that was a flattery. In parts the fence had broken down and for most of the perimeter a holey hedge was the only obstacle. Last night the man had simply walked through one of the open boundary gates behind the coppice in which he now knelt.

The sound of a fast-moving car on the secondary road less than a mile away reminded him of his task. Scuffling to his left made him also realize that he was not the only fauna in the little copse. Suddenly, a rabbit popped out from behind a bush. Instinctively, he remained completely still, just as Brown had taught him, but the rabbit sensed something was wrong and scampered back. A curlew called again. The man looked at his watch. The luminous hands said 5.10. He would have sold his soul for a good, stiff brandy.

Instead, Martin the Lookout slowly crept back to the nearest tree, stood up, hunched his shoulders against the cold and stared at the second hangar across the airfield, now coming more into vision as the horizon began to streak in yellow and pink.

Inside the hangar, Brown also looked at his watch. He too was cold, but at least he wasn't shivering. He looked round into the blackness beside him — at the five others who were huddled there. He still couldn't see them. The light from the small office, to the side and in the middle of the hangar, created a shadow behind the boxes and chests where they hid at the back. He knew they weren't asleep. Occasionally one would stir, but that wasn't the reason, he knew. Perhaps within minutes, certainly within the hour, the months, for him years, of planning would be put into practice, and they were apprehensive.

He, though, was more excited than uneasy. This tension was what he lived for. To him the quintessence of existence was planning an "operation", for every contingency, and then executing it. It was a test of his own abilities. Anyone foolish enough to get in the way would probably be killed. Had he lived in medieval times he would have been called "evil", but he wasn't born bad.

He took a quick look over the boxes. The two men were still inside the glass office, working on something probably. They certainly weren't talking, as the sound would have carried in the stillness of the morning.

Out in the centre of the hangar stood the Hawker Siddeley Argosy 220, wraith-like in the shadows. It looked like a rather portly, yet ghostly, albatross, its bulbous belly supported by a large wing and square tailplane section. This last feature of the aircraft made it resemble the rear end of the original Second World War Mosquito. But that was the only similarity between the two planes. The Mosquito was a fast, wooden-built fighter-bomber. The Argosy is a large, four-engined, short-range freighter with a wing-span of 115 feet and a maximum payload of 32,000 lb, about 14,545 kilos. With the 12,000 lb of freight and a third of the potential fuel capacity on board, Brown knew that she had a maximum range of about 750 miles. He knew how much was on board because he had watched it being loaded the night before.

The fork-lift that had come with the cargo on the lorry had worked well as it seemingly struggled to cope with the weight of each hexagonally shaped fuel assembly. Each was twelve feet long and about six inches across between the diagonals, and the lifter had been especially adapted to cope with this odd shape. Each assembly, he knew, weighed about 1,000 lb — about 450 kilos — and he had counted twelve trips from the truck to the cargo hold of the Argosy. The rear-loading capability of the plane made it a comparatively easy job. The loader simply drove into the cargo hold and stacked the assemblies in the prepared racks.

The job had been done inside an hour. The fork-lift was secured away aboard the lorry and it had left, leaving the Austin, plus its two passengers — security officers, both in plain clothes and both, Brown knew, armed.

Getting into the hangar had been child's play. He still couldn't believe how easy. Hiding behind the east hedge after dark, they had waited for the big, articulated lorry to arrive, plus the Austin Princess which followed at a discreet distance. They waited a further thirty minutes, while the transport was backed into the hangar and in order to allow the security team time to search the place. Then seven people had simply walked through the hedge, past the fuel store and straight to the back of the hangar. Brown was glad there had been no moon. They would have been forced to crawl and, with the packages they had carried, that would have proved difficult, although quite possible.

Brown had opened the padlock guarding the small, rear door of the hangar with a key, the impression of which one of his men had obtained on a previous trip; and, under cover of the noise of the fork-lift truck being started up, the six had entered to hide behind the boxes at the rear.

What to do with the padlock at this stage was a problem that had occupied a lot of thought. Brown's instincts told him he should have an escape route. But that meant retaining the padlock, which in turn meant that anyone testing locks wouldn't take very long to tumble to the fact that it was missing and their discovery would then be immediate. Brown had no doubt about their ability to escape, but the operation would be blown. He didn't think anyone was likely to be testing locks but he couldn't take the chance. So Martin had simply locked the door from the outside and walked off the airfield the way they had come.

There was no way out now except forward. But although his instincts rebelled, rational thought told him that it had to be this way. Whether they succeeded or failed, this was the last job that any of them would pull, therefore they had to commit themselves totally. He also knew that he would not fail.

As a young army officer he had realized very quickly that a life in the service of Her Majesty was not an attractive one. He had resolved that at the end of his short-service commission he would be out and away, to make a great deal of money. But how?

The answer had come to him one night while he lay in bed, and he had never changed it. He would have to steal. He wondered why he hadn't thought of it before. It seemed to him the most natural thing in the world. If the legitimate means of achieving wealth were not available, then he would have to use the illegitimate ones. Any scruples that he might have had before entering the Army, it soon beat out of him. The subservience to discipline created its own values, where survival, the Army's way, was the only route.

He had soon learnt, however, that the Army could teach a good deal and discovered that he had a talent for many things. He practised on the rifle-range until he could split an orange at two hundred yards, with a standard-issue rifle, ten times out of ten. But what he really liked was "war games", as he called them. On manoeuvres his platoon always performed impressively. This was mainly because Brown could lead men.

He had an excited and at times animated personality, and could tell tales round the camp-fire until the early hours. But above all, when he gave orders they were firm and explicit, and his men obeyed them to the letter — not because he was an officer, but because he was Lieutenant Brown. Like all great leaders, he had that indefinable quality of being able to be "one of the boys" yet somehow remain above them.

The final years of his commission had been spent waiting and planning. He talked more intimately to the non-commissioned officers and the men of his company, probing unobtrusively about their motives, their fears and their needs. He had also found out what they were prepared to do for money. When the time came for him to leave the Army he was a captain. He was also ready.

He had begun with a few petty thefts from houses, on his own, to provide enough working capital. It had been magnificently sensuous at first — observing the house from afar with binoculars for a few days and then, on a moonless night, silently drifting over the dewy turf, forcing the lock on the French windows, or using a glass-cutter and plunger, and looting the lower rooms, knowing that if he made a sound he might be discovered. It was a test of his competence and that was how he liked it. If he were disturbed, there was the knife in his belt. Then he would be gone the same way he had come — across the lawn at the rear and the fields beyond.

Eventually, though, the excitement began to go from houses, so he gathered his band together and robbed a few banks. They were more difficult but, provided you had enough imagination and thought of every contingency beforehand, it worked. Those who worked for him stayed, and all the time he was waiting and planning the big one — this one.

He glanced at his watch again. 5.33. Things would be happening soon. The most hazardous part of the operation was about to begin. The problem was crossing those forty yards of open concrete to the office without being seen. What's more, he had to wait until the flight-crew arrived. He didn't want to repeat requests to the tower that had already been made.

He couldn't take any chances, so he reached down to his right and found a small, cold hand.

"Now," he whispered.

Rustling movements in the dark told him that his command was being obeyed. Not that he expected anything else — it was just reassuring. Within minutes he knew that she would be naked but for a T-shirt, a very short skirt, stockings and a pair of high-heeled shoes. A somewhat incongruous get-up but, with a figure like Judy's, one designed to have the maximum effect on the men in the office. She would be cold for a while, but that was unavoidable. He probably wouldn't use her anyway, but he wanted every possibility at his disposal when the moment came.

He became aware of noises outside the hangar doors — the scuff of boot on stony concrete and the low murmurings that men reverently make at dawn. He really should have got Judy changed earlier. Still, she must be nearly ready.

There were three short raps. The noise reverberated around the confined area almost as one continuous sound. The two men in the office had heard them too and had been ready when the knocks came. It took the bigger of the two about twenty-five seconds to walk to the small inset in the huge, sliding doors, but no further sound was heard. The other was by the door of the office, gun in hand.

Brown could watch everything. With all attention riveted on the front of the hangar, neither security guard was going to turn to the back.

"Who is it?" shouted the guard at the door.

There was a short, guttural exclamation from outside.

"It's your pilot," replied an Australian voice. "Who the hell else do you think would be out here in this Godforsaken cold at this hour of the bloody morning?"

Brown noticed that the guard seemed to hesitate, but he stuck to his task.

"Name?"

"Oh, blimey, mate! You'll be asking for a password next. Greenfield. Now for God's sake, Rufus, open this bloody door."

The door was opened and two men, clad in heavy, leather flying gear, entered. One laughed and clapped the guard on the back.

"You know your trouble, Rufus?" said the Australian. "You have no faith in people."

Brown did not catch Rufus's reply, even if there was one. He had ducked down as they began to walk towards the glass office. The tension was building in him and he smiled in the dark.

"Take-off in thirty minutes," called the pilot, apparently determined not to be disheartened by Rufus's sullen disposition. "The wind is light, north to south, and the morning is fair."

Brown could imagine him smiling into the face of the man by the office door. He looked at his watch again. 5.39. He peeped over the boxes. They were all inside the office and he knew instinctively that this was the right moment. With the four men in one place and blinded by the light of their own room, the chance was too good to miss.

"Wait," he whispered, as he slipped a balaclava mask over his head. On rubber-soled shoes he rose from his hiding place. He was committed.

He slid along the wall and within thirty seconds was beside the office, crouching down to below glass level. He moved to the door, which was facing out into the hangar, and beckoned to his team. The next moment he was standing in the doorway.

The four men, all standing in the ten-by-ten feet space, made the place look very small. The pilot and the senior of the two security officers had their backs to Brown, bending over a desk situated against the wall. Rufus stood in the far, right corner looking at them, and the co-pilot was looking out of the door at the plane, three feet from the nozzle of Brown's automatic carbine.

The man in the balaclava mask wished he had more time to study the expression on the co-pilot's face, but he was blocking the field of fire. Quickly, before the man knew what was happening, Brown took one step forward, swung the butt of the carbine and struck the co-pilot on the cheek. There was a sharp crack as the jaw broke. The automatic was back in position long before the man collapsed to the floor, unconscious. It happened so fast, and Rufus was so surprised, that his hand hadn't even reached the lapel of his jacket before he was staring into the snub nose of the Schmeisser. The others hadn't even begun to turn.

"The first one to move gets a bullet in the head," said Brown.

The two at the desk began to straighten.

"I said, don't move," Brown insisted fiercely and they both stood still. "Now, very slowly, raise your hands above your head."

The two with their backs to Brown didn't react, but Rufus, who could see the weapon, raised his arms.

"I said raise your hands, now." The last word was shouted.

Gradually, with their heads turned towards Rufus, they complied.

"All right," said Brown, "now you two, turn round slowly until you're facing me."

They did that too. The pilot had a look of wide-eyed, open-mouthed astonishment imprinted upon his face. He stared first at Brown's mask and then at his mate, lying unconscious on the floor. From then on his terrified gaze focused on the carbine. The other took one look at the weapon, then looked into Brown's mask with an expression of thoughtful hostility. Aged about thirty-five, he was of medium height and build, with dark hair and blue eyes that didn't once turn to the man on the floor. He also seemed to be unafraid and that didn't suit Brown's purpose. Rufus was clenching his fists nervously.

"This," said Brown, raising his weapon a little, "is a Schmeisser automatic carbine. It was made during the Second World War. That makes it a bit dated. But as a killing machine, at this range, it's not bettered by anything manufactured today. Make one move without my permission and it will scythe you down within one second."

He paused for effect.

"Besides, there are three identical weapons also pointing at you through the glass."

Rufus and the Australian turned their heads, straining to see through their own reflections. Brown addressed himself to the calm security officer, whose head hadn't moved.

"You have probably worked out that it would not suit my purpose to fire. Too much noise. But we are going to take that plane, and if one of you does anything to jeopardize that, I shall shoot you all down without a moment's hesitation, because I shall then have nothing to loose. I shall also be very annoyed. Believe me."

They believed him. Even the calm one began to look worried.

"Now, I want you all, one at a time, to follow me. Remember those other carbines and keep your hands above your heads. You first, then you, then you last. Come."

They came — first the calm one, then the pilot, then Rufus, stepping over the co-pilot on the way, until they were all lined up outside.

"Tom?" called Brown.

A small, chunky figure detached itself from the group of armed men. He had been a corporal in one of Brown's platoons. Not possessed of a first-class brain, he made up for it in natural cunning. He was also as tough as old boots, as skilful with a knife as anyone Brown had seen and thoroughly dishonest. But due to some paradox of character that Brown had given up trying to fathom, he was devoted to his leader. On leaving the Army he had been dumped on the unemployment heap and when the chance had come to join Brown's band he had jumped at it. As the workhorse of the team, he was invaluable.

"Watch him," said Brown to Tom, pointing to the fallen co-pilot. "He may regain consciousness."

He turned to his prisoners. "You three walk over to that wall and put your hands up against it."

There were three of them covering now and there was no resistance. All the same, Brown kept fairly close to the calm one while he was being searched. When two guns had been removed and their faces were still towards the wall, Brown spoke again, in a matter-of-fact voice, as if he were a bored schoolteacher addressing an obedient and unresponsive class.

"You now have two choices. You can remain absolutely still while my colleague injects you with a substance that will put you out for four to five hours — the only effect you will suffer is a thundering headache when you wake up — or you can resist and die with either a knife or bullet in your back."

There was a short silence.

"Mac," said Brown, motioning the Scotsman to get on with it.

The calm one spoke. "How do we know the stuff won't kill us?"

"You don't," answered Brown, signalling to Wilson at the same time. "But we would hardly bother to wear masks if we were going to kill you."

"He's right," shouted the Australian. "Let him do it and get it over with."

The calm one was looking at Brown now, still unhappy, but then Wilson was there on his blind side, with one arm wrapped around his neck and a knife between the eyes. Wilson had been a sergeant and Brown had fought tooth and nail to get him into his platoon. Finally, he had managed it, with a little subtle blackmail on a brother officer, and neither man had looked back since. Wilson had no desire to be a "bourgeois" officer, yet Brown knew that he had more insight than any officer he had known. On an operation, he was Brown's right-hand man and usually anticipated his next move. No one knew his first name, except Brown.

Any resistance that might have been anticipated from the security officer disappeared. Mac followed in with a syringe to the man's

18

neck, and within a minute he was limp. There was no trouble from the other two.

"Don't forget the co-pilot," said Brown casually, as the Scotsman was injecting Rufus, and then he walked off to inspect the door inset.

"No. OK," answered Mac, but he had forgotten. He arrested the downward plunge of the syringe immediately, withdrew it and inspected the amount remaining by the office light. Nearly all the serum was gone. He walked over to the fallen figure and, with Tom's help, removed the heavy sheepskin jacket. He then rolled up a shirt-sleeve and injected what was left into the main vein, hoping that, as with the others, it would be enough to kill him.

Brown was pulling off his mask and anorak, and speaking at the same time, his voice raised so that it could be heard at the back of the huge hangar.

"Sash, don your 'chute and make sure the plane is OK. Judy, come here. Tom, front door."

He waited for the girl.

"Judy, collect Mac's syringe, all these masks and anoraks, put them in the disposable bag, take them on to the plane and get into your wet-suit. Mac, Wilson, let's get the heavy gear on to the plane."

As they walked to the rear of the hangar, the co-pilot became semi-conscious. He had the worst toothache he had ever known. He tried to move a hand to his face, but his arm wouldn't work. He just couldn't feel it. He thrashed his whole body in panic and the sudden, violent movement threw him from his side on to his stomach. The mist in front of his eyes momentarily cleared and he saw a pair of woman's legs, in high-heeled shoes, walking across the hangar. Then the fog came back, covering his mind as well as his sight, and he sank into oblivion.

Within five minutes, Brown, Wilson and Mac had transported all the bags from behind the boxes into the front of the main hold of the plane, out of the way of the fuel assemblies.

"OK," said Brown; "Mac, you're the nearest in size to that security officer."

"I was hoping you were going to say that," smiled the Scotsman. "The North Sea I can do without."

He began to undress immediately and Judy put his clothes in the disposable bag. Brown and Wilson jumped down from the aircraft and trotted over to the three bodies. Within minutes the calm one was stripped and Mac, his bare limbs shaking from cold, gratefully put on the shirt, tie, trousers, jacket and overcoat. They weren't a perfect fit, but the coat would hide everything, and, with a cap on his head —
Brown's idea of what smart security officers were wearing these days — he would pass muster. Brown removed the pilot's jacket and boots, and put them on himself, over his wet-suit. The boots were

tight, but he wouldn't have to wear them for long. They then dragged the four bodies behind the boxes.

Brown looked at his watch. 5.55 exactly. Not bad. Fifteen minutes to take-off.

"Wilson, on to the plane. Make sure everyone's got a parachute on and then give Sash a hand with the checks. Mac, back that pulling trolley into position and couple it up to the plane — and don't prang the Princess while you're doing it. I'll give you a hand with the doors in a moment."

Mac was laughing.

"Donna worry," he replied. "I would na damage ma own transport," and he trudged off happily across the hangar.

Brown treated himself to a growing feeling of inner satisfaction, although he wouldn't have dreamt of showing it. But that was as far as it went. Things had gone well up to now, but the next stage was a tricky one. When they opened the doors and pulled the plane out on to the dawn-splashed tarmac, they would be in full view of anyone looking their way. But it would still be fairly dim outside, if not dark, and it was unlikely that anyone would notice the difference between himself and the co-pilot. His wet-suit was jet-black, without a stripe, he had a flying-jacket and boots on and the colour of their hair wasn't all that different in the dark. His height was the only problem. No one would notice the change, he was sure, between Mac and the security officer. The other, Rufus, would simply have travelled with the plane. All this, of course, was assuming that anyone was up at this hour. A man in the control-tower, yes, but the front of the hangar was not visible from there and he would be surprised if there was anyone else about.

He signalled Tom to come over from the door and get on to the plane. Then he climbed aboard himself and helped Tom put on his parachute, which, like those of the others, had an attached life-jacket. Brown began to walk to the front of the hold and caught sight of Judy, seated on the heavy bags, her arms crossed in front of her in a futile attempt to keep warm.

"Cold, isn't it?" she called. "Is it going to be worse up there?"

He stopped and looked at her, wondering how she would react if she knew how cold she was going to be in about an hour's time. A wet-suit was no real protection against the cold of prolonged immersion in the North Sea at that time of the year.

"Yes," he answered, "I'm afraid it is."

He heard the trolley starting up and turned, climbing up to the cockpit where Sash and Wilson were seated, checking the aircraft. Sash looked around as he entered. Despite the cold there were beads of perspiration on his forehead and he hadn't been doing any of the heavy work.

20

"I hope these engines start," he said. "It's been a cold night."

"They have to start," replied Brown.

But he didn't like the negative attitude of the pilot. Sash could fly the plane blindfolded if necessary. He wouldn't have been chosen otherwise. He would be all right when they were on the runway, but he was nervous now and nervousness is infectious.

"Can you handle it?" asked Brown.

The implied criticism was not lost on the pilot and his hands gripped the stick tightly for a few moments. When he turned round to face his leader, everything except his eyes looked angry.

What Sash saw was a man of six feet two inches tall and very slightly underweight. He had a pale, unimaginative face, with full lips and a stubby nose, all framed by raven-black hair. Brown's small brown eyes were now looking at him enquiringly. The one thing which he had in common with the others was a bushy beard. To Sash he had always been an imposing figure, but absolutely no one criticized his flying abilities.

"Don't you worry. I can handle it."

Wilson glanced wryly at Brown, who placed a hand on the pilot's shoulder and said:

"OK. We're pulling her out now."

Chapter 2

THE SHORT, round figure in a brown trilby ascended the last dozen steps to the door of the control tower, and reflected that the climb became more of an effort every time he did it. It fitted into his general mood — tired depression.

Not that he disliked his job. On the contrary, he enjoyed the power and responsibility, and the perfection of it. It was firm and tangible, and he could see the end product. Every plane that took off gave him personal satisfaction. True, there weren't many aircraft these days to fill his day, but that usually meant that he concentrated more on each one. No, the job was suffering, but it wasn't the cause of his malaise.

He unlocked the door and walked in. He didn't bother to close it quickly to keep the cold out, but took his time, knowing from experience that the temperature inside would not be very different from that outside. The thermometer hung on one of the window uprights showed that it was only just above freezing point. He plugged in the two rather primitive, electric-bar fires and, reluctantly, the two extractor fans. The windows of an airport control-tower are one place where condensation must not be allowed to form.

The man removed his hat to reveal the classic bald head, with a band of hair running around the base of the skull. The thick overcoat he kept on. He sat down on his stool and looked out, under paradoxically bushy eyebrows, at the orange sky.

No, the job was suffering, but it wasn't the cause. The truth was, the job was the only thing he was good at. He certainly wasn't any good at holding his marriage together. If only they could have had children. He had been in favour, but she had always won the argument. They had either needed a new carpet for the hall, or a new bedroom unit in the spare room so that she would not be ashamed to invite her mother to stay again. How could they afford children? He knew there was another reason, but hadn't been able to work it out. At one time he thought it was because she didn't want any rivals for his affections, but that couldn't be it — theirs wasn't exactly an affectionate relationship at the best of times.

Now it was too late. They were both past forty and sex was regarded as a treat on birthdays and bank holidays, except, of course, Christmas Day, which was sacred. She had become more withdrawn than even her introverted character allowed and conversation between them centred on the shopping or the state of the weather. He had his work and she had her garden — the onions and lettuces in neat little rows, like sentries guarding her chastity. She said she did it to save them money, but he knew different. They were very alike really — both very orderly and pedantic — yet somehow they didn't meet.

Last night, things had seemed to come to a head. He'd told her there was a dawn flight and that it would probably be more convenient for him to sleep at the airfield. It was an exaggeration and she'd sensed it, accusing him of not loving her any more and only being interested in his work. What she said didn't hurt him these days, but he had left puzzled. He finally concluded that she hadn't wanted him to go, not because she wanted him at home, but because she didn't want *him* to enjoy himself when *she* couldn't. She always was perceptive about his moods.

Then he had lost heavily in a bridge game he had played until midnight, partnering the airfield cook, who lived in, against the two pilots of the special flight that morning. He should have known better than to gamble in his state of mind, but then George Grimble was everyone's fool. The cook, who had learnt the game in a Liverpool Salvation Army hostel, was a poor player and the cards had been against him. The slump had begun when, being dealt a quite miraculous fistful of picture cards, he had bid for a small slam. The cook mixed up the replies, they were doubled and went down by four tricks, vulnerable. From then on they couldn't get it together. When it finally looked as if the cards might be changing, the Australian had smilingly said that he must get his beauty sleep, and George had reluctantly paid up, double, since the cook was broke until pay-day.

He had gone to bed, but hadn't slept.

22

The warden's car, returning from checking the runways, brought him back to reality. He looked at his watch. Three minutes to six. Then he thought he heard the pulling trolley being started up in Number 2 hangar.

These BNFL people were always the same. Anyone else would be content to leave their aircraft on the apron overnight, but not these bastards. They had to pull it into the hangar so that they could load in secret. And why was everyone so close-mouthed about it? British Nuclear Fuels Limited, he was told it meant, but that didn't help him much. What was so damned secretive about a load of uranium anyway? He should be told. After all, he was the air-traffic controller.

The plane emerged at no more than a snail's pace, as the trolley struggled with the weight. A solid plane — Grimble liked it. An aircraft in the classic mould.

The 220 version, as this was, was powered by four Rolls-Royce Dart turboprops, each developing 2,230 h.p. With her maximum payload, she could climb at 900 feet a minute and, flying at her economic cruising speed of 280 m.p.h., she could cover 485 miles with a 230-mile diversion and forty-five minutes' reserve. But such were the economics of flying that if you reduced the payload to 18,000 lb, about 8,200 kilos, she could fly no less than 1,760 miles, with the same allowances. Grimble knew that she wouldn't be fully loaded, otherwise she wouldn't get off the short runway, and she was only going to Wick, a distance of about 250 miles, so she wouldn't be fully fuelled either.

The disgruntled man realized that he had better warm up and check his equipment. The place felt less cold now, but he kept his coat on.

He watched as the engines started up. One engine seemed to cough a little, but eventually all the propellers were turning satisfactorily. The sort of car that he could never afford cruised out of the hangar and stopped on the apron, behind the aircraft. He couldn't see whether anyone had closed the hangar doors.

In a few minutes the Argosy began to move out on to the taxi-road. Grimble began to imagine what the pilot was going to say when he called up. "Morning, George. Thanks for the beer money." Well, that was one possibility. The man in the tower set his face in a resigned grimace.

Suddenly, he realized why he hated the Australian so much. He envied him. He was jealous of his carefree, bachelor ways and his roguish good looks. Quite unexpectedly he felt a lump in his throat, as he wished and imagined himself the man in the aeroplane, flying into the blue, with a red-headed lass and a bottle of good malt waiting in the Highlands. Then, just as suddenly, he realized it wasn't to be. He gazed unseeingly at the chart-board and felt his eyes begin to water.

On the plane, Brown was with Sash and Wilson in the cockpit. The vibration and noise were worse than he had expected and he had to raise his voice to make himself heard.

"Sash, can you do an Australian accent?"

The pilot, his confidence returned after the heart-stopping hesitation of the near-port engine, looked quizzically at Wilson, sitting beside him. Then comprehension dawned.

"Sorry, old boy," he replied, looking back at his leader. "Not one of my specialities."

"Never mind," shouted Brown. "When you're due to get through to the tower, pass the earphones and mike to me."

It was essential that, even at this late stage, there was no hint of suspicion.

Back in the control-tower, Grimble watched the plane reach the southern end of the north-south runway and wheel round to face north. The balloon was just beginning to lift off the vertical as a northerly breeze began to blow, gently. There was a crackle of static and the loudspeaker barked at him.

"This is BNFL Special Flight to Wick. Permission to take-off. Over."

Grimble was slightly disappointed. The Australian seemed subdued. He blew his nose quickly and switched to transmit.

"Tower to BNFL. Permission granted. Wind still light, nor'-nor'-east. Over."

"Thank you, sport. See you again."

"Goodbye," said Grimble, "and take care," he added as an afterthought, regretting it immediately. It sounded silly. There was no reply.

He watched as the plane's engines working up the revolutions and, as the pilot released the brakes, she began to move, gathering speed as both pilots pushed the throttles forward to maximum. As she passed the tower though, she was still on the tarmac, hurtling towards the fence. Incredibly, the pilot seemed to have left it too late. Then, seconds before the end of the runway, the nose lifted and the great bird inched off the ground, missing the boundary fence by what seemed like a whisker. Grimble could see the limp wire vibrating.

Just like the Australian, he thought, and watched the plane climb steadily out of sight as it headed due north, without deviation. With the sunrise to its right, it had to be a marvellous sight up there.

Across his line of vision, the Austin Princess passed under the path the aircraft had just taken, as it travelled around the airfield on the boundary road. He watched it dazedly as it continued its journey, briefly disappearing behind some trees to the west, then emerging, more slowly, as it headed for Carlisle. Probably braked to avoid a rabbit, Grimble thought. Soft, these city folk.

24

Martin began to swear at the cold as soon as he got inside the car.
"Is that heater on, you Scots bastard?"

Mac turned briefly to smile at him.

"Aye, but try a drop o' this," he replied, reaching inside his coat. "I
hid it in ma underpants."

A small, metal flask emerged and Martin grabbed it eagerly.

"You crafty bugger," he said, "but I love you," as he brought the
flask to his lips.

After a couple of grateful swigs, Martin felt much better and he
settled back comfortably. Compared to the way he had spent the
night, the car seats were luxurious. Mac turned right on to the B6264,
en route for the M6. Martin suddenly realized that the Scotsman was
chuckling.

"It went well?" enquired Martin, a little suspiciously.

Mac didn't look round.

"Aye, it went bloody well," and he continued laughing.

Martin gazed through the windscreen. Then the relief rushed over
him as well and, with the whisky doing its work on an empty
stomach, he too began to laugh.

"And I'll tell ye what, ye Sassenach bastard," said Mac, attempting
to control his laughter, "you may have been a wee bit cold last night,
but by the Christ ye were not as cold as they're goin' to be in aboat an
hour, when they take their wee dip."

Both men looked at each other and laughed uproariously.

Chapter 3

AS THE ARGOSY transport rose into the clearing sky, Sasha Goodwin-
Smith was in his element. Even though he'd been to a good school,
his masters had never been able to give him a formal education. He'd
only been interested in one thing — flying. He didn't actually get to
do it until his middle teens, but by that time he knew more about
aircraft than his contemporaries knew about Latin, Greek, history,
English and mathematics put together. The local airfield was his
classroom. He read everything about aircraft that he could lay his
hands on and virtually nothing about anything else.

He scraped through O levels by the skin of his teeth, but he was not
recommended to continue for A levels, "not because he lacks ability,
but due to an almost total lack of motivation". The school was
immensely relieved when his father finally gave in to his son's
repeated pleas and withdrew him for flying lessons.

Sasha had no trouble qualifying as a pilot, but found that he
couldn't get a job with any of the reputable companies, due to his lack
of formal academic qualifications and a bad report from his school.
Moreover, his father had no contacts in the aviation industry. Still,

he told the young Sasha, he had made the choice himself, against advice, and he must therefore make his own way in the world.

But Sasha wasn't worried. He packed his bags for the Middle-East and was soon flying ageing transports from one Arab sheikdom to another. Since then he had flown everything, from two-seater mail planes in Australia to freighters and airliners in a number of the developing countries of Asia and Africa. The fact that he had no future had not concerned him. His fair hair always seemed to attract the African and Asian women and he was never far from a cockpit. It was the way he liked to live.

He glanced at the altimeter. 4,300 feet. It should take about six to seven minutes to reach 10,000, when he'd level off. She could climb faster, but this was the way Brown wanted it. Crossing the Scottish border now, course due north. He liked the Argosy. Fully loaded she was a little underpowered and could be a real bitch when taking off from mountain airfields. But being only a third loaded and with a third of the possible fuel, she handled excellently for a heavy freighter. This was a milk run and he was as happy as a king.

Sasha was also a little naive. Indeed, that was one of the reasons why Brown had chosen him. He was not part of the regular team as this was a one-off job requiring a pilot, and he had been told just enough to keep him happy. But he wasn't really interested in the cargo anyway, or the fate of the four men they had left in the hangar. His job was to fly the plane. Nothing more. The fact that Brown had promised him £100,000 at the end was also not far from the front of his mind and had helped him turn a blind eye to a lot of things. Had he known his fellow pilots were dead he would certainly have regretted it, but done nothing. Sasha was going to retire. He was also a coward.

In his ear, Brown shouted, "OK, Sash?"

The pilot looked up, smiling. "So when do you want the somersaults?" he asked.

Brown grinned before replying.

"You know what to do. Keep her on this bearing until we reach Portknockie. I should be back by then. If I'm not, send Judy for me."

Sash nodded.

"In precisely three minutes from my 'execute'," continued Brown, "take her into the steepest climb that you can manage for fifteen seconds, then put her back on the normal climb level. OK?"

Again Sash nodded, looking at his watch. Brown was doing the same.

"Execute," said Brown, then left.

Sash noted the position of the sweep second-hand and glanced down at the open map on his lap. In a little under fifteen minutes they should be over the Borders and passing fourteen miles east of

Edinburgh. Then it was across the Firth of Forth and, in less than another ten minutes, they would pass to the east of Dundee by a mere five miles. Then it was on over the Sidlaw Hills and Forfar to the distant Grampians.

As Brown entered the hold, he signalled the others to join him. He glanced at his watch as Judy struggled up.

"Go and strap yourself in beside Sash," he said and she left immediately.

He pulled the two men closer so that he could be heard.

"We have about thirty-five minutes to Portknockie. Perhaps less. There's a slight head-wind, but it shouldn't affect us very much at all. We must work on thirty minutes to be sure."

He looked hard at both of them before continuing. "That means only two minutes per rod. No more."

They both nodded and Brown looked at Wilson.

"Got the magnet?" he asked.

Wilson handed it to him.

"Right, let's get into position."

Brown led the way to the rear of the plane, glancing at his watch as he walked. The lights, which had been switched on soon after take-off, helped a lot, making the alloy fuel assemblies shine silver in their racks. When he reached the first port-side assembly he turned round to face it, so that he was now facing the front of the plane. Tom came round on his left and clasped the rack with his left hand. Wilson was already on his right, clutching the rack with his right fist. He felt their free hands lock together behind him and leant back to test the bond.

Again he looked at his watch. Less than thirty seconds to go. He reached out and released the retaining clip on the end of the hexagonal fuel assembly. Slowly, it swung open and he felt a tightening in his stomach as he saw the ends of the fourteen stainless-steel fuel rods, lying flush with the assembly. Each was twelve feet long and half an inch in diameter, and each nestled snugly in its own half-inch hole. He knew that a quarter-inch hole ran down each rod and that it was filled with half-inch long plutonium oxide pellets. The combined weight of each rod and the oxide within it was just over 30 kilos. If you multiplied that by fourteen and added the weight of the, admittedly light, magnesium fuel assembly of 25 kilos, you had a combined weight per assembly of close on 450 kilos, or 1,000 pounds.

He drew the huge round magnet to his chest, already feeling the strong pull from the steel bars and the rack. Then he heard the engines beginning to whine as their power increased, and the deck tilted quite sharply as the Argosy clawed higher.

Slowly, but as quickly as he could, he allowed the magnet to close on the rods. When it was just under a foot away, the pull became too strong for him to reverse and the magnet slammed on to the end of the assembly, the noise echoing around the hold. With the deck canting now at over 35 degrees, he pulled with all his strength and felt the rods sliding out.

He let out his breath and sucked in some air. Wilson was grinning broadly. Brown had been a little worried about this part and Wilson knew it. The rods would probably have come out without the extra angle, but it was best not to take chances. The deck began to return to its normal level and the engine note decreased.

"Right," said Brown, still panting slightly, "let's get this thing off." All three men grasped one half of the magnet edge.

"Ready," said Brown. "Now!"

He didn't need to say it. The swing of his body told them exactly when they should pull and, with a sideways and outward jerk, the magnet came free. Brown retained his hold and handed it to Tom.

"Disposable bag and let's go. You both know the routine."

Tom and Wilson moved to the front of the hold, while Brown began to slide the first rod from its container. The job was easy now that he could grip it. After six feet had been extracted, he grasped it with both hands and walked along until it was totally removed.

Wilson and Tom arrived with large bags in their grip. Each unzipped one and began to extract bright, orange, inflatable rafts, together with parachutes. One of the specially made rafts, with attached carbon dioxide gas cylinder, was fitted around the rod and zipped up. Then a parachute was attached and the whole lot, now a dead weight of something like 55 kilos, was moved to the rear of the plane. Another cylinder was then prepared. The same operation had to be repeated thirteen times.

Each member of the team, except Sash and Judy, had practised this so often that it was second nature to them, and Brown knew that this part of the operation could be completed in under fifteen minutes, if they really pushed it. But that was at ground level. As the plane reached its cruising height of 10,000 feet, the hard, heavy work became progressively more difficult in the oxygen-lacking air. Brown knew that for men not used to it, sustained or sudden, violent exercise at 10,000 feet could be crippling, but, this time, he'd had to take the chance. There was nowhere in Britain where they could have obtained the sort of training needed, and he had had to make do with severe physical exercise for the whole team.

He was glad he had, for as more cylinders were dragged to the rear of the hold, his breath began to come in short gasps and he felt the sweat breaking out under his wet-suit, despite the cold. The weight of the 'chute strapped to his back with the attached life-jacket made the task worse, and he wondered whether they should have put them on later.

He looked at Tom and Wilson, who seemed to be having similar trouble. The last meal they had eaten, apart from a few glucose tablets, was at lunchtime yesterday in a motorway restaurant. They had spent a sleepless night and now this crippling physical task. He hadn't known it would be quite so bad.

As he zipped up the eighth cylinder, he glanced at his watch. They were only just on schedule and he knew it would get worse.

"Come on, lads," he shouted, "we've got to work faster."

Wilson showed his teeth as he fought for breath and switched his eyes towards Tom. Brown did too and saw that the little man was already in a bad way. His face had lost its usual rosy glow and the way he lifted his feet made Brown doubt whether he would last. That meant that he and Wilson had to work harder.

He took a 'chute from Tom and buckled it to the next raft. There were no seconds to waste and he quickly jumped up to extract the next cylinder.

As he worked, his feet became more leaden, a pain in his back stabbed at him every time he straightened up and sweat began to run into his eyes, blurring his vision. He was also, apparently, becoming light-headed, for, as he glanced up, Tom appeared to vibrate like a man working a pneumatic drill.

After what seemed an age, the last cylinder was dragged to the rear cargo-door. Brown turned round, expecting to see Judy attempting to gain his attention, but she wasn't there. Wilson was propping himself up against one of the racks, his head low as he gasped for breath. Tom, miraculously, was still on his feet, tottering slightly, but showing a smile to Brown, his arms hanging vertically from his sloping shoulders. He looked like an ape.

Brown forced himself to move.

"Well done," he gasped, but doubted whether they had heard what to him sounded like a whisper in the din of the hold. He paused for several seconds while he regained some more breath, but his voice still sounded weak as he shouted: "Just the disposable bag now and we're set."

Wilson would see to it.

He clapped them both on their bowed shoulders as he passed and walked uncertainly towards the ladder to the cockpit. As he placed a heavy leg on the bottom rung, he glanced up and saw Judy, framed in the entrance at the top. She retreated as he came up. The climb was easier than he anticipated, but, even so, Judy's mouth dropped open as she saw him.

"Christ, John!" she exclaimed. "Are you all right?"

Sash swung round and said, "You don't look too good, old boy," a look of genuine concern on his face.

Brown, still breathing fairly deeply, ignored them. He could see the coastline approaching and the Moray Firth beyond.

"Portknockie?" asked Brown.

"You guessed it," answered Sash, still glancing at his leader.

"You know the flight plan. The second we pass over the coast, alter course to Wick Airport. The boat should be exactly twenty-five miles along that line."

There was silence for a while. Brown retrieved some more breath and looked out of the window as Judy stared at him. Sash concentrated on the coming turn, he had known exactly when the turn had to be made and had planned the angle beforehand. With one final glance at the map, he turned the aircraft fractionally to port and settled her down on that compass bearing.

"Wind going to give you any trouble?" asked Brown.

"No." Then after a pause, "Oxygen masks would have made it worse, you know."

Brown remembered that it was Sash who had advised him against using oxygen. He hadn't intended to anyway — the altitude was far too low and the masks would have been cumbersome — but the pilot needed praise.

"I know," said Brown, and smiled.

The grin was returned and Judy joined in. She had found a blanket from somewhere and had it wrapped around her like a cocoon. Suddenly, Brown became aware again of how much everything depended on him and his smile disappeared.

"How long?" he asked.

Sash looked through the window. "About six minutes." Then he bent down to his left and, straightening up, proferred some binoculars.

Brown braced himself against the bulkhead and raised the lenses to his eyes. The image was completely blurred. He adjusted the screw and the distant sea sprang into focus. It appeared as if the surface was hardly rippled. It probably was a calm sea, with such a light wind. All right for ditching, but not too good for sailing away. Slowly, he scanned the empty horizon, moving his body to left and right to see past the window uprights. Nothing. His arms were tired and he found it increasingly difficult to hold the glasses still.

"You should be able to see it now," said Sash, as Brown lowered the binoculars.

While his arms rested, Brown gazed out of the window, as if trying to see the yacht with his bare eyes. That it would be where it was supposed to be, he had no doubt. If there had been cloud they would have jumped and dropped through it, blind, at the planned rendezvous point, trusting that it would be there. Radio, or radio direction-finders, would have been a dead giveaway — if not now, then later.

He lifted the binoculars again and saw it immediately. In the upper left radius of the circle there was a minute orange dot.

"I've got it," he said, matter-of-factly, lowering his binoculars to fix its position. "Fine on the port bow."

Sash smiled, both with relief and at Brown's nautical expression. "Shall I alter course?" he asked.

"No. We may be out of sight of land, but they may have us on radar at Wick. Besides, if we go slightly past then the breeze will drift us down to the boat."

Looking through the glasses again, Brown was glad that he had decided on the orange sails — well worth the expense. They were beginning to take form now. Jerry had the Main and Number 1 Genoa up, sailing west on a reach so that Brown could see them more easily. He lowered the binoculars again.

Judy was still hunched in the blanket and Brown felt suddenly chill. The sweat inside his wet-suit was turning cold and, although the sea looked inviting in the bright, morning sun, he knew that at 7 a.m. in early May, the North Sea is far from warm. He turned his mind away from the unpleasant thought. It was inevitable and that was all there was to it.

He spoke to Sash: "Open the rear cargo-door."

Sash pulled a switch.

Brown focused on the yacht again until it disappeared from sight below the level of the console. It would be directly under the plane soon.

"You might as well put her on auto-pilot now," said Brown, "and switch out the cargo-hold lights. Your job is over, Sash. Let's go."

He unstrapped Judy and ushered her out of the cabin. He waited for the pilot and then followed, his face a mask of concentration.

They were waiting for him by the open freight doors. Wilson and Judy were looking at him and Tom was looking out of the door and the big drop beyond.

He estimated that they had just passed over the boat. This was not a moment for hesitation. In one sudden and continuous movement, he launched the binoculars out of the plane, jumped towards the raft nearest the door and pressed a button on the side of his wristwatch.

"Right, let's get these out," he shouted and they were spurred into action.

Wilson swiftly clipped the 'chute-lines, attached to each raft, to the nearest plutonium rack, so that the parachutes would open immediately. Tom quickly walked along the row, turning each CO_2 gas valve to inflate the rafts and, as he did so, Brown pushed them out. The last half-dozen took longer because they were further back, but in forty-five seconds they were all clear, including the disposable bag.

Brown flashed a look at Sash. "Any not open?"

He saw a quick shake of the head before he stood back and shouted:

"OK, then jump! And don't forget to open your 'chute as soon as you're clear."

Before the last words were spoken, Wilson had jumped, and Tom and Sash followed at two-second intervals. During that time period, Brown had gathered up the trailing 'chute lines and began to tie them in a rough knot around the rack. On finishing he turned round to find Judy still hesitating on the brink, despite her six training jumps.

It was so imperative that she jump quickly that time seemed to stop. She was standing on the edge of the cargo floor, looking back at him, and he couldn't move. It was as if there was some bond between them that would be broken if she jumped. He wanted to shout at her, to push her — do anything to get her off the plane. But he made no move. Then she turned and disappeared, as if there hadn't been a problem at all. Suddenly he too felt released. He counted two seconds, pressed the button on his watch and jumped into space.

A few seconds after he pulled the cord the straps bit into his life-jacket as the opening parachute brought him up with a jerk. He glanced at his watch. His finger had stopped the second-hand at sixty-three seconds. Their immobility must have been more imagined than real. With a bit of luck the whole lot would be strung out over no more than three miles of the Moray Firth.

He looked down at the floating white puffs, but didn't think to glance back at the plane. If he had, he would have seen an almost indistinguishable black shape, winging its undeviating way to the tip of Scotland.

Chapter 4

TROUTMAN STARED at the telephone. It was quite an aesthetic instrument really, for what it was: a jumble of wires and diaphragms, or whatever. The shell was so constructed that it seemed to blend in with man's idea of natural acceptability. There were no corners, for instance — just gentle curves. Other things that man makes, like buildings, consist almost entirely of straight lines, perpendiculars and angles. And then, when you wanted to dial your number, you put your finger in a hole and twisted your hand in a circle several times, until a bell rang and you obtained you reward. Yes, definitely an interesting, possibly even erotic, artefact, the humble telephone.

Erotic! He slapped his thigh and admonished himself at his thoughts. But, at the same time, he realized that it was a subconscious form of escapism, so that his mind didn't have to grapple with the problem that was presenting itself. A telephone was undoubtedly an inanimate object and, what was more, the one he was looking at refused, obstinately, to ring.

He looked at his watch yet again. 6.49. Drake knew the plan and he had rung on all previous occasions. Their plane was due to leave at 6.10. There could have been a little delay, but not *so* long, and anyway Drake would have let him know.

Troutman reached into his deep mackintosh pocket and extracted cigarettes and lighter. As he lit up, he made his decision. He picked up the telephone receiver and dialled the operator. If the phone was engaged when his deputy called, he would just have to call again. After only one ring a male voice answered.

"Is there any way you can check whether this phone is working properly?" asked Troutman. Hearing his own voice he realized how worried he was and hurried on. "I'm expecting an incoming call which has not arrived."

"Well, sir, I can phone you back. If you don't hear the telephone ring in thirty seconds, pick it up anyway and we can speak to each other."

The operator sounded bored and tired. Troutman wondered whether it was because he was coming to the end of a long shift or because he had heard the same sort of inane request many times before from distraught wives and mothers.

"Will it give us the answer? I mean, if *you* can get through then anyone can?" asked Troutman.

"Yes, sir," replied the operator, kindly.

Troutman was about to replace the phone when the operator said: "Can I have your number?"

He gave it and put the receiver down more heavily then he had intended. He *was* on edge. He took another, longer drag on his cigarette and tried to relax. The sound of the telephone bell made him jump and he answered it before it could ring again.

"Operator?"

Strange how he had unconsciously assumed that Drake would not be phoning.

"Yes. It appears, sir, that your phone is in order."

Why was it only now that he realized the man did not have a Scottish accent?

"Thank you," he replied calmly, and replaced the receiver.

He took another long pull on his cigarette and forced himself to think. He could phone Carlisle, but Drake would not be by the public telephone that they used, for the obvious reason that if he were he would have used it. And anyway, they could cross calls. The plane was either delayed for some reason or it had taken off on time. Either way, Drake should have phoned. The best way to find out was by going to the control-tower. They would most likely have it on radar by now, if it had taken off on time, and he could use their phone to rouse control at Carlisle if necessary.

In the meantime he didn't want to leave his present phone unguarded, just in case. He cast his eyes round desperately, but there was no one in the lobby. Wick Airport, he reflected, was not busy at the worst of times. At 6.55 a.m. it was almost deserted. Then he saw a mechanic, in stained, blue overalls, walking past one of the windows, an open tin of tobacco in his hands. Troutman rushed to the door and ran after him.

The man heard him coming and turned round suspiciously. He was young — about nineteen or twenty — with red hair and a short moustache. The sad, blue eyes looked Troutman over as he approached, then he looked down at his cold hands. With the taciturn disposition of the working man the world over, he concentrated on rolling his cigarette.

Troutman was conscious of the condensation of his breath on the still, cold air as it rasped in his lungs. He paused for a few moments, deciding how to put it to this young man, who seemed interested in nothing but his tobacco.

"Would you do me a great favour?" he asked, pointing through one of the windows. "Guard that telephone until I return. I shouldn't be away long. I've just got to go up to the control-tower."

It sounded like a desperate plea and the mechanic's apparent concentration on his roll-up had not wavered. On an impulse Troutman withdrew his wallet and extracted a five-pound note.

"Take any message for me and bring it to the tower, and don't let anyone else use the phone."

The mechanic had finished the construction of his cigarette. He popped it in his mouth, shut the tin with a loud click and raised his head. He looked first at the fiver in Troutman's outstretched hand and then into his face. He appeared to make up his mind.

"Well, if it means that much to ye, I daresay I could do it for nothin'," he said in broad Scots and ambled towards the door.

Troutman looked after him, convinced that the assertion of the tight-fistedness of the Scots must be a myth. He replaced the note in his wallet and began to run towards the control-tower.

As he reached the bottom of the stairs, he slowed. It occurred to him that it must be very cold, if he could put his mind to thinking about it. He didn't want to burst in if all was well, so he climbed the stairs at what he considered to be a respectable speed.

When he reached the top, his thighs aching, he stopped at the door. The two occupants were looking at him through the glass. They had obviously heard him clanging up the iron steps in his policeman's boots. Embarrassed, he threw away his cigarette and went in.

The heat hit him immediately and he quickly closed the door. A slight, grey-haired man of about sixty stood perfectly relaxed, his hands at his sides, in the middle of the room. He wore an overcoat, but no gloves. Behind him, seated at two emerald-green screens, was a man in his mid twenties, who was perhaps less appropriately dressed in a green anorak. Both were staring at Troutman. The grey-haired man spoke first.

"Can I help you?" he asked in a home-counties accent, and then, more forcefully, "The public are not allowed in here," fixing the newcomer with a piercing look.

It occurred to Troutman that there weren't many Scotsmen around.

"My name is Troutman. I'm Chief Security Officer for BNFL."

"Aah! So that's it," said the controller, and then: "I suppose you have proof of that?"

"Yes, of course." Troutman reached for his wallet again. As he handed the card over, trying to keep his voice as calm as possible, he said, "I'm a little worried about my plane."

"Needn't be," answered the controller immediately. He handed the card back. "We've just got her on the radar," pointing at the anoraked figure. Troutman felt relief flooding through him.

"How do you know it's the BNFL flight from Carlisle?" he asked, a little hesitantly.

The controller turned on a condescending smile. Troutman knew the type. Supremely self-confident in his technical expertise, but with about as much general awareness as a Yorkshire pudding. He would make few mistakes, but when they did come, they would be big ones.

"Because," said the controller, as if Troutman were a retarded child, "the blip should be exactly where it is and we are not expecting any other aircraft at this time."

He smiled at Troutman again before continuing, making the security man realize that he had rather unfairly maligned that venerable pudding.

"The plane crossed into the Moray Firth at Portknockie, which is exactly what it should do, and it is bang on time for a 6.10 lift-off, given a slight northerly. What's more, it has altered course very slightly and is now heading straight for where we are standing. In addition, it is at the correct height and Jamie here says that the blip corresponds to the size of the aircraft — an Argosy, I believe?"

Troutman nodded absently. He had been worried unduly. His policeman's training had taken over from reason. What could possibly go wrong anyway? Here it was, on route and on schedule. There had obviously been some sort of technical hitch in communication. Well, at least the controller hadn't asked him to leave, but then he'd want him to stay, to show Troutman how good he was.

As if in answer to his thought the controller said: "You can stay if you like."

He then walked towards the screens, picked up a microphone and flicked a switch.

"This is Wick control calling BNFL Special Flight."

He waited several seconds. There was no reply.

"This is Wick control calling BNFL. Do you read? Over." And again, the wait.

Troutman felt a tightening in his throat.

"Why aren't they answering?" he questioned.

The controller just repeated the message.

"BNFL, this is Wick control. Come in."

The silence was almost overpowering. The controller gazed out of the window towards the south, as if he could see the plane. Troutman stared at the microphone. The radar man peered myopically at his equipment. Interference began to develop behind the plane on both screens, but that often happened. The pilot wasn't answering, but at least they had radar, and the operator knew that his job was now becoming more important. He looked first at the left screen, that gave distance, and then at the one on the right, which gave height. Apart from that interference, which was now beginning to go, both screens were working well. The young man was new at his job. Radar operators didn't stay long at Wick Airport.

"Perhaps he hasn't switched his set on," ventured Troutman.

The little man turned round and gave him a long withering look.

"No," said the controller at last, "there must be something wrong with his set."

But he called up again, just to make sure.

Troutman was very worried now. First, the lack of a phone call. Now this. Too much coincidence, surely? And there was something at the back of his brain.

"Does this often happen?" he asked, braving the controller's wrath and hoping to stimulate his own mind.

"Sometimes," replied the older man, in what Troutman regarded as being a fairly reasonable tone. "There is often interference of some kind, but not on a day like this. Technical faults do occur in the pilot's radio but they are usually spotted before take-off."

"That's it," said Troutman suddenly.

Both men turned round to look at him.

"When he took off," continued Troutman, "wouldn't he call up the control-tower at Carlisle, to get clearance of some kind?"

Both men now looked at each other as if Troutman ought to be committed.

"Yes," said the controller, as if humouring a child, "he would."

"Then the fault would have been noticed when he was still on the ground," said Troutman. "The controller at Carlisle would surely have called through to let you know that the plane had no radio."

The little grey man opened his mouth to speak, but Troutman didn't give him a chance.

36

"So the fault must have developed during the flight. What chance would you say there was of that happening, Mr Controller, with a clear sky, no wind and on a straight, one-hour milk-run?"

The radar operator was standing as well now, looking at Troutman. The controller looked puzzled and perhaps a little worried.

"What's on that plane?" he asked suddenly.

The question caught Troutman by surprise.

"Never you mind," he said, waving an arm in dismissal. What was he arguing with this little man for anyway? But it was a lame reply and the controller stepped forward with triumphant gait.

"What are you afraid of?" he asked, boring his eyes into Troutman's. "A hijack?"

The security officer looked back into the red rims. Of course it was obvious. He had stupidly given it away by his insane behaviour. Well, perhaps he would get some authority if he told. The controller was still glaring up at him, waiting for an answer.

"Yes," said Troutman, trying to keep his voice as level as possible.

But the controller continued to leer at him.

"Then tell me this, Mr Chief Security Officer. Why is it that the aircraft is on course and on schedule for Wick? Why is it that it's not half-way across the North Sea by now?"

A good point. It might be a ruse on the part of the hijackers to fool him, but that would sound far too weak for this upstart of an idiot controller. He felt so frustrated that he wanted to hit the man, and was about to explode the tension inside him by shouting when the radar man spoke for the first time.

"We'll know in a wee while anyway," he said. "He's due to begin his descent about now."

Troutman wondered whether the controller was going to ask him to leave. He was still squinting up at him. Instead, he pivoted round like a ballet dancer and strutted over to the mike.

"Is he still on course?" he asked.

Troutman had to admire his control.

"Aye," replied the radar man, now seated again, his eyes on the right-hand screen.

There was the flick of a switch.

"This is Wick control calling BNFL. Over."

There were several seconds of silence before he spoke again.

"BNFL. This is Wick control. We are assuming that you cannot transmit, but there should be no difficulty. We have you on our screens and you are cleared for landing. You are dead on line for Wick airport, but you must begin to lose height now."

He looked at the right screen.

"BNFL, you are approximately six miles from north-south

runway. Wind is light, northerly, backing slightly to the east. It's as clear as a bell here and you should have no difficulty with visual landing."

He flicked the switch again, just in case, and they all stared at the right-hand screen.

Thirty seconds went by.

"He's no' coming down," said the radar operator, a little incredulously.

A crease appeared between the eyes of the controller. He continued to watch the screen as he flicked the switch again.

"BNFL, this is Wick control. You must reduce height to approach from the south."

The blip remained perfectly steady on both screens and, for the first time, the controller began to realize that something was very wrong. He moved his gaze to the security man.

Troutman's mouth was now completely dry and he also became conscious of the sweat breaking out all over his body. *My God, a hijack.* He had been convinced it would never happen. But why was the plane coming on?

"Can we see it yet?" he asked.

The controller walked over to a desk top and lifted some binoculars to his eyes. Troutman stood mesmerized by the sweeping green arms of the radar screens.

"There she is," said the controller, "coming straight for us."

Troutman moved over quickly and the little grey man handed him the glasses, pointing. The plane came into view at once, as Troutman didn't have to refocus at all. It galled him to realize that the sod of a controller had the same strength eyesight as himself. Strange how totally irrational thoughts impinge upon your reality in these situations. Then he was searching the aircraft for any tell-tale signs. But there was nothing to see — just an Argosy, flying in orderly fashion at 10,000 feet. He knew it wasn't going to stop, but he followed it until it was nearly overhead.

As the controller began to call up again, he moved outside, not bothering to close the door this time. He could hear the four Rolls-Royce engines clearly and he could see with the binoculars that all the propellers were turning. As the plane passed him he saw that the rear part of the cargo section looked odd. It took him fully five seconds to realize that the rear door was wide open. He watched it for a few more moments with the naked eye, then moved back inside.

This was the moment he had dreaded happening, the moment that he was sure couldn't or wouldn't happen. Yet he now had to make that phone call. The two occupants were looking at him.

"Any response or change of course?" he asked.

"No," answered the controller.

The hostility was still in his voice — probably more because he had been proved wrong than anything else, thought Troutman.

"Do you mind if I use your phone?" he asked briskly, clearly not expecting a negative reply as he walked towards it.

He reached for his wallet for the third time in half an hour and extracted a piece of rather crumpled paper. It was odd, but although he was acting quickly he felt like taking his time, as if what he did now didn't matter. He turned to the two technicians. The scene had changed completely. *They* were now the onlookers.

"What you have seen and heard this morning comes under the Official Secrets Act. So does what I am about to say on this phone. I would advise you to go outside while I make the call."

The young man started to move, but the older one motioned him back. The latter then thrust his chin out and folded his hands across his chest, defiantly.

Troutman shrugged, picked up the receiver and dialled the numbers backwards. There was a long pause before the bell rang. After the second ring it was answered.

"I'd like to speak to the Director," said Troutman.

"What director is that, sir?" replied the voice.

Troutman envisaged a long, pointless conversation with this minion and time was of the essence.

"Look here, sonny," he growled, "my name is Troutman. I'm Chief Security Officer for British Nuclear Fuels Limited. I have reason to believe there has been a hijack of plutonium and I need air surveillance immediately. I don't care where the Director is, or whether he's still having his beauty sleep, but get him now, d'ya hear."

The man at the other end appeared to hesitate, before saying:

"Could you give me your number, sir?"

He gave it. Then he had a sudden thought and gave the public telephone number as well, just in case the Director couldn't get through. The phone went dead. He replaced the receiver and slowly walked over to the radar screens.

"Is it still at the same course and height?" he asked, not really expecting that it wasn't.

The radar man, who was still staring open-mouthed at Troutman, came out of his reverie. He turned, scanned the screens and nodded his head.

"Write down his course for me, will you?" said Troutman.

He felt wretched and gazed forlornly out of the window. Even the controller had ceased to exist within his thoughts. He lit up a cigarette and just sat, staring at the "No Smoking" sign. Then the phone rang and he rushed to it.

"Troutman," he said tightly.

"This is the Director. What's happened?"

It was a voice you obeyed instantly and Troutman explained as succinctly as he could. But he felt some urgency creeping into his voice and at times he had to pause to run his tongue over dry lips.

"Have you been on to Carlisle?" asked the Director, when he had finished.

"No, I phoned you the moment the plane flew over."

"Good. Anything else that you think I should know?"

"No," replied Troutman again, thinking furiously. "I think the open freight-door must be significant."

"Yes. I'll handle things from now on. It's become a matter of state security. I'll be in touch, so stay available, where you are."

And with that the phone went dead in Troutman's hand again.

Well, it was out of his control now. He'd passed the buck. He licked his lips again and turned, looking the controller straight in the eye as he spoke. He felt strangely buoyant.

"If either of you two breathe a word of what you've heard here today, you'll be slapped in irons so quickly your teeth will rattle."

It gave him some small pleasure to see a nerve twitch in the controller's face. But the feeling was short-lived as he suddenly and belatedly focused on the fact that he'd had two men and two pilots at Carlisle, and he hadn't heard from any of them.

Chapter 5

JUDY WAS the last person to break the surface of the sea. The first panic-stricken thought that registered on her already numb brain was that she was drowning. When you hit water travelling at over twenty miles an hour, even wearing a life-jacket, your body totally submerges for a few seconds. Long enough for you to realize that you are under.

She thought of her father, a merchant seaman whom she hadn't seen for eight years. As a child she used to dream that he would die like this, his mouth open, calling her name and the frothing sea filling him up. It was that, really, which had made her give in to the neighbourhood boys when she was fourteen. She had developed early and been attractive even then. Later, her fair hair had curled naturally at the shoulder, framing big, green eyes and high cheekbones on a rosebud skin. She had what novelists call "natural" beauty, ostensibly because it needed no help from make-up, but really because the loveliness held an essence which defied description.

She threshed her arms and legs to get to the surface. The legs worked, but the arms kept getting caught up. She opened her eyes as little as she could and discovered, to her horror, that she was still under. She tried to thrust her body upwards again in renewed panic, her feet kicking wildly and her hands beating imaginary drums in front of her. But still the darkness. Why wasn't the life-jacket working? She wanted to breathe.

When Judy had reached puberty, she remembered, her mother had become hostile to her, entertaining her men from the textile factory where she worked while her husband was at sea, and threatening her daughter with all sorts of dire consequences if she told. On leaving school at sixteen, Judy had run away from Manchester, to London. She had seen neither parent in the five years since then. Too curvy for modelling and her deportment all wrong, she had undressed on film and made a mint. When she'd blown the money, a prominent politician, with a wife and four kids in the provinces, had supported her in a flat in Chelsea. That had cost her an abortion. Her general melancholy and a search for some sort of fulfilment had eventually led her to the French Mediterranean coast.

Now terrified and unable to hold her breath any longer, she opened her eyes wide and, with a relief that can only come to those who believe they are about to die, realized that she *was* on the surface. The trapped air in the 'chute had formed a canopy above her head, shielding the sun and creating a cocoon of darkness. She gulped great mouthfuls of air, breathing deeply. But the relief was soon to go, for as she relaxed she felt the cold penetrating her wet-suit — sudden, shocking, unbelievable cold. John. She thought of him, as she always did in times of stress.

They had met in Cannes. It had been the classic situation. She, the penniless nymph, lounging on the beach in seductive pose and he, the rich playboy, flicking sand off her excuse for a bikini. But she hadn't cared. He had provided her with the strength she didn't have. The blind persistence that she had acquired for finding something unseen and unknown, she also saw in him. It bound her to him. He had sent the crew of his yacht back to Britain by plane and the two of them had sailed it all the way back on their own. Those had been the most blissful four weeks of her life....

What was it about him she had sensed up there at 10,000 feet that had frightened her? What was it he had said? *Keep your body moving. Move your arms and your legs to keep the circulation going.* The darkness. She must move out of the darkness.

As quickly as she could with frozen hands, she unbuckled the harness and swam to the edge of the canopy, which was now collapsing on top of her. She had to pull her head under the water again to escape, her motions slow and laboured. She felt strangely colder in the sun.

Her limbs ached and her brain wasn't functioning too well either. She gazed towards the east, searching for her rescuers. It did not occur to her that it was the wrong direction. The arm movements became more laboured as the blood flowed less and less fast and the brain ceased to send messages of instruction. Her head dropped back as consciousness began to leave her. All bodily feeling had gone. In less than another minute her heart would have stopped. Then, through a silent haze, she heard Brown's voice.

"An armpit each, quickly."

Then he started asking stupid questions.

"Judy," he said anxiously, "can you hear me?" A pause, and then, "Can you move your legs?"

Stupid man. Of course she couldn't move her legs. She couldn't even feel them.

"Is she...?" someone shouted before he was dug in the ribs.

At that Judy opened her eyes and saw Brown's face. She dropped her lids against the brightness and tried to smile.

"No," said Brown, "but almost. We'll take a limb each and massage like hell."

The big rubber dinghy skimmed across the water and keeping balance was difficult when you couldn't use your hands. Besides, Brown thought that he ought to be directing operations. Sash, Wilson and Tom were rubbing furiously. He called over the second of the two-man dinghy team and told him to take over Judy's right leg. This enabled him to crawl up to the bows, two or three feet above the water. They were heading straight for the yacht which, its sails down, lay motionless. Far over on the starboard bow, he spotted the other inflatable, stopped in the water as it picked up another rod.

The operation was going well, but they had to move faster. The authorities would take some time to get organized. He would guess at at least half an hour after the plane flew over Wick. But when someone started to make decisions, everything in a line from Carlisle to the tip of Scotland and beyond would be surveyed. He wanted to be well away by the time they got around to the Moray Firth. The likelihood was that they would be slow to react, and a thorough air-to-ground/air-to-sea search would be difficult to mount at short notice. Anyway, they would concentrate on the Argosy. Eventually they would figure a parachute jump, but would be unlikely to give priority to the sea areas. He also reckoned that co-ordination would be bad. The people who understood the details of the plutonium shipments, and therefore how, when and where the plutonium was hijacked, were unlikely to be the same people who would lead the search. They would also have to find out what had happened at Carlisle in order to get some insight into what, exactly, had occurred, and that, too, would take time, especially since they would need to keep things quiet. And, anyway, Carlisle would compound their problems. Brown didn't envy them. Of course, there was always the possibility that he would be discovered by pure luck, but that was one chance you always took.

The yacht was fast approaching now and he signalled to the helmsman to slow down. The inflatable was skilfully glided to the yacht's stern cockpit and Irma, the only person left on board, secured the painter that Brown handed her.

There would be a tendency now to become lethargic, Brown knew. The immediate danger was over and relief would flood through the body like a tide, washing away the adrenalin. Reaction would set in. That must not happen. There was still a lot to do. Without greeting her, Brown called to the woman on deck.

"Irma, Judy is literally dying from cold. Take her into the peak cabin, strip her off and dry her."

Wilson and Tom, having secured the dinghy aft, were already beginning to lift the girl.

"Paul, George, get her into the cabin," said Brown. "Then get the white sails ready to hoist. Light-weather Main and Number 1 Genny. Got that?"

They both answered in the affirmative and jumped on deck. Judy was passed to them and they disappeared into the cabin. Tom was looking at him and Brown flicked his thumb towards the boat. With a remarkable degree of speed, considering what he had been through, Tom vaulted off the dinghy and quickly cast off fore and aft.

Brown settled down in the bows as Wilson gunned the engine and steered a north-westerly course in search of the other dinghy. He forced himself not to think of the cold that was creeping into his bones and slowing his actions.

As they approached the other inflatable, which was again stopped in the water, one of the two-man crew looked up. Brown cupped hands to mouth and the engine died to a murmur.

"How many?" shouted Brown.

"Twelve," came the instant reply.

Brown had already spotted two rods, nestling in their rafts, as they had approached. He cupped his hands again.

"Get those back to the boat. We'll get the other two," and Wilson accelerated again as Brown pointed.

Each rod-raft had had a stainless-steel ring fitted and reinforced into each end, and it was simplicity itself to cleat the rings on to the many ropes that Brown had fitted to the dinghy's rim. Then they were heading back at a much reduced speed. Even so, they managed to overtake Jerry's inflatable.

Back at the yacht, both rod-rafts were hauled aboard the dinghy and the stainless-steel rods extracted. Brown and Wilson handed them up to Sash and Tom, both in a dry set of clothing, who took them into the main cabin. There they were fitted into a cavity that was skilfully cut out of the top of the fibre-glass keel. The other inflatable arrived, and Brown and Wilson jumped aboard the yacht to supervise the loading of the rods. All fourteen were soon in the cavity. The top of the keel was then slotted back into place above them and, apart from a hairline crack, which they would temporarily seal in transit, the rods were undetectable. The duckboards and cabin floor were then replaced.

"Well," said Brown, emerging from the cabin into the sunlight, "she'll ride a little lower in the water, but with an extra 900 pounds of ballast, she'll stand upright in a Force ten."

He was glowing now and it was infectious. With the exception of Wilson and the two men puncturing the rod-rafts to a watery grave, everyone was laughing.

The two puncture experts finished and quickly moved to one of the inflatable dinghies. They removed the engine and, with everyone working with excited alacrity, it was moved, hand over hand, to Brown and Wilson, who stowed it. The inflatable itself followed, was deflated and stuffed in a large aft locker. Men were laughing and joking the whole time. Brown let it continue. The release of tension was practical now and he could always bring them back to a fast-moving team when he wanted. He would be expected to join in. No sour-faced leader, he.

With a joyous leer on his face he put his right foot on the starboard aft locker, looked down at the remaining inflatable, turned his head to his men and shouted:

"Where's the pigsticker?"

Some loud cheers went up and someone darted into the cabin. A stiletto knife, strapped to a four-foot length of bamboo, emerged and was passed, carefully, from hand to hand, to Brown. He grasped it with obvious glee, leant over the rail and carefully punctured all the air compartments of the inflatable. With the engine to weigh it down, it sank like a stone. There were some more cheers and some laughter.

Brown didn't feel cold any longer. He looked up at the burgee and raised his voice.

"Jerry, I do believe the wind is freshening. Let's have those sails up. Then put her over on the port tack. I want to sail sixty miles due east into the North Sea before we turn south."

He was above to give a hand with the mainsail when it occurred to him that there was something he should have remembered. Judy.

He walked through the main cabin and opened the for'ard doors. A somewhat bedraggled female, draped in several blankets, was propped up against the bulkhead. Irma, appearing the more flushed of the two, was sitting in front of her with a large glass of brandy in her hand. They both looked up as he came in. Irma glanced back at the other woman and Judy fixed her eye on Brown. It was several seconds before he spoke.

"How are you?"

There was another pause.

"I'm fine," she eventually replied in a husky voice. It was also a little restrained. She cleared her throat.

"Has she drunk some yet?" he asked Irma.

The woman nodded. "A little."

He turned back to Judy and said with a smile, "Try some more. It'll do you good."

With that he left, shutting the door quietly behind him. Wilson was looking at him rather absently as he exited the aft cabin.

"Towel yourself down and get some clothes on," Brown said to him, and there was an immediate response.

The leader sat back against the pulpit and relaxed as he watched his team at work, getting the fast boat underway. He had been foolish to bring Judy along. In the event, she hadn't been needed and had almost died. That would have been bad for morale. What was more, he didn't like making mistakes.

Chapter 6

STANDING in the centrally heated hall of his London flat, General Sir Giles Stoddard replaced the telephone receiver and looked at his watch. 7.29. He picked up the phone again to make his third call in ten minutes, dialling a Scotland number.

The bell rang once before a harsh voice barked, "Amis."

"Clive, Giles Stoddard."

Amis said: "Hello, Giles, how's tricks? Dashed time to ring, old boy. Haven't even...."

"Listen, Clive," interrupted Stoddard brusquely, "this is not a social call, I'm afraid. I'm at home, so I can't go through official communication channels. An Argosy plane that flew over Wick Airport about twenty minutes ago, heading approximately nor'-nor'-west, is full of plutonium and I've reason to believe it's been hijacked. It should have landed at Wick. Can you get some of your jets on to it as soon as poss? Wick still have it on radar."

There was a small pause.

"Can do," answered Amis. "Where do I get in touch?"

"You have the Control number?"

"Yes."

"I'll be there in twenty minutes or so. I'll phone you then. All right?"

"Just a minute," said Amis.

There was a pause of about five seconds.

"Who was best man at my wedding?"

Stoddard couldn't help smiling at the caution.

"How could I ever forget," he replied. "Making a speech about how wonderful you are is not my favourite pastime."

There was a short laugh at the other end. "Fine. Anything else?"

"No. I'll be in touch," said Stoddard and hung up.

He then immediately dialled Control.

"Pomfret?"

"Yes."

"This is Sir Giles. I've requested an immediate Fireball Alert. The aircraft that Troutman told you of is being taken care of. When I arrive I want all the communication networks manned. Is that clear?"

"Er, yes, sir."

Stoddard would have to have been totally insensitive not to feel the insecurity of the other man.

"This is urgent, Pomfret. You have my personal authority to draft anyone until I get there. Do your best. Any new developments?"

"No, sir."

"Good," and with that he put the phone down, grabbed his coat and left.

It was 8 a.m. when he pushed open the door of Communications Control. Everyone looked up as he entered. What they saw was a man in his middle fifties, about five feet eight in height, with a thickset figure. Sparklingly clear blue eyes shone against a mildly florid complexion and short, grey hair covered the squarish head in tight curls. A pipe protruded from a corner of his mouth, but everyone in the room knew that he never lit it until midday. The smart, grey suit was the same one he always wore. There would have been speculation that he went to bed in it if it didn't look so well-pressed every morning.

On the frustrating car journey over, Stoddard had listed in his mind the things he had to do and shuffled them into an order of priority. But he had to be here to do it. The reason why, in a war, your enemy invariably aims to destroy your command headquarters is because you are virtually lost without a centre of communications. From this hub, Stoddard could, in theory, control the rim. He had decided that he would be his own Director of Operations, when the holder of the office had retired, as well as being Head of the Department.

Pomfret, who, Stoddard knew, was supposed to go off duty at 8.00, was still manning the console. He'd done a good job in getting everyone together, especially since it was so early in the morning. Most of the equipment had an operator in front of it and the place was filling with more people, all looking to him for direction. He removed his pipe.

"Any new developments?" he asked Pomfret.

"No urgent ones, sir. Mr Jensen will be arriving shortly."

The voice was more confident now, but Stoddard noticed beads of sweat on Pomfret's brow.

The older man nodded and said, "Can you stay on for a bit?" knowing that Pomfret wouldn't have left now for anything. Before he could reply, Stoddard turned to his replacement, a man called Deansworthy.

"Give him a hand and get me General Amis in Scotland, immediately," he ordered.

"Sir," said Pomfret, "perhaps I ought to say that Air Commodore James wants to know what the flap's about. I said you'd call him back. And General Jacks is on at the moment, demanding to know why his whole unit is about to besiege Heathrow."

Stoddard suppressed a groan. At least his request for a Fireball Alert had been granted. But these sorts of questions were bound to come up and there would be many more. He turned to Deansworthy who was holding a phone towards him. Stoddard took it and said:

"Take over the console. Pomfret, try and quieten down General Jacks and deal with any other similar enquiries. I am not available."

Looking up, he saw his Intelligence Director, Jensen, coming in by the other door and put the speaker to his mouth.

"General Amis? What's happening?"

"We're in pursuit, but we don't have radar contact yet," answered the ebullient Amis.

"Let me know when you do. I shall also want helicopters and troops for an air-to-ground search soon, General. Can you manage that?"

"Thought you might ask," said Amis modestly. "I have five on standby, and some more coming."

"Good man. We'll link up by radio from now on. Also, if you don't mind, I'd like to be in direct hearing of your jets when they catch the Argosy."

"Can do," replied Amis.

Stoddard replaced the receiver and turned to Jensen, who had been listening.

"I'll tell you all about it in a second, Bill. For the moment, can you see to the radio contact — with Amis in Scotland?"

With what Stoddard thought was commendable restraint, his deputy hesitated, nodded and turned towards the radio operators. One of the console assistants, wearing tinted glasses, was looking at him, and before he could turn his head away Stoddard spoke.

"Get me the Chief Constable for Cumbria on the phone, now."

The young man turned at once to a book fixed to the desk in front of him.

"Try his home first," said Stoddard, as an afterthought. Chief Constables didn't usually begin their working day before 9 a.m. at the earliest. He glanced at his watch. 8.06. Nearly an hour had passed since the plane had flown over Wick and the doubts were beginning to multiply in his mind. Turning, he stopped a passing controller.

"Turf out all the maps between Carlisle and Wick." Then another afterthought: "Plus the Admiralty charts to the north of Wick, clear to the Pole."

Jensen was returning. He had a forceful face, the nose long and narrow, the jaw large and dark, and the eyebrows black and bushy. This was topped by contrasting reddish brown hair. He was of normal build, although he had a substantial paunch, which was catered for by the immaculately tailored, Savile Row, double-breasted, pin-stripe suit. He was what socialists see as a typical product of the English upper middle classes — public school, fashionable Cambridge college and a career civil servant. He was more than a little pompous, but Stoddard had a grudging respect for him. Respect because he had a good brain, grudging because he didn't like him. He recognized him as a necessary evil, whose connections, through what was euphemistically called the "old-boy network", were greater than his own. He himself had been down a similar route: prep school, Eton, Oxford, Sandhurst Military Academy, then into the Guards. He'd had a heavy Etonian accent at one time, which he now played down. Jensen didn't, and Stoddard had always thought it odd that he insisted on being called Bill. He had an infuriating habit of screwing up his eyes and grinning after almost every utterance.

"We have the radio link-up," said Jensen, and then, not being able to restrain himself any longer, "what's all this about?"

"Plutonium hijack. I'm going to explain it to the Chief Constable for Cumbria in a minute, so hang on."

"Mr Phillipson, sir," called the young man with the tinted glasses, holding out the phone, and then he realized that Stoddard probably hadn't a clue who Phillipson was. He reddened and added quickly, "The Chief Constable for Cumbria."

Stoddard took the phone and paused while Jensen linked himself into the same line.

"Mr Phillipson?" asked Stoddard politely.

"That's right. And who may you be?" answered the policeman in a northern accent.

Stoddard decided it was no time for modesty.

"My name is Stoddard. I'm the Head of MI5."

It wasn't strictly true. "Internal Security" was split up into so many horizontal sections now that it was difficult to know who was actually in charge. But he didn't think Phillipson would know that and it might impress him. In any case, his real position in the hierarchy would take far too long to explain.

"Oh, yes," came the non-committal reply.

The Chief Constable appeared to be unmoved. Stoddard took a deep breath and decided to be honest.

"I need your help urgently. An aircraft — a Hawker-Siddeley Argosy — has been hijacked. It contained plutonium from the reprocessing plant at Windscale. The plane took off from Carlisle Airport early this morning for Wick. As yet I have no idea where the hijack took place. I want that information. I must, therefore, know what happened, if anything, at Carlisle Airport. I'm phoning you because it's your patch and I need the information urgently. I should be obliged if you would take personal charge."

He paused, but Phillipson said nothing. Stoddard wasn't noted for his tact and Chief Constables needed to be handled with kid gloves. Phillipson, he thought, might think it was one big hoax, but he would still be curious.

"If you wish to verify my authority, Mr Phillipson, I'm sure you know how, but it would waste valuable time."

It was another five seconds before Phillipson said, "Do what I can," in a voice which implied that he hadn't actually made up his mind.

Stoddard nevertheless breathed a silent sigh of relief and continued.

"We won't be able to keep this out of the media eventually, but I'd rather it was later than sooner."

"Of course." Phillipson sounded more sure now. "Anything else?"

"Perhaps you could ring me here as soon as you have the information?" said Stoddard and he gave the number.

"I'll see to it myself," replied Phillipson and hung up.

Stoddard had wanted to impress upon the Chief Constable how desperately urgent it was to have the information, but he knew he couldn't. The policeman would be expected to work that out for himself. And Stoddard had to rely on Phillipson's quick organization in the area. A radio operator was signalling him and he walked over. Jensen followed him, looking worried.

"Sorry, sir," said the operator, "I didn't want to disturb your call. The jets have had the Argosy on radar for a couple of minutes. They should have her on visual any second."

He looked closely at Stoddard to gauge his mood. He knew from experience that the Old Man had a genuine manner and an almost lovable character, provided you were on his side. His face held an almost perpetual frown and he lost his temper frequently, but this acted as a sort of release valve for letting off tension and he was quickly back to normal. He also smiled a lot. What the radio operator didn't know, though he would have believed it if he had, was that, as a man of extremes, Stoddard was often quoted at mess parties as saying, "There is nothing worse than mediocrity," which would be followed by bouts of affectionate laughter. Seeing no hostility, the man replaced the headphones.

Stoddard bent down to the other operator who he knew was monitoring communications between ground and air. Transferring his pipe to his left hand he wrote on a pad, "Switch to loudspeaker." The operator immediately flicked a switch and removed his headphones. He realized there was no sound and turned a knob. The room was instantly filled with static.

"They haven't spotted it yet, sir," ventured someone.

Stoddard said, "Thank you," and smiled.

The pause gave him time to think and he sucked on his empty pipe. There were things he wanted to know about the plane, yes, but more than anything else he wanted to know how the hijack took place and how they could have done it. He needed to know more about the transportation arrangements. Jensen broke into his thoughts.

"Do we know enough about this plutonium?"

"No, we don't," answered Stoddard churlishly, but Jensen was persistent.

"What happens if the plane crashes, for instance? Is it dangerous? Could we have a contamination problem as well?"

Stoddard realized that that was a very good question.

"I don't know, Bill," he replied, running fingers through his short grey hair, "but see if you can get me Troutman, BNFL Chief Security Officer. He's at this number." He wrote it down on the pad. "There are one or two other questions I want to ask Mr Troutman."

Jensen grinned thinly and walked away. Through the arch in the next room, Stoddard watched several people laying out large maps on the briefing table. Suddenly the static became a voice.

"This is Red Leader to Base. We have target on visual. Height is ten-thou'. Speed 270. Course steady. Request instructions, over."

Stoddard tapped one of the radio operators on the shoulder and held out his hand. The shirt-sleeved man passed over the earphones and mike. Before he could speak Stoddard heard:

"Stand by, Red Leader."

"This is General Stoddard. Get me General Amis."

Amis must have been about to call up, because he was on within two seconds.

"General, we are under your instructions."

Despite the situation, Stoddard couldn't help smiling.

"Request you ascertain whether there is anyone flying the plane or whether it is on automatic pilot," said Stoddard.

"Wilco, out," replied Amis.

It occurred to Stoddard that Amis's operation was working well and he immediately heard instructions being given to the jets. Jensen spoke at his shoulder.

"Troutman's on."

50

Stoddard turned and called, "Pomfret, link into my call," and he walked over to the phone.

As he waited for Jensen to listen in, he was struck by a feeling of loss. That somehow this was all a waste of time. That he would be far too late. So far he knew virtually nothing. He mentally shook himself and none of the defeatist attitude showed in his voice.

"Mr Troutman?"

"Yes?" The voice was faint.

"This is the Director. There are a number of questions I wish to ask you, and when you answer I must ask you to speak up because the line is a bad one."

There was no reply.

"Can you hear me, Mr Troutman?"

"Er, perfectly. The bad line seems to be only one way," replied Troutman in a clearer voice.

"Where was the plutonium stored last night?" asked Stoddard quickly, to forestall any more trivial conversation.

"It would have arrived at the airport about 10 or 11 last night, by lorry, and then been loaded on to the plane immediately. So the plutonium would have been on the aircraft overnight."

The voice was still faint, but Troutman was obviously taking great care to speak clearly. Stoddard crushed his impatience to hurry.

"Can you be a little more specific, Mr Troutman, about the time of arrival of the plutonium at Carlisle and, indeed, whether it did arrive at all?"

There was a pause of several seconds. Stoddard forced himself to remain silent.

"No," came the eventual reply, "I'm afraid I can't." Another slight pause. "I haven't been in touch with my deputy since yesterday morning. He was my man at the airport. But he would certainly have phoned me if the cargo had not arrived at all."

Stoddard let that one go. There was no point in phoning Windscale to find out whether the shipment was delivered to Carlisle. They would probably say yes because their records said yes, but that didn't make the records correct. He knew enough about bureaucracy to know that you had to actually go to the horse's mouth to be sure of your information, and by the time he could institute that sort of enquiry he would probably have the facts anyway. Moreover, the same sort of investigation at the airport would pre-empt Phillipson's arrival. The Chief Constable wouldn't be too pleased about that and the press would probably get to know of it more quickly. He would just have to wait. The feeling of surrealism increased. There was still so little he knew.

"Mr Troutman, what form is the plutonium in?"

"It's in the form of plutonium oxide pellets, reprocessed and ready for immersion into the Fast Breeder Reactor at Dounreay. These are contained in stainless-steel rods in a fuel assembly, which is designed to fit straight into the reactor. There would have been twelve assemblies in all. They're each twelve feet long, about six inches across and they weigh close on a thousands pounds each."

Stoddard staggered a bit at that. He knew they were heavy, but 1,000 lbs! That raised an enormous logistical problem for the hijackers and pointed forcefully at a ground hijack. Now he had something to work on. But he wasn't finished with Troutman yet.

"One final question, Mr Troutman. How dangerous is it if the plane crashes?"

Again there was a long pause. It was as if Troutman were expecting the question but hadn't made up his mind how to answer it. When he spoke, his voice was so faint that it was almost inaudible.

"We have considered this possibility and tests have been carried out with successful results."

Stoddard glanced at Jensen and pulled a face. The latter, his ear to the extension phone, did the same.

"You mean there is no contamination problem?" persisted Stoddard.

He was fairly sure that Troutman said, "That is what our tests have shown."

"Does that apply if the aircraft catches fire and explodes on impact?"

The answer came back immediately, in a much clearer and firmer voice: "Since the aircraft is now flying over nothing but open sea, I wouldn't have thought that applied."

Troutman was beginning to bristle. Jensen pulled another face. Suddenly someone shouted.

"Sir. The loudspeaker!"

"...Control. There is no one flying aircraft. Cockpit deserted. Over."

Stoddard's thoughts were racing. So, either the plutonium was thrown out and the crew baled out, or the plutonium was hijacked on the ground and the plane was a decoy.

"Will attempt search of cargo hold through open rear cargo door. Over."

The pilot then bales out after setting the automatic pilot.

"Proceed, Red Leader. But don't get too close."

Given the weight problem, the latter possibility was almost certainly the case. But if the plutonium arrived at Carlisle before midnight it could be anywhere in the country by now. It could even be in London with a fast lorry! Road blocks would be pointless. The surrealism became reality as he focused upon the enormity of the problem and, just as swiftly, he knew what must be done. The pilot would have to be found. He lifted the phone.

"Are you still there, Mr Troutman?"

"Yes, what's happening?"

Troutman, Stoddard reflected, must have been able to hear the radio and general commotion, although probably not the words. He ignored the question.

"Was the route the Argosy took a straight one?" he asked.

"No," answered Troutman, to Stoddard's relief. "It was due to fly due north to Portknockie on the Moray Firth and then turn slightly westward to Wick."

Stoddard signalled an aide to come over while Troutman continued.

"The air-traffic controller here confirms that it was at least on route from Portknockie. Before that I can't say." Troutman was far more cautious in his answers now.

"Thank you," said Stoddard, really meaning it. "Stay on the line would you," and he put the phone down.

He turned to the aide, who was standing faithfully at semi-attention.

"Get me a map covering the whole of Scotland — a contour map with roads." And to Tinted-Glasses, "See if Phillipson's arrived at Carlisle Airport yet."

"He's on now, sir. Been waiting about half a minute," replied the operator.

The Chief Constable had worked quickly. As he was handed the phone, Stoddard became aware of the loudspeaker.

"Red Leader to Base Control. Cargo hold too dark. Repeat, too dark. Also, angle of sight obstructs most of hold. Over."

There was a slight pause.

"Roger, Red Leader. Stand by."

Stoddard handed the phone back to Tinted-Glasses and walked over to the radio. He wanted to know how many of the assemblies were missing. He wrote a message on the operator's pad: "Did the pilot see anything?" Amis might think it a stupid question, but he didn't care now. The odds were getting longer and longer.

He walked back across the room, passing Jensen studying a map of Scotland. He signalled him to listen in again and picked up the phone.

"Mr Phillipson?"

"Yes, Mr Stoddard?"

"Sorry to keep you waiting. What's the score?"

"Well, don't know whether this is going to come as good or bad news to you, but the 'ijack certainly took place 'ere, in one of the 'angars. Found three bodies behind some boxes at the back. One's already been visually identified as the pilot. T'other two 'ave papers saying they are security officers for British Nuclear Fuels Limited. Co-pilot appears to be alive, barely. Odd thing is, 'e's the only one with any physical signs of injury. My guess would be that t'others were injected with a drug of some kind. It's nice and quiet. Suit their purpose down t'd ground I should think. But can't say for sure until doctor gets 'ere. That what you wanted to know?"

Phillipson sounded quite pleased with himself and certainly more forthcoming than during their last conversation.

"Yes, you've been extremely helpful. There are two further questions. First, I'd like the take-off time and the heading. And...."

"Just a minute," interrupted Phillipson. Then, after about five seconds: "Carry on."

"And second," continued Stoddard, "the time of death."

"Thought you might ask me that," replied the Chief Constable. "Can't say definitely until doctor arrives, of course, but I 'ave been giving it some thought. Don't know what temperature was down in London last night, Mr Stoddard — quite mild, I shouldn't wonder — but there was a frost up 'ere. The 'angar, of course, 'ad no 'eating, and in my experience, bodies left in freezing conditions not only mask the exact time of death, but the approximate time as well. I've touched one o' them — 'e was like ice. Now...."

There was a slight pause and a mutter. Stoddard did not interrupt. Phillipson was obviously enjoying himself.

"I've just been 'anded information, Mr Stoddard, which says that the plane left at exactly 6.10, 'eading due north, by the way. That means that, at a minimum, they 'ave been dead two and a half hours, and in my experience the maximum that doctor will judge is considerably more. 'E'll probably say from one and a half to eight hours, but I've been known to be wrong."

There was another slight pause.

"Can you 'old on a moment please, Mr Stoddard?" and there was some more muttering.

Stoddard had that feeling of unreality again.

"Mr Stoddard?"

"Yes, Mr Phillipson."

"I've got some new information 'ere which 'elps us quite a lot." The Chief Constable obviously now considered himself part of the case. "The Warden of the airfield says that 'e saw the pilot and co-pilot walking towards the 'angar at about 5.45, just as 'e was going to check the runway. Now, if it was them, that means they were probably killed, or rather the pilot was killed, between two and a half and three hours ago. However...."

Stoddard waited for Phillipson's slow, but deadly logic.

"...the Warden also says that the BNFL lorry, which presumably was carrying the plutonium for transfer to the plane, arrived 'ere at approximately 10.15 and left at approx 11.50. During that time it was inside the 'angar and the doors were closed. So, although the killings didn't occur until much later, the 'ijack could 'ave taken place earlier, about 10.30. The plutonium needn't have been transferred to the plane at all."

Of course Phillipson was right. Although Stoddard had arrived at the same conclusion he felt no feeling of elation at having his deduction confirmed. The plutonium could be anywhere in the country by now. Then, for a sudden, shocking moment, he realized that it could even be out of the country. They had at least seven clear hours before anyone knew there was anything wrong, and nearly nine hours before he was in a position to do anything about it. The hijack had probably taken place just after the lorry arrived. The two security officers had been killed and dumped out of the way at the back of the hangar, and the drivers of the lorry similarly killed and thrown in the vehicle. The hijackers had then simply waited an hour or so, the time any onlookers would expect it to take for the plutonium to be transferred to the plane, and had driven the lorry out, with the plutonium still inside. The fact that the driver and his mate were not lying on the floor with the two security officers was an attempt to fool him into thinking that the hijack had taken place later. The rest of the hijackers had then simply waited for the flight crew to arrive, and killed them. A substitute pilot had then flown the empty aircraft to Wick, while the others left by another route. The security officers must have had a car if they weren't due to fly with the plane, and if there were more than two hijackers left, then they could have lain below the level of the seats until they were out of the aerodrome. They could even have delayed killing the security guards until the time they killed the crew, just to confuse. The plane was not just a decoy, it was part of a brilliantly conceived plan to give the hijackers a few extra hours. Why? He filed that away because Phillipson was speaking to him.

"... Mr Stoddard, are you still there?"

The Chief Constable sounded worried.

"Thank you, Mr Phillipson. I am very grateful. Some of my people will be coming up shortly. I should appreciate it if you would hand over the investigation to them."

"I understand," replied Phillipson.

"In the meantime," said Stoddard, "I wonder whether you can do me one last favour. Find out the description of the BNFL lorry and the car belonging to the security officers. Then put out an all-points alert."

"Already done it for the lorry, but not the car. I'll find out about that," replied the Chief Constable.

"They are both probably still on your patch," continued Stoddard as if Phillipson had not spoken, "having transferred the goods and themselves to other vehicles. You have my number if anything develops."

"Yes."

"Thank you once again, Mr Phillipson. Goodbye."

As he hung up, a very tall controller, who was standing beside Stoddard, said, "The pilot could see nothing in the hold, sir." On receiving no reply, he asked, "Where do we set up the road-blocks, sir?" and waited patiently.

"Everywhere," came the sudden, rather gruff statement. "I want every lorry capable of carrying a ton or more stopped and searched, anywhere and everywhere in the country. See to it."

Stoddard walked over to Pomfret, leaving the lanky controller rooted to the spot, open-mouthed. He made to call after Stoddard, thought better of it and walked off, scratching his head.

"Did you get all that, Pomfret?" asked the General.

"Yes, sir," came the confident reply.

Jensen looked up from the Scotland map as Stoddard approached, sensed his mood and asked quickly, "Are we talking about a one-man bale-out?"

Stoddard nodded curtly. So his deputy had come to the same conclusion. Well, it *was* rather obvious. He bent down to the map.

"In that case," said Jensen, "there are only three areas where he could have jumped. We know it must have been after Portknockie because he made a course alteration there. That's on the coast here, so the first possibility is into the sea."

The eyes narrowed and the lips stretched into a grin as he continued.

"I suggest that is unlikely. It would be cold and uncomfortable, and it would need a boat to pick him up. Also to be borne in mind, of course, is the fact that it's rather difficult to search a boat from a helicopter; and even if we did have a ship in the area, which I doubt, stopping a foreign vessel on the high seas is still piracy."

The grin became longer.

"The next and most likely possibility, in my view, is the small spit of land beyond Wick, before the Pentland Firth. It's about seven miles across and could be searched quite quickly. If he had a car hidden he could get out of the Highlands by only two routes: the A9 from Wick, or around to the north on to the A835 at Ullapool."

Jensen paused and looked at Stoddard again.

"What time would he have dropped here?" He pointed to the peninsula.

Stoddard thought for a moment.

"About 7.15. Say 7.00 for safety."

They bothed glanced at their watches. 8.48.

"So he's got an hour and a half on us," continued Jensen. "If we set up road-blocks at Bonar Bridge anu horizontally at Ullapool, we must have him."

Jensen narrowed his eyes again. The inane grin was still there. Listening to him, Stoddard could see the reasoning, but he had a feeling it was too obvious. These boys were as sharp as needles and must have foreseen the possibility. Nevertheless, there didn't seem to be any harm in setting up the barricades.

"Do that," he said.

Suddenly the room was filled with static again. The radio operator had obviously previously switched the air-to-base link off the loudspeaker so as not to disturb everyone.

"... Repeat. Argosy is diving uncontrollably. Am following down."

There was nothing but static for about thirty seconds, while most people looked at Stoddard. The General was apparently assiduously studying the map.

"Aircraft broke up on impact. No explosion. Over."

No one moved or spoke for a further five seconds. Stoddard turned and began to walk through to the chart room.

"Stand by, Red Leader."

O'Conner, one of the Chief Assistants, saw Stoddard coming.

"Get the co-ordinates, will you, O'Conner? And pinpoint it on one of those Admiralty charts you turfed out," said Stoddard, pointing his pipe at the table.

He then returned to Jensen, noting that one or two in the room were averting their eyes as he walked.

"What was the third possibility?" he asked his deputy.

Jensen resumed his survey, while Stoddard made vulgar sucking noises on his pipe.

"If you draw a line from Portknockie to Wick and continue it, you'll see that it goes over the Orkneys, touching the island of Hoy very briefly. Rough terrain, but a good place for a lonely parachute landing. The apparent problem then for him is that he has to get off the island, but he would have made prior arrangements. A small, fast boat after dark and he could be through the Skagerrak before we knew it."

That seemed to Stoddard to be the most likely possibility of the three, but he still wasn't hopeful. He walked over to the radio, noting that O'Conner was still hunting through the charts. Whatever happened, he had learnt from this. He switched the link to loudspeaker and picked up the microphone.

"This is General Stoddard. Get me General Amis immediately."

Amis answered in a few moments.

"What do you want me to do with my jets?"

It sounded as if he had expected Stoddard to come through earlier, but the latter was in no mood for truculence.

"I want some aerial cover of the crash area until the Navy gets there, General. How you handle that is up to you." He paused, thinking. "In the meantime, how many helicopters can you let me have?"

"Seven," replied Amis, "four of which are long-range and can carry troops."

"Good. I'd like two of the troop-carriers and one of the other 'copters to the island of Hoy. The whole island should be searched from the air and the ground. You're looking for one parachutist. No, possibly more than one. I'm sorry I can't be more specific than that. I want the other two big ones and a small one to search the whole peninsula from Reiss to Castletown. Get as many troops as you can to both locations, General. Another possibility is that he dropped into the Moray Firth, although, for obvious reasons, we think this is unlikely. But the remaining small 'copter is to search the area, including outward into the North Sea. If he dropped there, he will almost certainly have been picked up. Make a note of all shipping, including small boats. Try and get some assistance there if you can. All sightings to be reported to this control."

If there is one thing you never tell a General it's how to deploy his own troops. Stoddard realized that he had done just that. It was a long time since he had been used to an Army chain of command, and the strain of the moment had to be getting to him. What he should have done was explain the situation to Amis and let him take over. He could imagine the man at the other end fighting down his anger.

"I'm sorry, General," continued Stoddard, "but the situation is urgent. The aircraft was flying in a straight line from Portknockie to Wick and, as you know, did not deviate until it ran out of fuel. Deploy any other troops and equipment that become available as you see fit. You have the full authority of a Fireball Alert."

"Yes, sir," answered Amis and the line went dead.

Stoddard returned to Jensen, where O'Conner was pointing at a map. They both looked up as he approached.

"We've found it, sir," said O'Conner excitedly. About 120 miles north-east of the Faeroes and about 380 east-south-east of Iceland." He paused and pointed.

"Here, sir."

"What's the depth, man?" asked Stoddard impatiently.

"Twelve hundred fathoms, sir," answered O'Conner with a smile. Stoddard was stunned.

"Seven thousand feet!" he exclaimed.

"Yes, sir," replied O'Conner, completely unabashed. "A bit o'luck, really. Another sixty miles and she'd be down another four thou'."

He looked up. The Old Man was looking at him as if he'd stolen his whisky. There had been a tentative suggestion from one of the lads the other day that the General wore a girdle or belt of some kind to keep his stomach in, since in all other respects he cut a rather robust figure. Looking back into the angry blue eyes he could now see what a stupid idea that had been.

"O'Conner," said Stoddard in a rather strangled voice, "go back into the other room, will you?"

He knew that it would take the Navy days, perhaps a week or more, to get the equipment needed to dive to 7,000 feet to that exact spot, and then make the dive itself, even if the weather held. It just got worse every minute. As yet he had no evidence that any plutonium was even missing. It could still all be down in that plane. It was always possible that it was a gigantic hoax, to demonstrate the possibility of a hijack, and that all twelve assemblies were lying at the bottom of the Norwegian Sea. But somehow, he didn't think so. He felt sure the aircraft was empty, but there was only one way of finding out. He leant forward, both hands on the table, and thought.

"Bill, take some notes."

He waited while Jensen dutifully picked up a pad and a pen.

"Troutman is still on the phone at Wick. Give him my condolences and tell him that his two security officers and *both* pilots are dead. Then tell him to stand by for a jet to bring him to London. I need him down here as soon as possible. Arrange it with Amis, will you, and make the transport arrangements this end. Then brief half a dozen of our boys and get them to Carlisle and Wick, fast. We also need a naval vessel over the crash area as soon as poss' and a naval diving team with deep-water equipment. I don't even know if they have it. Then we need as many vessels in the Moray Firth and North Sea area as we can."

He paused.

"On second thoughts, I'd better see to the Navy side of things."

He turned and called to the console operator.

"Get me the Admiralty." And turning back to his deputy, "See to that now, will you, Bill." It was a statement, not a question.

Stoddard unconsciously struck the classic pose, with pipe held in mouth, and looked at his watch. 9.04. The morning had only just begun, yet he felt ready for bed. He knew that he would be up till midnight at least, because he also knew that the search was going to fail. He would do everything he could — ritually make the right moves — but the battle was lost before it had begun. He didn't know how much, if any, plutonium was missing. He didn't have a clue where it was. It could be anywhere in the country or already on some foreign ship at sea. He didn't know where the hijackers were. He didn't even know where the pilot-hijacker was and, even if he did catch him, that provided no guarantee of finding the plutonium. He was concentrating a lot of resources on finding one man who might know virtually nothing.

The search would have to be stepped up at goods yards, sea and airports. You cannot put a twelve-foot package in your pocket. Already the Fireball Alert would mean that troops would have moved into all goods transit areas. Passengers at the UK's major air-terminals would be thinking that there had been a revolution. That was to say nothing of the massive troop movements that would be taking place all over the country, to scour deserted coasts and airfields. Late breakfasters would be hearing it on the radio over their Shredded Wheat. It wouldn't be long before a smart reporter put it all together. As time went on, too, he would have to speak to the Prime Minister again and that would be painful. He was surprised that he hadn't been on already.

Then Stoddard thought of the weekend just gone, that he'd spent at his family estate in Hertfordshire, just as he did most weekends — riding horses, playing the piano, enjoying good food and wine, and drinking malt whisky. It was his form of escapism and he often thought of it in moments of tension. He was regarded as something of a squire in the county, although he refused to join the local hunt, and really lived for his job since his wife's death. There were no children. Somehow he sensed that he wasn't going to be able to get up to the country for some time.

"The Admiralty, sir," called Tinted Glasses.

With the force of mind that had helped him be good at his job, Stoddard pushed the doubts out of his mind, rose from his chair and, with a smile on his face, walked over to the telephone.

The electrical instrument panel above the cabin hatch glowed green in the dark. Beyond that Brown could see the dark outline of the sails against the star-spotted sky, but not the riding lights which were shielded from the cockpit. It was indeed a dark night. But quiet it wasn't as he listened to the sleek craft sliding into the swell. The water rippled down the hull and gurgled at his back in the boat's wake. Occasionally, the mast or a shroud creaked. Brown lay on one of the aft lockers, a coffee in one hand, wrapped up against the cold. The helmsman, steering by compass, tried to ignore him.

Late in the morning the helicopter had buzzed them and come down very low for an inspection. It had played havoc with the wind and the boat had rocked uncontrollably. They had shouted their outraged shouts at the pilot and shaken their justified fists, and he had gone away. All afternoon they had seen nothing. At 5.30 they had turned south and, a few hours later, night had come to mask their passage.

Then they had all got busy, peeling off the red plastic from gunwale to waterline, revealing the gleaming royal blue below. *Nessy* had become *The Gorgon* as the names were changed. It had been difficult work in the dark, with only torches for light, but worth it.

The wind had continued its move towards the east all day, until backing to the north again at dusk. Now it was blowing a steady Force 4 out of the north-east and *The Gorgon* was slightly back of a broad-reach — her fastest point of sailing.

Brown sipped his coffee, content.

II: BOMB

Wednesday, 7 May

Chapter 7

"NO. IT WOULD NOT, in my view, be possible for a terrorist group to make a bomb from fast-reactor fuel," said the tall, slight, black-haired man seated across the desk from Stoddard. His suit and shoes were also black. Indeed, the only bit of colour on his entire frame were the minute sky-blue dots on the inevitable black tie, set against the white shirt. Even his eyes seemed colourless. He sat with one long leg crossed over the other, hands in lap, perfectly relaxed, the small, clipped moustache refusing to move any more. He was a very high Scientific Officer in the Department of Energy and not pleased at being taken from his valuable work to give answers to questions from a "security man".

Stoddard gazed over his pipe at the third man in the room. Although by far the youngest there, he was almost completely bald. He was also much smaller and rounder in appearance than the other and wore a bright green tweed suit. The shoes were of fashionable design, made of brown leather. He was from the Atomic Weapons Research Establishment (AWRE) at Aldermaston, and so far he hadn't said a word. As Stoddard looked at him, he took out a large, green and yellow handkerchief and blew his nose.

When the handkerchief had disappeared, it became clear that neither man was going to continue the conversation. Stoddard said:

"Would you like to explain that to me, Dr Pond?"

The tall man sighed audibly.

"Well, what you have to do is highly complex. You have first to remove the oxygen from the plutonium oxide and then separate out the plutonium, which is a tremendously difficult operation. And don't forget," he bent forward to give weight to his words, "that this all has to be done under conditions of great care because of the problem of radioactivity from the plutonium. A large well-equipped science firm might be able to do it and one or two educational establishments like Queen Mary College, London. And, of course," glancing under furrowed brows to the man on his left, "AWRE. But I don't think any smaller group could do it, and I don't believe it could be done without people finding out."

Stoddard, who had been watching the smaller man's nervous glances at Pond, removed his pipe and opened his mouth to speak, but, having been reluctantly prodded into verbal action, the man from the Ministry wasn't going to stop now until he was finished.

"I would therefore regard it as an extremely tricky operation. If I felt I had to have a bomb, I'd go and steal one from some military establishment. I'd regard that as being more worthwhile, and certainly less dangerous, than trying to make fast-reactor fuel into a bomb."

As Pond sat back, now purse-lipped, Stoddard refrained from mentioning that the security surrounding military bases was a great deal more effective than that guarding reprocessed reactor fuel. He turned to the smaller of the duo, who seemed to be expecting it, because the points of his shoes had begun rubbing together on the floor.

"Dr Ogilvie," said Stoddard gently, "how do you feel on this?"

Ogilvie shot a quick glance at Pond. "Well, um, this is not exactly my line of work at all," he replied in a Welsh accent, "but I would say that what Dr Pond has said is essentially true."

He stopped and looked at the ground. When he began again his head was still lowered.

"It *is* an extremely difficult operation, even if you do have the knowledge. But," he looked up and attempted to smile at Stoddard, "who knows?"

It was a stupid thing to say and he realized it. His face flushed and he looked at his feet again. Stoddard felt sorry for him.

Pond gave him a withering look of absolute disdain, stood up, and said, "Will that be all, Sir Giles?"

He wasn't expecting a negative reply and Stoddard certainly wasn't going to give one.

"Yes, of course, Dr Pond. Thank you very much for coming." He didn't bother to shake his hand, just stood up and smiled benignly. The tall man turned and left without ceremony.

Ogilvie had made no movement. He was still bent over his knees, too embarrassed to look up. Stoddard walked over to the window and looked down at the milling traffic, his right hand holding the pipe and his left in a trouser pocket.

He had seen Ogilvie's file before he had come in. Once into his PhD in some obscure branch of nuclear technology, he hadn't needed to apply for a job. The government had recruited him for Aldermaston. They had known he was homosexual and the British security services were very sensitive about that sort of thing since the Vassall scandal. But homosexuality was no longer a crime, the social norms regarding it had considerably changed and, anyway, Owen Ogilvie was too good to pass up.

Stoddard turned to look at him, wondering about the best way to tackle it. The General had reached the top of the tree partly because he had the right background (of which he was quite well aware), partly because he had a much better brain than the normal commissioned officer, but mainly because he understood men, their motives and desires. He removed his pipe.

"Ever met Dr Pond before?" he ventured.

Ogilvie looked up with a brave smile. "No. 'Fraid not."

"Me neither, and frankly I hope I never shall again," Stoddard added feelingly.

Ogilvie laughed slightly and looked into Stoddard's eyes. The General smiled too and hoped the little man saw no hostility there. He decided to push on while the going was good.

"Your record says that you are good at your job. Is that true?"

"That's for other people to judge," replied Ogilvie immediately.

There was a small silence. Stoddard decided to try again.

"Someone told me once that Einstein did most of his original thinking before he was twenty-three. Is *that* true?"

Ogilvie laughed again. "I don't know. Probably. It certainly seems logical."

"Oh, why's that?" asked Stoddard.

"Well, after the early to mid twenties the brain deteriorates physically. A man can still increase his knowledge and, indeed, his adaptive thinking; but his capacity for, as you rightly put it, 'original thinking', actually lessens. There are exceptions, of course."

Stoddard, who knew all this, replied with a smile, "I promise I won't tell AWRE that you're over the hill."

Ogilvie laughed fully this time.

Stoddard looked away. He wasn't too concerned with amateur bomb-making, because he was pretty sure that the stuff was already out of the country, or certainly destined for overseas, but he didn't like uncertainties. He sat on the corner of the desk and looked down at Ogilvie, seriously.

"I need to know whether Pond is right. Can you tell me?"

Ogilvie began fidgeting again.

"I'd like to, Sir Giles, I really would. But I honestly don't know. I certainly wouldn't be as definite as Dr Pond."

He looked worriedly down at his hands again. "You see, I've never made one out of this sort of material. I can see that it's possible, given the right sort of information."

The Welsh accent was strong now as he struggled to continue.

"You see, I've led — I lead — a rather sheltered existence. If I want something I just have to ask for it. I would think that the availability of this sort of information on the open market was nil. On the other hand, a government scientist, or even *ex*-government scientist, would surely be discovered before he completed the process, even if he did know how to, which I doubt. We don't make bombs from this sort of material, Sir Giles. I doubt whether there is anyone in the country who ever has done. But the real answer is, I simply don't know."

He looked at Stoddard more confidently.

64

"There is one other thing too. In my opinion, Dr Pond understated the difficulties. He only mentioned the chemical process. There are far more techniques involved in making an atomic bomb, I can assure you. You need a high degree of sophistication in metal-working and electronics — neither of which I have."

"I see," said Stoddard. He stood up and smiled. "In that case I won't detain you any further."

Ogilvie stood up immediately and Stoddard showed him to the door.

"Can you make your own way back to Aldermaston?"

"Yes, of course," answered Ogilvie. "I'm sorry I couldn't help you further."

"You have been a help."

The little man nodded to himself and scuttled away. Stoddard was left wondering at the thought that if it was not possible to make a bomb out of the stuff, then why steal it?

The basement workshop was twenty-four feet by twenty. At strategic positions against the walls stood three Calor-gas heaters, as the place was cold and damp. Stacked against three walls were metal shelves, stretching right up to the ceiling. On two of these series of shelves were various kinds of machine tools, bottles and gas cylinders. The other one was half filled with files and books.

Against the far wall — the wall opposite the door above the corner stairs — stood what appeared to be a large, transparent, plastic bag, that almost reached to the ceiling. It was about eight feet wide and ten feet long when fully extended and it was, in fact, an adapted oxygen tent. A variety of objects could be seen inside and a number of electronic leads led from it.

The big, low, metal workbench was sited off-centre in the room, due to the protrusion of the tent. On one side of it was placed an oblong of slotted angle iron, three feet long, two feet wide and eighteen inches deep. Attached to one inside corner of the frame were two square boxes. Many electronic leads ran from these boxes to a panel across the width of the frame, on which were scores of electronic connections. There were a number of small cylinders in the frame and on top of the upper box was a switch. Even more electronic leads wound from the assembly to a mechanism called a double-beam oscilloscope with long-stay traces, and to a digital timer.

There were two men in the room. The one who was bending over the assembly was called Caren Macdonald, a twenty-four-year-old graduate in cybernetics. He had orange hair and freckly skin and was rather plump. With his fingernails bitten down to the quick, he worked with a fanaticism which almost rivalled that of the other man. He was Keith Vaisey, of medium height and build, with dark-brown hair. But there the normality stopped. A plane crash at fifteen had left him badly disfigured about the face and he had false legs. He had managed, through tremendous motivation and no little ability, to get to university and graduate in physics. Now forty-two, he had been unemployed for two years. During that time he had researched, in his own home, in nuclear physics.

He was impressed with Caren's work. He liked professionalism and admired his skill. Once he had explained to the young man what was required he went and did it and, indeed, they had just more or less completed the construction of a simultaneous detonation system, or at least as much of it as they could without the other "parts".

The problem was to achieve detonation of all the explosive lenses at the same time — in fact, in less than a "nano" second after the plutonium hemispheres had been brought together. Detonators were notoriously inconsistent and there weren't any on the market which had this degree of accuracy. So it necessitated building high-quality electronic control units to enable synchronization to occur. The metering equipment and the oscilloscope had shown a quite remarkable degree of simultaneity.

Vaisey sat back, pleased. This was a vital stage in the construction. No matter how well he handled the plutonium side of things, if the lenses did not explode simultaneously, the resulting explosion would be less than the maximum possible, and the device might even fail to go off altogether.

Thinking of the plutonium side, he began to worry again about the time limit. He had told Brown that he needed more time for the construction of the rest of the mechanism, so that all they would have to do after the hijack would be concerned with the plutonium itself. But a delivery was being made and Brown couldn't wait. Apparently only seven or eight deliveries were made a year, and if they didn't take this one they might have had to wait another six to eight weeks. And that, Brown had said, was too long. Vaisey didn't know why, but that was that. He would just have to work harder and faster. The plutonium would be coming soon and they had only just begun.

Anyway, for the moment, he was satisfied. As the scientist in charge, it was his responsibility if the bomb failed to work. He didn't expect it to be used, Brown had said, but he wanted those pompous cretins in Whitehall to know that it would have worked. Besides, it might well have to.

Caren stopped working and put down his screwdriver. He looked at Vaisey and nodded.

"I'll away an' make supper. Cheese and pickle?"

"Fine," answered Vaisey, looking at Caren intently. He watched him climb the stone steps. So far he hadn't been able to reach him. He'd thought that the week of confinement would lead to certain developments, but the red-haired man had stayed distant, Vaisey's one advance being repulsed with an indignant expletive.

He levered himself on to his feet with powerful arms and walked, stiff-legged, to the other end of the bench. He sat down on the stool and resumed reading where he had left off. The book was *The Plutonium Handbook*, Volume 2, published by Gordon and Breach. He had bought it, together with Volume 1, in London, over the counter of a perfectly respectable bookshop in Charing Cross Road.

Scattered around the worktop were a number of other volumes, all American and bought quite openly. The most well-thumbed among them were: *The Los Alamos Primer* by the Atomic Energy Commission, declassified in 1964; *Manhattan District History: Project Y, the Los Alamos Project* by the Office of Technical Services, US Department of Commerce, declassified in 1961; *Source Book on Atomic Energy* by Samuel Glasstone; *Rare Metals Handbook; The Reactor Handbook* (four volumes); and *The Curve of Binding Energy*.

Together, they contained all the information he needed.

Chapter 8
Friday, 9 May

ANN STUART looked at her watch. 5 p.m. Her normal time for leaving the office, providing there was nothing urgent on, which at the moment there wasn't. She hesitated. That Romeo from down the corridor would be waiting at the lift for her to appear. She had finally given in last week to his repeated requests to go out, mainly because she was bored. Now she regretted it. After dinner and two bottles of wine he had put his hand on her thigh. She had liked it and allowed him to keep it there. It was naughty really, because she had no intention of letting it go any further. In the taxi, she had thanked him for a wonderful evening and suggested that they were not suited. But he wouldn't take no for an answer. She was going to have to be cruel and she didn't like that, especially since it was partly her fault.

Having been educated at private all-girls schools until the age of eighteen, she had been taught rather traditional values and they had stuck. Those who were unaware of the devotion she gave to her job often called her old-fashioned, because she believed that women should be women and men, men, although she found great difficulty when asked to explain what this meant. She was devoted to the classical novelists and loved the theatre, going at least once a fortnight, if possible. Secretly, she read romantic novelettes and, despite the tragedy of her marriage, which had ended in divorce two years earlier, she wanted to marry again and live a simple life in rural England, bringing up children. But she was aware that if she didn't remarry soon, she'd become wedded to her desk. She loved her job and there were scores of women in the building who existed in a semi-nun-like state. She was also aware that she was already on that slippery slope of self-sacrifice, as she now seemed incapable of forming close relationships with men.

She knew that men found her attractive, though. She had light skin colouring, contrasting with raven hair. The lips were generous, slightly pouting, and her eyes were brown. She always thought that her features were too big — her hips, breasts and mouth in particular — but she hadn't found them a handicap. She knew she was pretty, but certainly not beautiful.

Then, quite suddenly, she was angry with herself. There was only one reason for her delayed departure. This man, Matthew Calder, was due to meet the General and she wanted to meet him in the flesh. She had read his file when Sir Giles had finished with it, and had had a good look at the photograph. She knew that she was stupidly romanticising about a man she had never met, like a frustrated schoolgirl. But Calder intrigued her.

Peter Striker had been in that morning, exhausted and very disorientated from lack of sleep. He said they had finally picked Calder up in Mexico. Apparently he'd ridden out of the desert on horseback, looking like a bandit, and they'd whisked him away so fast that he hadn't had time to pick up his normal clothes. He had travelled all the way to London in jeans, riding boots and poncho. Striker had said that people kept giving the man suspicious glances, expecting that they were going to be hijacked. At one point the Captain had come back to have a look and Striker had had to show his identity card. Calder, with straw hat over his face, hadn't moved the whole trip.

He had refused to see Sir Giles until he had "slept off his jet lag", so Striker had come in to report on his own, before he himself went to bed. With some quip about her joining him, he had left, crashing into the door-jamb on his way out.

As she followed her thought by looking at the door, there was a knock on it and it opened before she could answer. She wondered who he was as the man walked in. Then it struck her that photographs could be very deceptive. True, he now had a black beard, a dark-brown tan that looked incongruous in May London, and his brown hair had contracted fair streaks — from the sun, she reasoned, not from the hairdressers. He was tall and dressed casually in white polo-necked sweater, red leather jacket and brown trousers. Not the usual sort of get-up she saw in the building and he looked at variance with his surroundings, although, strangely, not out of place.

She took all this in very quickly as he approached the desk, but she must have been staring for too long, because be began to smile. It was odd, but it wasn't the teeth that shone against the darkness of the face, but the eyes. She should have said something by now.

"My name is Calder. I'm here to see General Stoddard."

She managed to speak. "He's expecting you," and she flicked a switch on her intercom.

"Sir Giles, Mr Calder is here."

"Ah, good. Send him in."

She flicked the switch back and looked at Calder again.

"Through that door," she said, pointing.

He walked towards it and, his hand on the door knob, looked back at her for a few moments. She smiled. He did the same, turned and went in.

Stoddard walked round from behind his desk and considered the man he had met once only, seven months previously, at a controversial lecture given by Calder at the In-service Training Centre of the Ministry of Defence. It had included a warning about the dangers apparent in unlawful possession of fast-reactor fuel. Stoddard had invited him to lunch afterwards and been impressed by his knowledge and by the man himself. He had recognized in Calder a kindred spirit and felt that the younger man sensed it too.

Now, his presence in the room was immense. Perhaps it was more imagined than real — an old man's last, desperate clutch at a straw of hope, that became bigger than it really was. Both men grinned and shook hands.

"It's good of you to come," said Stoddard.

"You've got to be joking," answered Calder. "After the trouble and expense you've been to to find me I dread to think what would have happened if I'd refused."

Stoddard smiled. "Scotch?" he asked.

"I have a feeling I'm going to need one."

Stoddard walked over to a filing cabinet, unlocked it and withdrew a bottle of good blend, together with two glasses. To Calder, the General looked older and more strained. There was some dark around the eyes and he was a little thinner.

"No water, I'm afraid," said Stoddard.

"That's fine."

The General handed Calder the thick glass, one-third full.

"Apparently you caused quite a stir on the flight from the States."

Calder smiled. "I felt sorry for your two messengers who were sitting next to me. I was badly in need of a bath."

Stoddard also smiled, though hesitantly, as if his mind were on something else. The small-talk had finished.

"Striker and the press were a little vague," said Calder. "What's happened, exactly?"

Stoddard looked at the leather of his desk-top, motioned Calder to sit down and told him everything. He was a good teller. He knew which points to emphasize and which not. What's more, he did it in sequence, which made it interesting, only summarizing towards the end. As an ex-professional in the art of oral communication, Calder was impressed.

The General paused when he'd finished and lit his pipe. A cloud drifted across to Calder until the fire got going. Stoddard stuck it in the corner of his mouth, held on to it and puffed between sentences.

"My biggest mistake, of course, was not realizing that the rods could be removed from the assembly. I didn't know that until Troutman told me later. If I had known, I could have seen the possibility of an air-drop and intensified the search over the flight-path. I could have set up road-blocks in strategic positions. Instead of having about eight hours' start, as I had thought, they had only about two."

Calder sensed the anger and frustration that had built up in Stoddard.

"It wasn't your fault," said the younger man. "If anything it was Troutman's for not telling you early enough."

Stoddard was standing at the window, nodding slowly.

"Perhaps," he replied, "but the point is that it happened and it shouldn't have."

Calder knew that it was self-recrimination, not self-pity.

"I don't think it would have made any difference," he said.

Stoddard swung round from the window as Calder continued. The pipe was pointing out of the mouth like a weapon.

"The man who masterminded this operation is no fool. He must have foreseen the possibility that you might think it was a parachute drop and he would have made plans accordingly. He would also think it likely that you would make the mistake that you did, because he must know the scattered nature of the security concerning plutonium oxide. That would give him extra time for the getaway. But he could not possibly have afforded to take the chance, especially after the thought and investment that he must have put in."

Calder paused. "He would have got away even if you had known."

Stoddard looked away. When he turned back there was a grim smile on his face. A pigeon fluttered silently down on to the ledge behind him.

"Perhaps I needed someone else to say that," he said.

Calder waited a few moments.

"I take it they were standard fuel assemblies," he asked, "with fourteen twelve-foot rods in each one?"

"Yes."

"Then they probably denuded one assembly."

"Why?" asked Stoddard quickly, but removing his pipe slowly.

"Because that's how much plutonium they'd need to make a reasonable sized bomb."

Stoddard stared at Calder for a number of seconds. He didn't know whether to be glad or sorry that he'd sent for him.

"I've been told by experts that it's impossible to make a bomb from fast-reactor fuel," said the General.

Behind him the pigeon began to groom its feathers. Calder pulled a face and his voice took on a resigned tone.

"I'm not surprised. They either have an economic axe to grind or they lack overview. Probably both."

Stoddard thought of Pond and Ogilvie.

Calder said, "No, that's too simplistic."

He drained his glass before continuing.

"The hoverfly beats its wings 175 times a second. According to the experts it's impossible. When Galileo said that the sun did not revolve around the earth, he was branded as a heretic. It wasn't just that the experts of the time didn't want to believe it; as far as they were concerned it was simply impossible."

The bird arched its wings to clean underneath.

"Man establishes laws of nature or contrivance," Calder went on, "that are essential to his survival and progression, at every stage of history. He needs them like he needs food, as a foundation — a raft of sanity on an unsteady sea. He cannot accept that *they* are not true, because that would erode the very basis of the justification for his existence. But they invariably are untrue. Almost every law or rule that we have ever established can be, or has been, questioned or disproved. I've heard too many so-called experts claim that something cannot be done, and, quite frankly, I'm pissed off with it."

He switched his gaze from bird to man. When he spoke again his voice was steadier.

"It can be done, General, believe me."

Stoddard was strangely pleased at the emotional outburst. It was reassuring to know that Calder was capable of strong emotions like everyone else. Silly, really. As he looked into the steady eyes, he had no doubt that the man behind them was right.

"I believe you," he said seriously. "Have some more Scotch."

"Thanks," replied Calder, holding out his glass. "It might be worth considering the implications of a bomb later on, but for the moment I want to ask you some questions."

"Fire away," said Stoddard, refilling his glasses.

"Have you any clues at all as to where they dropped?"

"Clues, no," said Stoddard immediately. "My own view is that the jump area was over the sea, or the Moray Firth to be exact. They could have kept to their flight path and still been out of sight of land. Difficult and bloody cold, but not impossible if you are determined enough, and we know they are that. The fact that we haven't found any evidence at all — not even a piece of parachute cloth — again points to the sea. And, of course, a boat is an ideal vessel for carrying twelve-foot rods. They wouldn't need to enter Britain again. With the start they had, they could have sailed for almost any foreign port. Once in the open sea the chances of detection are slim, even if we did have a blanket search of the area, which we didn't until later. It takes time and all this is with the benefit of hindsight."

Stoddard sucked vigorously on his pipe to keep it alight and continued in a less bitter tone.

"It would have needed split-second timing to land in the sea, but it's possible. It would also explain why we didn't find a trace of the pilot. He would already have completed his last course alteration at Portknockie. All he had to do then was set the automatic-pilot and jump out with the rest of them. It would also explain why the rear cargo-door was open. If the pilot was still on board at Wick, he would almost certainly have closed it."

Stoddard sat down slowly and glared at Calder before continuing.

"Funny how one works it out when it's too late. I must be getting old." He smiled. "Of course, I could be completely wrong — about the sea, I mean, not about getting old."

Calder, already having decided that Stoddard, among other things, had one of the finest analytical minds he had come across, thought, again, that it probably wouldn't have made any difference if the General had worked it out at once. But this time he considered it polite not to say so. Instead, he asked:

"You said you had some helicopters in the air. What about shipping?"

Stoddard continued looking at Calder for a few seconds, before reaching for a file on his desk.

"Four vessels were seen. Two we have found and cleared. One of the others was a foreign fishing vessel; Polish. We're following that up, but so far all we've got is a flat denial. I must confess I'm inclined to believe it. I can't see any reason why the Poles should get involved in this sort of thing. The other was a sailing vessel, a yacht, about forty feet or so according to the pilot: One mast, red hull, with the name of *Nessy*. Seems unlikely, but we checked it out. Can't find it. Lloyds have no trace of it and it's not registered anywhere, it seems. That in itself is not unusual. Owners are always changing the names of their boats and not telling even their insurance companies. We're still looking for it. We've given up the air-to-sea search now. No vessel of any kind, though, is allowed off our shores without a thorough search. And that goes for aircraft as well."

Again Stoddard paused and looked at Calder intently before continuing.

"As you can imagine, the man-power usage, not to mention the possible diplomatic repercussions, are immense. But that's not what bothers me. It's good training for the men involved, and I couldn't care a monkey's toss about diplomatic bloody problems. The thing that worries me is not finding it. And I don't think I'm going to, not the way I've been trying. In fact, I'd be very surprised if it isn't already in another country."

Calder looked out of the window again. The bird's head had completely disappeared under a wing. Beyond it the sky was mauve and cold.

"The Navy presumably is still diving?"

"Yes," answered Stoddard, his voice returning to normal. "They say it will probably take at least another couple of days. But those are rough seas and if it gets too choppy they will have to suspend activities. Theoretically, it could be weeks."

Stoddard compressed his lips and his voice became bitter.

"The more I think about the plan — the hijackers' plan — the more I realize how good it was."

"How did they know when and how the shipment was going to be made?" asked Calder quickly.

"Ah, yes, *I* wondered about that. They had to have someone inside the security set-up itself, because the transit security boys are not told until three days in advance when a delivery is going to be made. What's more, they don't know before then whether the shipment is going by road or by air. We discovered that only guards who have been with BNFL for two years or more are chosen for the transit jobs, which tends to rule out anything but a long-term infiltration. That's most unlikely and, anyway, risky from the point of view of the hijackers; there was no guarantee that their man would get a transit security clearance. So, there was only one guaranteed way they could have known."

He stopped to see if Calder could fill in the answer. The younger man suitably obliged.

"Threats of violence on the family of one of the guards. 'No harm will come to them if you give us the when, where and how of the next shipment.'"

"You guessed it," said Stoddard heavily. "We checked all the families. One of the wives had a broken arm and looked very ill. She said she had fallen by the coal bunker, so we knocked up a few of the neighbours. Apparently, she and her seven-year-old son had been away for about three weeks. It took some time to extract a confession. They were terrified. Three heavies had broken her arm in the husband's presence to demonstrate their genuine intent."

Stoddard's voice was even more bitter now and he had let his pipe go out.

"It's the worst kind of human activity and a policeman's nightmare. There's virtually nothing one can do to prevent it — not while there is just a glimmer of hope that the man's family is going to be returned in one piece."

"I don't think they were being humanitarian by returning them," said Calder, in a voice that, in contrast to Stoddard's, was totally devoid of emotion. "They killed at the airport quickly enough. I'm sure they would have preferred to kill the wife and child as well, but they might want to use the trick again and we'll know that they keep their word."

Stoddard noticed that Calder's eyes shifted rapidly when he thought hard.

"Indeed," continued the younger man, "it seems to me that the fact that they did release them indicates that we *will* hear from them again. No clues from the woman, I suppose?"

For the second time since their conversation had begun, Stoddard became vaguely uneasy. He still clung to what he considered was the well-reasoned belief that, if the plutonium was not out of the country by now, then it soon would be. To him, it all pointed very strongly to a foreign terrorist group.

"No," he said, placing his pipe on the blotter and picking up the file again, "no real clues. They wore masks, only one of them ever spoke, in a 'foreign' accent, and anyway they kept the woman and boy in one room. She had no idea where. Food and water were pushed through the door. She overheard one sentence in the whole three weeks, through the door, in an 'English' accent. I quote: 'Get that off to Paddington,' unquote. She didn't know what it was. If that's a clue it's a pretty vague one."

Calder was thinking, chin in hand.

"There's one thing," he said. "The *Guardian* said that four men were killed at the airport. You said that the co-pilot lived."

Again Stoddard hesitated before replying.

"We lied about that because we thought the co-pilot might give us a clue. But again, it came to nothing. The man who hit him wore a balaclava mask and he heard nothing said."

The General opened the report again.

"He came round for a few moments. All he saw," said Stoddard looking up, "this is what he claims, was a woman walking across the hangar. Then he blacked out again."

Stoddard folded the file.

"Is that all?" said Calder in disbelief.

"No," answered the General, without taking his eyes off Calder.

"He said that she had the most fantastic pair of legs that he had ever seen."

Both men stared at each other for a few moments in silence. Then they laughed. Stoddard picked up his pipe and placed it in his mouth without bothering to relight it.

"One thing, though," he said. "He was injected with the drug too, so they obviously intended to kill him. But they didn't. A mistake. I find that a little comforting. Unless, of course, they just wanted us to think they intended to kill him."

Calder stood up and walked over to the window. The bird didn't see him, its head tucked under the other wing, and he stood perfectly still, looking at the lights of the city beginning to show.

"I don't really know why I sent for you," said Stoddard behind him. "All the foreign departments are making enquiries abroad, where I believe the plutonium is, or shortly will be."

He looked hard at Calder's back, expecting argument, but none came.

"Also, of course, I have my own department, and almost the entire armed forces, to say nothing of the police, working around the clock searching for the bloody stuff."

He tapped out the contents of his pipe into a large glass tray. "But, as I've already said, I don't think we're going to find it, or them."

There was silence for about five seconds, then Calder turned away from the window and walked slowly over to the chair in front of the desk. Stoddard noticed the calm way in which he settled, arms perfectly relaxed along the arms of the chair, eyes gazing back openly.

The General busied himself in refilling his pipe. During their previous meeting, he had discovered that Calder had four major interests in life: environmentalism, women, chess and sports, in descending order of importance. He played most sports, especially rugby union and cricket. He was also a keep-fit fiend, although health foods were strictly out. He ate well, drank most alcohol moderately, but didn't smoke. His environmentalist views were closely connected with his view of the world and his idealism, and Stoddard judged them to be the major source of his motivation. He held life and the development of social and cultural existence as being distinct from, and more important than, economic goals. That, unfortunately, technology is seen as the god and man as its tool, instead of the other way around. It was these views which had forced him to resign his post at the In-service Training Centre for top security and military personnel. At that time he had been involved in doing a special study, in his own time, on environmental pollution, especially the nuclear variety. On looking at Calder's file, Stoddard had discovered that, although his first degree was in physics, he had an MA in International Relations.

As he continued to fill his pipe, the older man thought, too, of the quick, concise way in which Calder had asked the right questions. This business had to some extent damaged his confidence in his own ability, but if there was one thing he felt that he did know about, it was men. And the man sitting calmly in front of him was definitely someone he wanted on his side, especially when one considered that there was probably someone very much like him on the other side.

Calder heard the rasp of a Swan Vesta match being scraped along sandpaper and watched the General lighting his pipe. A cloud drifted across again and Stoddard began to talk at the same time as he was sucking, between words, as only the real practitioners can do.

"I wanted to talk to you, but that isn't all, I know now. You said it yourself, partly. I distrust experts as well. Yet I'm surrounded by them." He grinned. "I'm one myself."

Calder smiled too.

"Don't get me wrong," continued the General, examining the glowing bole with satisfaction. "I believe in organizations, up to a point. They can be extremely *efficient* and I think mine is, but on certain investigations they can be *ineffective*. It's well over four days since the hijack — nearly five — and we have got absolutely nowhere. I can't allow that state of affairs to continue."

Calder suddenly realized the terrifying responsibility that Stoddard had. Whatever happened in the field, whatever he asked anyone to do, it was Stoddard who was to blame if anything went wrong, or if the results were not achieved. It also occurred to him that the pipe was finally failing to fulfil part of its unconscious purpose, and that the General was going to lose his temper. He was surprised that he had held it for so long.

"You warned me it would happen," said Stoddard, "and I know you have certain specialized knowledge. What's more, I have no way of knowing whether or not Mr Hijack knows every move we are going to make. He seems to have allowed for all contingencies and I have no intention of taking for granted the assumption that he could not possibly have infiltrated my organization."

Calder was nodding slowly. "You want me to operate on the outside," he said.

"Exactly. But I want more. Above all else, what I need is a fresh mind. Someone whose outlook is not narrowed by technique. Christ!" he crashed his left hand down on the desk, "what I need are new ideas, because I don't have any more."

Calder was smiling. "You know, General, for one awful, terrifying moment, I thought you were going to let me go without asking me to do anything."

He got up and walked to the window again. The pigeon was still concerned only with its grooming. He placed a hand low down on the pane and it flew away. He wondered whether its brain would work out which feather it had got up to. Stoddard couldn't hold himself back any longer.

"Do you have any ideas?"

The younger man turned. "At the moment, just one or two vague glimmers, but I'd rather follow them up first, if that's all right with you?"

"Perfectly," said Stoddard. Calder was obviously going to be cautious before presenting anything.

"I will say this, though, General. I've a feeling the plutonium is going to remain in this country."

Stoddard nodded. "Perhaps you're right."

There was a pause before Calder spoke.

"I'll need an assistant, someone to do some legwork. He has to be the sort of person who has access to police information and knows what to do with it."

Stoddard didn't hesitate.

"I can give you Striker. He had a year's training with Special Branch before he came to me. What's more, he's an American on loan to us for a few years and unlikely to be involved. One of our boys is over there."

Calder thought for a moment.

"Has he been involved in the investigation at all?"

"No. He was looking for you from Monday afternoon. I expect he's still in bed."

"Fine. Then Peter Striker will do."

Stoddard baulked slightly at the somewhat casual way in which Calder appeared to accept the services of a highly-trained agent.

"When do you want to see Striker?" asked Stoddard.

"I'd be obliged if you could tell him to come round to my place at 8.30 tomorrow morning."

Stoddard placed his pipe on the blotter and walked over to an old combination safe crouched in a corner of the room. Calder watched as he turned the knob several times, opened the door and extracted a thick pile of £5 notes. He walked over to Calder and held them out to him.

"Five hundred pounds. Operating expenses. You'll need it. Let me know if you want any more."

Calder hesitated momentarily. Then he took the money and placed it in the inside pocket of his jacket.

They walked to the door together.

"I hope you're not right about it being an internal hijack," said Stoddard, "but either way I'll give you all the help I can, although essentially you're on your own."

The General opened the door.

"Ann! You're still here," he said, surprised.

"Yes, sir. I thought you might need me," she answered, smiling uncertainly.

Stoddard looked at his watch, then at his secretary in a familiar, speculative sort of way and she, unaccountably, looked down at her desk. He was always able to read her like a book. Of all the men that had been through that office, he thought, but he'd known that it would happen one day. She was too damned good-looking.

The trend away from attractive secretaries that had swept through Whitehall recently had not affected him. He saw no point in attempting an outward demonstration of chastity and lack of interest in things of the flesh, merely to fall in with a hypocritical, probably transient and anyway dubious notion of piety, the main reason for which was to impress superiors. Well, he had no one above him to impress, and Ann did give him little interludes of self-indulgent pleasure when, at various times during the day, she came into his room.

"Well, perhaps you'd better show Mr Calder out," he said, then turned and shook the younger man's hand.

Calder smiled at him and he wondered whether anyone could get used to those eyes. Then he closed his door, sighed and walked back for the solace of his pipe.

Chapter 9
Saturday, 10 May

CALDER WOKE instantly, without any movement or disturbance in his breathing. His eyes were open in the near-dark, but that was the only overt difference between sleep and wakefulness. Several times in the past he had awoken like this and had learned to listen to his instincts. His brain was working furiously, trying to fathom the reason for his disturbed repose — what sound he had heard, or what thought had subconsciously occurred to him like a flash of inspiration in his slumber. He could remember nothing. He listened, every muscle ready to move immediately. But again, there was nothing.

He had woken like this two days ago in the Mexican desert. That time he had identified the sound in his memory: an almost human scream as the natural selection of the desert had worked to the detriment of some creature or other. He had found it difficult to return to sleep and knew it would be the same now.

He swung his legs out of bed and switched on the bedside lamp, his eyes immediately sweeping the strange room. After all, something had stirred him. He measured the trip to the door, extinguished the lamp, stood up slowly so as not to make the bedsprings creak, and moved silently across the room. Then he swiftly opened the door and pounced through, crouching. He waited a full minute, until the muscles of his thighs protested, but the only sound was from his own breathing.

Feeling rather silly, he looked at his watch. The luminous hands said 1.15 a.m. He switched on the lights and systematically searched the obviously female flat. Nothing. He even checked that the windows were locked and that the front door was fixed from the inside.

Restlessly he returned to the bedroom and, in the light from the front room, took in the sleeping Ann on the double bed. Like him she was naked, but unlike him she was a picture of beauty as she slept. He remembered the night before and the suppressed passion with which she had made love. Quickly but noiselessly he dressed, then looked at her again before leaving, her heavy breasts lying across her chest, her arms outstretched and the concave of her stomach disappearing into the sheet. He looked for a long time, then let himself out.

On the parapet outside the bedroom window, the cat continued his journey. His passage had disturbed the sleeping bird and it had fluttered away into the night. Some lights had gone on, but no one seemed to have noticed him.

The gloved hands inside the adapted oxygen tent worked like automatons, the man manipulating them almost lost in the folds of translucent plastic, as he sat as close as he could to his materials. These included an electric induction furnace, hydrofluoric acid, metallic calcium flake, nitric acid, crystalline iodine, quartz glassware, magnesium oxide, a cylinder of argon gas and high-temperature crucibles. Brown's men had bought them at various retail outlets, on the open market.

Vaisey was very tired. He had been working on the chemical process almost continuously since very early on Friday morning, and it was now the late, small hours of Satuday morning. He found that he didn't need much sleep these days, but he needed to take a break soon.

He had just completed the first stage of a highly complex process that he had copied many times in the last twenty-four hours. This first stage had converted a fairly small quantity of raw plutonium oxide into concentrated plutonium nitrate.

He now finished measuring a litre of hydrofluoric acid and poured it into a quartz flask. Then he led a rubber tube from the furnace, that contained the plutonium nitrate, to the flask and placed it on a burner. Soon, hydrogen fluoride gas began to fume. He then switched on the furnace, watched the temperature rise to 524 degrees centigrade and steadied it. He then waited for about twenty minutes until the conversion to plutonium fluoride had been made, then switched off the furnace.

Vaisey now prepared a graphite crucible by lining it with a thick magnesium oxide paste. Then, using no more than the steel calipers on the end of the heat-resistant gloves, he removed the ceramic crucible containing the plutonium fluoride from the furnace and replaced it with the magnesium oxide crucible. The oven was switched on and the paste dried.

While the crucible was returning to something like room temperature, Vaisey withdrew his arms from the gloves. He removed the black-rimmed spectacles from his Halloween face and rubbed his eyes. Yes, this would definitely be the last one. If he slept for the rest of the morning he could be back on it that afternoon. Then he should have enough plutonium 239 that night or the following morning. It never occurred to him that he might be working too hard. The job simply had to be finished quickly. His amazingly strong will would see that it was.

The spectacles went back on the stump of a nose and the arms filled the gloves out once more. The cooled magnesium crucible was filled with measured quantities of metallic calcium, crystals of iodine and the plutonium fluoride. The specially adapted crucible lid was sealed and the interior filled with argon gas. It was then placed into the furnace and heated to 700 degrees centigrade. The temperature was steadied and Vaisey waited for about sixteen minutes, until a violent reaction occurred in the crucible and its temperature rose very quickly to 1,630 degrees centigrade. At this point the furnace was switched off, the crucible removed and cooled.

Vaisey had puzzled for some time over how to speed up the cooling period. He had finally decided that most attempts to artificially impose cold to the degree of sophistication that he could manage might damage the natural chemical process, but he had eventually hit upon the idea of using an ordinary, small household freezer, turned up to maximum. It was a little slower than he would have liked, but once he had worked out exactly how long it took to cool to room temperature, he was able to use the time usefully.

Extracting himself from the tent again, he used the stool on which he was seated to lever himself on to his legs. He waddled to the workbench and began to study a computer print-out.

In order to prevent the danger of accidentally assembling a critical mass, and therefore creating an explosion somewhat prematurely, the plutonium oxide had to be converted in small quantities. But when he had enough plutonium 239 it had to be cast into two identical hemispheres, the dimensions of which had to be exact. So, he had hired computer time. All the computer programmer saw was a set of, to him, meaningless differential equations and one of Brown's men.

After about fifteen minutes, Vaisey returned to the tent.

It was a lump of P-239. He put it with the others and sat perfectly still for a moment or two, doing nothing. He liked being in his converted glove-box. With the mechanical arms added to his mechanical legs he felt more machine than man and the thought did not displease him.

Then he left for the stairs. Using his arms only, he pulled himself up by transferring his weight from one arm to the other on the iron railings. Even at his age, he could make any gymnast look pretty sick for upper-arm strength.

At the top, he switched off all the electricity and looked back to make sure that nothing but the Calor-gas heaters glowed in the dark. Satisfied, he closed and locked the door.

When the front door-bell rang, Calder, dressed in denim shirt and jeans, had a piece of toast in his left hand and Striker's file in the other. He just managed to stop himself from turning his left wrist to look at his watch, in case the thick marmalade fell off. Instead, he transferred the toast to the plate. 8.30 a.m. on the nose. He got up and walked to the door.

Standing there was Peter Striker in a smart blue suit and tie to match, looking like a Pan-Am commercial. With his straight blond hair and moustache, thin nose and the best looking teeth that money could buy, when he smiled, which he did as often as he could, he also looked like a Hollywood mogul's dream. Calder wouldn't have been surprised to hear that he had a haircut and manicure once a fortnight. But Calder also knew that this smooth exterior hid a very hard man indeed. His file had said that he had been educated at private schools in the United States and at an Ivy League University, and that he was super-fit, having no surplus fat whatever. His sporting interests included jogging, pistol shooting and the martial arts. In this latter skill he was proficient enough to be an unarmed-combat instructor.

"Come in," said Calder and led the American into the front room of the small flat. Striker was taken by its neatness. Two whole walls, from floor to ceiling, were given over to wooden shelves, all filled with books. The wall-to-wall dark brown carpet was cheap, but clean and unworn, and the cream-painted walls blended in with the woodwork. In one corner of the room was a small colour television set. In the centre, between a tobacco-coloured, cloth studio couch and matching chair, was a superb chess table which, from a distance, appeared to be made of ornate teak; it was on castors and the top was covered in green baize. Lying on this was a thick, leather chess-board and what looked like imitation ivory pieces.

"Come through to the kitchen," said Calder. "Coffee?"

"Thanks."

The Englishman poured from a percolator into a mug, and pushed over a tin of sugar, a pint of milk and a spoon. Then he sat down and resumed munching his toast.

Striker helped himself to sugar, stirred, picked up the mug, noted the writing on the side which said, "Coffee drinkers are sexier", took heart and sipped slowly. It was no good; he had to ask.

"Who *are* you?"

Calder finished his chewing, unhurriedly.

"A difficult question to answer," he said, taking another bite. "However, if you were to ask me, '*What* am I?' the answer would be easier. As you can perhaps surmise from this humble abode, I am a simple teacher."

He twisted his mouth wryly before continuing. "Temporarily unemployed."

Striker sipped his coffee. "With independent means?" he asked.

"You must be joking," answered Calder immediately. "You probably earn twice as much as I do. What makes you say that?"

Striker received the full glare of Calder's eyes as the man waited for an answer, and he suddenly felt out of his depth. His halfhearted attempt to impress Calder might go badly wrong.

"Mexico," he said.

"Ah, the General said you were a good detective," said Calder, but he didn't smile, in case Striker might think that he was being patronizing. "As a matter of fact, I won a chess tournament and decided to blow the cash prize on a three-month holiday. Do I pass?"

Striker beamed:

"What did the General tell you?" asked Calder, leaning back in his chair, his face impassive.

"More or less everything, and that I was to do anything you asked." He drummed his fingers on the table, lazily.

"How do you feel about that?" asked Calder. "After all, you are the professional and I the amateur."

Striker gazed into his coffee mug, then flashed his smile again.

"It does seem strange," he answered, "but there's one thing I've learnt about the General: he sure knows what he's doing."

Calder stayed silent, waiting for Striker to continue, but he didn't, just kept gently tapping the table with his fingers.

"I'm going to need your advice," said the Englishman.

He got up and leant against the sink.

"And if ever you think I'm wrong, lay into me hard, because we can't afford to make mistakes."

He paused slightly.

"I'm travelling down to Surrey this morning to speak to a friend.

He's an import/exporter, or something. Buys in one country and sells, for himself and other people, in another. He was once asked whether he could sell some enriched U-235."

"What's that?" asked Striker quickly.

Calder bit his lip.

"It's a particular grade of uranium that has been through a reprocessing plant. In that state it's the raw material for a nuclear bomb. It has very similar properties to the plutonium we're looking for. Also, if it was enriched 235, it had to be stolen and if it was being offered on the open market it could be for only one purpose, and that's to make a nuclear bomb."

"You mean," said Striker, "they might have tried to get some plutonium by other means, before they decided on the hijack?"

"Spot on. In the meantime, I want you to find me the biggest criminal in London."

Striker's fingers stopped drumming.

"The biggest criminal in London," he intoned, as if repeating part of a shopping list.

Calder walked over to the table and picked up his coffee mug.

"I'll be perfectly honest with you," he said. "The General thinks it was a foreign terrorist group. I don't. He may be right, but even so, they needed some British help. It was a big operation and it all took place in the UK."

Striker didn't say anything, just shifted uncomfortably on his chair.

"But," continued Calder, "they might be totally British. Either hired labour for some terrorist group or working for themselves. We've got to find that out by Monday."

"We sure have," said Striker, mimicking John Wayne and hunching his shoulders.

Calder looked at him hard. He liked Peter Striker. His manner was happy-go-lucky and he apparently saw life as one big joke. But Calder had realized on the trip from Mexico that his sarcasm and extrovert manner were part of a sophisticated sense of humour which helped him keep the world in perspective, a façade he hid behind. He'd told Calder that his family motto was going to be "*Carpe diem*" and it wasn't just to demonstrate that he'd had a classical education. His philosophy was to live life to the full, as if each day was to be his last, but only sexually. He drank nothing but the occasional beer and had only a rare cigar. His major interest in life was, apparently, to have sex with as many pretty girls as possible. He was a man who was full of energy, finding difficulty in relaxing. When sitting, for example, he would prop his head up on alternate arms and move his fingers a lot. When standing, he shifted his weight constantly.

"Do you know where to get that information?" asked Calder.

"I have a few friends at the Yard," replied Striker wistfully.

"Well," said Calder with a smile, "I see you've got your Dick Tracy suit on, so go out and super-detect."

Striker stood up, clicked his heels and gave a perfect salute. Calder walked out into the hall and wrote on the telephone pad. He returned to the living-room where he found Striker examining the chess set.

"Do you play?" asked Calder.

"Only if I can't avoid it?" replied Striker. "What's this?" He took the slip of paper that Calder was holding out.

"My number here and where I shall be going this morning."

Striker decided it was time for him to go. Calder may have asked for his advice, but all he wanted was his assistance. Also, although the blond had found that the traditional American image of the straight-laced Englishman was largely a myth, Calder certainly fitted the bill.

"Adios," said Striker smilingly and left.

Ten minutes later Calder was in his Vokswagen Golf and heading for the A23 to the south. The 1600 engine had started after only the second turn, which wasn't bad after two months. It was good to be behind the wheel of a car again, especially since he was going outside London where he could do some real driving. The sky had clouded over and the wind was from the west, probably bringing some rain from the Atlantic. Incredible to think that, less than two days earlier, he had been sitting astride a horse under the hot sun of the Mexican desert. He sighed and, as the traffic was nearly stopped in front of him, pulled into a garage to check tyre pressure, oil and water.

Back on the road, he switched on the radio to take his mind off what he was doing. He didn't want to think too deeply about it at this stage. The ideas were really only embryonic. They could easily be questioned now. When they were followed through and things still didn't gel — that was the time to drop them.

Two and a half hours later, he was surrounded by the horse brasses and warming-pans of a pub in Bletchingley. It had taken some time to socialize with Julian's wife and four children in the garden of their eight-bedroomed Georgian house, but eventually they had got away and were one of the first groups in the pub.

Julian Foster was a big man in height and girth, without being fat. His facial features were rugged and dominated by one of the worst broken noses Calder had ever seen. Foster always claimed that it had happened in a rugger scrum and that he was so drunk for so long afterwards that he forgot to get it fixed. But for a number of reasons, not least of which was the fact that he was a teetotaller, no one believed a word of it. He had a mop of untidy, straight hair that was beginning to grey in various patches. Dressed in dark-blue cord trousers and scarred, blue crew-necked sweater, he was an imposing figure.

In terms of income he and Calder were worlds apart and, whilst their politics were not diametrically opposed, there were fundamental differences. But somehow they liked each other and had been firm friends for several years.

"Cheers," said Foster, holding up his grapefruit juice. "This is all very sudden. I take it this little jaunt down to the wilds of the stockbroker belt is not for social reasons?"

Calder sipped his pint and wondered how his friend was going to take it.

"You know of the plutonium hijacking, of course?" he asked.

"Of course," replied Foster a little guardedly.

"Well, for some reason, the security services seem to think that I might be able to help them find it."

Foster didn't react. He just sat looking at Calder. If he thought it strange that someone he'd believed for years was a polytechnic lecturer — someone who had told everyone in the rugby club the same story — should now be working for the security services, he certainly wasn't showing it.

"I am making an entirely unofficial approach to you," Calder went on, "because I think you may be able to help me find it."

"How?"

"You were once offered some enriched U-235. You told me about it, remember?"

The big man nodded.

"I'm working on the assumption," continued Calder, "that some time before they decided on the hijack, the hijackers made enquiries about how to get hold of some reprocessed P-239, or enriched U-235, on the international market. We both know there's some about. If they did, then they might have spoken to your contact who offered you the uranium. He might be quite well known."

"He was more likely working for a contact of a contact," said Foster.

"OK, but at least he might know someone who knows someone. I know it's a long shot, but it's worth a try."

Foster was looking down at the table.

"You must be really stuck for leads," he said earnestly. Then he sucked on his lips. "It might be difficult," he said, looking up.

"I know," said Calder, "and I'm not asking you to get involved. All I want is a telephone number."

"No," replied Foster, "that's not what I meant. I've met him. He's important. That means he will deny all knowledge and be able to summon help if necessary. He is not going to hand over a name and I doubt whether threatening him will make any difference. You could get into trouble. How far are you prepared to go?"

"I'm prepared to pull his fingernails out, one by one."

Both men looked hard at each other. Foster drained his glass.

"Does that make you better than them?" he asked fiercely.

"Let's not moralize, Julian. Why do you think the plutonium was stolen? No one mounts that sort of operation for fun. Have you any idea how much damage a nuclear explosion would do in the middle of Tel Aviv, or Cairo, or London? If the wind was in this direction, the radiation would be so bad that growing vegetables in the gardens of Bletchingley would be out of the question unless the surface earth was removed. That's not to mention damage to the internal human organs from inhalation."

Calder paused, leaving Foster alone with his thoughts, staring into his empty glass.

"Can it be done?" asked the big man, with a frown. "Made into a bomb, I mean?"

"Yes," answered Calder, "and so can enriched 235. If your man was trying to sell it, it must have been stolen and there is only one possible use for it."

Foster looked at the table again. Calder picked up their glasses and walked over to the bar. When he returned, Foster looked as if he had made up his mind.

"All right," he said, "you win. But we'll have to do it my way. It will cause far less suspicion if I phone him myself. I'll tell him that if he still has the stuff — which of course he won't — I might have a buyer. Then you bug any calls he makes, or whatever it is you chaps do."

Foster raised his glass with a smile. Calder smiled back in admiration.

"No, Julian. I appreciate the offer, but no. It would be too dangerous and you know it. Without wishing to sound melodramatic, you have a family."

Foster gave a short laugh. "With my insurances, Jane and the kids could live in luxury for the rest of their lives."

Calder didn't laugh. "That isn't what I meant. They could get at you *through* your family."

Foster didn't laugh at that one.

"Why are you so bloody, damned clever?" he said angrily.

There was a small silence while Calder sipped his beer.

"So how are you going to get the information?" asked the big man.

Calder looked into his beer this time.

"I don't know yet, but I'll think of something."

Striker was waiting inside Calder's flat when he returned, sitting in an easy chair reading *Winning Chess*, by Chernev and Reinfeld.

"I didn't think you'd mind, so I let myself in," he said cheerfully. "It would have looked suspicious, you know, me waiting outside your door."

"A trick you picked up at Princeton?" asked Calder.

The blond man put on a look of amazement.

"Wow, how'd ya guess? No way one can survive there without being a whizz with a hairgrip or coathanger. But you really ought to get that lock changed, you know. Anyone could walk in here." The American smiled blandly.

"Thanks for the tip," said Calder in a voice which suggested he had no intention of taking the advice.

He sat wearily before speaking again.

"What did you find?"

Striker put the book down and reached inside his jacket pocket, extracting and unfolding a piece of crumpled A4 paper as if it contained the revelation of the century.

"You boys don't have the Mafia over here as you know, or anything like it, so organized crime is a fairly divergent business. I say," he said, mocking a rather good home-counties accent, "you couldn't put the kettle on, could you?"

Calder got up and walked through to the kitchen, amused that despite the American's forwardness he hadn't had the nerve to make himself a cup of coffee.

"However," continued Striker as he followed, "there are two or three large set-ups. My contact at the Met was reluctant to commit himself on who he thought was the strongest or biggest. Eventually, he decided on the least well-known of the big boys, working on the assumption that the more you stay out of trouble, the cleverer you are. George Cox. He's a legitimate businessman. Owns a chain of restaurants, as well as a chain of prostitutes, and has a couple of strip clubs. He's also a crook. We know he's been behind a number of bullion robberies, but there is no evidence. He's never even been in a court, let alone jail. The few of his men who have been caught in the act seem more afraid of him than of going down, and he'll reward them when they come out."

Calder began to make some instant coffee.

"He's English and has a wife with whom he lives in a mansion in Bedfordshire. Surely you don't believe that he did it?"

"No," said Calder. "I don't know Mr Cox, but I don't think he could have the brainpower or the expertise to mount this sort of operation, to say nothing of the leadership and direction necessary to carry it out without leaving any clues."

Striker winced as Calder continued.

"It was, in my view, if you'll excuse the pomposity, a military operation, not something that could have been done by your common criminal. I'm just hoping he is going to give me some information."

The American was looking at him open-mouthed now.

"Has he ever dealt in drugs?" asked Calder.

"Er, it's not on his record," answered Striker, looking at the paper. Then he looked up quickly before speaking again. "You're not going to ask him for help?"

"As a matter of fact, I am," said Calder as he switched off the kettle. "Does his record say where he will be on a Saturday night?"

"No, but I asked, just in case. Saturday night is pay night. Apparently he always spends it in a suite of rooms behind a nightclub that he owns. Would you believe it's called The Blue Lady?"

"I believe it. Anything else?"

"Not really," replied Striker coyly as he picked up the coffee mug with the sexy notation.

"As chance would have it," he continued, "I know The Blue Lady. Had to go there on business once or twice. You know the sort of thing that arises in our job — following someone or chatting them up."

Calder laughed. It was the second time Striker had seen him laugh, yet he was a little surprised at how completely uninhibited it was.

"You know, your powers of extra-sensory perception are really extraordinary good," said the blond. "But let's get things in proportion."

He walked through to the comfortable chair in the living-room and Calder followed.

"It's a classy joint. Tuxedos and dicky-bows, and the artistes are only the very best, believe me."

The last two words were said with some feeling and a glassy-eyed expression came over the blond man's face. Then he looked up as if the thought had just occurred to him.

"You wouldn't need any assistance, I suppose?"

"Well," replied Calder with apparent reluctance, "I guess I've got to keep the workers happy. Besides, if I've got to smell of moth balls tonight, I don't see why my able assistant shouldn't."

Using Striker's membership, they managed to book a table for 8 o'clock and, shrugging off the attempts of two attractive ladies of doubtful virtue, were shown to seats just below the small stage. The atmosphere, Calder felt, was congenial, but cloyingly opulent. Most of the guests were of portly build and the small band of black musicians playing in the corner wore perpetual smiles.

To Calder's surprise they dined well. The dressed crab was delicious and the fillet steak even better. The out-of-season strawberries were a little crisp, but with the remains of a good red wine they went down smoothly. The meal was served throughout by a topless waitress who, although she didn't have a great deal to show, was extremely pretty. Calder felt somewhat uncomfortable, munching his steak while a bare-breasted female leaned over him to pour wine, but Striker appeared not to notice.

At 10 p.m. precisely, the low lights were dimmed even further and the footlamps shone purple. There was a roll of drums and two men, wearing nothing but G-strings, came out carrying a black girl. Completely naked, she was lowered to the floor on her knees, her back to the audience. The straight, muscled back gleamed in the light and her skin shone — covered in oil, Calder reasoned. Slowly, the two white men backed away into the shadows. The whole of the big room was silent and the girl remained motionless.

Then, a single bass drum began to beat and the girl's upper body began to writhe in time with the tone, her arms outstretched and her head still. Slowly she rolled over on to her stomach and pushed herself up on hands and knees, as if trying to resist the rhythm. Two of the most enormous breasts that Calder had ever seen dropped beneath her hard, compact frame.

Suddenly, she threw her head back, clenching her teeth, and her upper body moved again. Her breasts began to ripple obscenely as she straightened, running hands over nipples as they travelled to a point above her head. More drums entered, stepping up the rhythm, but the bass beat didn't falter. Calder knew that his pulse was probably keeping time to it.

The girl had her legs splayed now as she rose to her feet, her whole body undulating like a black sea. Then she stilled her upper body as her hips moved to the increased pulse. Calder marvelled at the way the huge breasts remained almost motionless, despite the sexual urgency of her stomach, hips and thighs.

The drums beat faster as her whole body began to pulsate, her breasts also vibrating now in pendulous tempo. Calder could see rivulets of sweat between them, clearing a path through the oil, and he became conscious of his hand grasping the stem of his wine glass too hard.

Then the girl opened her mouth and screamed as the drums thudded their complicated pernicious sound, and she lowered herself to the floor, side on to the audience, her knees bent and legs splayed, limbo style. Calder could hear her cries as she leant back, making her whole body bend, still moving to the rhythm. Hands crept across her belly and, suddenly, she thrust her body upwards in an arch as a long scream came from her throat. The drums stopped and the lights went out at exactly the same moment, but the scream continued, echoing around the darkness.

There were a few tentative claps and then the whole audience applauded loudly. When the restaurant lights went on, the two white men could be dimly discerned, carrying off the drooping body, an arm over each shoulder.

It had been an impressive display. It must have lasted at least ten minutes, yet the time seemed to go in no more than two. Calder was glad that he had finished his meal before it had begun. Striker was grinning at him.

"You know my one regret about tonight," he said. "After you've finished debagging Cox, I'm going to find it very difficult to renew my membership."

Calder grinned back. He had temporarily forgotten why he was there. He turned to look for their waitress. She was snaking her way throught a cordon of seemingly uninterested diners, some drinks balanced dexterously on a small tray above her head. Calder raised his arm and she saw him immediately. He watched her deliver the drinks to a party of laughing, sweating Germans and walk quickly over. She bent over slightly so as to hear what he had to say.

"Yes, sir?" she asked happily.

"I'd like to see the manager," said Calder.

Worry showed immediately in her eyes. The gleaming smile disappeared. Calder quickly placed a hand on hers.

"Don't worry," he smiled, "it's not a complaint."

He was relieved to see the teeth again as she let out a small laugh of pleasure and moved off.

"That was just a starter too," chimed Striker, staring morosely at the stage. "The others are even better."

He turned back towards the table, extracted a packet of thin cigars and gave one to Calder before helping himself. As they lit up, Striker looked keenly at Calder.

"I don't know how you're planning to work this, but I suggest that we both go in together," said Striker.

A man of about thirty, with oily hair and a bandito moustache, appeared at his elbow.

"Good evening. I'm the manager. Can I help you?"

The eyes were watchful. Calder stood up to find that he was looking quite a way down at the man.

"My name is Calder. This is Mr Striker," gesturing with his hand.

The manager made no attempt to shake hands, but grinned condescendingly at Striker.

"Would you join us for a moment?" asked Calder.

The eyes were confident as the man looked up.

"Thank you, but I'm rather busy. Perhaps if you just tell me what it is that you require."

"Your name is?" asked Calder.

The man hesitated slightly. "Robinson."

"Very well, Mr Robinson, perhaps you could ask Mr Cox if we could have an audience with him."

The manager didn't falter.

"I beg your pardon? Did you say Mr Cox?"

"Yes," said Calder politely.

"I am afraid I don't know what you are talking about," said Robinson. "There is no Mr Cox here," and he began to walk away.

"Don't walk away from me, Mr Robinson," said Calder.

Something in his voice made the man pause and turn. His eyes flickered over the bearded face.

"I suggest we stop playing around," continued Calder. "Mr Cox is at this moment not fifty yards from us. We are making a civil request to see him. Mr Striker and I are unarmed and our mission, I assure you, is a peaceful one." He smiled.

The small man looked towards the door. When he turned back his expression had hardened.

"Why should Mr Cox see you? He, too, is a busy man."

Calder hesitated and looked towards the stage. What he said was important. He hadn't told Striker, but he was prepared to force his way in if necessary and that would hardly be an ideal beginning to a request for help. Still looking at the stage, he said:

"Tell Mr Cox this. We do not come bearing gifts. Indeed, I think it's fair to say that he will not gain from our visit in any way that I can see. But if he does not see us, he stands to lose his whole empire. We want to help him stand still, but it is imperative that we see him now."

He turned back to the manager, who was looking at him rather oddly. Then the man glanced pointedly at Striker and left.

"Well, of one thing I am sure," said the American as he blew a smoke-ring at the ceiling. "My membership *is* terminated."

Calder smiled. "Your membership is not the only thing you might lose tonight, if they don't let us in peacefully."

Striker raised his eyebrows and glanced over at the exit. Two very big men, with necks like tree trunks, had stationed themselves by the stairs, looking in his direction. He swivelled his head to look at the door near the bar, where he found that a couple more had suddenly materialized. Slowly, he turned back, bent forward and casually flicked the ash off his cigar.

He looked at Calder, who was gazing into the distance above the stage, and wondered how he would manage. He knew from experience that in most circumstances he himself could handle two, but with three he generally needed help. Calder seemed to have no nerves at all, but surely he was too intelligent to attempt a forced entry without some probability of success?

Then the sheer force of Calder came across, as he sat there, perfectly relaxed, his mind on the problem in hand. He blinked slowly and looked at Striker, the eyes piercing and the corners of the mouth turned up. Suddenly, the blond man realized that although he wasn't frightened of the men at the door, he *was* afraid of Matthew Calder. It worried him that he didn't know why and, even more, that he realized he would follow him to Hell, without knowing the reason for that either.

The music changed from soft piano to something more sophisticated, as bright lights brought the stage alive. A girl, dressed in Victorian middle-class fashion, holding a parasol, waltzed on.

Striker was surprisingly looking the other way as he spoke.

"You won't believe what she does with that parasol. Especially since I don't think you're going to have time to find out."

Calder looked round to see a heavily built man, whose function in The Blue Lady was fairly obvious, walking purposefully towards them. Calder stood up, waiting. The man stopped, confidently, like someone content in the knowledge of his own physical prowess.

"Mr Robinson will see ya now," he said. The voice was East-End cockney.

He turned and they followed, through the bar door into a small ante-room, where two more men waited. They were roughly shoved against a wall and thoroughly searched. Then they went along a corridor, with only three doors leading off it. At the end they turned sharply right and walked to a door in an alcove. There a man knocked and they entered another ante-room. This one was decked out like an office, with filing cabinets, a typewriter and desk. Behind the last object sat a man of a smaller and different stature to the others. He raised his eyebrows quizzically, received a curt nod and closed the drawer in which his hand had been placed. He then stood up, walked over to the other door and knocked. In the silence which followed, Calder heard a muffled, "Enter," and they were ushered in.

The room was huge — at least thirty feet by fifty — and tastefully decorated, provided you could live with the colour scheme. A deep, red pile carpet accentuated the red and gold wallpaper. The wall-lighting shed pools of illumination on the many oil paintings. To the right was the glow of a real log fire surrounded by a marble fireplace. Near this were two comfortable, red leather, Chesterfield couches. At either side of the hearth stood a red and gold standard lamp. There were no windows and only one other door. The unmistakable strains of Mozart filled the room.

Sitting in front of Calder, behind a desk, was a man who could only have been George Cox. Striker had not mentioned his age and Calder was surprised to see he was so young. He realized that he had subconsciously expected to see someone elderly, but this man was in his late thirties, even if his prematurely almost bald head made him look a little older. He had wide, flaring nostrils, hollow cheeks and a sensuous mouth, and the arms that leaned on the desk bulged with muscle under the dinner jacket. He looked as hard as nails.

92

In the middle of the room stood a Charles Atlas in blue T-shirt, and to Cox's right was the short Mr Robinson.

"Mr Cox?" asked Calder.

The man behind the desk did not answer, just sat back in his chair and gazed at the two newcomers. Then he rose and walked slowly over to the fireplace, where he warmed his hands with mock satisfaction. Calder wondered how much of it was for effect, to establish that his position of authority in the room was not just guaranteed by the muscle man. He felt Striker shift behind him.

"Who are you, Calder?" asked Cox, without turning from the fire. The accent was cosmopolitan.

Calder shot a glance at Striker and noted he was looking at the guard.

"I'm working for the government. So is Mr Striker."

Mozart deepened in the room. Calder let himself surrender to it, sharing something with the man at the fire and sensing part of him. Cox retrieved a glass of what looked like brandy from the mantelpiece, and turned towards them.

"What part of the government, exactly?" he asked.

"The security services," answered Calder.

Cox nodded. To Calder, it seemed that he was answering a question that he had already asked himself.

"You can prove it, of course?"

Calder looked at the roughneck.

"If your gorilla here won't jump to conclusions, my colleague has an identity wallet in the inside pocket of his jacket."

Striker reached inside and gave it to the muscle man, who took it over to Cox. His boss examined it for some time before walking over to Calder and giving it to *him*.

"Very interesting," said Cox. "I've never seen one of those before."

They were of a height and the man looked straight into Calder's eyes. Then he turned away uncomfortably and walked back towards the fire.

"Come and sit down and tell me what you want," he said.

Calder glanced at Striker again. The blond man, for once, looked perfectly relaxed, feet slightly apart and hands at his side. He was still looking at the heavy.

"I want your help," said Calder, as he approached the hearth. "But I must emphasize that this is a completely unofficial request."

Cox suddenly burst out laughing. His whole body shook.

"I hardly think that MI5 would be asking me officially for help, Mr Calder." He laughed again. "It might soil their nice clean hands."

His face hardened before he spoke again.

"But I'm sure your business is dirtier than mine, despite that."

"In this case, Mr Cox, you're quite right. We know about your interests and we are not concerned with them — although I can't, of course, speak for the Metropolitan Police. But compared to what we are dealing with, you *are* the vestal virgin."

Calder realized that he had almost gone too far as the man's face hardened again, so he pushed on quickly.

"You will have heard of the plutonium hijack?"

"Of course," answered Cox and then he smiled. "You don't think I did it?"

"No. But I'm asking you to help me find out who did."

Cox burst into a fit of laughter. It was a long time before he stopped.

"I must confess, Calder," he said, "you take the cake for nerve. You come in here, as bold as brass, tell me that you represent the side of law and order and then you ask me to find the perpetrator of a hold-up."

He walked towards Calder and stopped about a yard from him. His face was fierce but his voice was controlled.

"Give me one good reason why I should."

Calder looked back into the brown eyes in his usual way. He saw hatred there and intelligence, but not fear. Cox was used to being on top and Calder did not want to alter that. Besides, he felt a strange liking for the man. He was more a product of society than the other way around. He probably had a resentment against the so-called legitimate world for producing him in the condition that it had, and the accusation had its point. What's more, he had risen to the top of his profession in a very tough environment. As did successful businessmen.

The music was reaching a crescendo. Calder turned to look at the guard.

"I'd prefer as few people to know as possible," he said, looking back at Cox.

The latter glared at Calder until the sound died down, his nostrils flaring, before he signalled the guard to go.

"But Robinson stays," he said forcefully.

Striker shifted his weight. Calder nodded and gathered his thoughts.

"I don't know whether you know, Mr Cox," he said, "but the material that was stolen was reprocessed plutonium 239. With a certain chemical conversion — which is difficult, but can be done by a competent scientist — it is the raw material for a nuclear bomb."

He walked over to the fire and stood in front of it.

"We don't know who stole it. It may have been a foreign power or terrorist group, or," he paused slightly, "it may have been a British group. We simply don't know. But we must eliminate possibilities. There would certainly need to have been British help for the job, even

94

if it wasn't all British. A certain amount of recruiting might have gone on within the criminal fraternity. We thought that you, with your connections that are denied to us, might know something or be able to find it. Any clue would be useful."

Cox shifted his position and scowled before he swigged at his brandy.

"Before I continue," said Calder, "please turn the concerto off. It would be a blasphemy to listen to it with what I am about to say."

Cox remained perfectly still for several seconds, looking at Calder. Then his face visibly softened and he signalled Robinson. The short man bent to the desk and the room became silent, apart from the crackling fire. Calder felt that part of him had gone. So, he hoped, would Cox.

"Our fear is, Mr Cox, that if it was a British group, it can have only one object: nuclear blackmail. We don't know how much, as yet, was stolen, but assuming the bomb that may be built is about the smallest possible, it would contain about ten kilos of plutonium. In normal circumstances, that would produce an explosive power of about twenty-thousand tons of TNT."

Cox wasn't drinking his brandy now, Calder noticed. Striker was looking at him with a puzzled frown on his face and Robinson was impassive. He himself felt strangely calm.

"I'll spare you the technical details, but if such a bomb were exploded in Central London, let's say in the boot of a car in Horse Guards Parade, behind 10 Downing Street, the effect would be catastrophic.

"Most people and most things within a radius of one and three-quarter miles from that point can be expected to be destroyed by fire — from flash burns or simply burnt by fire — or crushed by falling masonry, or cut to ribbons by falling glass. The 'blast wave' and the 'fireball' would see to that. If anyone in that circle is lucky enough to survive the initial explosion and resulting firestorm, the gamma rays or neutrons — very intense and powerful initial radiation — that would be released at the same time, would probably finish them off. Almost everyone, and everything, within that three-and-a-half-mile circle would be destroyed and, of course, the effect would be greater the nearer one was to the centre.

"I needn't point out that Soho is well within that circle, and insurance companies don't pay out on nuclear explosions. This building would simply cease to exist. So would most things from the top of Tottenham Court Road in the north to the Oval cricket ground in the south, from Park Lane in the west to Southwark Bridge in the east."

Cox was still not drinking his brandy. He was just staring at Calder. Striker was strangely immobile.

"Then," continued Calder, "the worse effect of all would still be to come. There would be residual radiation fall-out. Depending on the strength of the wind, it would fall in a cigar shape over a distance of about a hundred miles. I don't know whether you know the effects of radiation on the body. The main one is to cause cancers of various kinds, which are usually incurable.

"I don't know how many people live, or work, or visit within that circle — two hundred and fifty thousand? Five hundred thousand? A million? It would doubtless depend on the day and the time of day. Very few would survive and the eventual radiation, which would spread over a much larger area, would perhaps eventually kill even more. We are not just talking about your businessman in the Strand, but also a child playing in her garden in Bedfordshire."

Calder moved to one side and noticed that Cox's gaze didn't alter. He was staring into the fire. Robinson hadn't moved and Striker was looking at Calder intensely.

Suddenly Cox drained his glass and looked Calder straight in the face. When he spoke he seemed perfectly calm.

"I'm going to have another brandy. Would you two gentlemen like one?"

Calder looked at Striker and said, "No, thank you."

Cox walked over to the decanter on the mantelpiece and began to pour.

"You have produced your reason, Mr Calder. I shall think about it and made some enquiries."

Calder nodded, slightly surprised. Somehow, despite his confidence, he hadn't expected it to be so easy.

"We can't ask for more," he said. It was time to go.

"Give your telephone number and address to Robinson on the way out," said Cox. "I'll call tomorrow evening."

The quiet, watchful Mr Robinson was looking at Calder very carefully as they moved towards the door.

"Mr Calder?" called Cox from the fireplace.

They all paused and looked back.

"I suppose I'm a bit of a villain." He was looking at the brandy in his glass. "That's the main reason I've felt unable to have children."

Then he looked into the fire.

The room was spacious and expensive. In the middle, covering most of the parquet flooring, was a large, greenish Persian carpet and, surrounding it, several pieces of chintz furniture. The space was lit by a single standard lamp and the glow of a colour television set that was perched in one corner. Six people sat in the room watching the late film: five bearded men and a woman. It was not quite midnight.

The atmosphere, Judy felt, was definitely unfriendly. Being the

96

only woman, and an extremely attractive one at that, you would think that she would be happy. But she knew that John wouldn't like her to get too friendly with the others. Yet he had hardly spoken to her since Monday. Once she had asked his permission to go for a walk, but that had been vetoed. She was a prisoner and she didn't like the feeling of oppression that had set in with the group since their return. Eighteen men enclosed in one house, with nowhere to go and nothing to do, was not a good recipe for congeniality, she knew. The daily exercise in the large enclosed garden was not enough to get rid of the excess energy, and there had been intense competition as to who went on the job with John and poor Vaisey the following night.

She looked down at her carelessly crossed legs, glanced up and saw Martin looking at her. She thought about what it would be like with Martin and, feeling beautifully mischievous, slowly drew her legs up underneath her on the soft chair, exposing the length of one thigh.

She looked up again and saw that John had just come in. He was looking at her. Had he seen and interpreted her movement? He had been giving her the same look now for a week. He had changed. He was colder. And she had to admit that the feeling was mutual. On the boat the distance between them had become even greater. But she still acted the part of faithful girlfriend. It saved a lot of friction. She didn't like the set-up now, but she knew how to survive.

John was signalling to her. Dutifully, she got up and followed him down the corridor and up the stairs to her room. There he locked the door and told her to strip. She did so. Then, without being asked, she bent over the bed with her rear in the air. She had found it rather animal at first and exciting, but it had now become rather monotonous.

He knew from experience that he could enter her immediately. She had four orgasms before his fingers pinched the flesh at the top of her thighs and he let out a long sigh.

Swiftly, he withdrew, zipped himself up, turned her around, smiled and kissed her. Then he walked out. It had been a relief of tension. Nothing more.

Chapter 10
Sunday, 11 May

STRIKER COULDN'T see out of the car windscreen, as the rain had distorted its translucence. It was coming down heavily now and there was a definite drumming on the roof. Condensation had been the major problem and he had had to have a side window continuously open to prevent the car steaming up. A small pool was beginning to form on the passenger carpet and the cloth seat looked as if it would never be the same again. But that couldn't be helped. He had to have clear vision to see out of his side window and he needed immediate forward sight if he had to move off quickly. The drumming got louder.

Keeping his breath away from his door window, he looked again at the solid gabled house, patches of it just discernible behind the newly-leafed beech trees. He had been there since 9 a.m. It was now nearly 11.00 and he had a thumping headache. Calder had insisted that he was up at 7.30, despite their late night. Not that Calder had slept much. He had been up even later, waking headquarters, arranging links with Special Branch, borrowing equipment and organizing a phone-tap of the house at which he was now looking. It was the residence of the man Calder's friend had put them on to, and by all accounts he was a legitimate businessman, completely unknown to the police. Not a thing had stirred since he had arrived, although, through binoculars, he had observed that curtains had been drawn about half an hour before.

On a wet, Sunday morning, Hampstead, it appeared, did not emerge from its lethargic affectation. Strange, Striker thought, how middle-class norms and values were so similar in all Western, industrialized societies — so exportable. Only the working-class were different. Hampstead did not differ markedly from the sort of area in which he had been brought up, in Los Angeles, where his father was a successful lawyer and his mother a society beauty. Only the weather, of course. Later on, about midday, he figured, one or two of the residents would drift along to the local or the golf club bar, perhaps a little earlier than usual since gardening was obviously out.

A bedraggled dog — incongruously, yet somehow fittingly, a mongrel — cocked its leg at a gatepost for no more than two seconds, to mark its territory, before limping on home.

The car radio barked at him. "Blue Wing. This is Red Wing."

Striker unhooked the microphone.

"Receiving you loud and clear, Red Wing," he answered, exaggerating his US accent.

"I'm going to call in exactly five minutes, Blue Wing."

"Acknowledged, Red Wing. Anything else?"

"No. Out."

A man of few words, Matthew Calder. God, what was he thinking? Striker started the engine and immediately put the heater and fan full on the windscreen. Then he switched on the wipers and reversed about a hundred yards up the road. This had been arranged beforehand. When Andrews received the call, he might get suspicious and look out of the window to see if he was being watched. A strange car parked just outside the front door would not look good. In his new position, Striker decided to keep the engine running. This

98

enabled him to close the near-side window and keep the heater, fan and windscreen wipers on.

The inside of the car was now very noisy. He opened his window a little and watched the entrance to the house.

The plan was that Calder would phone Andrews and explain that he had acquired some P-239 and ask whether he knew of a buyer. Andrews, they had reasoned, would do one of three things. What they were hoping for was that he would phone his contacts to find out whether he could place the plutonium. In that case Calder would listen in. Alternatively, Andrews might make contact directly. That was what Striker was for. Alternatively also, he might decide to do nothing until Monday. After all, English Sundays were rather sacrosanct. But Calder was hoping to impress a sense of urgency upon him.

The next thirty minutes went by extremely slowly as Striker watched the end of the drive. He was about to call Calder for news when the car radio spoke again.

"This is Red Wing calling Blue Wing."

"Blue Wing here. Anything?"

"No. Your end?"

"No."

There was a pause.

"OK. Maintain surveillance. Out."

Just then, a silver-metallic Mercedes swept out of the drive — if anything had been coming the driver would have been hard-pushed to stop — and accelerated away from Striker up the road.

"Red Wing. He's just emerged. Am in pursuit."

With that, Striker dropped the receiver back on its rest, slammed the 2-litre Ford Cortina into first gear and sped off. He held it in each gear for a long time before he reached top and was hurtling after the speeding Mercedes. He saw its left indicator winking at the top of the road before it disappeared. Striker braked late and turned after it. He managed to close to within two hundred yards and grabbed the receiver.

"This is Blue Wing calling Red Wing."

"Receiving you, Blue Wing."

"Am coming towards you. He's heading south towards Central London."

"OK. Out."

Striker had to keep the pedal fairly well down to the floor to keep up with the Mercedes in the sparse traffic, but he managed without a great deal of trouble, although he had to shoot a red light to stay in sight. Finally, they entered Knightsbridge and turned into Princes Gardens. Andrews stopped outside a big Georgian terraced house and got out.

The blond man cruised by and stopped on the other side of the road. He looked back, saw Andrews reach the top of the steps and press a black bell that was set into the cream wall. Then he appeared to hesitate, push the door and walk in. Striker turned the car round and parked it right behind the Mercedes, about nine feet from the bumper. Then he picked up the microphone.

"This is Blue Wing calling Red Wing."

"Receiving you loud and clear, Blue Wing," came the stronger reply.

"Subject entered house in Princes Gardens, Knightsbridge." He gave the number. "Request instructions."

"Just follow and report, Blue Wing."

Striker replaced the communicator with drawn lips. There was something wrong. The front door had appeared to open as soon as Andrews pushed the bell, or it was already open.

Suddenly, Andrews burst out of the door at a run. He stopped, as if realizing that he was outside and clambered down the steps to his car. On reaching the street he glanced quickly, furtively, to left and right. The front door of the house was still open.

On impulse, Striker decided to disobey orders and use his initiative. He left his car and began to walk towards Andrews. The heavens seemed to choose that moment to rain even harder. The older man saw him as he was opening his car door and just stood there, a look of sheer horror on his pale face. The complexion was whiter than it should have been, Striker decided, as if it had been drained of blood. He was about sixty, with a full greased-down head of straight white hair. The nose was long and thin, the eyes a bloodshot blue and the lips also had a tinge of the same colour. It was the face of a retired admiral, but Striker knew that he probably didn't know one end of a ship from the other. He was dressed in black overcoat with a beige scarf at his throat.

"Mr Andrews," said Striker in his best English accent, "I want you to shake hands and smile, as if we were old friends."

Both the smile and the shake were pitifully weak, but adequate in the circumstances.

"Now, I want you to slowly walk over to my car and get in the passenger side. And be careful, Mr Andrews; I do have a gun under my jacket."

Andrews obeyed tamely, his arms hanging at his sides and his head drooping. Striker managed to get in his side before Andrews sat down. The latter appeared not to notice the wet seat.

"Good," said the American. "As you might have gathered, I'm a policeman. What went on in there?"

Andrews looked at Striker intently, as if he were relieved in some way. Then another thought appeared to cross his mind. He turned and stared through the windscreen. Striker waited.

100

"He's dead," said the grey man absently. He turned to look at the blond again, fear in his eyes. "But I didn't kill him. Honestly. He was dead when I arrived."

Striker believed it.

"Anyone else in the house?" he asked.

"No. I didn't see anyone." Andrews frowned. "He has servants. But I didn't see any of them, and the door was open when I arrived."

Striker unhooked the microphone.

"Blue Wing, calling Red Wing."

"Go ahead."

Striker took a deep breath and kept to the English accent.

"Have apprehended suspect as he ran from the address previously given. He says that there is a body inside, but no one else. Request assistance before proceeding."

There was a pause.

"I'll be there in ten minutes."

In that time Striker tried to prise some more information out of his captive, but he was now saying nothing. Striker strapped some handcuffs on him and waited for Calder. In the meantime he kept an eye on the house and tried to ignore his worsening headache.

Calder parked behind the Cortina and let himself in by one of the rear doors.

"Any life, from him or the house?" he asked Striker.

"None from neither, if that's grammatically correct. He wants to see his solicitor."

"Does he?" answered Calder.

Striker had never seen Calder in this mood. He looked at the old man and almost felt sorry for him.

"If he doesn't co-operate," said Calder, "he'll be lucky if he *ever* sees his solicitor. Now, listen to me, Andrews. We are all going into that house to have a look at this body. Let's go."

The anger, Striker realized, was only just under the surface. Calder had been almost deferential to Cox, but he treated this apparently respectable businessman with ill-disguised venom. He was being hauled out of his seat now by Calder, and Striker quickly followed, feeling uncomfortable.

They went down a dark corridor which led into a large, even darker room. The blinds were still down. Striker could just make out the wood-panelling and the big, empty fireplace. There was also a red and purple, patterned rug and, on it, right in the centre, a body, fully clothed. Andrews, he noticed, was staring at it with his mouth and eyes wide open.

Calder switched on the lights and Striker didn't have to go any closer to see that the man was an Arab of about middle-age. He was also very dead. A pool of blood lay around his head and there was no doubt that his throat had been cut.

Calder pushed Andrews into a chair and bent over the body. So did Striker. It was very cold. He'd obviously been dead for hours. Certainly a long time before Andrews arrived. Calder was looking at him. Then he stood up and walked over to a telephone, on a small table to one side of the fireplace. Striker hadn't noticed it. Calder dialled a number and waited. The blond rose and looked over at Andrews. His strength appeared to have gone. He just sat, looking at the carpet, head in hands.

"Hello. This is Calder."

A pause and then he gave the address.

"On following a suspect, we have found a murder victim. The man our suspect was going to see. He's an Arab. I don't know how you want to play it and I know it's a Sunday, but if it's possible, I suggest you send a small team round before we notify the police. There might be something of interest."

Another pause.

"Yes."

Then he put the phone down. Andrews, Striker noticed, had become attentive.

"If you're not the police," said the grey man rather uncertainly, "then who are you?"

"We'll stay here until they arrive," said Calder to Striker.

Andrews was extremely nervous and glanced over at the blond American for assistance, having worked out that Calder was the danger man.

"Who is he?" asked Calder, pointing at the man on the floor.

"I'm not saying anything until I have seen my solicitor," replied Andrews, looking at the door. But his voice was shaking and he was unsure of himself.

"Let me put you in the picture, Andrews," said Calder. "We know what you do and a lot of it comes under the Official Secrets Act. Do you know what that means? You come under the category of 'spy' or 'foreign agent', and if you're lucky enough to get a trial, it will be held *in camera*."

"You can't prove anything," interjected Andrews a little too confidently.

Calder, with hands hanging at his sides, was seemingly perfectly relaxed as he continued.

"Then, of course, there is the public trial for murder."

The grey man stood up. "You can't prove that either! He was dead before I arrived."

"My assistant here observed you running from the house," Calder went on. "And this, immediately after receiving a phone call offering some plutonium for sale."

Andrews looked away as the penny dropped.

102

"I don't think it would take the police long to make the connection between you and Mr X here, do you, Andrews? It looks very suspicious. Bound to be a trial."

Calder paused for effect. Andrews had sat down again and was looking at the carpet.

"You may just get off the murder charge, if you're lucky, but the publicity would be ruinous," continued Calder relentlessly. "And I would make sure that you got it."

Again he stopped momentarily.

"And there's one other thing, Andrews."

He stepped purposefully over to the now dejected man, grasped him by the shirt and tie, and hauled him to his feet. Striker moved instinctively towards them, then stopped himself. Andrews's face was barely a foot away from Calder's. They both appeared to be shaking slightly, for different reasons. The words were not merely spoken, but spat.

"I hold little shits like you in nothing but contempt. Creatures who sell fuel for nuclear bombs on the open market are not people, they're the arsehole of humanity. If I had my way, I'd take you to the deepest hole I could find and let you starve to death. But even that's too good for you. As it is, I'd take the greatest delight in rearranging your face and believe me, I'd enjoy it."

Andrews shivered. He was also clearly struggling, but Calder's grip was not allowing him any movement.

"As it is, you have precisely three seconds to start telling me all you know about that man and the rest of your filthy business, or I'll make a start on your teeth."

A pause.

"Well?"

It was said with terrible portent and Andrews was not a man of courage. He cracked. Calder released his grip and his victim grovelled on the floor, staining the carpet some more with his vomit. He told all.

The dead man was a wealthy Arab named Khalid Aziz who owned the house they were in. Andrews had twice acted as a broker in selling him some enriched uranium 235, three years or so previously, and they had kept up a business and social relationship that did not involve nuclear elements. He had come to see him on three counts. On receiving the call that morning, he thought that Aziz had been the one to put the caller in contact, in which case he wanted to know who he was. Secondly, and if not, he thought he might be able to sell the plutonium to him. He also wanted to talk to him as a friend, because he was a little worried about his security.

"How many deals of this nature have you made?" asked Calder, while Striker took notes.

Just the twice with Aziz, it seemed. It was difficult material to come by.

"I've had one request for it recently, but was unable to find any," concluded Andrews.

Striker stiffened and swapped glances with Calder.

"Why didn't you call that person — the one who wanted the U-235 — after I phoned this morning?" Calder wanted to know.

Andrews looked up pleadingly.

"I might have done, but I don't have his number or his address, or even his name. You've got to believe me. People are very cautious in this business. They hold back information about themselves until the last possible moment. He phoned one day, just like you, and refused to give his name and number. That's why I was suspicious about your call. He said he would phone again in a month."

Andrews stopped.

"And did he?" asked Striker pleasantly.

The grey-haired man looked up, either surprised at the direction of the question or the change of accent. He nodded his head several times before speaking.

"Yes. But only once more. I never heard from him again."

"How long ago was the last call?" asked Striker. "Be absolutely sure, Mr Andrews."

This time he shook his head.

"I can't be sure, I'm sorry, but it was around...October or November of last year. I would not have made a note in my diary."

Striker looked at Calder. The latter pushed his hand forward, encouraging him to continue. Striker looked back at the pathetic old man.

"We will be asking you to put down a transcript of the conversation, Mr Andrews, but can you remember anything about the man — any clue as to who he might be?"

Striker looked down at his writing pad before continuing.

"Needless to say, it will stand you in good stead if we can say that you were helpful."

Andrews looked at Striker, then Calder, then back to Striker again.

"I don't know," he said. "What can you tell about a man from a telephone conversation?"

"Quite a lot," answered Striker, but Andrews appeared to be thinking.

"It was such a long time ago."

He paused and they waited.

"There was one thing. I remember thinking at the time that he had been in the Army."

Striker and Calder swapped glances again.

"You know," continued Andrews, "officer type — used to giving orders. Had a way of saying things."

He paused again.

"I was in the infantry, you know. Captain," and with that he appeared to go into a trance.

A footfall sounded in the corridor.

"He'll have to be interrogated with a tape-recorder," said Calder, "but we'll let these boys handle that," and he turned towards the door.

Striker was seated in one of Calder's comfortable chairs, drinking some of his dry ginger. Vaughan Williams was playing on the stereo. It was 7.30 p.m. and they were waiting for two things. Most importantly, George Cox was due to ring and they were also expecting a transcript of the interrogation of Andrews.

Calder was looking at the chess-board, deep in thought. The anger of midday had disappeared and he was almost his normal self, whatever that was. But Striker felt that their relationship had subtly changed. He wondered whether Calder was seeing the whole investigation in terms of a chess game. Would he, Calder, be the white queen or a knight? Andrews would probably be an expendable black pawn, or perhaps a white one.

He looked up to see Calder looking at him. Their eyes held.

"You disapprove of the way I handled Andrews, don't you, Peter?"

Striker looked down at his glass. This could get very heavy, he thought.

"I don't know how much of your anger was controlled or genuine," he answered with a smile.

"A bit of both, I think," said Calder. "But I must admit, I was only just in control of myself." He turned to look at Striker, a wry smile on his face. "Does that make it better or worse?" he asked.

Striker hadn't lost his grin.

"I don't know," he said, shrugging his shoulders in an attempt to lighten the atmosphere.

To himself he thought that it at least showed Calder was human. Out loud he said:

"It got what we wanted."

Calder laughed before speaking.

"Since when did the ends justify the means in your philosophy?"

"Perhaps I was trying to ease your conscience," smiled Striker.

Again Calder laughed.

"Come on," he said, "let's play chess. I want to think."

"That's what I like about you," said the blond man, "the way you flatter your opponents."

Calder signalled Striker to start with the white pieces as they moved over to the chess-board. Striker hesitated and picked up the white king. It was no use. He had to say it.

"There is one thing about you."

The sudden seriousness in his voice made Calder look up.

"You make fundamental decisions for other people — moral decisions — that might affect them quite significantly. But you never seem to hesitate about making them. I'm not so sure that I could do that."

Calder was looking at him intently now. Striker remembered their meeting in San Claro and how the eyes had bored into him then. It was the same look and he found it just as difficult to counter. The eyes told you nothing, yet they told you everything. They were neither hard nor soft, weak nor strong; just open. A gateway to *your* soul as well as his.

"Is that a question about me or you?" asked Calder.

To Striker's relief, the telephone rang. Calder merely blinked, hesitated until the second ring, then turned and moved into the hall.

"Hello...yes, is this Mr Cox?"

There was a long pause. Then Calder turned and looked at him.

"I'm very grateful to you, Mr Cox. Would you write down the dates of those raids and send the information round to my address tonight....Thank you....Yes, it does....Yes, I will. Again, thank you," and he put the phone down.

He stood there for a moment and drained his glass. Then he picked up the receiver again and dialled a number.

"General? Matthew Calder. I think we ought to have a talk....That will be fine. Goodnight."

This time, after replacing the receiver, he walked through to the living-room.

"I'm seeing the General in his office at 9.30 tomorrow," he said, walking over to the cocktail cabinet. He handed Striker the half-filled dry ginger bottle and tipped some more Scotch into his own glass before he spoke again. The American waited patiently.

"Cox has been making extensive enquiries. There have been a number of what he calls 'recruiting drives' over the last two years or so, but he's not worried about them. Apparently the 'recruits' were either petty villains who wouldn't be any use to our man — the fact that they are not permanently employed, he says, is testimony enough to their incompetence — or, he knows where the others went and, in his view, those groups would not be capable of this sort of operation."

Calder took a swig before continuing.

"He also has some very interesting information about a number of bank raids in the last year or so that he and the rest of the criminal fraternity are very puzzled about. The perplexing factor, apparently,

106

is that no one knows who committed them and that is extremely rare. What's more, no one connected with any of the raids has ever been caught. The word is, and Cox pointed out that this is only surmise, that the 'gang' is not from your actual criminal fraternity at all, but that it is, and I quote, 'an army group'."

"Ding dong," said Striker.

"Yes," answered Calder with a smile. "Now let's start this game. I said I have to think and I do that best when I'm playing."

Striker returned the white king to the board and advanced his pawn two squares.

"Do you know," said Calder, "some people actually believe that chess players imbue their pieces with life of their own, as if they were real men and women in a real-life situation? What these folk don't understand is that it's mainly the assumption that the pieces are lifeless and totally divorced from reality that provides the attraction of the game."

Striker was, for once, completely lost for words. He advanced his queen's pawn one square to counter the attack of the black knight on his king's pawn. Already he was on the defensive. He knew that he was still afraid of Matthew Calder and he still didn't know why.

Felixstowe Docks are much like any other; dark, dank, dirty and wet might be a good description. But, lit gently by the lights of the moored ships that reflected in the black water, the place could, just possibly, have a fairly-land image for anyone romantically inclined. It did, paradoxically, have a kind of enchanting quality about it.

Romance, though, was the last thing on Brown's mind as he walked along the wharf, close to the wall. You needed the eyes of a cat to see him, dressed as he was all in black, with rubbed-soled shoes and black cowl over his head. Most criminals, when engaged in skulduggery, dress in ordinary clothes; then, unless they are actually caught red-handed, they can claim innocence. However, Brown didn't want to be seen at all. If he *was* seen, it would be obvious that he was up to no good, but then the unfortunate person who saw him wouldn't live long enough to give the game away.

Brown stopped by a gate and listened. All he heard was the gentle slop of the slight swell against the wharf stanchions and the hum of distant traffic. The fresh, salty smell of the sea came to his nostrils. He was glad the rain had stopped.

The gate was strongly held by a padlock and chain, and along the top were several strands of barbed wire, as, indeed, there also were on the wall. Brown looked inside. There was a small square yard and to the left an equally small factory/workshop. He stood immobile for five minutes, watching and listening. Then he banged hard against the wall, twice.

Similarly dressed black figures began to emerge from the darkness. One detached itself from the others and bent down to the lock. Within ten seconds it was open. The chain took much longer to remove because silence was necessary. The gate made a small squeak as it was swung open. It had to be wide open because three men had to go through abreast, as Vaisey was carried to the side door of the workshop. When they had all passed through, the lock-picker, standing inside, reset the padlock on the outside. Two men stationed themselves on either side of the gate, in the shadows, just in case anyone unwisely decided to snoop.

Within minutes the side door lock had been picked and Brown, Vaisey and the four remaining men entered the workshop. The place had been picked because the high, boundary wall would block out light from the side windows, but that left a couple of skylights. Brown gave a signal and three men, two with pre-cut sheets of dark plastic under their arms, disappeared outside.

Using a torch only, Vaisey moved to an impressive-looking lathe-type apparatus. He examined it closely and then moved on to another machine. The implosion assembly, into which the hollow hemispheres of P-239 had to fit, needed to be made of stainless steel and had to be exact. That meant the use of professional metal-spinning equipment and it was the one job in the construction of the bomb that he couldn't do in his own workshop.

He turned to see one of the men return and put a thumb up at Brown. The latter switched on the lights and looked around. Then he walked to a set of switches and pulled them. A soft hum arose as the power for the machinery came on.

Vaisey nodded at Brown and looked at his watch. 10.16 p.m. Brown wanted no trace left of their entry or their task. That meant that there needed to be enough time before dawn to clean up the equipment, sweep away excess material and remove the plastic sheets from the roof windows. He hefted his bag on to a nearby bench, and removed the raw material and a long list of mathematical calculations. It was going to be a long, hard night.

Chapter 11
Monday, 12 May

AS CALDER pushed open the door to Stoddard's outer office Ann was sitting behind her desk smiling at him. With her clear eyes and fresh white blouse, she looked as bright as a new pin.

"Hey, you're too much for me on a Monday morning," he said with a frowning smile.

She didn't laugh, just kept showing her teeth and said:

"You ought to try thinking good of people for a change. It helps one sleep at night."

The barb was not lost on him. He wanted to walk round the desk and touch her.

"Tonight?" he asked.

" 'Fraid not. Evening class."

"Political philosophy?" he ventured.

"Wine-making."

"I want to kiss you."

"I know." She was still beaming.

He looked towards the door. "Is he in?"

"No," she replied between even teeth and let him stew for several seconds. His eyes shifted from side to side as he sought out the reason, though whether it was about the General's absence or her motives for not telling him why, she wasn't sure.

"He's at the zoo," she said at last. "He often goes there when he wants to think. There's a car waiting for you at the main entrance."

She wondered whether he would work out that she could have got the doorman to tell him. He smiled thinly and walked towards the door.

"I always think it's the smell," she said.

That *did* throw him. He stopped, looked back at her and creased his forehead.

"That helps him to think," she added. "Zoos always smell — haven't you noticed?"

He opened the door.

"I can make Tuesday," she called.

He turned and laughed.

"Seven o'clock?"

She nodded, still smiling, as he left.

The black Rover 3-litre actually had one of those glass partitions which cut off the rear compartment from the driver. Calder had thought that they only existed in the imagination of writers of fiction. The car also smelt of tobacco. Perhaps Ann was right.

The driver said that Sir Giles would be by the polar bears, and Calder spotted him from a distance, an unlit pipe in his mouth and an Austin Reed mackintosh over his shoulders. When Calder was still forty yards away, he looked round, as if sensing that someone was coming. Behind him a huge white bear perched on a rock about twenty feet above a blue pond.

"Morning, Calder," said the General brusquely and removed his pipe. "I'm coming to believe your surmise was right. It *was* a British operation."

The iron-grey hair looked darker in the morning light. The white bear slowly raised his head to the overcast sky, then looked down at the water as if to jump.

"I've finished here," said Stoddard formally. "Let's walk back to the car."

Calder felt like a bridegroom who knew he was about to be told that he'd been left at the church.

"We've handed over the Arab to the Metropolitan Police. Andrews, we've let go."

Stoddard glanced defiantly at Calder, expecting an argument. The younger man said nothing. The General was clearly in forceful mood and Calder decided that, on this occasion, discretion was the better part of valour. He kept step as they walked towards the entrance.

"Three of the servants have turned up," continued Stoddard. "They're all Arab. Apparently they fled when they got up in the morning and found their master sprawled in his own blood. I think they were expecting some sort of Islamic justice. Anyway, the police are handling it now and they will keep us informed if there are any connections with our little matter. Frankly I doubt it and I'd be surprised if they find the murderer. Probably some sort of Moslem feud."

He stopped and looked up at Calder.

"The Navy have come up with the vital information, at last."

Calder stiffened and looked back at the bear. He hadn't jumped.

"You were right again. The rods were missing from only one fuel assembly. The empty assembly is still there."

They approached the car and Stoddard gestured for him to get in. No wonder the General was in a mood this morning, he thought. Enough plutonium oxide for ten kilos of plutonium had been stolen and there could only be one possible reason for that. When they were both settled on the large back seat, the car moved off smoothly. Stoddard began speaking again.

"It also tends to indicate that they are British. If it were a foreign group, why not ship the whole lot? Why just fourteen rods? The logistics of the actual operation were difficult enough to plan and accomplish. Surely they could have pinched the whole lot with a different kind of operation? Besides, MI6 have found nothing. There seem to be no foreign connections at the moment. Have you found any?"

"No. And there's something else," said Calder, thinking he ought to say something.

"It's a military group," said Stoddard.

Calder reminded himself never to underestimate the General.

"If they are British," continued Stoddard, "they have to be military, or rather, ex-Army."

He examined his pipe as if viewing it for the first time.

"It was jumping the British hurdle that was important. After that, the assumption was almost inevitable. The criminal community don't have the organizational ability or discipline, not just to carry out the operation, which was difficult enough, but also to keep quiet about it afterwards. I should have seen it earlier. I should have recognized the style."

He turned to the younger man and noticed that he was looking at him in an odd way. What's more, he'd hardly said a word.

"What do you think?" asked Stoddard.

Calder cleared his throat.

"I agree. Andrews mentioned something to Striker and me — before your boys arrived — that's not on the transcript. He received an enquiry for plutonium about October of last year. He had the feeling that the speaker had been an officer in the Army. He was one himself apparently."

Stoddard was looking at him intently.

"In addition," continued Calder, "a contact of mine, from the criminal fraternity in London —" he hesitated and fingered his beard — "by all accounts the biggest, informs me that, in his view, it is most unlikely that any of his partners in crime did it. Nor has there been any recruiting of specialist criminal personnel, that he knows of, that could be relevant."

"This is rather speculative," said Stoddard suspiciously.

Calder refrained from pointing out that the General's own surmise was hardly based on firm evidence. Instead, he said:

"Yes, but he also told me something else: that there have been a number of successful bank raids in the last year or so that no one in his business can fathom. He doesn't know who they are, nor have any of the robbers ever been caught."

"I'm ahead of you," said Stoddard, his eyes alive.

"My contact," continued Calder, "said there is a rumour, which he is very much inclined to believe, that they are an army group."

Stoddard was nodding.

"Have you got the dates of the raids?" he asked, unable to keep a certain restrained excitement out of his voice.

Calder extracted a piece of paper from inside his jacket and handed it over. It was the page that Cox had sent. Stoddard placed pipe in mouth as he began to read.

"That was why I wanted to see you," said Calder, feeling a bit like a spare part. "If we can match up the dates in some way with people leaving from a particular regiment, we might be able to get a cross-reference of some sort on who the officer, or officers, are behind this. Clearly the 'band' will have been hand-picked and all well known to the officer in charge. It's a huge job to trace them, but the Army must keep records."

Stoddard was still looking at the piece of paper. The car seemed to travel at a constant speed, as if the traffic didn't exist, and they had nearly reached their destination.

"This is your line of country, General. You understand it. I don't. What's more, you can open doors in a moment, whereas it would take me months at the Ministry of Defence just to get permission for an investigation. You may have to check on the whereabouts of all those who left in, say, the last two years — perhaps three."

Stoddard was still reading.

"Yes, I'll handle this," he said absently. He was clearly thinking ahead.

The Rover pulled in at the kerb and they both stepped out. In the lift, Stoddard was silent, still looking at the sheet of paper. But as soon as he entered his office he came alive.

"Ann, the rest of my activities today — cancel them. If necessary, give them to Mr Jensen." He looked at her and smiled. "You know what to do."

She nodded.

"All that is except the Fitch case," said Stoddard. "I'll deal with that in a moment."

He paused.

"Thinking about it, you'd better cancel my business for tomorrow as well. I'll come and sort *that* out with you in a moment. Also, order my car for an hour's time. I'm going to be away for a couple of days."

Stoddard was looking into the distance now.

"Will that be all, sir?" Ann asked.

Calder looked at her, thinking she was being sarcastic again, but her face was deadpan.

"Yes, thank you," answered Stoddard and walked through into his own room.

Calder hesitated. Suddenly he realized what a vital person Ann was in the General's whole security set-up. The thought was strangely uncomfortable.

She stood up, lifted a tray on which was a percolator of coffee, cups, spoons, milk and sugar, walked over and handed it to him with a smile. He walked through and placed the tray on the General's desk. She was fascinating.

"Shall I do the honours?" he asked.

"Yes, help yourself," answered Stoddard.

The pipe was now lying on the blotter. He flicked the piece of paper with the back of his hand and said:

"This is the best piece of news I've had all week." He looked at his watch. "Almost exactly a week," he added rather more bitterly.

Calder handed him his coffee and saw him help himself to milk only. He took a slow sip and looked at Calder steadily.

"This information is accurate?" asked the General.

Calder stirred his third black coffee of the morning, while he thought about the answer.

"As to the exactness of the dates, you'll see that my informant was a little unsure, but you can check that easily enough with the police, now you have the rough dates. With regard to the substance of the information, it's accurate."

Calder sipped and glanced at the General. Stoddard was looking at him in that disarming way he had — pipe in mouth and calm, blue eyes. He was one of the very few people Calder had met who could gaze back at him without shifting. At length the General said:

"Forgive an old man's scepticism. Two questions. Why should the biggest criminal in London give you this sort of information, and how come he happens to be an acquaintance of yours in the first place?"

Calder didn't smile.

"I met him for the first time on Saturday night. He gave me the information because I described to him the effects of an explosion of ten kilos of plutonium in Horse Guards' Parade."

There was a pause while they continued to look at each other expressionlessly.

"He's a hard man," continued Calder, "but he became quite human towards the end."

There was another small pause before Stoddard spoke.

"I had a feeling you would annihilate my brief moment of elation sooner or later."

"Sorry," said Calder, "but if it is a British group, it has far-reaching consequences."

Stoddard sat back in his chair, coffee cup in hand, ready to listen.

"To begin with, it increases the possibility of their making a bomb in this country. Indeed, I would say that it was a probability. Why else steal the stuff if not for nuclear blackmail? Besides, I keep thinking of the guard's wife and child at Windscale. Why take the chance of releasing them alive if they weren't going to use that piece of generosity as evidence that they keep their word? It also provides an additional explanation as to why they went to so much trouble to steal the stuff in the first place. If they had waited long enough they could possibly have picked up some U-235 or P-239 on the open market."

"What do you mean?" asked Stoddard, looking genuinely puzzled.

"Well, if you got a threat tomorrow that there was a home-made nuclear bomb set to go off in, say, Central Manchester, unless you hand over, would you believe it?"

"Probably."

"Why?" asked Calder.

"I see what you mean." The General shook his head, his lips tight. "No hijack and my natural scepticism might come to the fore. That doubt as to the bomb's authenticity might foil their whole plan. The hijack in itself provides evidence that the threat is real."

Calder was looking out of the window.

"I should have thought of that," said Stoddard, sipping his coffee.

"It's only just occurred to *me*." said Calder. "And anyway, I'm not too keen on it. As it happens, hijacking reprocessed plutonium seems to be easier than obtaining fissionable material elsewhere."

Calder also sipped, unhappily. Stoddard did not exactly look bright either as he, too, gazed away to the window, his mind occupied. The younger man knew what the next question was going to be and was already thinking of his answer.

"You told me three days ago that a bomb could be made," said Stoddard. "Are you sure?"

Calder stood up, still holding his coffee. He moved to the window and spoke as he walked.

"Yes, I'm sure. It would need a highly competent scientist, one that isn't just an expert in physics and chemistry. He would have to be good with his hands and he would need considerable skill in electronics. Perhaps a team would be needed. But it could be done. Indeed, my guess is that it already is being done. They will have had enough time beforehand to prepare the basic connections. The chemical conversion and finishing touches wouldn't take long."

Stoddard's cup returned to its saucer more loudly that it should have done. Calder turned to see the General standing up, his anger which had been simmering finally boiling over.

"But how would that be possible?" he demanded. "Where would they get the information? Surely it's classified?"

Calder felt angry too, as if the other's ire had triggered off a chain reaction. He walked across to Stoddard and looked hard into the steel-blue eyes.

"Classified? All the information needed is available through legitimate bookshops. Most of it's American. On the inside cover of this de-classified material there is a note of disclaimer, absolving the United States government of any responsibility for the use of any information enclosed within. I have the required volumes on one of my bookshelves at home. The only difficulty I had in obtaining them was finding the money."

He placed cup and saucer on the tray and walked back to the window before continuing. He was still angry.

"The Flowers Commission in 1976 said that the equipment required might not be much more elaborate than that already being used by criminals in the manufacture of heroin."

There was another long pause.

"What's more," continued Calder, still looking unseeingly out of the window, "this is just the beginning. The Fast Breeder Reactor Programme is in its infancy. The only FBR we have is the experimental one at Dounreay. The first commercial Fast Reactor is still at the planning stage. A public enquiry is being set up on its siting. We have, at the moment, about ten tons of plutonium in circulation in this country. In the year 2000, when the programme has really got going, it's estimated that there will be about 250 tons and the eventual, future total is ten times that. Can you imagine the security problem there, General?"

Stoddard said nothing.

"The new Pressurized Water Reactors that are being built at the moment are nothing but a short-term smokescreen. Any government that favours nuclear power must favour the Fast Breeder, because the fuel for conventional reactors, uranium, is running out, whereas the Fast Breeder, to a large extent, creates its own fuel, plutonium, as it goes along. Also, there are huge profits to be made in the export market for selling this sort of technology."

Calder paused.

"The trouble is, plutonium is the deadliest substance known to man."

Feeling suddenly guilty, Calder turned from the window and walked back to the desk, smiling apologetically.

"I'm sorry," he said, "I know you don't make energy policy."

"I'm sorry too," answered Stoddard, grinning. "I just pick up the pieces."

Calder nodded and sat down.

"Besides, we're wasting time," he said.

"Yes," said Stoddard. "I'll have my work cut out finding the right bloody regiment. Once I've done that, finding the right man won't take long. With a man we get a name."

Calder was looking at the ground and the older man got the distinct impression that he wasn't paying attention.

"What is it?" the General asked.

"Something has just occurred to me," said Calder, getting up. "If the bomb is being constructed, then there are certain specialized materials needed. They must have got them from somewhere. I'll write up a list and get Peter on to it."

He reached the door. "There's one other thing. Do you still believe it was a sea drop?"

"Yes."

"And you've only checked the boats going out."

Stoddard hit his forehead with the palm of his hand. Of course. Since they were now thinking it was a British operation, with Britain as the destination, he needed to check all the shipping that had come *in* over the past week.

"Remember that yacht you mentioned being in the Moray Firth?" asked Calder.

"Yes."

"It would need to have special features to carry those twelve-foot rods. They weigh between a third and half a ton. Just above the keel would seem the only place. That way they might add to the stability instead of ruining it."

Stoddard nodded, sombre-faced. Calder smiled and left.

The geiger-counter outside the basement door was still reading "safe" as Vaisey entered. He was feeling good. The job last night had gone well. What's more, he had just consumed a superb chicken brunch on top of six wonderful hours' sleep. That Irma could cook. He waited for the fluorescent lights to struggle to full power before strong-arming his way down the steps. He was looking forward to the day.

The plutonium had now to be cut into two hemispheres. The sphericity of the moulds, moreover, needed to be just as exact as the implosion assembly. Then they had to be polished and lacquered to avoid corrosion. When he had done that, the reflector, which had to be fitted to the inside of the assembly, had to be made. This would be done by melting high-tin-content solder into the assembly and the shape moulded to take the two plutonium hemispheres. When formed, the reflector would be removed and drilled to allow for the apertures for the plutonium assembly tube and the initiator.

Vaisey sat down at the workbench and glanced at the computer print-out. Then he lifted the implosion assembly and studied its beauty. He was sufficiently aware of his own motives to know that the whole project had now become a crusade, as well as a justification to other people of his existence. But he didn't care. He was enjoying it. At that moment, he made up his mind. The bomb would be exploded, regardless of whether Brown gave his permission or not.

He heard the door open, but did not look round. Caren, he knew, was coming to watch him work. He smiled to himself, glanced over at his glove tent and moved confidently off the stool.

Calder placed *The Plutonium Handbook* on the floor with the rest of the pile and looked at the list he had compiled of the materials required to make a home-made atom bomb. It was enormous because he had included everything, even the innocuous items, like solder. Striker would be arriving any minute to pick it up. He would have been sleeping that afternoon and evening, so that he could work through the night. Some of the stuff might have been stolen and hopefully the police would have a record of such thefts.

He needed an early night, but, although he felt physically tired, he knew that he wouldn't sleep until his mind relaxed. He stretched his limbs slowly and eased himself off the couch. Then he walked over to the television and switched on the 10 o'clock news.

As Brown slammed the door behind him, Judy burst into tears — not just tears of chagrin, but body-raking sobs of absolute despair. The knot in her stomach got worse and the remorse she felt would not go away. It was ten minutes before her body stopped shaking and she was able to think about her predicament.

It wasn't just the sex. Heaven knew, she was what is colloquially described as a nymphomaniac and had learnt to live with it. She had worked out how to use it to her advantage and enjoyed doing it.

It wasn't even that she hated John. Anway, she wasn't really sure whether she did or not. This whole thing recently had changed him. She was secondary to it and always would be. Or perhaps she'd known that all along. Had he really changed that much?

She had also come to realize fully last night, while watching Irma cook dinner, what they were doing. Kevin had also let slip that the men in the hangar were dead. He had implored her not to let Brown know that he had told her. Once it had been a romantic dream with John but, now that the relationship had turned sour, the discovery of the reality of their deed became horribly oppressive.

But it wasn't even that that depressed her so much. Or perhaps it was. Was this what her life had become? She had no purpose again. The old neuroses, the old fears, had returned.

Feeling suddenly cold in her nakedness, she drew up her feet and burrowed down between the sheets. She drew them above her head until she was cocooned in darkness. Soon she felt warm, but not secure. Her body shook again at the blackness of her heart. There was only one thing, she knew, which would make her feel content, and her hands crept down to her middle.

Chapter 12
Tuesday, 13 May, and Wednesday, 14 May

THE ITALIAN restaurant was already half-full when they walked in. Spring had suddenly and surprisingly burst upon the city, and the diners had been quick to dress appropriately. Some of the men wore open-necked shirts, the collar turned over the jacket, gigolo-style, but most of the others had removed their jackets. Flowing, lightweight summer dresses adorned the women, with baggy forearm-length sleeves and knee-length hems. They were coloured in numerous pastel shades, of which blue and green dominated. The candlelight was, as yet, superfluous, but the light from the street combined with it to make a sort of magical glow. The rich, aromatic smell of herbs beckoned.

"I can see why you chose this place," said Ann, as she was helped into her chair by the head waiter.

"Its main advantage is yet to be revealed. It possesses the most delicious Italian house wine in the whole of the UK," said Calder.

She laughed.

"And I thought that you were a sober individual."

"I don't think the General would have employed me if I were that respectable."

"True," she answered coyly.

She picked up her napkin before continuing.

"He's terribly Byronic and I'm rather fond of him. In fact you have a lot in common."

She looked up expectantly, but he changed tack.

"It occurred to me yesterday that you have a crucial position in his set-up. I haven't met any of the others, except Striker and Fox — not even Jensen — but it seems to me that you are the central pin around which everything revolves."

So much for romance, she thought.

"Actually, I'm probably even more important than you think. I'm not just executing decisions, you see. I also have to make quite a lot of them. Not major ones, but many of them are important enough to affect considerably the working of the Department if I made a mistake."

"Does the General know that?" he asked.

She thought about it. "He must do. Although we've never discussed it. I think he prefers not to, simply because it suits his purpose and, strangely enough, he does have confidence in me."

"I see."

"No, you don't," she said cruelly. "You see he employed me for —" she hesitated briefly — "three main reasons, in the following order of importance. First, because I'm quite intelligent and have a much better than average memory. He wasn't very impressed by my degree in English, or my previous administrative experience, but he *was* interested in my memory. One's creativity tends to suffer, but it can be a considerable advantage to a secretary."

He nodded as she continued.

"I'm the sort that wins 'Mastermind' competitions, but if you asked me to create some original prose, I'd struggle."

She paused.

"Secondly, he places a great reliance on what he calls my honesty. I suppose he connects it with the fact that I'm a clergyman's daughter. At least, that's what he said at my interview — the fact that I was honest, I mean, not that I was a clergyman's daughter. He said he was impressed by the way in which I was completely open with him in my answers to every question."

She frowned and felt suddenly flustered. She looked down at her lap.

"What's the third reason?" asked Calder.

"Ah, well, that's even more embarrassing," she said, looking down at her napkin again. When she looked up her expression was set in mock arrogance.

"Being a typical male chauvinist pig like yourself, he prefers a secretary who is reasonably good-looking." She hesitated. "He likes my legs."

Calder laughed out loud. Several people from nearby tables turned to look.

"Did he tell you that?" he asked.

"No," she answered primly. "That is my surmise."

He couldn't help smiling. "He's right though," he said.

"About my legs?"

"No. About being open and honest."

He smiled again and she stuck her tongue out.

Just then the waiter came over to take their order, already carrying the wine. By the time the coffee came they were into their second bottle.

"So," he was saying, "after graduating you became a career civil servant?"

She nodded.

"And how did you come to apply to be the General's secretary?"

"Oh, you don't apply for that sort of job. They pick you. I suppose I should consider myself lucky."

She looked at the far side of the room. She wanted him to be unsure as to whether she was kidding or not, and she was getting that feeling again whenever he looked at her. But that was the second time he had brought the conversation round to the Department. It was almost as if he wanted to keep off any topic that recognized anything more than a sexual relationship between them. Well, perhaps he was right. She was acting like a schoolgirl again.

He was fondling his beard — a characteristic he had, she'd noticed, whenever a thought suddenly struck him.

"What is it?" she asked.

"You're going to think I'm very slow," he said, "but I've just realized why, in the two times we've been out together, you've never asked me about my past."

She was smiling defensively.

"Why should that be of interest?"

"You already know," he continued as if she hadn't spoken. "You've read my file."

"On the contrary," she said, smiling genuinely to take the edge off her previous statement, "most things — probably the most important things, in fact — are not on your file. You can't expect an official document to tell a great deal about a person's character."

He could have used a lot of predictable lines at that point, but he didn't and she loved him for it. Instead, as she looked across, his mouth formed into an ironical smile and he turned his eyes away. It was a gesture that he performed often and she loved that too.

"I believe that you have rather taken my breath away," he said, still smiling.

She linked into the role he expected of her.

"Don't say that. It could have disastrous consequences."

They smiled conspiratorially across the table.

"You have a point," he said. "We're wasting time."

"I thought that was all you could do until Sir Giles returned — wait."

He was rescued by the waiter, who appeared silently at his elbow. His English was heavily accented.

"Excusa me, sir. Mr Calder?"

"Yes."

"Telephone for you, sir."

"It's Striker," said Calder to Ann. "I gave him this number."

She smiled benignly. He walked over to the bar and picked up the phone.

"Matthew Calder here."

"Matthew, Peter. Sorry to call you there, but I didn't know what time you'd be getting back."

Calder felt a pang of guilt. Here he was, wining and dining, while his partner was flogging his guts out down at Scotland Yard.

"That's all right," answered Calder innocently.

"Besides," continued Striker, "I thought it might be, you know, a bit difficult if I rang you at home later."

"What have you got?" said Calder quickly.

"Well, according to the computer there have been very few thefts of the items on your list. Not much dough in them. There may have been some more but some of the items are so trivial that the theft might not have been reported. However, two I have unearthed, after considerable sweat and sandwiches."

Calder felt that pang again. Striker really knew how to rub it in.

"What a lucky man I am to have an assistant who is so diligent. Are you going to give me the information, or am I to bribe you for it with an Italian meal?"

Striker guffawed.

"No, thanks. Italian food's too fattening. I'll settle for a night out at The Blue Lady. Do you know, when this is all over, I might even get a discount on next year's membership."

"You're on. Now, Peter — the information?"

"Oh, yeah. Well, a fairly large quantity of baratol went missing from an engineering firm in Peterborough about two and a half weeks ago and, the day before, so did a double-beam oscilloscope from Aston University in Birmingham. While they were there, they also filched some electrical circuitry."

Calder's mind was racing.

"Incidentally," continued Striker, "a small firm specializing in metal-spinning was broken into, just as you suggested. Two nights ago. I've only just discovered it, as it's not yet on the computer. The oddest thing is that nothing was stolen. At least it was odd to the local cops. The only way the owner knew anyone had been inside was because he read the electricity meter before leaving on the Saturday and made a note of the numbers. Always does, apparently, God knows what for. Parsimony, I suppose. Anyway, the place was closed on Sunday, but when he came to check the meter on Monday evening, he was surprised to find that rather a lot of juice had been used. Especially since they had a lighter day than usual.

"He asked all his workers whether they had noticed anything odd in the morning. One operator said that he 'felt' — I quote that word specifically from the police report — there was something different about his mechanism that morning. You know, the odd shaving in the corner and the blob of metal where he didn't usually let it fall. It had occurred to him that it might have been used, but he thought that he was being stupid, so he hadn't mentioned it. The owner phoned the police yesterday evening and that's all I know."

Calder's heart was beating unnaturally quickly.

"Where was this, Peter?"

"Oh, sorry. Felixstowe. Ring any bells?"

"No."

"Me neither."

"Birmingham, Peterborough and Felixstowe," said Calder. "I wonder whether they have anything in common. They must do. It's too much coincidence otherwise. I certainly feel that the Felixstowe thing is what we're after. It has their stamp about it. If it is them, it means they're not as far advanced in their construction as I thought. We need to know more."

"I was wondering whether I should go down there and scout around, in my usual unobtrusive way," said Striker.

"Yes, would you, Peter? Have a word with the owner especially. You've got the info' on the implosion assembly. Ask him whether this machine is capable of spinning that. If it is, put something under the local law and get them to do a thorough fingerprint job and search. I doubt whether they'll get anything, but it's worth a try."

"OK, pardner," said Striker in Western drawl.

"Do you think there will be anything more on that list?" asked Calder.

"Frankly, no, but I'll put one of my buddies on it while I'm away."

Calder smiled to himself. "If I were you, Peter, I shouldn't go till morning."

"That's very gracious of you, sir. You mean I can actually get some sleep?"

"I think so," said Calder grudgingly. "Just enough to recharge the old batteries."

"Yes, sir," answered Striker, in true military style. Calder could imagine him standing to attention at the other end with hand tapping forehead.

"The General not back yet?"

"No," said Calder a little too abruptly. "Anyway, anything else?"

"No."

"OK, then. Thanks for the information, get a good night's sleep and give me a ring from Felixstowe."

Calder thanked the manager for the use of his phone and walked back to his table.

"I've paid the bill," exclaimed Ann proudly.

"I must ask Peter to phone again at appropriate moments," said Calder.

"It depends what appropriate moments you mean," she replied and swept past him to the door.

Standing on the pavement, she asked whether Striker had had good news. He hesitated, as if struggling to focus on her question.

"Possibly," he answered. Then his face came more alive. "In fact," he continued, "it could be a very big lead."

"You weren't thinking of that though, were you?" she asked perceptively.

He spotted a cruising taxi and pushed his arm out.

"No."

She continued to look at him.

He turned to her and smiled. Then his face clouded over as he spoke.

"As you said, all we can do now is wait."

The sun was halfway to its zenith before the mist finally cleared off the water, bathing the yacht station in its light. Dark glasses were imperative, as the river danced in sparkling brilliance. They were certainly necessary if you wanted to see the gulls and terns. These, now that the mist had gone, were coming in for a late breakfast on the rich pickings of the yacht basin.

It was the sort of morning that Tom Arkright liked. Cool at the beginning, then coming awake slowly, until the mist finally cleared and you could take your jacket off, revelling in the sun's warmth. It was like seeing the dawn without having to get up early. It had been a long, harsh winter and it was great to see the good weather setting in at last.

He was standing at the end of one of the many small, floating

122

jetties in the marina, squinting at the birds feeding. The terns were always the most impressive, their acrobatic skill enabling them to judge their descent to the water so perfectly. Even the tiniest crust could be snatched from the surface by their sensitive bills.

He knew that he, too, was being watched. He'd been searching the boats since 8 o'clock that morning, which had caused a lot of indignant protests, especially when it was realized that he wasn't allowing anyone to leave, either on foot or by boat, until all vessels had been investigated. This Emergency Powers Act gave him more weight than he'd ever had before. If they protested, he could just slap them in jail, with no *habeas corpus* to worry about.

Well, he and his four-man team had completed about three-quarters of the boats and he wasn't having his lunch until they'd finished the lot. He knew what they'd be thinking as they stared at his back, but he didn't care. He even took a little sadistic pleasure in making them suffer a bit. Having been Sergeant of Police at the local station for eleven of his forty-four years, he was secure in that position. He knew that these people needed him more than he needed them.

He left the dipping terns and stepped across to the next yacht, on the other side of the jetty. It was a magnificent thing in dark blue called *Gorgon*. He looked at the checklist that the marina Superintendent had given him. Berth 95, *Gorgon*, owned by Mr D. Stephens, 13 Keit Road, Paddington, London. A young man, who had been coiling ropes on the foredeck, came along the side.

"Morning, Sergeant," he called happily.

The accent, Tom noted, was just like that of the others — southern.

"Sorry to bother you, sir, but as you 'ave probably gathered, we're asking people if we can search their boats."

"I'm not the owner," said Jerry, "but I'm sure he wouldn't mind. Come aboard. What are you looking for?"

Tom stepped on to the vessel carefully. He still hadn't got used to clomping about in Wellington boots on a boat. The owner of the first yacht had lent them to him so that he wouldn't mark the nice paintwork on the other boats, but they were too small and cramped his feet.

"I'd rather not say, if you don't mind, sir," answered Tom seriously.

He stepped into the cockpit-well and looked into the main cabin. A special hollow compartment above the keel, they'd said. Even he knew what a keel was. He looked at the figure in T-shirt and denim shorts.

"I wonder whether you'd mind if I 'ad a look at your bilges?"

Not a flicker of anxiety crossed the young man's face.

"Sure," he replied, and bent down to remove the wooden floor and duckboards.

Tom, too, bent down and examined the fibreglass. It was quite clear, from the stains and consistency of the worn appearance of the surface, that there were no joins and no hollow compartments. In fact it looked just like every other bloody keel he had examined that morning, except the two where he had actually had to wait while they pumped the water out.

He stood up, surprised that he could rise to his full height of six foot four.

"That's fine, sir. Thank you very much. I'm afraid you won't be able to leave until we've checked everyone, though."

He smiled for the first time.

"That's OK," replied the young man merrily.

Tom, somewhat disappointed, levered himself out of the cabin and steadied himself in the well, preparatory to stepping on to the jetty. He could never sail on one of these things.

"Sergeant?" asked Jerry, who had silently appeared beside him: "What would have happened if I had not invited you on board?"

His face was beaming innocently. Tom walked on to the gunwale and jumped from the boat before turning.

"You couldn't 'ave 'eard. Per'aps you've been away."

Jerry said nothing.

"Don't you know there's been plutonium 'ijacking?"

"Yes, I did hear something about it," answered Jerry with difficulty.

"Aye, well, Parliament passed Emergency Powers Act so we'd 'ave no trouble finding it. I can walk into any 'ouse, or boat, with or without owner's permission."

Tom turned and walked up to the ketch moored alongside.

Jerry shrugged and moved back into the cabin. He'd done a good job on that keel, even if he did say so himself. Brown had insisted, in the weeks beforehand, that he develop a skill with fibreglass, and he could only now really appreciate why. Even if you got down on your hands and knees, the crack was totally undetectable, and he liked the work he had done wearing in the new glass so that it merged with the rest. Brown had inspected it. His respect for that man went up another notch.

He replaced the duckboards and flooring, then opened the door to the for'ard cabin. Judy, a sheet held to her throat, looked up, wide-eyed.

"It's all right," he said, "he was as thick as he was tall."

She had arrived in the night and made him swear he wouldn't tell Brown. He had agreed, then, and it would be a terrible shame when he did phone. But he knew where his priorities lay.

He looked at the shape under the thin sheet. There was no hurry. He couldn't leave the marina yet anyway. He'd phone this afternoon. All he could do now was wait.

Calder had spent all day reading on the construction of an atom bomb, plus Glasstone's book, *The Effects of Nuclear Weapons*. It was depressing and, although he had read it before, it frightened him more this time. Then, it had been theoretical; now it was a possibility.

Feeling the need for a return to sanity, he wanted to phone Ann and get her to come round. But he knew he couldn't. Not only was he expecting a call from Stoddard or Striker, but he had to be prepared to move immediately. He didn't think that Ann would be too happy at being interrupted in the middle of an embrace. She still hadn't forgiven him for letting Striker know the number of the restaurant. He smiled at a memory of the night before. That was better.

He was worried about the General, though. Two whole days and not a word. This waiting was making him pensive, but what else could he do?

As Brown drove to the marina, the sun was well down on the horizon. It had been a glorious day, with just a gentle breeze to prevent the air from becoming muggy. The leaves on the trees seemed to have grown greener and longer, just in one short day.

None of this was on Brown's mind, however. He treated the weather very philosophically. Since it was something over which he had no control, it was not worth bothering with. If it rained, it rained. If it was a fine day, then good, but since there had been no achievement in it for him, there was no real enjoyment. Harnessing the weather for one's own purposes, though, that was different. That was why he liked sailing so much. But he gained no pleasure from a fine day, as such, just as he didn't care whether England won the World Cup.

No, Brown was reflecting on the second and most difficult part of the operation so far: the period of the bomb's construction. It was the most difficult stage because the team was largely inactive and therefore fretful. What was more, he had tipped his hand with the hijacking, yet he could not move again until the bomb was completed.

Of course Vaisey had been right when he had said that most of the bomb's construction should have taken place before the hijack, to save time, and it was a pity that they'd had to commit themselves when they did. But it was unavoidable. Vaisey, being a scientist — albeit a very good one — couldn't understand the problem of keeping a team of men, already keyed-up, waiting around for six weeks or so until the next plutonium delivery, even if it might have been by road — rather easier to hijack. There had also been the problem of the security guard. There was always the risk of his making a slip; and the longer they were to hold on to the hostages, the greater the likelihood became.

Anyway, the construction had gone smoothly and quickly, and

there was still no sign that the authorities had any mark on them, though they obviously had a smart boy on it. All yachts above the keel, Jerry had said. Perhaps they had already made the mental jump to "non-foreign", which might cut the search time down. He must work on the assumption that they had.

However, he was sure, for a variety of reasons, that the bomb would be completed in time. Three to four days more had been Vaisey's last estimate earlier that day, for connecting up and final testing. Say another two days to allow for complications. That meant six days at the very outside, which would take them through to Tuesday.

He had kept out of the scientist's way and let him work at his own pace. A lesser man would have felt a compulsion to hurry him. But men like Vaisey formulated their own timetables, which were anyway horrendous. They worked as hard as they could because their work was their *raison d'être*. They had very little else to live for.

Vaisey had just completed what he had described as the "trickiest" part of the whole construction, the shaping of the thirteen explosive lenses. He had designed them some time before apparently, when he and Caren had built the simultaneous detonation system. He'd had to use baratol, an explosive that could be cast very precisely, which was essential; but it was difficult to work with, especially since each lens had to be so finely shaped and identical to the others. But he had managed it, as Brown had known he would. He had been right about Vaisey.

His only real mistake was Judy. He had been more worried than he cared to show on discovering her missing. He knew why she had gone, and it wasn't to inform the authorities. But he had, nevertheless, been relieved when Jerry had rung. She might have blabbed to someone. He had called the search parties off, but she would have to be got rid of. Pity, she was such a good lay. Anyway, he couldn't do it yet. It would be bad for morale. He would have to keep her locked up for a week, though, while they waited for Vaisey. All he could do now was keep on waiting.

Chapter 13
Thursday, 15 May

THE PHONE BELL woke Calder immediately. He peered at his watch. 4.55 a.m. He'd found difficulty in sleeping and had only been under for about three hours. Quickly, he slipped out of bed, donned his dressing gown, walked out of the bedroom, through the lounge and into the hall. The bell had rung ten times when he picked up the receiver.

"Hello," he said, a little surprised at the huskiness in his voice. The earpiece barked at him.

"Sorry to get you up so early. Can you come round?"

"General?" He suddenly felt very alert and realized that he hadn't stopped thinking about it, even when he was asleep.

"Yes."

"Tell first."

There was silence at the other end. Then:

"I've got him."

Calder made himself relax. "Your place?" he asked.

"Yes, do you know where it is?"

"No."

Stoddard proceeded to give the address and directions.

"I'll be there in thirty minutes," said Calder and put the phone down.

It was just getting light when he rang the General's doorbell. Stoddard, fully dressed in crumpled, grey suit and unshaven, opened the door wide. In the dim, overhead light from the hall he looked terribly tired. This impression was far from dispelled when Stoddard had ushered him into an immaculate and large room that was more brightly lit. He stared at the older man.

"If you'll forgive my saying so, General, you don't look too well."

Stoddard tried to smile.

"Thank you for your concern. I've only had a couple of hours' sleep since I last saw you, but I'm too much on tenterhooks to feel it at the moment."

And it was true that there was a sort of faint ebullience about him, despite the large loops under his eyes and the general pallor of his skin.

"Coffee?" asked Stoddard, walking over to a mahogany bar.

Calder gave a soulful sigh, the meaning of which would have been apparent to anyone. Stoddard began to pour from the percolator.

"Help yourself to milk and sugar," he said and walked over to a large, low, glass table set by a grey-brick fireplace.

"I'd only just got back when I called you," he said and began to sip his coffee, gazing down at the mass of papers on the table.

Two things were clear to Calder as he spooned sugar into his cup. First, the General's mental powers were not up to par. He was behaving like a man in a dream. Besides, his pipe was nowhere to be seen. And, second, this in itself added to the sense of unreality he felt about the whole scene. The fact that it was so early didn't help. Was he really going to hear about the man who, in his imagination, had dominated his waking and sleeping thoughts for nearly a week? God, it was still only five and a half days. His attention was drawn to the table.

"John Brown," said Stoddard suddenly. "John Brown." He looked up at Calder. "Ironic, isn't it?" he said, then looked down again.

Calder felt unable to speak.

"Well, he isn't," continued Stoddard absently.

The younger man thought that he ought to try and get in on the wavelength somewhere.

"Isn't what?" he asked, equally absently.

"Mouldering in his grave," said the General. "Far from it. Brilliant man."

He looked up.

"That's what really made me certain about him. Sorry, I'm forgetting my manners. Please sit down."

"I'm fine, thank you."

"It was, I must confess, a difficult job," continued Stoddard before Calder had finished speaking. "I won't bore you with the technical problems I had in getting my hands on the records in the first place. I decided to go back three years and was prepared to go back further if necessary. I had the dates of the robberies, of course, which meant that it was pointless, working on the assumption that they were committed by our boys, to go any further forward. That gave me a period of about eighteen months, during which time a great many officers and men left the Army."

Stoddard took another sip of his coffee, placed it on the fireplace and put both hands in his trouser pockets in a most unmilitary-like way.

"I concentrated on the enlisted men, to see if I could see a pattern in a particular regiment. I couldn't. Wasted a whole half-day. It wasn't until I began dissecting each regiment into its companies, and looking at that level, that I struck pay-dirt, so to speak."

He looked up, as if surprised by his own use of the vernacular.

"A bit of luck really. It was fairly early on my list, but then I needed some luck at that stage. Examining this regiment," he held up an insignia and Calder raised his eyebrows, "I noticed that two companies had rather higher levels of leaving than the rest. That in itself is nothing unusual. Indeed, it's one of the things that is looked at anyway, as a check to find where the problem companies are. But one of them was particularly high around this period and not at any other time, whereas the other had a consistently high leaving record, stretching back over many years. What's more, the first company had a disproportionate number of 'lifers' who bought themselves out."

Stoddard was animated now.

"I didn't expect anything so obvious as their release money all coming from the same source, but I checked anyway. What I found was that some had paid cash. Since it amounts to a large sum of money, this would be unusual even for one, but when it turned out to be three within the space of six weeks I knew I was on to something.

"The key, though, was the officer, or officers. Once I'd found him, the rest would fall into place. Ignoring the others who had left and concentrating on the three cash-payers, I unearthed all the officers they had been associated with. Our man stood out a mile. I found him even before I learnt that he'd left about a year before the others. All three were under him for some time. Captain John Brown."

He looked up.

"Actually, there was another possible: a lieutenant under Brown's command — Cosmo Binge."

He shook his head.

"I later found that he died in a car accident two years ago. The Army is no place for a man with a name like that."

He shook his head again.

"Sorry, being callous. Anyway," he leant down to the table and picked up a buff folder, "when I read this file, I became convinced that Brown was our man. I think I would have picked him out even if he hadn't had the connections."

Stoddard waved his hand.

"I don't need to tell you," he said, "that we are not just looking for an average Sandhurst 'hocker'."

He walked over to Calder and handed him the file. Calder put down his cup and glanced at the pages as the General continued.

"Although a little old-fashioned, Sandhurst is still one of the best military schools in the world. But I've always believed that leaders, like musicians, are more born than made and certainly before the tender age of sixteen. I was looking for someone who was not just good at his job, but very good, nay, brilliant. But more than that. He also had to be an outsider. This is a rogue elephant, don't forget."

"A rare combination," mused Calder.

Stoddard looked up quickly, clearly not expecting to be interrupted.

"What do you mean?" he demanded.

Calder regretted his interjection.

"Someone who is good at his job is usually acceptable by definition. To a large extent, you have to behave the way people above you expect in order to reach the top of the ladder yourself. There are exceptions, of course." Calder smiled.

"Exactly," replied Stoddard, who clearly thought he was one of the exceptions. "Brown has both these...qualities. He was a brilliant officer. Of that there is no doubt. Cadet of the year at Sandhurst and he holds something of a regimental record from when he was a lieutenant, largely for the success of his platoons on manoeuvres. He is also, by the way, a crack shot.

"The rogue-elephant side of his nature doesn't come out in the report. I had to talk with some of his old chums for that. To say that he was unpopular with junior officers would be an understatement. Two showed open hostility when they realized that I was no longer serving and they could tell me the truth. One of them refuses to say why he disliked him, even after I started to hint at dire threats."

Stoddard looked at Calder with surprise on his face, as if he found it difficult to believe that a subordinate officer would openly defy him.

"Anyway, I decided to interview some enlisted men while I was there and it's a complete contrast. I could only find a few who were still about, but they all remembered him and spoke of him with affection. One of them, then a private, now a sergeant, said that he was the best officer he had ever served under."

The General looked up again.

"A leader of men, Calder. And someone who does not suffer fools gladly. More coffee?"

The bearded man shook his head.

"Anyway, just to make sure I had the right man, I continued to check, in the other companies and regiments. I had a team of helpers by this time and it was easier. We came across a few possibilities, but they were all blind alleys. One of them turned out to be the manager of a Rochdale furniture store, with a wife and four children. It was pointless. As I've already said, there was only really one possibility. I was just being excessively careful. No, Brown's our man. I feel it."

He stopped and looked intently at the man reading the file. Seeing no opposition, he continued.

"Being sure of that, I checked on all men serving in his company, in addition to those I already knew. As you can imagine, I came up with quite a list. I converted them into an 'A' list and a 'B' list, according to how long they served under Brown and how close they were to him. Only a small number of list 'A', to say nothing of list 'B', will be in his band, of course, working on the assumption that not every man who leaves the Army is a crook."

He glanced wryly at Calder. This time the younger man looked up from Brown's file and smiled.

"So far I haven't checked any of them except Brown. Both his parents died when he was seven and his only known relative is an elderly rich aunt at Shrewsbury who brought him up. She's not there. None of the neighbours know where she is. Haven't seen her for months apparently. Brown, of course, is also nowhere to be found."

Stoddard walked over to the mantelpiece and drained his coffee. Suddenly he felt very tired indeed. He took his cup over to the bar and refilled it.

"No photo, I'm afraid," he said. "It's at the Department being duplicated. So are the snaps of some of the others that I'm sure of. Within two hours they will be distributed to every police force in the country."

His guest, he noticed, was not reading the file in front of him any more, but looking ahead without focusing.

"You're right," said Calder. "This is our man."

Stoddard said nothing. Calder placed the file on the table and picked up his coffee before continuing.

"We'll have to handle the investigation and arrests ourselves."

"Already being done," interrupted Stoddard quickly. "Sorry, I should have told you. No point in secrecy now. Jensen, my deputy, is setting up a team. I'm taking all these files round to the Department when we've finished."

Calder nodded. "Who, or what, do you expect to find?"

"What do you mean?" intoned Stoddard, in a way that implied he knew the answer.

Calder fingered his beard.

"I hope this isn't deflating General, and I hope I'm wrong, but I don't think that sort of investigation is guaranteed success."

Calder drained his coffee and walked over to the percolator.

"I think," he continued, "that our man...Brown, will have foreseen this eventuality — that his identity might be discovered and, consequently, that of his men."

Stoddard said nothing — just gazed myopically at Calder.

"He couldn't possibly risk dispersal after the hijack for that reason. Oh, we'll find plenty from your lists, but they won't be the ones we want."

He paused for longer this time. Stoddard was nodding at the floor. Finally he spoke.

"I knew before I phoned you that you were going to say that. That's why I got you over."

He grinned crookedly, before continuing.

"But I'm not as depressed about it as all that. His gang may be in hiding with him, but we might find some evidence — from their lodgings, a relative, a lover — as to where their hideaway may be."

Calder hesitated again and sipped his coffee.

"I hope so," he said, "but I think Brown is far too clever to have allowed any of his men to know where they were going. On the other hand, he can't think of everything. You may be right. There could be some clues."

He didn't sound hopeful. Then his right fist hit his left palm, the sound filling the room.

"Christ, Calder, be positive," he said viciously to himself and began to pace up and down the long room.

Stoddard, despite the loud slap, felt that his brain had ceased to function. He saw Calder stop, place a bent forefinger into his mouth and bite on it. It was a gesture Stoddard would never have imagined his performing. Calder was speaking.

"Was there anything else — in your conversations with his friends in the mess? No clues as to where he spent his holidays or who he wrote to? Did he have a girlfriend, for example?"

Stoddard shook his head. He felt wretched.

"He kept very much to himself, apparently."

He looked at Calder in sympathy. He remembered an officer — the only one who seemed to get on with Brown — saying that he used to feel sorry for him.

"One of his fellow officers said he never received any letters, even though he used to write quite a lot himself. Never said where he went on leave either. Always used to go to Paddington first, though, apparently."

Stoddard paused, thinking.

"But the London station for Aldershot is Waterloo, isn't it?" he asked.

"Yes," said Calder, whose brain was racing.

"Paddington," he said. "Paddington again. Didn't the security officer's wife say something about sending something to Paddington?"

"Yes," answered Stoddard, suddenly alert.

"How did he know?" asked Calder absently.

"Who?"

"The officer."

"Oh, I didn't ask. I can easily get in touch again."

Calder was nodding, still pacing the room, his head bowed. Stoddard noticed that although he was clearly totally absorbed with his thoughts, the number of steps he took were the same in each direction, each leg turning at exactly the same spot every time.

"I think you may have something here, General. Any why should he write a lot of letters and not get any back? Nobody's that unpopular."

He stopped suddenly and appeared to look intently at the huge, copper chimney that rose from the kitchen area.

"It might not be the station at all," he said. "I wonder whether it's an accommodation address? Somewhere that Brown might use as a sort of clearing-house. It would certainly account for the fact that he received no letters."

"It's a possibility," said Stoddard, enthusiastically.

"He might not use his own name, of course," continued Calder.

He turned from the chimney and looked at the General.

"But if we had his photograph...providing he didn't disguise himself."

He punched his left palm again.

132

"We won't get anywhere worrying about it. I need to contact Striker. Can I use your phone?"

Stoddard held out his hand.

"There's an extension on the bar," he said.

Calder walked over to it, but turned to the General before he lifted the receiver.

"Striker was in Felixstowe yesterday, interviewing people about a metal-spinning firm that was broken into. I'm certain it was used by Brown and whoever is making the bomb for him."

He began to dial.

"I'm also hopeful that two important materials needed for the bomb's construction were stolen from Birmingham and Peterborough."

Calder looked at Stoddard again as he waited for the connection. The grey-haired man was holding his coffee cup very limply and his expression of interest had gone. The bell began to ring at the other end. The General looked like what he was — a man on the brink of total mental exhaustion.

"I'll give you the details later," said Calder and didn't think that he'd been heard.

A strangled voice answered.

"Peter? Will you get round to the Department as soon as you can? Yes, I know I am, but we may be on to something.... Because you're crazy about me...."

Calder laughed out loud and replaced the receiver. As he walked towards Stoddard, the older man looked up quickly, as if awakening from a deep thought, or from sleep. He smiled crookedly again, waved at the mass of buff files on the table, and said:

"I'd better get these round to the Department."

Then he turned to the door.

"No, General," said Calder, stopping him in his tracks. "You're not going anywhere except to bed."

Stoddard's perplexed expression turned to one of hostility as he rounded on the younger man.

"Since when did you start giving me orders?"

Calder's face relaxed into a smile. His voice was gentle.

"Since now. You've worked miracles in coming up with this information in two days. You're dead on your feet and you know it. I'll be perfectly frank with you, General. You're no good to me at the moment. Your mind isn't working and it's not going to start up again until you get some sleep."

Stoddard had softened a little, but Calder could still feel a sense of duty.

"Does Jensen know of me?" asked Calder.

"Yes, but only vaguely."

Calder was still smiling, enjoying himself, as he spoke.

"Since my position is somewhat temporary, I don't need to worry about prospects of promotion. Your orders, General, are as follows. First, you pick up that phone and tell Jensen all about me and my status. He and I are going to have to work together today. Second, you leave the phone off the hook. I shall tell Jensen you are not to be disturbed except in an absolute emergency and I shall call on you when I need you. I shall then deliver these files to Jensen myself and we can get the investigation going. Third, you go to bed, don't set the alarm and sleep until you wake naturally."

Stoddard finally relented. "I suppose you're right."

He looked at Calder fiercely, but there was no hostility in his eyes. The younger man merely grinned at him.

"You'd better get going then," said Stoddard as he walked towards the telephone.

Calder grabbed the files and made to leave, hesitating in the doorway. Stoddard stopped dialling.

"Don't worry," he said, trying not to smile. "I'll go to bed."

Calder grinned again and let himself out. The General continued to dial.

There were eleven known accommodation addresses in the Paddington area. Calder and Striker had drawn a blank at eight. It was 5.40 p.m. and they were stopped outside a TV rental store, watching the start of the BBC evening news. The manager always kept the shop open until 6 p.m., in hopes of catching the rush-hour pedestrian traffic, and he always kept some sets on to attract the cathode junkies after their harsh day of reality.

Brown's face suddenly appeared on the screen, then that of five others, whom Jensen was by now fairly sure were his accomplices. Calder couldn't hear what was being said, but he didn't need to. Jensen had decided to release the names and photographs and claim that they were wanted in connection with the plutonium hijacking. It was a calculated gamble and there were good arguments against it.

To begin with, Jensen had had to seek the Minister's permission. The news of the hijacking was ten days old, and the newspapers and television (and consequently the public) had begun to forget about it. Advertising Brown and his cronies on TV would bring the whole thing back into public focus again. There was also the possibility that the advertising might force the hijackers underground, where it would be more difficult to find them. It had been argued by someone on Jensen's staff, moreover, that the advertising might make them more desperate, because it would indicate to them and, most importantly, to Brown, that they could never work in the country again. Calder had been impressed by that argument, even though he considered that Brown would already have worked it out.

But eventually he had come down in favour of the publicity. To begin with, someone *might* recognize them. And, it might panic them a little and slow them down. Brown might have worked out that he could never live in this country again, but the others might not have. They might, for example, decide to disperse. That might, paradoxically, make it easier to find one of them and therefore Brown as well, than if they all stayed hidden away in some retreat.

The picture switched back to Brown again and for the umpteenth time that day Calder reflected on how ordinary he looked. The only indications of the sort of man that lay behind this rather boring countenance were the eyes. They were brown and small, and gave just a hint of the mind lurking behind them. It was nothing that Calder could put his finger on, but he felt that they acted as a kind of calculated trigger for the rest of the face to come alive. Army photographs were not exactly known for their artistic qualities.

Calder jabbed Striker on the shoulder and they moved off along the grimy street. He wondered why it was that road-sweepers didn't seem to work as hard in inner London as they did in the suburbs. Perhaps it was just that people dropped more litter. Another one of the hidden effects of urban deprivation. The problem, he knew, was timeless; the absolute poverty of the late eighteenth and nineteenth centuries being replaced by the relative poverty of the twentieth. He also knew that there was no panacea, no sudden solution. Then he stopped in his tracks. He didn't like the way his thoughts were going, so he looked around for a street sign.

"This is it," said Striker accommodatingly, looking up from his "A-Z" map.

Calder raised his head to the surprisingly bright sign plugged into the wall, set at right angles to their direction. It read "Keit Road".

"Yes," said Calder. "What number do we want?"

"Thirteen."

They turned right, into the road and saw the group of shops immediately, across and to the left. As they approached, Calder picked out number 13 — the first in line, beside the hairdressers. A rusted, red and yellow Goldflake sign was nailed to the side brickwork.

Any pretence the shop might once have had to being painted green had long since gone. There was more bare wood than paint and such of the latter that had survived was flaked and dull, although it was more green than any other colour. The sign on the frontispiece, in big black letters, said "E M Powne" and, in smaller letters, from corner to corner, it had once read "Newsagent, Confectioner and Tobacconist". But the letters, in parts, had gone and some others were badly faded, so that it actually said, "....agent, .onfectioner and To..c..nist". Magazines were pinned to boards in both windows. Behind one window some Ronson lighters, of incongruously modern design, were on display. In the other were pipes of numerous types, several maps and various bric-à-brac. The sign on the door said "Open". Striker pushed it and a real bell clattered above his head.

There were no customers inside the dingy shop — just a weasely-looking man standing behind the counter. Unless he was standing in a hole, he couldn't have been more than five feet two inches tall. He had a receding hairline, a thin face with large ears and a pointed nose. The eyes were anonymous. He was dressed in a studded, striped shirt, without the collar, and a far from clean, grey waistcoat, unbuttoned. The expresion on his face was one of abject misery. He knew who they were and they couldn't be anything but bad news.

Calder looked around. The counter on his left was devoted wholly to tobacco, including brands that he thought had long since vacated the market. Powne had to be a bit of a specialist. To his right was the confectionery, the chocolate laid out on the counter, and the "bullseyes" and "candy twists" filling huge jars on the shelves behind. Calder had thought that this type of shop had long since gone out of business, but today had opened his mind. He wondered if Powne still weighed peardrops by the quarter. Turning, he saw that the space behind each window, on either side of the door, was taken up with maps. There was quite a collection, including two full racks of Ordnance Surveys. The place had an order to it, although it could have done with a clean. He turned back to see Striker holding his false identification wallet across the newspapers and magazines.

"Special Branch," he said.

The little man's face brightened a little. He now just looked miserable. Calder thought he probably knew that Special Branch were usually more gentle than the uniformed lot.

"Yus, guv, what can I do you for?"

The voice was moderately confident.

"We understand that you act as an accommodation address," said Striker.

The man paused warily.

"What's a Yank doin' in Special Branch?"

"Answer the question," said Calder quickly.

Powne blinked rapidly.

"Yes, I do do it," he said, "occasionally, for a few selected customers."

"Ever been used by a man named Brown?" asked Striker.

The man hesitated again.

"Now look, fellas, this is private stuff, you know. I mean, people are intitled to their privacy, ain't they?"

As soon as he'd said it the little man appeared to realize his mistake. He looked down and began to fiddle with a large, leather-bound book in front of him. Then he looked up at Striker. The blond man took one deliberate step forward. Powne took one quick step back.

"I hope you're not going to give us any trouble, Powne," said Striker, pausing for effect. "You do realize, don't you, that I can throw you in jail and have my men...*search* the place?"

The small man appeared to sigh. "No Browns," he said.

"Are you sure?"

"Positive, honest."

"Show me your book," said Striker.

Powne bit his lip. Calder noticed that his front teeth protruded.

"I don't keep one. I know I should, but I ain't never got round to it. I've got 'em all in me 'ead anyway. Honest."

"Very well," said Striker impatiently, "ever get any from Aldershot? And don't tell me you never look at the postmark."

The little man was thinking.

"I might 'ave 'ad," he said dangerously.

Striker hesitated. Then he pulled out his wallet and extracted two £5 notes. He held them up between forefinger and thumb.

"This is just to demonstrate our good will," said Striker. "But it can rapidly disappear if we don't get the truth."

Powne looked at the money and really did lick his lips. He appeared to make up his mind.

"Yus, I used to receive letters from Aldershot. Quite a lot at one time. None now though, that I can fink of."

"How long ago would that be?" asked Striker carefully.

"Oh, about two, three, four year ago."

Calder felt his heartbeat quicken. Just about the time when Brown would have been recruiting.

"And who were they addressed to?" continued Striker.

"A geezer named Stephens — D. Stephens, with a ph. Now, do I get the money?"

Striker turned to look at Calder. The latter was afraid to say anything, just in case he broke the spell and woke up. Instead, he extracted four more fivers of his own and passed them over to Striker. The little man watched this silent performance, licking his lips again and pulling his nose.

"I might have some more for you," said Striker, smiling and fanning out what was now a set of six.

Just then the door-bell clanged. Calder and Striker swung round instinctively. A huddled figure in mottled pink coat and red slippers shuffled past them to the counter, head bowed. She could have been anything from forty to sixty-five years of age. Powne was quick to recover.

"Evenin', Mrs P," he said, handing over an *Evening Standard*.

He took no money.

"Go carefully now," he added.

She turned and walked out. The door clanged shut. She had said nothing and appeared not even to have noticed the two extra men.

Striker realized that he was still holding up the six £5 notes and cleared his throat. The little man seemed to sense that, for the moment, he had the upper hand.

"You were saying?" he said to Striker rather carelessly.

Calder stepped forward and held out a photograph of Brown.

"That the man?" he asked.

Powne looked at it for several seconds, then at Calder. He then looked at the money, still held up in Striker's hand and back to the photograph again. Finally, he looked at Calder and bit his lip.

"I take it you want me to tell the truth, like?" he asked.

"Yes,"

The little man took a deep breath.

"Well, I don't know is the truth. 'E always wore dark glasses — even in the winter. Yeh, 'e wore an 'at an' all. You know, one o' those floppy fishin' 'ats."

He hesitated.

"I suppose it could be 'im," he said finally.

"How big is he?" asked Calder, remembering that Brown was six feet two.

"About your size. Per'aps a bit taller. 'E was a big fella."

Calder reasoned that anyone over five feet six inches was probably big to Powne. He also noticed that the little man was using the past tense.

"When was the last time Stephens came?" asked Calder.

"Oh, a long time ago now. In the last year or so someone else 'as collected 'is mail for 'im. 'E's much smaller than Stephens. 'E 'as dark glasses an' all, an' a bobble 'at. In fact, 'e came in last week. Can't remember what day. 'E 'ad a beard, I remember distinctly."

"Why do you remember distinctly?" asked Calder.

"'Cause 'e bought a map, didn't 'e?"

"He bought a map," repeated Calder moronically.

He was going to look at Striker, then changed his mind.

"What map?" he said desperately.

Powne was looking perplexedly at the money, which now appeared to be clasped rather too firmly in the blond man's hand.

"Er, a map o' Norfolk," said the little man, still staring at the money.

138

Calder felt his heart miss a beat and forced himself to keep his voice steady.

"Of all of Norfolk?" he asked.

"No, it was one of the Ordnance Surveys over there," pointing.

"How do you know it was of Norfolk?" persisted Calder.

"Because I saw where 'e took if from, didn't I? — the top o' the second row on the right. That's Norfolk," said Powne indignantly.

There was a silence while Striker turned and looked at Calder. Neither spoke, until Striker asked:

"Why did you happen to notice that he took that particular map?"

"Look, what is this, the Inquisition?" said Powne, rather too confidently. "I've answered your questions, ain't I, and I ain't got no money yet?"

Calder stepped forward and fixed the little man with a long stare. The latter turned away eventually and his hand began to shake on the book.

"No offence meant," said Powne, suddenly very defensive.

"My friend asked you a question," asked Calder quietly.

"Well, if you'd bin takin' in letters an' parcels for a man for six years, who always took the trouble to disguise 'imself before 'e came in, wouldn't you take an interest in anyone who collected 'is mail for 'im?"

Calder nodded.

"I rather think I would," he said.

"In fact," continued Powne, "I could tell you exactly which map it was, if you like."

The little man was obviously trying to redeem himself. He glanced at the money, still firmly clasped in Striker's hand, and looked at Calder.

"I keep the complete set of OS maps, as you can see," pointing again.

This time Calder turned to look at the maps he had already noticed. He thought that Powne probably took some pride in the mauve display.

"There were a few other gaps," continued the now generous Powne, "so when this geezer bought this Norfolk map — I only keep one o' places like that — I decided to do some reorderin'. I wrote down the numbers o' the ones I needed on the order form. I've got a copy inside," he added and turned.

He was nearly through the inner door when Calder stopped him.

"Just a minute," he said, "we'll come too. You *were* closing, weren't you?"

Calder looked at Striker, who got the message. He walked to the door and turned the sign over so that is showed "Closed", then slipped the catch. Powne watched this procedure like a cornered animal, shrugged his shoulders and walked into the inner room.

In contrast to the shop itself it was very untidy. Cardboard boxes filled most of the space and were stacked against three walls. A large table, that Powne obviously used as a desk, was set to one side. It was piled high with various pieces of paper in, it seemed, no particular order. A grey filing cabinet, with the middle drawer open, stood alongside. In the far corner was a sink. The remains of a meal lay on the draining-board, together with an electric kettle, a mug with a spoon inside and plastic food containers. The room smelt heavily of tea leaves, although, as far as Calder could see, Powne didn't sell any tea.

"'Ere's the order," said the little man, holding up a large piece of paper. "I ordered ten 176s — that covers this area — five 177s — that covers East London. One 198, one 89 and one 133. That must be it — 133."

He looked at the chart on his desk.

"North-east Norfolk," he said finally.

Striker looked at Calder, but he appeared to be looking into the distance. The blond man held out his hand and took the piece of A4.

"How can you be so sure that it was 133 that this man took?" he asked.

"I told you," answered Powne, more in frustration than anything else. "I saw where 'e got it from on the rack. None o' the other numbers are anywhere near it."

Suddenly, the sharp report of Calder's fist hitting the palm of his hand filled the room.

"My God, it's got to be," he cried dramatically.

Striker looked at him, concerned.

"Peter — Felixstowe and Peterborough," shouted Calder.

Both men looked at each other. Powne momentarily forgot his money and stared at Calder too.

"Of course," said Striker, "they're both close to Norfolk. In fact, if you put a compass point on Norwich and draw a circle, it probably falls through both towns. It's too much of a coincidence."

He frowned before continuing.

"Birmingham doesn't fit though."

"No," said Calder, "but Peterborough is in a straight line home from Birmingham to Norwich, and Peterborough was done the day after Birmingham."

"You have an observer on Powne's shop, I take it?" asked Stoddard.

Both Calder and Striker nodded. The latter wasn't used to seeing his boss in pyjamas and dressing-gown, and for some inexplicable reason he felt embarrassed. What made it worse was that Calder didn't seem at all self-conscious. Striker felt himself in one of those environments where his personality was caged. He was also aware that he was jealous of Calder's self-assurance in any situation.

"Three, on eight-hour shifts," said Striker a little nervously. "They have orders to notify us and follow. We have a back-up team ready to take over the minute anyone shows."

"Also," interrupted Calder, "Jensen has nothing on our suspects yet, except that a large number of them seem to be absent from their place of residence. The incident room has had a number of calls since the TV broadcast, but there's been nothing useful so far."

Calder looked at Striker.

"It's early days yet, but I don't think that line of enquiry is going to be fruitful, for the reasons I mentioned this morning, certainly not in the short term, and we are running out of time."

He hesitated.

"It's true that if it was them in Felixstowe, and I'm convinced now that it was, then they are not as far advanced in their construction of the bomb as I'd previously thought. But even so, there is really no way of accurately guessing when the thing will be finished. It could be two days, or a week or more."

He looked hard at Stoddard.

"What I'm saying, General, is that I believe we must have an alternative strategy — now."

It was Stoddard's turn to nod.

"Why do I get the feeling that you're going to ask me to do something unpleasant?" he said.

Striker noted Calder standing perfectly still, looking at the General. His friend had said that the old man had been exhausted this morning, but apparently he had slept for well over twelve hours and looked far from tired now. He was standing with his back to the fireplace, legs apart, hands in dressing-gown pockets. The eyes were as clear as Striker had ever seen them. They almost twinkled. Yet there was something different about him, something missing. Of course: no pipe. Perhaps he didn't smoke in his pyjamas.

He and Calder had discussed their tactics on the way over. There was only one thing to do, they knew. Actually, it was Calder who had suggested it. Striker had simply agreed. They were too close now to let Brown get away and were convinced that he was holed up in north-east Norfolk. It even fitted with the yacht theory and parachuting into the Moray Firth. Brown could have sailed straight down the east coast and there were plenty of deserted beaches up there to off-load a vessel. The fact that a massive, nationwide search had failed to find the yacht proved nothing. If anything, it could mean that he was simply extremely resourceful and they knew that anyway. Calder didn't hesitate any longer.

"I think you should organize a thorough search of the whole of the area covered by this map," he said, pointing down at Ordnance Survey 133, already open on the low table, "at dawn tomorrow."

"I don't know whether it's possible," he continued, "but I think it should be preceded by a complete seal-off. There are about ninety or a hundred roads leaving the area, as you'll see, which makes it difficult; and there are scores of tracks, which must also be covered, especially since Brown probably has a Landrover, or something like it. That also means that some could escape simply by driving through a ploughed field, which means that literally the whole border of the map has to be covered. That, in turn, means helicopters, continually patrolling the perimeter. That's difficult because the south, horizontal border is twenty-five miles long and the west, vertical border, twenty-three miles."

Calder paused, apparently to assess Stoddard's reaction so far. The General bent down to look more closely at the map and Striker noticed that he was beginning to go a little thin on the crown.

"Yes," said the older man, "patrolling these three land borders is a major problem, but there are three others that also need thinking about. To begin with we have this long coast to guard, which stretches for, what, twenty-five, thirty miles? That means boats and lots of them, not to mention more helicopters."

He looked up at Calder.

"And don't forget that 'copters are useless for observation purposes at night."

Calder bent down as well, looking puzzled. Only Striker remained standing.

"Then," continued Stoddard, "we have the fact that the top half of Norwich is also included on the map. Many roads there leading out of the area. Do we, therefore, go south of the map and seal off the whole of Norwich, which might be easier in the long run, or do we adhere strictly to the area on the map?"

It was a rhetorical question, but Calder interrupted anyway.

"I'm inclined to forget Norwich altogether. They won't be in the town. They must be away from prying eyes. That would make our seal-off easier."

He paused and frowned.

"On the other hand, there's nothing nosier than a village community. You can be more alone in a town than you can in the country. Sorry, General, I don't know. Perhaps we should seal off the whole of Norwich."

It was the first time Striker had known Calder unsure about anything. Stoddard seemed to look at him keenly before continuing.

"The fourth major problem is, of course, the sheer size of the operation. About five hundred square miles, I'd say, which must be totally isolated and searched meticulously."

The General looked at Calder again. Striker screwed up his courage. He had to mention the Broads.

"Excuse me, sir," he said, "but I think there may be a fifth major problem."

He squatted down to the map, feeling his hearbeat quicken and sensing Calder and Stoddard looking at each other over his head.

"I know part of this area," said the American. "I went sailing on some of these Broads last year."

"Get to the point, man," growled Stoddard.

"Yes, sir. The point is that this is a holiday area. It's called the Norfolk Broads. This whole south-east area here is a maze of interlocking rivers, dikes and lakes, and in the summer it teems with thousands of boats, some of them containing accommodation for up to ten people, or more."

He looked up and saw Stoddard and Calder look at each other again as he continued.

"The problem is, of course, searching all those boats when they are continually moving about. I don't know how you intended to do it, sir — search in kilometre blocks I expect, as the map is set out that way — but unless you can find some way of preventing the boats from moving, you'll have a continuous, flowing transport system, moving into and out of areas which have already been searched."

He looked up again. Calder and Stoddard were both looking at the map, so he went on.

"You can seal the boats off all right by simply blocking the junction where the rivers Thurne and Bure meet, here. You'll have a lot of unhappy holiday-makers, not to mention the commercial holiday operators, but you'll prevent boats moving out of the area. Also, of course, if the search goes over the weekend, the traffic will become a major headache. Being a popular vacation area, there is a continual stream of holiday-makers. Even though it's only May, you'll find it's still popular. I should think that a bulletin, telling people not to travel to the area, might help."

Striker stood up and looked at the other two. He felt flushed.

"Thank you, Striker," said Stoddard. "I'm sure we could think of more problems as well, if we all thought hard enough."

He moved off to the other side of room and stopped in front of an oil-painting of a grand, old house, set in extensive grounds. It had been done by a gifted amateur, Striker suspected, and he wondered whether it was connected with Stoddard's family. No one spoke for some time and Striker swayed nervously from foot to foot. Both younger men were looking at the older and the latter was gazing at the painting. He was still doing so when he began to speak.

"I take it you have thought about what this would mean? The social and economic upheaval that would be caused to the inhabitants by such an operation. And that's not to mention the question of life and death situations caused by the lack of mobility. It means completely immobilizing everyone within an area of five hundred square miles for... I don't know how long. This sort of thing has never been done before."

He turned to look at them and spoke across the room.

"That is not to mention the cost and effort involved in diverting troops, civil police forces and equipment. One thing is certain, by the way; it couldn't be organized by dawn tomorrow. Dawn on Saturday is the earliest, if you're lucky."

He looked down at the carpet and shook his head. Then he walked towards the two men and stopped very close to Calder. When he spoke, it was as if he were angry.

"Is that bomb in that area?" he demanded, pointing at the map.

"I believe so," replied Calder woodenly.

"And you would recommend searching it?"

"There is no choice."

Stoddard swung round on Striker.

"And what do *you* think, Peter?"

The blond man didn't know whether to be more surprised at being asked for his opinion or being called by his first name. But he was determined to remain impassive.

"I agree with Matthew," he said after a little hesitation.

He felt Calder looking at him. Stoddard lifted his head to the ceiling, took a deep draught of air through his nose and smiled.

"In that case," he said, "since the top brains in my Department are unanimous, what else can I do?"

He looked at his watch.

"8.35. This decision will have to be taken by the PM himself, but I'll have to contact the Minister first. I hope they're not dining somewhere, because I'm going to disturb them."

He paused and smiled again.

"On second thoughts, I hope they are dining somewhere. I want them in a good, pliable mood, because they are not going to like what I'm going to tell them."

He looked at Calder seriously, then picked up his pipe from the mantlepiece and began to fill it. Striker realized then that some things never change.

"We'll just have to pray that they see things the way you do," said Stoddard.

Then he winked and thrust the pipe into the side of his mouth.

"Don't worry. I'll scare the arses off them. They'll agree, eventually."

He paused as the two younger men grinned.

"I'd better get dressed. This is going to be the biggest operation of

144

its kind in British history, and I'm going to make sure that no one organizes it except me."

Chapter 14
Wednesday, 21 May

ALL DAY THE SUN had shone from a cloudless sky and now it was evening as Calder pulled up outside the pub. It was still humid and he needed a long, cool drink. The beer garden was full of lounging soldiers in full camouflage, their packs and weapons back at their camp across the road. It reminded him of scenes during the First World War, although he was born well after the Second.

He left his car unlocked and walked through the garden, weaving his way through the smiling soldiers. They gave him strange looks, dressed as he was in casual jeans and shirt, but he had become used to that. Stoddard had given him a roving commission and he had moved around the area, sleeping in his car.

Some of the local pubs had run out of beer but this one had a brewery practically next door. The public bar was packed to the seams with soldiers and there was a sort of queue at the bar itself. Suddenly, as he began to muscle his way to the counter, he felt profoundly depressed. The operation had been delayed until dawn on Sunday, largely due to political reluctance. That meant that it had been going for four days, there were just forty square kilometres left and they hadn't found them. They'd found a few things that no one expected, but no Brown and no bomb. That meant, in turn, that either he had been wrong and the whole thing was a mistake, or they were here, but somehow they were cleverer than he had thought. They could still be in that forty square kilometres, of course, but somehow he wasn't hopeful.

Yet, he was sure he was right. They had to be here. And the police at Felixstowe had reported that the only fingerprints on the metal-spinning mechanism were no more than a day or so old, the others having been completely erased.

The most likely possibility was that they had been by-passed. The major problem with an operation of this sort was making sure that everyone knew what they were looking for and he suspected that many didn't. It was inevitable really. He'd told Stoddard that communication might be a problem. No; that was unfair. Organization on the ground, if not the planning behind it, was in General Carey's lap and, anyway, if they didn't find that bomb it was everyone's problem. What's more, it looked as if they weren't going to find it and that meant that the number of choices open to them was becoming very limited indeed.

He reached the bar finally and realized that there was no choice of beverage either. The landlord was pulling pints continuously. You just took it and paid the robust barmaid beside him. So much for a civilized pint.

He forced his way out of the crush, his drink held high, and walked straight outside into the relative peace. He spotted an empty patch of grass and made a beeline for it. He sat down slowly and sipped his pint cautiously. It was surprisingly good. Then he focused his attention on a group of squaddies about five yards to his right. One of them was getting very excited. The cockney twang of London was clearly recognizable.

"An' I'm not jokin', I couldn't take my eyes off 'er. Showin' a leg, right up to 'ere she was." His hand came down to a point half-way up his left thigh. "An' she didn't seem to mind neither. 'Arry 'ere," he started to laugh, "was pretendin' to examine the carpet — very studious like — but, all the time, 'e was tryin' to get a look up 'er skirt."

The whole group guffawed and someone punched the blushing Harry on the shoulder.

"You dirty little bugger," said someone else.

"I'm not jokin' though," said the original speaker, "she 'ad the most fantastic pair o' legs I've ever seen. Beautiful."

Calder had the mug to his lips when something screamed at the back of his brain and he was back in Stoddard's office when he'd just got back from Mexico. His throat refused to swallow and he squirted beer all over the grass. The co-pilot of the Argosy had used exactly the same words, when he'd come round for a few seconds in the hangar — she had the most fantastic pair of legs he'd ever seen!

He found himself looking over at the small group. They had fallen silent and were returning his gaze. From the look on their faces they didn't think much of spitting good beer over the lawn. He could see their point. So she had good legs, just like hundreds of thousands of other women in the country. But they had both said *fantastic* legs. Oh, what the hell. He'd better say something intelligent anyway, before they thought he was mad.

"When was this, soldier," he asked, "when you saw the woman?"

The young man, not unnaturally, hesitated. He'd never seen Calder before and, dressed as he was, he didn't look like anyone in authority. None of his friends spoke. They just looked at Calder and then at the soldier who had spoken. Calder guessed that he was probably their leader and that he might get a little uppity, to demonstrate to his pals what a tough guy he was.

"What's it to do with you?" he replied.

Calder sighed audibly and fished in the top pocket of his open-necked shirt. He extracted his very high-powered pass and tossed it

146

across to the group. They passed it to each other reverently. One or two began to look at their uniforms.

"I was hoping to avoid that bit of drama," said Calder, holding out his hand.

The soldier who had spoken got up on to his knees and gave the pass back. He no longer looked recalcitrant.

"You ain't army or nothin', are ya?" he asked.

"No, I'm not army," replied Calder.

The soldier looked even better.

"Now," said Calder, "when did you see the woman?"

"This mornin'. We was searchin' this 'ouse."

"What time?"

"About ten."

"How old was she?"

"Oo, about twenty-five I'd say."

"How far is it — the house?"

The soldier turned away and thought. One of the others pointed a finger and answered.

"About two miles up that road, although you have to make a few turns."

Calder followed the finger. The pub was on a crossroads.

"How many were there in the house, besides the woman?" asked Calder, hoping to keep up his own enthusiasm.

The original speaker got back in the act again.

"Just a crippled old man in a wheelchair. Oh, an' a butler. Now I think about it, 'e was rather odd. 'E 'ad a beard like. Whenever ya see 'em in films, they never 'ave beards, do they?"

Then he focused on the fact that Calder had a beard as well, but was quick to make amends.

"Not that I've got anyfing against beards like, but ya don't expect to see 'em on butlers do ya?"

No, you don't, thought Calder to himself.

"The old man," he said. "Did he have a beard as well?"

The soldier paused. One or two of the others answered in the affirmative.

"Yeah," answered the soldier, "'e did now I fink about it, but I didn't notice at the time. Grey it was."

"And you searched the whole house?" questioned Calder.

"Yep, and — as far as I know, mind ya — we didn't find nothin', except those three."

One of the others — the one who had directed him to the house — interrupted.

"A bearded butler, a beautiful bird and a crippled old man. Funny, isn't it?"

"Yes," answered Calder thoughtfully, "very funny."

There was no reason why the butler shouldn't have a beard, nor the old man, come to that. But there were a lot of them about — the mail collector from Powne's shop, for example — and a beard made a natural disguise. And, of course, there was no reason why the women of Norfolk shouldn't have fantastic legs. There might even be a reason why a beautiful young woman should be living with a crippled old man. She could be his granddaughter. But even so. Somehow he *knew* Brown was in north-east Norfolk and it seemed that he'd been missed. Was it worth making a fuss about? Well, he knew he wouldn't sleep tonight unless he did something about it and, if he did, it was better to do it with fifty men armed with rifles at his back. He made up his mind, stood up and looked down at the small group.

"What's your officer's name?" he asked.

"Lieutenant Wellbeck."

"And where can I find him?"

He'd noticed one or two of the group looking past him. Now they were looking over his left shoulder.

"I've no doubt you can find him in the saloon bar, sir."

The voice came from above and behind him. He turned to find an enormous man, wearing sergeant's stripes, looking down at him. Calder was six foot and this man was at least a head taller. He was about thirty-five and running slightly to fat, but only slightly. He had shoulders like a gorilla. Calder looked into the face and decided he was intelligent too. He didn't flinch from the appraisal, which didn't surprise Calder at all.

"Thank you, Sergeant," said Calder. "If I were you, I'd advise my men to drink up quickly."

He walked off in the general direction of the saloon, leaving the big man to look after him with a puzzled expression.

A temporary hand-written sign had been nailed to the saloon-bar door. It read: "Officers, policemen and civilians only". Calder's opinion of Lieutenant Wellbeck dived even before he'd met him. He pushed on the sign and searched the room. A group of three officers was standing at the bar to the left, a few nervous-looking regulars occupied a table in the centre and, scattered around the rest of the room, were half a dozen off-duty policemen. By comparison with the public bar, it was a haven of peace and quiet.

He noticed that all three officers were lieutenants as he approched them. One had already seen him as he had entered and the other two were now acknowledging the direction of his gaze. He stopped and stood for a few seconds, his eyes taking in the whole group. It was important that he make a good impression.

"I'm looking for Lieutenant Wellbeck," he said to the group in general.

"That's me," answered a wavy-haired young man in his early

twenties. His uniform hung from his frame rather than fitted it. His face was pale and smooth, and surprisingly podgy. He held a glass of Scotch up in one hand and a cigarette in the other.

Calder removed his pass again and held it out for Wellbeck to see. His eyes widened and the other two leant forward to have a look.

"My dear chap," said Wellbeck, "even I haven't got one of those."

Calder put it away as he spoke. His voice had an edge of urgency to it.

"I just heard one of your soldiers talking about a house that you searched at 10 o'clock this morning. It contained, according to him, a butler, a crippled old man and a woman."

Wellbeck's face lit up.

"Oh, yes," he said, "she was a real cracker."

One of the others laughed and Wellbeck sipped his Scotch.

"It may be nothing," said Calder, "but I'd like you and about fifty men to come with me now and search the place again."

The atmosphere suddenly changed. No one spoke for a few moments while they all looked at Calder.

"What you showed me was a pass," said Wellbeck. "I cannot see that it gives you any authority."

"Quite right, Freddie," said the one who had laughed before. "I think he's questioning your judgement."

The third man turned away. Calder gave the last speaker a withering look and turned back to Wellbeck. The latter took a deep drag on his cigarette. Calder felt the door open behind him and Wellbeck looked over his shoulder.

"What is it, Sergeant?" he said irritably.

Calder didn't look round.

"The men are ready, sir."

Calder recognized the big man's voice.

"Wh…what for?" stammered Wellbeck.

"To go wherever this gentleman wants them to, sir," replied the sergeant.

Calder couldn't help grinning and half-turned to acknowledge the man at the door, who shouldn't really have been there anyway, according to the landlord. But then, Calder suspected, he'd probably got used to the fact that only maniacs tried to throw him out of pubs. Everyone focused on Wellbeck.

"Been ordering my troops about, have you?" said the lieutenant indignantly to Calder.

"No, sir," came the immediate reply from the door. "I did it on my own initiative."

Wellbeck ignored his sergeant, just glared at Calder.

"I have no orders. I'd better get permission," said the lieutenant, making no move at all.

"Where are your senior officers?" asked Calder.

"Not here," answered Wellbeck sharply.

"Then there is no time to get them," said Calder urgently. "It'll be dark in about forty minutes. We must move now and quickly. I suggest you exercise some initiative, lieutenant."

Wellbeck looked as if he was about to have a fit. He was torn between the prospect of a comfortable evening getting drunk in congenial company and that pass, which he'd noticed was signed by General Carey himself. The man in front of him might be connected with the big brass. He certainly had an air of authority about him. But, he wasn't in uniform, was he? Therefore, technically....

"You'd better go, Freddie," said the officer who had so far remained silent.

He drained his glass and placed it down on the bar.

"I'll come as well," he added and smiled genuinely.

Calder wondered what he was doing with the other two.

"Thank you, Lieutenant," he said gratefully. "What's your name?"

"Frobisher."

Calder nodded.

"Oh, all right," said Wellbeck suddenly.

Calder nodded again.

"How many men can you muster between you?" he asked.

Frobisher thought carefully. "About forty-five," he said.

"That'll do," said Calder. "Who's senior of you two?"

Since Wellbeck looked so young he was expecting Frobisher to answer.

"I am," said Wellbeck forcefully.

Calder stopped himself from biting his lip.

"Fine," he said, "then let's go. I suggest that all the men are armed and we commandeer enough vehicles to get us there as quickly as possible."

He turned away.

"I shall give the orders, if you don't mind," said Wellbeck shrilly, still making no move from the bar.

Calder turned on him. He was angry now.

"No, Lieutenant Wellbeck. I shall be giving the orders. And if you question that, I should get on your field phone and call General Carey. With a bit of luck he might boot your arse from here right back to Sandhurst."

Calder turned away again. Wellbeck opened his mouth to speak, then shut it. The bulky sergeant was still standing by the door. If ever a man was smiling without using the normal facial expressions, then that was what he was doing. Calder stopped about a yard from him and looked up.

"Thank you Sergeant. What's your name?"

"Oakes, sir."

Calder couldn't help smiling to himself, despite the situation.

"I should have guessed," he said. "Did you hear what I was saying just now?"

"Yes, sir. Enough vehicles for forty-five men, all armed. Two troop-carriers should do it, sir. Plus a Landrover for you and the officers?"

"Yes, Lieutenants Wellbeck, Frobisher and I will travel in the Landrover. You will drive."

Oakes looked across at Wellbeck for confirmation or denial. The lieutenant was looking at him, but he wasn't saying anything.

"Yes, sir," said Oakes, smiling.

"And, Sergeant," added Calder. "Make sure that you and each officer has a walkie-talkie and be as quick as you can. We must do this before it gets dark."

"Yes, sir," said Oakes and he strode off down the path, barking orders as he went.

Frobisher rushed past, presumably to organize his own men and Wellbeck followed at a more leisurely pace. Calder suddenly centred on the possibility that he could be going off on a wild-goose chase. He might not have been so insistent had it not been for Wellbeck. Well, he was committed. He'd better be right, or one or two people would have a field day. But finding the bomb was more important than saving his dignity.

Within twelve minutes they were nearly there.

"How far is it down this lane?" asked Calder.

Wellbeck thought about it. Fortunately his sense of direction and distance were better than his ability to make decisions.

"About 450 yards, I'd say. On the left."

"Stop," said Calder and Oakes braked.

Calder took in the lie of the land. He had not time to reconnoitre. It was straight in now or nothing. The lane could barely take the width of two vehicles. There appeared to be a small track about twenty yards on the left, which hopefully led to somewhere round the back of the house. Anything past the entrance to the track though was screened by trees and shrubs. To the right of the lane was an old iron fence and a grazing pasture. It rose slightly and then disappeared over a hill after about two hundred yards. There were a few trees in the field and it had been heavily grazed, but there were no cows. Further down the lane — about a third of a mile it seemed — the field leant into a wood. The lane bent round to the left, but Calder guessed that the wood probably went right down to the road. That meant that it probably continued across the lane as well, along the side of the house.

He looked at the sky. The sun had already set, but there was still about twenty-five minutes of reasonable light left. It might not be enough. He turned to Frobisher.

"Lieutenant. Take your men up that track and see if you can come up to the rear of the house. I'm afraid I don't know what sort of terrain you'll find."

He looked down at the map before continuing.

"The map doesn't make it clear. That wood down there is marked, but nothing else. It's important that you're not seen, so don't be afraid to stay back. Your job is merely to stop any rabbits bolting out of the back door."

Frobisher nodded. Calder looked at his watch.

"I can only give you ten minutes to get into position," he said. 'I'm sorry. I know it's not enough, but the light is fading rapidly."

Frobisher nodded again and jumped down.

"Oh, Lieutenant," called Calder.

The young man — no more than twenty-three, Calder estimated — looked back.

"Don't be afraid to shoot if you have to."

Frobisher's eyebrows seemed to come closer together. Then he left.

"Lieutenant," said Calder to Wellbeck. "Set up a road-block, right here. If anyone breaks into that field you'll have a clear field of fire, for about a third of a mile, up to that wood. If anyone gets in there we've lost them. To avoid that, you'll take half your company along the lane, round the bend and past the house. There you'll set up another road-block this side of the wood. We'll just have to hope there are plenty of trees shielding you from the house, as there are here. If there aren't, you'll have to go into the wood. You must keep out of sight."

Wellbeck nodded confidently. He had become accustomed to the situation now. He wasn't going to call Calder "sir", but he'd carry out his orders. After all, that was what he'd been trained to do. He made to jump out, but Calder's voice stopped him.

"I suggest you and your men drop off while the driver continues some way past. If anyone is listening in the house he can hear the lorry receding into the distance. The driver can then turn the lorry and form a road-block."

Wellbeck looked at him blankly, got out and called, "Sergeant."

The big man instinctively made to move. Calder gripped his arm.

"No," he said, "he stays with me."

The lieutenant looked daggers at him and left. Frobisher and his men filed past at a trot. Then Wellbeck, shouting orders, caught his attention.

"I wish he'd keep his voice down," said Calder absently.

The two men sat in silence for nearly a minute. Oakes looked over at Calder, who seemed to be deep in thought.

"And what do *we* do, sir?" asked Oakes politely.

At first Calder gave no indication that he had heard and spoke without looking at the burly driver.

"We walk up to the front door, Sergeant."

"Yes, sir," answered Oakes, as if Calder had asked him to pass a cigarette.

"Well, not quite like that," continued Calder. "First of all, you will open the bonnet of this vehicle and cut a slit in the top hose. Then we follow Wellbeck, at a discreet distance. By the time we reach the entrance to the house, we should be steaming like a Turkish bath. We then have a legitimate excuse to pull over and knock on their door."

The big man nodded.

"We then play it by ear," added Calder.

That was painfully true. He had no set plan for when they reached the house. He couldn't begin to doubt himself, but he was prepared to admit that he wasn't perfect. He turned to the professional sitting beside him.

"How am I doing, Sergeant?"

Oakes turned and looked Calder in the eye. He twitched his mouth and said:

"You're not army — that's obvious. But you're doing all right. I was right about you back in the beer garden." He paused. "When most people meet me for the first time, they're afraid — I can tell. You weren't."

Calder didn't know what to say.

"Just one word of advice though, sir, if you don't mind."

"Go on."

"Lieutenant Wellbeck. I know him fairly well by now." He stopped and frowned. "The mood he's in, he's likely to go in, guns blazing at the slightest opportunity, just like he was leading the Seventh Cavalry. It might be worth having a word in his ear."

Calder nodded and put his head out of the window. One lorry was already broadside across the road and men were in the ditch along his side. He jumped down and walked to the back of the Landrover. Wellbeck was just about to pull himself into the cab of the remaining lorry. Calder beckoned him over and he approached suspiciously.

"On no account break cover until you get a signal from me or Sergeant Oakes," said Calder.

"Is that all?"

"Have you got your radio?"

"Yes."

"Then that's all," answered Calder and walked back to his vehicle.

He wondered whether he was being too hard on Wellbeck, especially since he was going to be quite angry when he discovered that Calder had no formal authority at all. Well, it was too late now. As he was settling himself in beside Oakes, the lorry eased itself narrowly past, then accelerated up the road.

"OK, Sergeant, the hose," said Calder.

Like many big men, Oakes moved with surprising quickness. Within seconds he had jumped down and had the bonnet up. Calder hadn't even wondered how he was going to cut the hose. That a man like Oakes would have some sort of sharp instrument about his person, official or unofficial, he had no doubt. Almost immediately there was a hissing from the engine area and Oakes slammed down the bonnet. He leapt back into the driver's seat and put the vehicle into gear.

"We'd better get going," he said, "before this thing seizes up."

He moved quickly up through the gears and in little more than a minute they were approaching the entrance to the drive of the house. Calder could see it now through the thinning hedge. Steam was definitely leaking out of the joints of the bonnet. Wellbeck had disappeared round the bend.

"There's no gate," said Calder. "Pull into the drive just a little and to one side."

Oakes slowed down to walking pace, then did as Calder suggested.

"OK," said Oakes, "let's give them a show."

He jumped down and threw the bonnet up, having to retreat swiftly as the suddenly released steam rose in a cloud.

Calder switched the engine off and jumped down. The house, about a hundred yards away, was half hidden by an enormous pine tree, about twenty yards from where the Landrover had come to rest. But he could see enough to know that it probably contained about a dozen or so bedrooms and probably had extensive grounds around the back. Some outbuildings to the right, that looked as if they had once been stables, formed an enclosed quadrangle.

He reached Oakes and, with him, bent over the engine, just like any motorist who had broken down and was examining the problem.

"If anyone comes and looks at this hose," said Oakes, "they're going to know it's a put-up job."

"They won't get the chance," said Calder, who turned round to look at the house again. "We've given them as long as we can."

He looked down at the walkie-talkie, nestling in a pocket on Oakes's thigh.

"I'll get my rifle," said the big man.

Before long they were both moving up the tarmac drive towards the front door. Oakes, if it hadn't been for the automatic rifle slung casually over his shoulder, looked as if he was out for an evening stroll. Calder felt tense. He didn't know what he was going to do once he was inside, even if it was the right place. He had the glimmering of a few ideas, but right at that moment he did not want to follow them through. He consciously emptied his mind of all the immediate problems and just concentrated on putting one foot in front of the other. Slowly, the tension died and he let the evening creep in upon him as he heard a chaffinch and then another.

Thirty yards from the house he paused and stared up at it. It was old, covered in ivy and did not look well maintained. The piping needed a coat of paint and so did the window frames. The garden, though, was immaculate.

"Any movement?" he asked.

"I've been watching the windows, sir. Not a sign."

They moved on and Calder felt a tightening in his belly as he approached the large wooden door, shadowed under a stone arch.

Ignoring the bell set into the stone, he walked up to the door, lifted the huge, carved-brass knocker and slammed it down twice on the woodwork. The sound echoed hollowly throughout the house and Calder felt immediately that it was empty. That told him nothing, of course, except that it was unusual for a house of this size to be completely deserted. You would expect at least one servant.

They waited for a full half-minute, then looked at each other. Calder waited a little more, then stepped up and knocked again. It sounded even more empty this time.

"The bell might go direct to a room at the back," suggested Oakes.

Calder shook his head. "Bells can be too easily booby-trapped," he said.

When, after another minute, nothing had stirred. Calder came to a decision.

"There can't be anyone here. If there is, then they must be hiding, in which case we might as well break in anyway."

He tried the handle on the door, but it was firmly locked.

"I'd ask you to put a burst through the lock," he said, "but Wellbeck would probably charge up the drive. So let's go round the back and break in quietly."

It took them far longer to walk round to the back garden, which was about three acres in area and ringed by trees, than it did to break a French window and walk in. There was no alarm.

The room appeared to be spacious and well decorated with chintz furniture, but no detail could be seen with clarity, as the light was fading rapidly. Calder crunched across broken glass to the light switch and flicked it on. Nothing happened. He moved out into a long, dark corridor and found the switch there, but that too produced no illumination.

That settled it. The house must be empty. The electricity supply had been turned off. That was odd, because big houses usually had freezers.

He caught sight of Oakes, framed against the remaining light, and said:

"Let's find the kitchen."

They walked down the corridor, ignoring the many rooms leading off and found themselves in the lobby at the front of the house. The inside of the house, in contrast to the outside, seemed to be well-maintained, clean and reasonably, if rather sparsely, decorated. By setting off down another corridor, Calder found the dining-room and hence the kitchen.

The light was too little to enable Calder to see very much at all, except a sink near the only, small window, a large table in the centre of the room and, at the far end of the large space, near the door, in the darkest corner, a long, low, chest freezer.

He walked over and lifted the lid. It was about a third full with what looked like meat, vegetables and bread, yet it was definitely not operating. He extracted a pre-packed chicken. It was still frozen. He must have stood there for some time, the chicken freezing his hand, before the burly sergeant walked in.

"Why turn off a freezer that's a third full of food, Sergeant? There must be at least two hundred quid's worth here. Answer — you don't need it any more."

He suddenly felt angry. So near, yet so bloody far. Christ, it was pathetic. Oakes was about to walk over, but changed his mind as the light from the window caught Calder's face. He just held out his hand instead.

"I thought this might be interesting, sir. I found it in the wastepaper basket next door. It's a sort of study."

Calder walked over, zombie-like, and took the crumpled, buff envelope. He turned it so that he could see in the light from the window. It was addressed to Mr D. Stephens, 13 Keit Road, Paddington, London.

He stared down at it, mesmerized. Then his anger rose again, this time uncontrollably. He turned and threw the frozen chicken into the freezer. The bird hit the underside of the lid with tremendous force and it slammed shut. He walked over to it and placed his hands on the surface, forcing himself to remain calm. Funny how he should throw the chicken *into* the freezer. He could have thrown it anywhere. He became conscious of the envelope, now crumpled in his left fist. Well, he could call off the guards on Powne's shop. If Brown was prepared to leave addressed envelopes about, he wouldn't be using that accommodation address again.

But why should they leave? The house had already been searched. It was clean. They could have stayed here indefinitely. It could have been that Brown just didn't want to push his luck and had decided to move on. But that wouldn't do. There was only one answer. They didn't need to stay any more, which again led to only one conclusion. Quite simply, the bomb was completed.

He lifted his head and looked unseeingly at the dark wall behind. As each piece of the map had been searched, so the security cordon had moved too, like a tightening noose. At least, that had been the idea. That was why there were a few surplus troops now. So, when the soldiers moved up, Brown and his cronies had simply hidden themselves and the evidence of a full house, put up a front of a woman, a crippled old man and a butler, waited for the place to be searched and for the cordon to pass by, gave it another three to four hours for safety, packed themselves into their cars and left at irregular intervals. The bomb was also, probably, in the boot of a big car and could now be almost anywhere in the UK. It was all so bloody simple. He'd missed them by about six hours. He didn't feel angry now, just empty.

"You still there, Sergeant?" he asked quietly.

"Sir," said the big man, equally quietly.

"Get on that two-way radio of yours and call in the troops. I don't want them to come into the house or touch it though. Before anyone else comes in here I want to check it myself, with a geiger-counter."

He turned to Oakes. "You had yours on when you checked the house this morning, I take it?"

"Yes, sir, and it's still in the Landrover."

Calder nodded.

"I'm puzzled as to why they didn't arrange to burn the place down before they left, Sergeant. They clearly didn't intend to return and it would destroy evidence. I'm probably being overly cautious, but I want an explosives expert to check this place over before anyone throws any more switches or turns on that electricity supply."

"Sir."

"Then go down to the Landrover and get on that field radio. Mention my name and ask General Carey to get here fast."

"I'm afraid I didn't get your name, sir."

"Calder."

Oakes nodded. "Anything else, sir?"

"That's enough for you to be getting on with," said Calder, turning to look at the big man. His face was featureless in the near-dark.

"This is the place, is it, sir?"

"Yes," answered Calder tonelessly.

"What put you on to it?" continued Oakes.

"You won't believe it, Sergeant, but it was a pair of beautiful legs."

He clapped Oakes on the shoulder as he walked past.

"Thanks for your help," he said.

It was becoming almost impossible to see and he stubbed his toe on the step. He left through the front door and walked slowly down to the Landrover. There, he searched for and found a battery-operated torch. It was big and powerful, as one would expect. With its assistance he then found the geiger-counter and returned to the house. He passed Oakes on the doorstep, still speaking into his hand-radio. Behind him he heard the sound of a lorry.

He switched on the geiger-counter on entering the house and noted that it showed no more than a normal reading. He went through to the kitchen again and searched for the cellar. With the aid of the torch he found it quickly and watched the counter carefully as he opened the door. Still normal.

His torch showed a fairly ordinary cellar, with prosaic looking boxes, dusty sacks and various odds and ends. He descended the steps. Against the far wall was, however, a far from normal wine rack. It was nearly completely full with about two hundred bottles.

Calder shone the torch around the walls. It seemed a rather small cellar for such a large, old house. He moved over to the wall against which the wine rack was propped and shone his torch into the corner. Yes, that was it. The wall was built after the outside wall. The bricks were of a slightly different colour. He walked over to the corner and felt both walls. It was a different texture too, rough and dry, whereas the other was worn smooth by the mildew and damp of nearly a century. It didn't take a genius to work out that the new wall was probably a false one.

He spent fifteen minutes probing it, but there was clearly no entrance. There had to be one from another room, upstairs. He was a little concerned that Oakes was taking so long, but knew he was capable enough.

It took him another ten minutes to find it, although he should have seen it sooner. A wall stanchion in the huge forward lounge shouldn't have been there. True, it melded in with the rest of the woodwork, but there was just no reason for it to be in that particular spot. It took him a few seconds more to find the lever — a wooden knob, set low down in the wood. He turned it and heard a soft click. He pushed the wall and it moved silently, like an ordinary door on well-oiled hinges. There was still no sign of Oakes.

Calder shone the torch through. Immediately in front of him was a series of steps that would take him down about seven feet. At the bottom was a small, flat place and then a steel door. To one side of the door, set into the wall, was a geiger-counter. His own sounded a little more agitated but not appreciably so. It still read safe. The other almost certainly measured radioactivity within the cellar.

A little stunned, he descended the steps and looked at the dial. It didn't register anything and he realized that it wasn't switched on. He reached out to push the button, then arrested the movement as the realization struck him that it was the perfect booby-trap. Brown knew by now that they were on to him, which meant that he must also know that the authorities knew that he was making an atomic bomb. The natural thing to do, therefore, would be to press that button to discover the degree of radiation within. That triggers an explosion and, all at the same time, Brown destroys evidence, spreads radiation into the neighbourhood and demonstrates his earnest intent.

Calder would give anything to see inside that room, but he would have to wait until an expert checked out the geiger-counter. Anyway, he really knew what was inside: all the necessary equipment for making an atomic bomb. And the bomb would be gone — finished. He was almost certain, but he had to be sure, before the night was out.

He heard someone shouting his name up above.

"Down here," he shouted back.

He was ascending the steep steps, which, extravagantly, had hand-holds on either side, when the unmistakable figure of Sergeant Oakes became framed in the entrance to the false wall-cavity. Calder was careful not to shine the torch directly into his eyes.

"Jesus," said the big man, "so this is where they were hiding."

"Yes," answered Calder, turning and pointing his torch at the cellar door. "In there. And I'm not surprised your boys didn't find it. It took me half an hour and I was looking for it."

He felt profoundly depressed.

"We had a little trouble with the radio, sir, but we've raised General Carey now. He was at Cromer and should be here in about five minutes or so."

Oakes lowered his head.

"What's the problem?" asked Calder.

"It's Lieutenant Wellbeck," answered Oakes immediately. "He's been giving me some trouble and I'm finding it difficult to keep him out of the house. I think he feels that his authority is being questioned and he's threatened to demote me to private twice."

"I'm sorry, Sergeant," said Calder. "I've caused you a lot of problems. I'll sort out Wellbeck."

Just then some headlamps lit up the front of the house.

"Don't apologize, sir. I wouldn't have missed it for anything."

Calder saw that the man was grinning as the sharp light reflected off his teeth and he smiled too.

"The radiation count is OK inside the house," he said, "but I can't guarantee that room. Pick two of your most reliable men and have them stand guard on the door. They must not touch anything. Also, no one, not even the General, is to pass without my permission. Then station some men around the house."

"Already done, sir."

Calder nodded.

"No one except those two guards is to set foot in this house until it's been checked by experts. Where is that explosives man, by the way?"

"We don't have anyone qualified enough here. Lieutenant Wellbeck mentioned it to General Carey."

"Fine," said Calder, "then let's go and do battle with Wellbeck."

They reached the front door. Oakes signalled to a group of men and left to give orders. Calder stood there on the doorstep for a moment, in the full glare of the headlights that someone had left on. He willed himself to think positively. All right, so he'd missed them this time. And, true, time was now running out fast. But he would simply have to build up again from square one. He could think of things that could be done now, but he had to get back to London and talk to Stoddard first.

The sound of a helicopter disturbed his thoughts and he allowed his mind to drift with it as it came closer. A powerful light stabbed down from the undercarriage, just forward of the vertical, and the machine landed. Calder continued to watch as the engine note dropped and two figures stepped out under the slowly flapping rotors. One of them was clearly in uniform. The other was smaller, with light-coloured hair and wearing a combat jacket. He looked familiar. Then he glanced Calder's way and stopped the uniformed man, who seemed bent on reaching the immaculate row of soldiers standing at attention by the pine tree. *He* carried on, but the man in the combat jacket started to walk towards Calder, and was no more than fifteen yards away before Calder saw that it was Stoddard. Calder also realized that he was never more glad to see anyone in his life.

III: THREAT

Thursday, 22 May, a.m.

Chapter 15

SMOKEY JOE pushed his cart along the Horse Guards to the next pile of litter. He'd come by a few minutes before and brushed the discarded paper into little mounds along the curb, to make it easier for shovelling. As usual, he was in no hurry. There was always another lot of rubbish around the corner.

He became aware that his roll-up had gone out, so he stopped, propped his shovel against the cart and relit it. Then he extravagantly removed his pocket-watch and checked the time. Four minutes to ten. He would stay where he was now, watch in hand, until Big Ben's tenth chime. It was a ritual he never altered.

Smokey looked over at St James's Park and noticed two men, just leaving the park by the War Memorial, walking towards him. One was much older than the other and looked very distinguished. He was wearing a grey suit and his head was topped by short silver-grey hair. The other was bearded and dressed in a dark-brown corduroy jacket, brown trousers and tie, and white shirt.

They were in earnest conversation and appeared not to notice him as they headed directly for the cart. Then the younger man looked up and the other moved over slightly. As they approached the kerb the bearded man looked more closely at Smokey, who touched his cap and kept looking. The younger man smiled. To Smokey there was something strange about him. Then the troubled eyes moved away as he scanned the traffic and they cross the road.

"You should have seen the PM's face when I told him about that booby-trapped geiger-counter," said Stoddard as they entered Horse Guards Parade. "I think it finally brought home to him that we're dealing with a man who is deadly serious and for that I think we ought to thank him — Brown, I mean."

Calder looked puzzled. The older man caught the expression.

"Before that I was having all sorts of problems getting things done. But now," he waved his arm dismissively, "I seem to have no difficulty. When I told him about your conclusions he didn't say a word — just sat staring at the table. Finally, he came to his senses and said he wanted to know the effects of 'this atomic device' if it were exploded and, taking advantage of my new-found influence, I suggested I had just the man for the job."

Stoddard was grinning broadly. Calder felt uneasy.

"When he asked me about your qualifications I told him the truth. And I said that you had made a special study of the area in question."

The General cleared his throat.

"I also told him that you had resigned your post at the Centre because you saw the dangers of nuclear proliferation through nuclear power and were frustrated when the people in control wouldn't listen. That pinned his ears back. What's more, I said that you could tell him what he wanted to know at 10 o'clock this morning, without the need for any preparation."

Stoddard stopped at a black gate set into a high, brick wall. He looked down at the pipe in his hand.

"I rather built you up, I'm afraid."

"Thanks, General," said Calder crookedly. "What I don't understand though is why. There must be scores of people who could do it. The Cabinet Office itself has nine scientific personnel on its payroll and that's to say nothing of the Prime Minister's Private Office. At least one of them must know something about nuclear explosions."

Stoddard's smile had gone.

"Yes," he said, "and two of them will be there this morning — looking you over no doubt."

Calder made no reaction at all, just gazed back at the older man, who, in turn, was looking him straight in the eye.

"I've already told you," said Stoddard fiercely, "that two weeks ago a very senior scientific adviser told me that an atomic bomb could not be made from reprocessed plutonium oxide. Perhaps that will give you an answer."

Stoddard's face showed pure agression.

"I just hope he's not there this morning," he added venomously.

With that he turned and placed the pipe in his jacket pocket. They were cleared by the policeman on duty and Stoddard opened the gate. It was the rear entrance to 10 Downing Street. Calder shut the gate behind him and followed Stoddard across the garden.

As he walked along the narrow path Calder felt apprehensive. After all, it's not every day you get to give a talk to the Prime Minister and some of his Cabinet colleagues. He was also a little tired, but then he'd been up all night. They hadn't left Norfolk until 3.30 a.m. and all he had had time for on his return was a bath and a sizeable breakfast. Stoddard had breakfasted with the PM at 8.00 and then phoned Calder as he was washing up. Come to think of it, the General should be tired too, but he looked like a man with eight solid hours behind him.

Big Ben began to chime.

"We're going to be late," said Stoddard and quickened his step.

Across the road, Smokey Joe looked from the gate where the men had disappeared, to his watch. He nodded ten times in extravagant satisfaction and returned to his daydream.

Within five minutes Calder was standing in what was obviously a briefing room. Two large windows at one end didn't quite shed enough light on the oblong space and fluorescent tubes were needed. Ostentatious wood surrounds were much in evidence along the borders around the cream walls. Along one long wall was a huge fireplace and, above it, hung an enormous, ornate mirror. A white screen stood at one end of the room and a film projector at the other. There were also a few TV monitors scattered about. On the floor was a plain, wine-red carpet over parquet wood and, in the centre, were sixteen straight-backed, leather-covered, red chairs around an elliptical table.

Seven men were seated there, some of whom were among the most powerful in Britain.

Calder was standing at one end. Halfway down, nearest to him on his right, sat Stoddard. Next to him and further down were two scientists, who had been introduced simply as Drs Crawford and Benavici. The former was about sixty-five, bald, diminutive and pale. A pair of bi-focals perched on the end of his nose and he was watching Calder suspiciously over the top of them. He looked like the stereotype of a nuclear physicist. Benavici, on the other hand, was young, large and dark, and clearly of Italian descent. The brown eyes had flashed at him briefly as they were introduced. They now looked at his own fingers, which fiddled nervously on the blotter. Calder wondered whether either of them was Stoddard's boffin.

Next to Benavici, near the end, was David MacPherson, the Home Secretary — known to his public simply as "Mac" — a thick-set man with curly, brown hair and a ruddy complexion which blended with his light-green check suit. By training he was a barrister and a man steeped in the belief of the freedom of the individual. It occurred to Calder that there must be a little worm working away inside his brain, due to the rather totalitarian measures he had been forced to adopt since the hijack and because of the even more Draconian actions that he must suspect would now be required to find the bomb. He appeared to have a headache — the forehead was wrinkled and the eyelids slightly closed. Calder didn't feel sorry for him. MacPherson was the member of a Cabinet which had allowed the Nuclear Power Programme and, while he wouldn't go so far as to say that the man deserved what he was getting, he wasn't going to hand him a handkerchief to cry into.

On the left of the smoothly polished table-top, nearest Calder, was Norman Stiles, Secretary of State for Energy. He was fifty-one years old and five feet five inches tall. This last feature, connected with the fact that he was somewhat overweight, made him a cartoonist's dream. To the press he was known as "the Barrel" and was drawn in various guises — being filled-up with some obnoxious substance, being rolled along the ground or, most commonly, bowling over the entire Cabinet or the House of Commons in a skittle alley. One way he did live up to his nickname was that he always seemed to be laughing. With his ubiquitous pipe continually turning up one corner of his mouth, he gave the impression that he was a little simple, but to Calder he had always had one of the sharpest brains in his party, even if at times his rebellious nature caused him to have a bad press. At times, too, he showed flashes of brilliance and it was well known that he was a potential rival for the party leadership. He was also the only man in the room, as far as Calder knew, who had spoken out publicly about the dangers of nuclear power, and for that Calder felt a rather biased affinity.

Next to him, further down, was the bespectacled John Corcorran, Minister of Defence. Calder suspected him of being one of the most influential members of the government — not because of his post, which is, on the whole, a relatively minor one in the late twentieth century, but because of his intelligence and personality. He was a hawk, or perhaps "owl" would be a better word, and he had firm views on morality and the state of the nation. Calder knew that he was about fifty-five, although his wavy hair was completely black. He had piercing blue eyes behind the dark frames and a just perceptible scowl almost permanently on his long face. He was immaculately dressed in dark blue suit, white shirt and dark blue tie, and Calder knew that the black shoes would be spotless. Corcorran was not a man with whom he would care to deal on a one-to-one basis.

Finally, at the end of the table, in the middle of them all, sat the Prime Minister, Bernard Lecast. He was a big man in height and girth, who would have to have had his suits made to measure even if he couldn't afford it. Calder knew that he was nearly seventy, but he didn't look it, and although his hair was white, there was still plenty of it. His career in politics had been long and hard-fought, but he had been almost the natural choice for leader when his predecessor had resigned because of ill-health. He had made mistakes, but most of the time had been prepared to admit them and, although he was close to retirement, he showed a capacity for adaptation. The cynical called it pragmatism, his supporters flexibility. In any event, you couldn't run the first coalition in Britain's post-war history by being dogmatic.

Whatever was true, one thing was clear to Calder — something that could not be conveyed through a television screen. Lecast had a presence which dominated the table. Even if he were not sitting at its head, there would be no doubt as to who was in charge.

All the men looked cautious and tense, although there were no signs of fear, with the possible exception of Benavici. Well, thought Calder, that would soon change. His mind was suddenly crystal clear as he removed some notes from the inside pocket of his jacket. He looked at Stoddard to sense his mood but he was looking at his blotter.

"The floor is yours, Mr Calder," said Lecast.

"Thank you." Calder hesitated briefly while gathering his thoughts.

"I'm afraid," he said, "there is a bit of so-called 'jargonistic' information that I must give you at the beginning. I'm sorry if I'm telling some of you what you already know, but it is important that all of you understand the whole situation."

He turned to the white board standing beside him and lifted the felt-tipped pen that rested in the groove of the easel. He wrote at the top of the board, "Effects of 20 Kiloton Nuclear Ground-Burst". As he spoke, he summarized the main points on the board, throughout.

"As you probably know, in conventional terms, one kiloton is equivalent to the explosive power of one thousand tons of TNT. So, a twenty-kiloton bomb, which is what we have to face, is equivalent to twenty-thousand tons of TNT. It's a very small nuclear bomb, but still extremely potent. Just to say that it represents that much explosive power in no way describes its capacity."

He glanced around the table. Everyone except Benavici was looking at the board.

"We are fairly sure it's about a twenty-kiloton bomb," continued Calder, "because we know how much plutonium has been stolen."

He paused.

"Actually, that's not, strictly speaking, true. We know how much plutonium oxide was stolen and we know how much plutonium 239 can be converted from it — about ten kilos. Now ten kilos represents two hundred kilotons, but we would expect only about ten per cent of the plutonium in our bomb to be involved in the nuclear reaction. I don't think it will be less than ten per cent but it could be greater. One has to make a calculated guess somewhere."

Stiles was nodding and Calder felt encouraged.

"If you are looking for absolute accuracy in this talk, gentlemen, I'm afraid that I'm going to disappoint you. There are just too many variables. Ten per cent is, I think, a reasonable estimate, based on the state of our knowledge and the availability of that information."

No one spoke. Calder looked at the two scientists and so did Lecast, but there was no reaction. Calder then glanced at Stoddard to gauge the General's mood but he was gazing at the blotter again.

"So," he continued, "we have about one kilo involved in the nuclear reaction — ten per cent of the total ten kilos — which is equivalent to twenty kilotons. That's very useful because Hiroshima and Nagasaki were both twenty-kiloton explosions, which means that we have considerable empirical evidence."

He paused and looked at the listeners again, his eyes flickering back and forth. There didn't seem to be anyone obviously floundering.

"Fine," said Calder. "I can now move on to what you want to hear — the effects of a nuclear explosion of a bomb of this power. There are mainly four: thermal radiation, the blast or shock wave, initial radiation and residual radiation. These sound technical, but they're not difficult to understand really. The first three occur in all nuclear explosions and the last doesn't, but I'll explain that when I come to it."

He turned to write on the board, hoping he wasn't sounding too patronizing. It was difficult to say it any other way.

"First, thermal radiation. This would be the first effect and although it's called 'radiation', it isn't, in the normal sense in which we use the word. In fact it's non-radioactive heat that at one point reaches the sort of temperature achieved by the sun. It's in the form of a fireball that travels at the speed of light. Up to three seconds after the explosion it cools to an insignificant temperature, but in that short time the damage has been done. It causes two types of burns: flash-burns, caused directly by the fireball itself, and burns caused by the fire that the fireball creates."

He paused and surveyed the table.

"I've got to make an assumption here, that, at the moment of explosion, average atmospheric conditions are prevailing and that the terrain is reasonably flat. That, of course, is a false assumption, because average atmospheric conditions, like all averages, are fictitious. I would ask you to appreciate that the effects may be more or less, depending on these conditions."

He paused again, but no one spoke. *OK, here we go*, he thought. Looking at Stoddard, he said:

"Assuming these conditions, second-degree flash-burns can be expected at a distance of one and a quarter miles from 'ground zero' — that's the point at which the explosion occurs."

The General didn't react, but MacPherson sat up in his chair.

"A one-and-a-quarter-mile radius!" he exclaimed.

Everyone except Lecast and Stiles turned to look at him.

"That's right, Mr MacPherson," answered Calder. "In fact it could be worse," he added cruelly. "At Nagasaki, first-degree flash-burns were recorded at twice that distance, but that was an air-burst, where the flash-burn effect is greater. Twenty to thirty per cent of fatalities at Hiroshima and Nagasaki were due to flash-burns."

He took a deep breath and let a silence develop. MacPherson was still sitting up in his chair and they were all staring at the board,

166

transfixed — all, that is, except Benavici. His hands were moving more and he started blinking. Stoddard's expression was still annoyingly non-committal as Calder continued.

"But flash-burns are only part of the effect of thermal radiation. The other is 'ordinary' burns caused by fire. In Hiroshima, everything combustible up to 2.2 miles from ground zero was completely destroyed by fire. In Nagasaki, it was only a quarter of this distance. But London, for various reasons which I won't bore you with, is more like Hiroshima in this respect."

He paused.

"I mention London only because it seems to me the most likely target."

MacPherson had already slumped back in his seat and was staring at the far wall. Everyone, including Benavici now, was immobile. If Lecast's secretary had walked in at that moment with no clothes on, he felt sure they wouldn't have noticed.

"Connected with this," continued Calder, "is the 'fire-storm', which blows back into the area. The explosion causes a sort of vacuum, but the laws of physics tell us that the air must come back. In Hiroshima it was manifested by a wind that blew back in after twenty minutes, in varying strengths, for about six hours. It's good and bad news: it limits the range of the fire, but it also increases its intensity. My estimate is that, given average atmospheric conditions in London, the fire would consume everything combustible for up to one and three-quarter miles from ground zero. Fifty per cent of the deaths in Japan were estimated to be by burns and two-thirds of those who died were badly burned."

Lecast cleared his throat and swallowed heavily. The room was so silent that even the second sound was quite distinct. Calder sensed he was about to speak and waited.

"Let's get one thing absolutely straight," the PM boomed eventually. "You're talking about a circle, what, three and half miles across, totally consumed by fire?"

"That's correct."

"My God," said Corcorran slowly, "and you said it was a small bomb!"

Calder knew he used to be a lay-preacher. Crawford interrupted unexpectedly.

"About the smallest it is possible to make and still be reasonably effective."

All except Lecast and Stoddard looked at the elderly scientist, who was still looking at Calder. The latter caught his eye and decided it was friendly.

"And how would you reckon the survival rate of anyone within that circle?" persisted Lecast.

"It's very difficult to estimate," answered Calder, "but I'd rather do it at the end, if I may. I have so far only described the effect of thermal radiation. There are three other factors."

The audience fidgeted nervously. Stoddard was still avoiding his eyes. He heard the Prime Minister take a deep breath before replying.

"Carry on," he said flatly.

Calder nodded.

"The second effect, the shock or blast wave, would hit people within a second or so after the fireball. In ten seconds the blast would travel two and a half miles from ground zero and slow to about forty miles per hour. Its effect is similar to that experienced during an earthquake — basically, buildings collapsing and people being crushed. Indirectly, of course, it's another source of fire. In Nagasaki, buildings collapsed at 1.4 miles from ground zero and there was severe structural damage at 1.6 miles. I would expect that in London, severe structural damage would occur at up to one and a half miles, given average atmospheric conditions."

Calder noticed that Crawford was plucking at his lower lip, but he didn't say anything. Neither did anyone else. They were just gazing at the board meekly. He got the impression that the politicians had finally begun to appreciate something of the scale of things, and the worst was yet to come.

"Thirdly," continued Calder, trying to be matter-of-fact, "initial radiation. To begin with, and to simplify it a little, two types of radiation are produced — Gamma rays and Neutrons. Gamma rays travel with the fireball at the speed of light and are effective for about a minute, when they decay to relative insignificance. Neutrons travel slightly slower, but are just as effective and last just as long. With a twenty kiloton bomb, Gamma rays can be expected to travel for about two miles, but at that distance the effects are not very great, at least in the short-term. With our bomb, and at a distance of half a mile, you would experience 1,000 roentgens of radiation, which produces hundred-per-cent fatalities. After this distance the Gamma rays would decay very quickly. At three-quarters of mile, 300 roentgens would be experienced, which produces thirty-per-cent fatalities in two to six weeks. The effects for Neutrons would be similar."

Calder paused. There was no reaction from his audience and there didn't look like being any. Stoddard just stared at the whiteness of his blotter. Calder must seem, to him, like an armed robot, churning out revolting information. Why the hell had he made a study of this subject anyway? He hated it. And the listeners hated listening, although they were compelled to do so. He took a deep breath.

"Depending on the atmospheric conditions and distance from ground zero," he continued, "anything from two to eight feet of concrete would be necessary for protection against Gamma rays. They can penetrate almost anything. Even this would be less effective for Neutrons, although wet soil more so.

"However, this in no way covers the total effects of initial radiation because of the various effects of relatively low doses of radiation on the human body. I'll deal with those in a moment. In Japan, up to fifteen per cent of initial fatalities were thought to be the result of initial radiation."

Calder saw Lecast turn to Corcorran and the dark man returned his gaze. No expression passed between them that he could identify, but he knew what they were thinking. MacPherson looked sick. Stoddard could have given Calder a look of sympathy, but he didn't.

"The fourth and final effect is residual radiation. This is called 'local fallout' and only occurs with a ground-burst. So, since Hiroshima and Negasaki were both air-bursts, we have to rely on the evidence of American tests, although many countries, as you know, have exploded surface bombs.

"When a nuclear bomb is exploded in the air, all the residual radiation — usually Alpha and Beta particles — is taken straight up to the troposphere (fifty thousand feet) due to the updraft from the gigantic thermal. This is then carried by the wind and deposited in a few weeks, in very fine particles, over a wide area. It can even circle the globe in an easterly direction in four to seven weeks. Not enough is known about this tropospheric fallout, but it is thought to be so decayed and diluted as to be relatively harmless."

Calder looked at Crawford before adding:

"I'm not sure about that in the long term."

The elderly scientist made no reaction, but Benavici looked at him for the first and only time. Calder held his gaze for a few moments until he looked away. Then his hands began to move again.

"With a ground-burst, on the other hand," Calder went on, "which ours would almost certainly be, the residual radiation is taken up in the same way, but this time particles of earth and debris go with it and this is too heavy to remain in the air, let alone the troposphere, for very long. The Beta and Alpha particles become attached to this debris and fall back to earth in a steady shower. The rate at which they descend obviously depends on their weight and the strength of the wind, but they cause widespread contamination."

Stoddard had raised his head and was now looking at Calder. The General looked down again and nodded, as if he had finally grasped something that had been eluding him.

"This is really the sting in the tail," continued Calder, "because, in my view, it is potentially, in the sense of long-term fatalities, more effective, if that's the right word, than the other three effects put together."

Only the two scientists weren't staring at him now.

"With a fifteen mile per hour wind, which is 'normal', fifty per cent of the residual radiation would be expected to fall within two hundred miles of ground zero."

He felt everyone stiffen. MacPherson leant forward in his chair again and this time so did Corcorran.

"Downwind, at a distance of 2.3 miles, given a wind strength of fifteen miles per hour, everyone exposed would die, at 5.3 miles thirty per cent would die and at fifty miles some would die over a much longer period. At its widest point the radiation band would be about five miles."

Calder turned from writing the figures on the board. Benavici was still fidgeting, but everyone else was still. They weren't even blinking. He pushed on relentlessly.

"I am sure you know some of the long-term effects of a relatively small exposure to radiation, but I think it is worth mentioning them. Our knowledge here is rather shaky, but it is known that radiation causes death by leukaemia and other cancers. It can also cause cataracts, retardation of children, genetic mutations, bone defects and various other illnesses."

Stoddard was looking at him again.

"Plutonium has a half-life of 24,000 years. That's the time it takes for the nuclei to reduce their radioactivity by decay to one half. So plutonium lasts for hundreds of thousands of years before it decays to relative insignificance. It also produces various isotopes, some of which can get into the human body through the food and drink chain, from contaminated ground. And that contamination, as I've already mentioned, would be a narrow band anything up to two hundred miles from ground zero, depending on the weather.

"The number of roentgens needed to cause cancer is not known exactly, but it is known that plutonium workers and people who have been exposed near test sites in the United States and elsewhere have suffered, in proportion, much more than the general population. Some of the cases are well documented, some not. You, of course, know this to be true because you have had access, and I have not, to the unofficial reports of the recent Aldermaston and Windscale scares."

Again, Lecast and Corcorran looked at each other.

"Is there much more?" asked Lecast heavily.

"That's it," replied Calder.

He had tried to present it objectively and unemotionally, but that was getting progressively more difficult.

"To give you some idea of what I'm talking about, Hiroshima had a population of 255,000. Of these people, 70,000 were killed and the same number injured, some very severely. I would expect the percentage casualty rate from our bomb to be greater."

He paused, considering his next statement.

"I think it is also important to realize that I'm not just talking about the destruction of an area three and a half miles across, but also about the widespread contamination of a much larger area. In addition, if the wind is coming from the north, Alpha and Beta rays are going to cross the Channel and enter northern France."

"In my view," said the relentless Calder, "and this is an estimate based on many variables, no one in a circle a mile across would survive, two-thirds of those within a three-and-a-half mile circle would be killed or injured, but I think that just as great a number would eventually die from cancer from the radiation, or be affected in some way by it. Central London would be uninhabitable for many years — perhaps for ever — and widespread decontamination would be necessary in an area about five miles wide and over a hundred miles long. Deep ploughing can do something, but you cannot completely decontaminate an area by human means. Time is the only healer. A very long time. It would certainly mean depopulation.

"Finally, I must say that terrain and weather can make a great deal of difference to my figures and it might not be London at all. It might not even explode, but personally I wouldn't count on it."

With that he replaced the felt-tipped pen, returned the notes to his inside pocket and stood with his hands at his sides. The lecture was, at last, over.

No one spoke for at least ten seconds. Calder examined one of his hands and felt Stoddard looking at him. Finally, Crawford and Stiles looked to Lecast. The latter took another deep breath and scratched his forehead.

"Well," he said, "I don't know about anyone else but I could do with a cup of coffee."

"A stiff whisky would be more to my liking," said Corcorran. He turned to Calder. "You tell a nasty tale."

The Defence Minister was looking at him, Calder felt, rather as he would a creature that had crawled from under a rock. He looked back steadily and said nothing. Lecast pushed a button on the table intercom.

"Let's have some coffee in here," he said simply, removed his finger and interlaced it with the others. Then he looked around the table. A sea shore stone probably had more expression than he had on his face. He spoke very quietly.

"Shall we not concern ourselves with details, but with the overall concepts?" He paused. "Dr Crawford. Is there anything you wish to say?"

The elderly scientist gathered his thoughts and looked at the table as he spoke.

"I wouldn't disagree fundamentally with anything that Mr Calder has said. However, there are one or two details...." He looked at Lecast and smiled. "Scientists," he said, "are even more notorious than politicians for their lack of unanimity."

Only Stiles laughed — a sort of short guffaw. It occurred to Calder that Crawford was only second to Stiles as the most relaxed man in the room.

"I wonder though," continued Crawford, "whether I can ask Mr Calder to bear in mind two points, if he will forgive my arrogance. As they are details, largely concerned with rainfall and humidity, I will send them to him rather than bore you all."

He turned to Lecast before continuing and looked him straight in the eye.

"In relation to the overall catastrophe, Mr Calder is quite right. It would be the worst in British history, if we discount things like the Black Plague. What you do about it is up to you, of course, Prime Minister, but this bomb must not be exploded."

Calder thought that his earlier estimate of Crawford's calmness might have been wrong. Moreover, no matter how he flowered his language, there was no doubt that he was telling Lecast what to do.

"Thank you, Dr Crawford," said the PM. "Dr Benavici?"

The nervous, dark man sat up as if someone had kicked him in the back. He moved his lips for a few seconds before anything came out.

"I have nothing to add," he said eventually in an English public-school accent.

"Well, Doctors," said Lecast, "if there is nothing more...."

Both scientists moved their chairs back and stood up. Benavici turned and walked straight out. Crawford walked up to Calder with his arm outstretched. The latter shook it. The elderly scientist held on for a fraction longer than was normal and looked into Calder's face. He nodded very slightly, turned and left. Calder thought he had an ally and felt pleasantly surprised. Lecast motioned him to sit down and he began to wonder why he too hadn't been asked to leave.

"Now we have dealt with the accuracy of what Mr Calder said, we can decide what we are going to do," stated Lecast firmly.

He looked down at the table suddenly.

"I'm sorry, Mr Calder. I am forgetting my manners. You have shocked me so much, I don't mind telling you, that I have not thanked you for explaining things, at such short notice. I don't know about the others, but I do feel that I now know what we could be in for. From what Sir Giles tells me, you found the process of telling it just as gruesome as we did listening."

He glanced awkwardly at Corcorran.

"But it had to be done and for that I'm grateful."

Stiles nodded. Stoddard had renewed his acquaintance with the blotter.

At this point there was a knock at the door and a coffee trolley was wheeled in, equipped with tea as well. Lecast stood up and so did the others. No one spoke as they helped themselves. It was almost as if the crisis didn't exist or had been relegated to second place and Calder couldn't help wondering at this most English of habits. He tried to imagine it happening in the Oval Office or the Kremlin. The trolley was left where it was and they returned to the table.

"Of one thing I have absolutely no doubt," said Lecast seriously. "We must give in to them, whatever their demands. The sort of disaster we have just had described is too appalling to contemplate."

"I agree," said Stiles. "Holding out to hijackers is one thing, but this is substantively different."

MacPherson nodded.

"You are sure there is going to be a threat, Sir Giles?" asked Lecast.

Everyone looked at Stoddard. He hadn't said a word yet and his pipe was out of sight. Calder found that odd now he focused on it. The General looked up at Calder, then at Lecast.

"Yes, sir, I am. Probably in the next twenty-four hours."

He paused.

"It may seem odd, but we have to be grateful for one thing. As you know, Prime Minister, we are pretty sure that they are not terrorists. If they were, the political demands they might make would be more difficult to meet, and might even be impossible to comply with if they involved a foreign power. And, even if terrorist demands were met, you could never be completely sure that they wouldn't explode the bomb anyway. We are almost certain that their leader, Brown, will be after one thing — money. And he won't come cheap."

"So we have got to hand over to a gangster," said Corcorran bitterly.

"Oh, you can be sure of one thing, sir," answered Stoddard. "Ruthless Brown may be, but he is not a gangster. He has one of the most calculating and brilliant minds I have ever come across."

"Is this why your investigations have not found him?" persisted Corcorran.

Stoddard hesitated. Calder knew that Corcorran had some direct control over the foreign security services, like MI6 and the myriad of foreign off-shoots, but that Stoddard reported mainly to the Home Secretary and the PM.

"Since we found the workshop last night," answered Stoddard, "in which the device was made, we have lost all trace. We have a few ongoing investigations up our sleeve, but, to be frank, I'm not hopeful."

Corcorran opened his mouth again, but Stiles got in before him. "How would it be detonated?"

Stoddard immediately looked at Calder with a sort of priestly smile which the latter found a little disarming. He replaced his cup on its saucer, leant his forearms on the table and proceeded to answer the question that he had already settled in his own mind.

"It could be done by a variety of means. It could be pre-set to detonate at a given time, but I think that's unlikely. Brown wouldn't have any flexibility and that wouldn't suit him at all. Alternatively, it could be plugged into the telephone system and exploded by dialling a certain number. But...."

Lecast interrupted.

"Just a minute. You mean it could be detonated by mistake, by someone simply dialling the wrong number?" he asked incredulously.

Calder nodded.

"It's possible," he said. "I don't think Brown will use that method though, partly because of the reason you mention, partly because it's subject to too many potential mechanical breakdowns." His mouth twisted into a grin. "Telephones are sometimes out of order. But the main reason is because it wouldn't be mobile. It would have to stay in a building, plugged into the telephone system and Brown himself would have to stay near a phone. Mobility may be important to him, so he will probably use a radio signal. He can tune a receiver to a certain signal, at a certain pitch, on a certain frequency. The odds on that signal being made by accident are astronomical. With micro-technology the receiver need not be very big at all. Then all he would need is a powerful enough medium frequency transmitter and he could send the vital signal over huge distances."

"Good Lord," said Lecast, "he could be in another country."

"Yes," said Calder. "He wouldn't even need to be by the transmitter. He could still keep his mobility. All he would need is a simple VHF transmitter, which would give him a fair distance and would fit into the palm of his hand. The tuner would be pre-set and locked on to the medium frequency transmitter. All he would have to do would be to press a button, the VHF signal would be sent to the big transmitter, recognized and translated, then a medium frequency signal would be sent to the receiver attached to the bomb. Within a second of him pressing the button the bomb would explode and he would be nowhere near it."

Lecast silently drew his hands over his face, stretching the skin. Corcorran still looked as if he wanted to kill someone. MacPherson looked sick. Stoddard merely looked at his blotter. Stiles, who was leaning back comfortably in his chair, switched his gaze from Calder.

"Sir Giles," he said, "what makes you think that Brown will not set off the bomb anyway?"

Calder looked at Stiles as he refilled his pipe from a tobacco pouch resting on the ample folds of his stomach. He could have been in his front room at home with his favourite slippers on.

"I don't think he is that type of man," answered Stoddard.

He must have thought to himself that that sounded a bit lame.

"Besides, he has no reason to do so if he gets his money. But the truth is, I admit, we simply don't know for certain."

He looked at Lecast and then back at Stiles before continuing. The confident smile was still there.

"We will continue to look for him and we may find him. But if we don't, as you said, we must pay up and hope. In the meantime there are measures which we can take. To begin with, we can seal off all the inner cities and search them thoroughly and meticulously. We can also check all traffic, in and out. Manpower might be a problem, but we still have the troops standing by in Norfolk."

Lecast and Corcorran swapped glances as Stoddard continued.

"I agree with Mr Calder that London is the most likely target and, after that, other inner cities. Brown may choose to demolish a small town. We don't know. But we have to make a start somewhere. One thing is certain: he is not going to tell us what city it is in, even when we get his demands. That means, incidentally, that evacuation will be impossible."

He paused to let that sink in. Calder noticed that Corcorran was glaring at the General.

"We may find it by searching every dwelling and building in the inner cities," continued Stoddard, "and we need to instigate a search of every sizeable vehicle in every part of the UK. I am told that it can fit into the boot of a big car."

He looked at Calder, who wasn't surprised that there was no reaction to that statement. They'd had too many shocks. Even so, he *was* surprised that no one had asked about its size. Stiles lit his pipe.

"These measures, Sir Giles," said Corcorran, his face like thunder, "will totally disrupt the economy and social life of Britain. This will be much bigger even than your little affair in Norfolk, which eventually found the place too late. The country will literally come to a standstill. People will die from lack of mobility."

Calder felt angry. And why was the hawk suddenly playing the dove? He glanced at Stoddard, whose face was still set in its relaxed smile. To a stranger it would look like a callous disregard for human dignity.

"Yes," said Stoddard, "they might, but that, in my view, is infinitely preferable to the loss of hundreds of thousands of lives."

Stoddard, the General, weighing up human sacrifices, apparently without a care. Lecast came in quickly, glancing at his Defence Minister.

"I think you're being a little unfair, John. After all, it very nearly succeeded. We only missed them by about six hours and that in itself shows it was justified. But," looking at Stoddard now, "I also think John has a point here, Giles. If you feel that Brown is not going to use the bomb if we submit to his demands, why institute these terribly drastic measures, which have very little chance of success?"

It was a good question, that Calder knew he wouldn't like to answer. They all looked at the General, who seemed in no hurry to reply. Corcorran was leaning back and peering at him down his nose.

On the car journey from Norfolk, Calder had found out some more about Stoddard. He had a firm idea of his place in the order of things, having no hesitation about calling people "sir" and expecting his subordinates to do the same with him. Calder, apparently, was one of the growing list of exceptions — "a younger generation that has inherited a different and more confusing world". Stoddard was English to the core and fiercely patriotic, believing in British-type "democracy", the monarchy and public schools, and probably wore his considerable array of medals on Armistice Sunday. But he had far too robust an intellect to be fanatical and was aware that the system had flaws. Calder was mildly surprised to find that he understood the differences between Marx and the type of "socialism" practised in the Soviet Union and Eastern Europe, as well as the similarities. He also recognized that "Communism" had many advantages over "Capitalism", but, on balance, preferred Adam Smith to Lenin and, having made the decision, was prepared to defend it to the death.

Eventually, the General lifted his head from the blotter and placed his clasped hands upon it. When he spoke, it was with total confidence, as if he had just come down from Mount Sinai.

"Quite simply because we cannot afford to take the risk. We don't know what his demands are yet and, besides, until we know his set-up, we can never be *sure* that he won't explode it anyway. If he did, it would certainly take care of earnest pursuit."

He paused and seemed to look at Corcorran.

"We cannot gamble with hundreds of thousands of lives. I realize that you have political responsibilities, but this is war. A rather warped war admittedly, but a war nonetheless, which has the classic symptom of killing the innocent rather than the guilty. And in war one has to make decisions which involve human lives. It's crude, calculated and barbaric, but it's necessary. You have to sacrifice some people so that more will live. In war, it is the one factor that makes a leader different from his subordinates and the main reason why he ages more quickly."

Calder had never known Stoddard to be so profound, yet he was perfectly calm. It was emotive, but unemotional. The mild smile had not left his face the whole time. Lecast and MacPherson were looking at the General, and Corcorran at the table. Stiles, Calder noticed, was staring across at Stoddard, his mouth slightly open, his forgotten pipe going out as it lay in his palm on the table.

"I agree," said the smoker suddenly.

Lecast looked at him and then at his Home Secretary. MacPherson took a long time before he nodded, his face deathly pale.

"What do *you* think, Mr Calder?" Lecast asked.

Calder felt that the PM hadn't yet made up his mind and that the question was more a breathing space, to allow him to do so, than because he really wanted his opinion. But then, he realized that he was appalled at the prospect of the totalitarian state that the General was advocating, however temporary it might be. And would it just be temporary, when the Plutonium Economy really arrived? The point was that they shouldn't be in the position now where they were forced to consider such measures. However, since they were, was it the lesser of two evils? Could he vote against Stoddard?

They were waiting for his reply. He felt Stoddard's eyes on him and he looked at him, in turn. Then he knew that his boss knew exactly what he was thinking.

"I agree with the General," he said flatly, wondering whether he did or not.

They were expecting him to continue, but he had nothing more to say. Stiles flicked his lighter and relit his pipe. Lecast stretched the skin on his face again and glanced at Corcorran. The latter looked up and shook his head violently. Calder suddenly appreciated what a difficult job being Prime Minster was. The Premier blinked rapidly for several seconds, then turned to his Minister of Defence and spoke in a resigned tone.

"Sorry, John." Then he looked up at Stoddard. "Very well, Sir Giles. I shall have to inform the whole Cabinet, of course, and decide what to release to the press, but that's my problem."

He paused, then said:

"I didn't think we'd be re-elected anyway."

It took a few moments for that to sink in, but when it did, Calder flushed with anger. Then the PM smiled and Calder realized that it had been a joke. Stiles chuckled, removed his pipe and blew a smoke-ring at the ceiling.

"In that case," he said, his mouth curling up at the edges, "we can't do anything until we hear from our 'gangster' friend." And he winked slyly at Calder.

Chapter 16
Thursday, 22 May, p.m.

MOTORWAY SERVICE stations are much the same wherever you are and this one, on the M6, was no exception. The tarmac and concrete were littered with oil stains, the petrol was expensive, the toilets were just clean enough, but smelt occasionally and the food was passably non-exciting. But then, what more could you do with a place where folks never stayed, just passed through?

For the four travellers, however, it was a welcome, lunchtime respite from the boredom of motorway travel. The cafeteria was about a third full and emptying as the diners finished their meals. Martin, Mac, Sash and Judy were taking their time over their second cup of coffee. They were in no hurry to get to their destination. None was noted as having a garrulous nature and conversation had died. Mac and Judy sat opposite each other, near the window and gazed out. Martin and Sash beside them stared into their cups. The only notable thing about them was that all the men had beards.

Judy had thought about standing up and shouting rape, but that had no guarantee of success. They could simply inflict pain surreptitiously and tell anyone who inquired that she was drunk or insane. A man had arrived in a yellow sports car about half an hour earlier. She'd thought about chatting him up as he left, on the pretext of going to the loo. But that was even more risky. The timing was too exacting and, although he looked brave enough, you could never tell with men.

"This needs livening up a bit," said Mac.

He reached inside his coat, extracting the familiar metal flask and poured a generous helping into his cup.

"You'll get us arrested," said Martin, but he didn't seem too concerned.

Finally, Judy had decided that it had to be done by going to the ladies' loo. Once inside she had a number of possibilities. The windows might be big enough for her to climb through, but she doubted it. Besides, they would probably check them. She had £150 in her purse. She could try and buy a disguise — an exchange of clothes — but again there were problems. Women were notoriously fussy about giving up their clothes and wearing others, even for £150. That, of course, was providing the clothes fitted in the first place and qualified as a disguise. It was a possibility, no more.

The most likely solution was to ask the first woman she came upon to call the police, on the grounds that she was being followed, then lock herself in a cubicle. What could Martin and co do? It was a little primitive, but then John always said that the best plans were based on simple principles. It would serve him right if she took a leaf out of his book. Anyway, it was the only thing she could think of that might really work.

She willed herself to act naturally, stubbed out her cigarette and turned to Sash, sitting beside her.

"I take it I can go to the loo?" she asked sarcastically.

She hoped it wasn't too strong, but then she'd been locked up in her room for nearly a week and she was expected to be bad-tempered.

Sash looked at Martin, who nodded. The pilot stood up and watched Judy wriggle out of the booth. When she had left, Martin looked up.

"Don't sit down, Sash lad," he said and tossed his head at the retreating figure in short, summer frock and matching shoes. "Your turn, I believe," he added. "No need to check the windows — I've already done it."

He smiled inanely and Sash did the same. He didn't like this thing with Judy, but then what could he do?

She stopped in the foyer, ostensibly to look for the toilet sign and saw that Sash was about twenty-five yards behind. She turned a corner and, for a fleeting moment, thought about dashing for the door. Her watchdog would think she had entered the Ladies. She would have at least five minutes' start and she knew she'd get a lift within minutes. But it was just too far. He would have turned the corner before she got to the entrance. No, there was only one place to go. She stopped at the door with the doll monogram and looked back. Sash was standing at the corner, watching. He looked slightly embarrassed and could not hold her gaze. She pushed the door and walked through.

A woman left as she entered and then she realized, in a moment of panic, that she was alone. There was no one in sight. She examined all the locks on the cubicle doors and they all read "vacant", so she turned and looked at the entrance-door. She would talk to the first person through.

Just then a small, round woman with short-cropped, mousy-coloured hair entered, opening her bag as she did so. Judy rushed up, making the woman retreat a few steps and leading her to drop her bag in the process. There was sheer terror in her eyes.

"Please, you must telephone the police. I'm being held prisoner. I don't know what they might do to me."

The stricken woman hesitated, clearly torn between the apparently genuine agitation in the fair-haired woman and the thought that she might be mad. She looked down at her fallen bag. Judy bent down and picked it up.

"There's a man outside," she said, "with fair hair and a beard. He's one of them, and please, you must ring. Dial 999."

The woman looked at her bag, still in Judy's hands, then at the cubicles. She bit her lower lip, snatched her bag, looked again at the frightened Judy and left quickly.

"Please hurry," called Judy as the woman was halfway through the door, then looked in her own bag for her purse. She prayed that she had a two-pence piece, found one, let herself into a cubicle and locked it.

Outside, the woman looked round. Over by the entrance there *was* a man with fair hair and a beard and he did appear to be watching the Ladies. He was certainly watching her now. She looked around for a phone, then back again. He didn't look like a villain though. Rather a nice-looking man actually, with similar colouring to the woman. She'd ask her husband.

Sash had observed the woman exit the toilet rather swifly and then stop. She'd only entered a few moments before. She began to stare at him, then glanced at the telephone and back at him again. He acted on impulse and walked up to the woman, smiling. She seemed rooted to the spot, her eyes wide. He put on his best public school accent.

"Don't tell me," he said, "she gave you the man-following-her routine again and will-you-please-telephone the police. Am I right?"

The woman smiled too, relieved.

"Yes," she answered and then, a little more carefully: "You know her?"

Sash let out a short, polite laugh.

"I'm her brother," he said. Then his face became serious. "She has been in and out of hospital all her life. I had a feeling she was going to do something like this. That's why I stationed myself outside."

He looked at the toilet door and sighed.

"She really believes it, you see. The last time was at Heathrow. We all spent the night in jail. Usually, when we travel, Mother comes now, but," he lowered his head, "that wasn't possible this time."

Sash smiled again, bravely.

"How will you get her out?" asked the woman.

"Suppose I shall have to call the police myself and ask them to bring a policewoman along."

His smile broadened.

"Perhaps they'll believe me if *I* phone *them*," he added. "Sorry you have been troubled."

His face took on a new seriousness, he nodded his thanks and walked over to the public telephone. She turned and looked at the loo door. Well, she wasn't going back in there again. She'd just have to last until the next service stop. She walked back into the restaurant, passing the nice man as he was dialling.

Sash placed his finger on the bar just as someone said, "Emergency, which service?" He suddenly realized that his heart was racing. He hadn't thought that he had it in him. It was because he did it without thinking, he supposed. He couldn't go in to tell the others about the problem, because it would look suspicious to the woman. But then he didn't have to move anyway. When neither he nor Judy returned, they'd come running soon enough.

He had waited about three minutes, still with the phone to his ears, when he noticed the woman returning. Beside her, incongruously, was a man as tall as Martin. Two kids followed in their wake. He saw her pointing at him out of the corner of his eye. His heart did a somersault and landed on its back. The man was looking at him suspiciously. Sash waved at the woman and began talking rubbish into the phone, putting on a look of frustration. To his immense relief they walked past.

He watched them go and replaced the phone, repositioning himself outside the Ladies. Within a minute, Martin and Mac arrived.

"What's up?" asked Martin knowingly.

He told him.

"Jesus Christ," said Mac. "That's all we need. If we had no' had to pick up that gear in Manchester we'd be there already."

"Where's this woman now?" asked Martin.

"She's left with her family."

"Good. We can't cause a fuss," said the tall man, looking at the toilet door. "But we've got to make an effort."

Mac swore at the floor again.

"If we have to make the choice," continued Martin, "between leaving her here and being arrested ourselves, we leave her here. None of us has told her where we're going, have we?"

They both shook their heads.

"What's more, she doesn't know where the bomb is. Only three people know that: John, Wilson and Vaisey. He knows what he's doing, does John. Jeeze though, I wish he was here now."

He bit his lip. He had to decide what to do.

"You did well, Sash," he said. "But you've got to have a final go."

"What do you mean?" asked the fair-haired man suspiciously. "What do you want me to do, walk in there and bring her out?"

"Judy's case is in the car," said Martin. "Go and get it and take it into the Gents. Lock yourself in a cubicle and...."

"You've got to be joking," said Sash indignantly.

"It's got to be you, Sash. You're the only one who can even get near her size and your blond beard doesn't show as much as ours. You should be all right if you keep your hands over your face."

"And I suppose that is going to look perfectly natural," said Sash.

He crossed his arms in obstinate disobedience.

"I can't do it," he said.

Martin closed in on one side and Mac on the other.

"Oh, yes, you will," said Martin, "because I'm telling you to."

"Besides," added Mac through broken teeth, "you're prettier than we are."

Martin pulled out the car keys. Then he had second thoughts and they disappeared back in his pocket.

"I'll walk over to the car with you," he said. "Mac will stay here and make sure she doesn't slip away. When you've got into something suitably feminine, bring the suitcase out with you, repacked with your clothes as well, and give it to me. When you go in, we'll be waiting over the far side, by the service exit, so that no one can read our number. If anything goes wrong, run for the car."

Sash had become resolved to the idea.

"How do I know you won't just run without me?" he asked, suddenly seeing a picture of himself, dressed up in woman's clothes at a motorway service station and stuck without a car.

Martin sighed.

"For the same reason, stupid, that we're taking so much trouble to keep hold of Judy. You know even more than she does. Come on, let's go."

Martin had been officer material in the Army. Brown had implied it. An ability to show initiative in tricky situations, he had said. Yes, he could have made lieutenant. The plan was excellent in the circumstances and, as he walked over to the car, he felt strangely elated. If he thought there was anything odd about being more pleased with the plan than he was disturbed at losing the reason for that plan, he didn't show it. He also hadn't considered one of the basic rules of command: that even the most brilliant scheme was only as good as the men who carried it out. Being officer material was not the same as being an officer.

Judy, meanwhile, was getting worried. She had lost count of how many minutes had passed since she had locked herself in the cubicle. Surely the police should be here by now? They had patrols going up and down the motorway all the time, didn't they? She had a minor heart-attack every time the door opened, which it did with amazing frequency. But surely Martin wouldn't come into the Ladies to get her?

She was fairly sure the place was temporarily empty when the door opened again. Almost immediately she felt her door being tried.

"Hello," said a voice. "This is the police. Was it you who called us?"

Relief flooded through Judy and she reached for the bolt. Then something stopped her. The voice sounded female, but there was something about it that she couldn't put her finger on. She stood back, her heart thumping in her chest. There was no harm in being cautious.

"How do I know you're police?" she asked defiantly.

There was a muffled expletive and a body slammed against her door. The bolt held. She heard the door of the next cubicle being tried, then *her* cubicle became dimmer as someone appeared over the door. There was the sound of material ripping. She looked up, terrified, unable to shout. It was Sash, his head in the hood of a cloak and one leg astride the door. Suddenly a woman screamed.

Sash had been wise enough to don long clothes. The dress reached the floor on Judy, but it didn't on him. His shoulders were scrunched up at an odd angle, although his hips were all right. Over this he had put a coarse, dark cloak he had found, and put the hood up. It hid a multitude of sins. Unfortunately, the one thing he could not get to fit him were Judy's shoes. She took a size five and, although Sash was not a particularly big man, there was no way his size eights could be squeezed in. So he had left his shoes and socks on. and hoped they wouldn't show under the cloak.

The woman had entered the room just as Sash lifted his leg up on top of the door. Her attention was immediately drawn by the sound of the dress ripping down the back, but she couldn't really have missed him anyway. What she saw was a muscular leg, covered in short, blond hairs, wearing a man's shoe and sock, halfway over a toilet cubicle. She did the thing that came naturally and screamed.

Sash realized, in that moment, that he had failed. He could, just possibly, have forced Judy out and to the car while they were perfectly anonymous, but with a hue-and-cry already instigated it was impossible. He, too, did what came naturally and ran — past the screaming lady at the door, past the staring, incredulous by-standers in the foyer, into a startled, portly gentleman entering the building and sending him flying, past the petrol pumps and across the seventy or so yards of tarmac to the waiting car. A rear door opened as he approached and he dived in. The vehicle then accelerated away, past the "No Entry" signs, up the ramp of the access road and away to the distant countryside. In the Ladies, the woman was still screaming.

Fifteen minutes later, Judy had become accustomed to the hum of voices on the other side of the door. One or two phrases she could hear distinctly, like, "poor girl", and, "the police have been called". But she was still shaking.

The voices became hushed and there was a knock on the door.

"Open up now. This is the police."

Judy was trying to concentrate. A woman's voice again. Fearfully, she repeated her last question.

"How do I know you're police?"

She heard someone sigh loudly, then:

"Anyone got 2p?... Ah, thanks, luv."

A coin was placed in a lock meter and she heard the door of the cubicle next to hers being opened. Then someone stood on the toilet seat. She daren't look this time.

"What's the problem, luv?" came the voice from above.

Judy did look up. The black and white squares on the policewoman's hat were unmistakable and underneath them a friendly, chubby face smiled down.

"'Ave ya got the runs?" it asked.

Judy burst into tears.

Calder emerged from his bedroom in underpants and switched on the television. He was just in time to hear the newscaster say, "Good evening".

"The government has announced," continued the newsreader, "that the inner city areas of nine major cities in England have been cordoned off and are at this moment being systematically searched. All traffic in and out of these areas is being checked and traffic on all roads is similarly being stopped."

The picture switched from a studio to an outside broadcast unit, showing a long queue of traffic waiting to leave inner London.

"Large queues are already developing as motorists, caught unawares by the surprise decision, are waiting to drive home. Apparently public transport is not affected and motorists have been advised to use buses, the underground and trains tomorrow morning. All private vehicles should leave the inner city areas tonight though, if they usually do so, otherwise the boots of these cars are likely to be broken into. By the same token, motorists living within these inner city areas are advised not to stray too far from their vehicles until further notice."

The newsreader came back on.

"The government have apologized for the inconvenience and say it is a training exercise."

A picture of MacPherson, looking at least ten years younger than he had that morning, appeared and, alongside him, the typewritten government statement.

"According to an official statement from the Home Office: 'The Government was taken by surprise by the plutonium hijacking on the 5th of this month and must be sure that they can handle a similar emergency again. Such security measures, by their very nature, must operate with surprise. Hence it was not possible to give any advance warning, even though it is only a training exercise. The government apologizes for the obvious inconvenience, which will last three to four days, and hope that the necessity will be understood.'"

"Meanwhile," went on the broadcaster, "nine of England's major cities — London, Birmingham, Manchester, Liverpool, Sheffield, Leeds, Newcastle upon Tyne, Southampton and Bristol — are sealed off. Towns and cities in Wales and Scotland are unaffected, but they are subject to road-blocks."

"They'll never get away with it," said Ann.

He turned. She was leaning seductively against the door-jamb, wearing one of his best white shirts, the tails covering her front and back to a point about a third down her thighs. The side slit left a tantalizing strip of flesh up the hip and her nipples pushed proudly against the material, creating deep shadows. He forced his mind back to her statement.

"Probably not in the long term," he said, "but what else can Lecast say? That all those inner cities are in danger of being devastated by a nuclear bomb?"

She shrugged heavily. The shirt rode up and her breasts quivered.

"Coffee?" he asked, not taking his eyes off her.

She nodded and smiled.

He wandered into the kitchen. When he came out she was sitting primly on the couch, leaving just that little bit to the imagination. The screen showed the Queen opening a new hospital in Northampton. They both watched moronically. The kettle boiled and Calder returned to the kitchen. *Nationwide* had begun when he got back. Ann made to speak, but he waved her to silence as he listened to their proposed programme.

"Sorry," he said, placing a coffee in front of her. "It would appear that they are not going to discuss it. Were there any announcements made about special programmes later on?"

"No," she answered. "That appears to be it."

"Then the BBC and IBA and the press must be in on the cover-up. The Government must have come down really hard, or perhaps they simply let them in on the secret and they're doing their best to stop panic. They'd leap at the story otherwise. Infringements on individual liberty and all that. It's the only way they can hope to keep it from leaking out too soon. It doesn't take a great deal of grey-matter to work out why these cities are being sealed off less than three weeks after a plutonium hijacking. Journalists must be eating their pencils in frustration and it would soon come out in a studio discussion."

Ann frowned.

"Individuals up and down the country must be suspicious now," continued Calder, "especially after the 'training exercise' in Norfolk. You're right. They can't hope to get away with it, in the long term, but they might just pull it off for three or four days, and that's all the time we shall need."

He paused and grinned. She was glad when the telephone rang.

It was 10 p.m. when Striker pulled into the police station, which was not bad going. The traffic had been heavy from central London to the M1, but once on the motorway he had broken the speed limit the whole way, apart from two sections where there was only one lane open because of repairs. Two hours and five minutes later he was at the Stoke turn-off. There had been one cordon and two road-blocks on the way, but each time he had been able to use the police access lane and they had hardly held him up at all. The biggest problem had been finding the right police station. Stoke, it appeared, was not just Stoke. It consisted, in fact, of five towns, only one of which was Stoke, but all of which, together, went under the generic title of Stoke.

He noticed the desk-sergeant come involuntarily to attention as he walked in. Stoddard had obviously been on the phone to smooth his path. The sergeant put on his responsibility face.

"My name is Striker. I think you are expecting me."

If the uniformed man was surprised at the American accent, he didn't show it.

"Yes, sir," he answered, pushing a button on his desk. "Superintendent Bridges is in charge, sir."

Striker looked round and took his bearings. It was interesting how police stations looked the same, wherever you were. Similarity of function he supposed. But he was not allowed to elaborate on these reflections, because a man came out of a side door. He was about forty, with fine, sandy hair and a clipped moustache.

"Bridges," he said simply.

"Striker."

They shook hands and the blond man showed his identification. Bridges nodded and ushered him through a different door. They walked down a corridor and Striker was told what had happened at the service station. Apparently there were no clues as to the identification of the vehicle or its subsequent journey.

"How is she?" asked Striker.

The Superintendent hesitated.

"Quite well, physically, although she won't eat anything — just drinks tea. She put up quite a fit of hysterics when the arresting WPC went off duty. Taken quite a liking to her. Only person she'd speak to, in fact. Hasn't said a word since she left."

He stopped outside a door marked "D" and lowered his voice.

"She refused to tell us at first who she was. It was when we told her that in that case we might as well release her that she told us some of the story. When she mentioned the name Brown, we at first didn't believe it. We questioned her a bit more."

He lowered his head.

"I don't think we were too hard. Anyway, she said enough for us to realize that she was probably telling the truth, so we left it there and phoned you people."

He looked unhappy, but whether it was about the girl, Striker wasn't sure.

"I'll go in alone if you don't mind?" said the American.

Bridges nooded and opened the door. It was an interrogation room, about fifteen feet square. The walls were off-white and totally bare. In the centre was a Formica-covered table and two canvas chairs. Sitting on one, facing the far wall, was the girl, her head held in her hands. She didn't stir as he came in. The woman police constable left.

Striker closed the door and walked round to the girl. She looked up at him. What he saw was a strained but attractive face. The skin under the eyes was a puffy red and a rather poor attempt had been made to repair the tear-stained make-up. The eyes themselves were bloodshot and frightened, and the tousled, fair hair could have done with a comb.

She put her hands on the table and sat back, her eyes not leaving him as he sat down.

"Hello," he said, searching her face for a reaction.

She said nothing, just looked at him. He glanced at the table and back at her face. He spoke very softly.

"I'll lay it on the line for you. My name is Peter Striker and, as you can no doubt gather from my accent, I'm not with the police. At least, not exactly."

She looked at the table.

"I've come from London," continued Striker. "I have a car outside and I'd like you to drive back with me tonight."

She looked at him again.

"I'm going to ask you a few questions now, some of which you've already been asked. They won't last long and then I won't ask you any more. At least, not until you've had a good night's sleep. You can snooze in the car if you like. It's quite comfortable."

He paused.

"They are very important questions. A lot of people's lives may depend on them. Do you understand?"

He saw the fear come back into her eyes again.

"Where did the hijack take place?" he asked quickly.

She hesitated a long time. Then her eyes flickered from side to side.

"Carlisle Airport," she said.

It was a pleasant voice. He found placing British accents difficult, but hers sounded like what most southerners call "northern".

"How did you leave the plane?" he asked.

He saw the fear again — or was it terror?

"Parachute." The voice was breathless. "Into the sea."

That almost settled it. He waited for a few moments, his eyes never leaving her.

"Do you know what we're looking for?"

"John Brown," she answered plainly.

"Do you know where he is, or any of his gang?"

She shook her head. "No. They didn't trust me."

"So you have no idea where the bomb is either?"

"No," she said immediately. "I wish I did. Believe me, please."

He smiled before answering. "I do."

He saw a window open in her face and, inextricably, felt himself blush. She seemed to smile.

"That's all for now," he said quietly, looking down at the table, then up again. "Will you come with me?"

"Yes," she answered and stood up to reinforce it.

He followed suit.

"It's a three-hour journey," he said. "Perhaps you'd like to...."

"Yes, I would," she said, still looking at him.

He walked past her to the door. Outside, the WPC was waiting patiently.

"Would you show this lady to the toilet? I'll meet her at the desk."

Judy scrutinized him closely as she passed and he watched her walk carefully up the corridor. The final confirmation. He met with Bridges, signed her release papers and received a photocopy of the transcript of all her statements.

She looked different when she returned. Her hair was still in disarray, but the face was clean and some of the strain had gone. The desk-sergeant handed over her bag and Striker removed his anorak.

"You'd better put this on," he said. "It's cold outside."

She looked at him closely again, then turned as he slipped it over her shoulders.

They walked out into the night. There was a fresh scent in the air. She stopped on the step for him and he placed an arm around her. He didn't consciously do it. It just seemed the most obvious thing to do.

Chapter 17
Friday, 23 May, a.m.

AT 9.25 A.M. a man wearing dark glasses and a red and white bobble-hat, walked through the front door of the *Daily Express* offices in Fleet Street. He headed straight for the porter's desk and handed over a small package, about two and a half inches by four, and half an inch in depth. It was wrapped in brown paper.

The porter took it suspiciously.

"For the Editor," said the man and left.

The porter turned it over, weighed it in his hand and shook it. He shrugged his shoulders and put it to one side. Then he picked it up again. It was marked "Urgent". Well, the messenger, would be back soon.

Along the street the man entered a phone box. He brought out a piece of paper from his coat pocket, lifted the phone and dialled. He replaced the paper and fished in his pocket for a coin. A 10p piece came between his fingers and he extracted it, pushing it into the slot as the pips sounded.

"News desk, please," he said.

There was a short pause.

"Hello. A small package has just arrived at the porter's desk, addressed to 'The Editor' and marked 'urgent'. If I were you I wouldn't waste any time in opening it."

Upstairs in the newspaper offices, the young reporter stared at the dead phone, replaced it, scratched his head, then headed for the stairs.

In the lobby, the porter was still waiting for the messenger to return when the journalist walked up.

"Have you just received a small package for the Editor?" asked the young man.

The porter picked it up. "It seems all right."

"I'll take it," said the other.

The porter handed it over and watched the man depart. He shrugged his shoulders again and returned to his paperwork.

Upstairs, the reporter tore off the brown paper. He had no hesitation about opening it — the editor was in a meeting and so were the rest of the senior staff. And, after all, it *was* marked "Urgent". Inside was a cassette tape. He dragged over his own portable machine, slotted in the tape and switched on. Anyone observing him might have noticed him stiffen. They would certainly have seen his eyes get wider as he sat motionless.

After four or five minutes he stopped the machine and looked at the door marked "Editor". So they were in an important meeting, but he could interrupt them for this. It had to be the hottest thing he'd ever got his hands on. He grabbed his portable, walked briskly to the door, knocked and walked in without waiting for a reply.

The call came through for Striker at 10.50. A man entered the room where he was interviewing Judy with a colleague. The blond man looked up and switched off the tape-recorder. The man approached and placed a hand on his shoulder.

"The Old Man wants you. In his office."

Striker looked across at Judy. They had arrived back in London in the early hours. She had slept most of the journey and, rather than take her to the Department, they had gone straight to his flat. She had had a bath and then a good night's sleep, while he had tossed fitfully on the sofa. In the morning they had showered and breakfasted slowly, then done a little shopping in order for Judy to buy some articles of clothing. They had arrived at the Department at 10 o'clock. He had insisted that he conduct the "interrogation" and, to his surprise, found that he had no opposition. He was fairly sure she wasn't going to add to their knowledge in any vital area, but it had to be done nonetheless.

"I'll have to go now," he said to her.

She nodded.

"I'll be back soon and we'll carry on."

She nodded again.

"See if you can find some coffee will you, Jim?" he said to the man sitting next to him. Then he left.

Ann was at her desk when he walked in. She smiled and flicked a switch.

"Mr Striker, sir," she said.

"Fine," answered Stoddard. "Send him in and come yourself, will you? Route all the calls through to here."

The General was being businesslike. She flicked a few switches, raised her eyebrows and followed Striker through. Bill Jensen was seated in front of the desk and Matthew was standing by the window, looking at the desk. He didn't move as they entered, or acknowledge them. The General was fiddling with a portable cassette recorder.

"Any luck with the girl, Peter?" he asked. "Take a seat, Ann."

It occurred to Striker that the Old Man had a professional set of priorities. And he had called him by his Christian name again. It was funny, but he didn't find him anything like so awesome now he was fully dressed and in his office, pipe in mouth. Then he noticed that Stoddard had broken a lifetime's habit as he saw smoke rising from the bole.

"I'm afraid not, sir," he answered guardedly. "I've asked all the important questions already and really there are only two: where is the bomb and where are the people who have hidden it? She has no more idea of the answers than we have. She's giving a lot of information that we wanted once, but it's really too late now."

"You're sure about that?" asked Stoddard. "She's not lying?"

Striker looked at him hard. "No, sir. She's not lying."

There was an awkward silence.

"She's innocent, sir. She's terrified of the whole business and she's also aware of the consequences. She'd tell me if she knew."

He felt himself shift uncomfortably. Ann was looking at him, a faintly quizzical expression on her face. Stoddard was still touching the recorder, as if he had something else on his mind. Striker thought he ought to be a little more helpful.

"The only possible hope is that she does know something but

190

doesn't realize it. You know, the chance word or remark dropped in casual conversation that had no significance at the time."

"Well," said Stoddard, "we didn't think it would be a breakthrough. Keep on it. As you say, something may show through. Send me a full transcript and have it on my desk by five."

He sighed.

"We haven't had any luck with our other enquiries either, have we, Bill?"

"No," said Jensen. "I'm afraid...."

"Yes, I know," interrupted Stoddard. "It's no one's fault. I thought that we might get something useful out of all those names and addresses, but we haven't even got a lead to the house in Norfolk, let alone to where they are now." He glanced at Calder. "The Arab, Khalid Aziz, was a dead duck as well."

Striker looked at Calder too. The bearded man's face was expressionless and he hadn't moved. He was still standing, hands at his sides, looking at the surface of the Old Man's desk.

"Anyway," continued the General, "the reason I have asked you all here is this," pointing at the cassette recorder.

"This tape arrived, by hand, at the *Daily Express*, at 9.30 this morning. I've already sent someone round. He'll get a description of the delivery man and we'll put out an all-points bulletin, but I don't hold out any hopes there."

He pressed a button.

"I've heard it," he added and sucked vigorously on his pipe.

All of them, including Stoddard, stared at the machine. All they could hear at first was the rustling sound of the tape travelling through the amplifier. Then, a deep, well-modulated, yet somehow metallic voice began to speak.

"Good morning. This is John Brown. It seems immodest for me to say so, but I don't think I need an introduction. I am sending this tape to you, the editor of the *Daily Express*, for no particular reason, except that you will know the appropriate person to give it to. I advise you to do so immediately, not least because the longer you wait the greater the risk to human life, but also because the person you give it to may be annoyed at any delay."

There was a pause while the tape crackled.

"To whom it may concern. As you no doubt know, I have built, from plutonium oxide, hijacked on 5th May, an atomic bomb. I see no harm in telling you that it contains ten kilos of P-239. No doubt you have experts, as I have, who can tell you something of the devastation that would be caused by the fission of that amount of plutonium. And devastation I assure you there will be, unless you meet my conditions. These are as follows.

"First, all road-blocks other than those around the inner cities will cease at 1200 hours on Saturday 24th. The reason for that will become apparent to you in a moment.

"Second, you have thirty-six hours from midday on Friday 23rd in which to deliver to me £25 million worth of the best quality, uncut diamonds."

Striker looked at Calder as the voice went on. His face still had no expression.

"When I say the 'best' quality, that is precisely what I mean. It seems almost pointless to say that I have an expert on my team who can tell the difference between 'gem quality' and those things destined to drill people's teeth. They must be a mixture in terms of size, although there must be no small ones. In other words, they must be gems that, when cut, will be 'Fine Blue-whites', 'Top Crystals', 'Capes' and so on, but they must not be flawed or of poor colour."

There was a pause.

"I hope that is all understood, because if I find one poor-quality stone, I shall have no hesitation in exploding the bomb. I hope you believe that."

Brown allowed another pause to develop. Striker could imagine him, sitting down recording it and seeing the people in this room looking at each other — which was precisely what they were doing. All except Calder, that is. He hadn't taken his eyes off the recorder.

"Thirdly, you will deliver these diamonds to the back of a lorry. In order to find it, take a robust vehicle along the M4 out of London. Make the Newbury turn-off and in Newbury take the A343 from the roundabout that also feeds the A34. Follow this road for precisely six and a half miles, until, nearly at the top of the hill, you will come to a left-hand fork directing you to Crux Easton, Woodcott and Egbury. Turn into this side road and stop immediately, waiting until exactly midnight. Then follow the road, without deviating, until you come to our first phosphorescent, orange arrow. Follow the arrows to the letter and you will come to the lorry. The tailgate will be down. Place the diamonds, which must be in twenty kilo lots in transparent plastic bags, in the back of the lorry. Then leave the way you came.

"You will make no attempt to follow and there are to be no bugs. Also, don't be stupid enough to try and stake out the position beforehand. You won't know exactly where it is and if we spot you, I shall push the button.

"Fourth, you will initiate no search for myself or my men for a further forty-eight hours. You may continue to search for the bomb though, if you persist in wasting time. The road-blocks will, of course, have ceased as per my first instruction. In addition, all sea-ports, airports and coasts will be freed of all surveillance. If anyone tries to stop any of my men you know what will happen.

"That is all. Follow these instructions completely and exactly, and

I give you my word that I will not explode the bomb. Also, within a few days, the *Express* will receive a letter giving its exact location. If, on the other hand, you do not follow these instructions, in any particular, the result will be catastrophic, and I'm not all that sure that history would blame me. This is the only communication there will be between us."

There was a sharp click and the message was finished. Stoddard was the quickest to react. He reached forward out of the smoke and switched off the machine. Then he ejected the tape and held it in his hand.

"I'll get a copy made of this," he said. "Then I might as well go through the motions of giving it to the technical boys for some sort of clue."

Striker saw Jensen nod.

"I'd like to hear it through again," said Jensen, "but it seems more or less what we expected."

As he listened to the man continue, Striker focused on the fact that, to him, Jensen always seemed like a robot. His hair was the colour of wet rust, but he was sure that had nothing to do with it.

"It seems to be a good example of what we already know to be true, that Brown's *modus operandi* is simple, exact and faultless. I don't think we can complain about his demands. Indeed, they seem rather modest. I suppose the question is, do we play his game or don't we?"

Striker couldn't see his face, but he knew what the expression would be. Stoddard looked fierce.

"We have no choice," he said. "We have to play it his way. We simply cannot afford to do otherwise. I dread to think what will happen if we slip up."

The phone rang and Ann picked it up. It gave an excuse for a comfortable pause, while the four men considered their acquiescence and accepted it into their being. Ann talked in low tones so that she did not disturb anyone. Striker looked at Calder. He still looked unconcerned, but there was tension in the voice as he spoke.

"Will there be any difficulty in getting diamonds of that quality and quantity in thirty-six hours?"

"Not really," answered Jensen immediately. "Oh, it will be difficult, but we can manage it. London is still the diamond capital of the world."

"I thought it was Amsterdam," said Striker without thinking.

Jensen seemed pleased by the comment, and looked round at the blond man with narrowed eyes and benign grin.

"That's where they are cut," he said. "Our friend wants uncut diamonds, because they are, to a very large extent, untraceable, and London is the place for uncut diamonds."

He paused and looked at the ceiling, clearly gathering his thoughts before continuing. Most of the room now was quite thick with smoke.

"No, HMG will have to cough up to the diamond merchants, of course, at top of the market prices, but there will almost certainly be that quantity available."

"Exactly what would be the weight of that amount of diamonds of that quality?" asked Calder. He still hadn't moved.

Jensen's eyebrows came together as Ann replaced the phone.

"Difficult to say exactly," he said. "The last time I had to look into the diamond trade was not long ago, but with inflation and the pound changing all the time against the dollar — the US dollar is the major currency in the diamond trade — it's difficult."

He bit his thumb delicately. Everyone there, except Calder, knew that he was going to come out with exactly the right answer.

"I would say," he hesitated for five seconds, while he mumbled figures that no one could interpret, "about 225 kilos, or nearly 500 pounds."

"Jesus," said Striker involuntarily.

"Yes," continued Jensen, turning towards him, still with the grin on his face and his eyes screwed up. "It is rather a lot. I can see why they need a lorry. We shall need something similar ourselves."

To Striker it still seemed incredible.

"But how would they unload all that on the market without it being noticed?" he asked.

"They wouldn't," answered Calder. "Each member of the gang — we know already that there are about fifteen to twenty.... Has the girl given you any clues there?"

Striker was taken off-guard.

"Um, eighteen she said, but she thought there might have been a few more in other places."

"Let's say twenty," continued Calder. "Each one will get a share and then they'll go their own separate ways, to the four corners of the globe, with forty-eight hours' grace to get there. I expect Brown himself will take at least fifty per cent and he'll know how to get rid of them — slowly, over a period of time. Each member of his group wouldn't get more than half a million pounds worth each — about five kilos or so. That's about, eleven pounds?"

He looked at Jensen, who nodded, smiling, so he continued. To Striker, he seemed to talk unnaturally.

"Provided each one doesn't try to unload all his share at one go, I imagine there are plenty of undercover operations that would be willing to take small amounts and possibly even large ones. Alternatively, they can simply put them into a safe-deposit box for years as a hedge against inflation. Diamonds are small, manageable and, above all, exchangeable. They're even better than gold in that respect."

194

"Yes," said Stoddard without looking at Calder. In fact he seemed uninterested in what was being said — just in his pipe.

"On the other hand," continued Calder, "I agree with you, Peter, in that it does seem rather crude and clumsy. Surely there are easier, although perhaps more complicated, ways of taking possession of an untraceable £25,000,000 sterling. Can't it be done through the banking system?"

Jensen pinched the bridge of his nose and looked at Stoddard.

"I believe it is possible," he said, "but it would be very difficult, in this situation, to keep it untraceable. Besides, I believe it requires a crooked banker." He smiled thinly. "I'm not saying there aren't any of those, but perhaps they are not within Brown's circle of acquaintances."

The grin was broader than ever now.

"Nothing would surprise me about that man," said Stoddard heavily. "I'd like your girlfriend to hear this, Peter — to see whether it really is him."

It was a casual, innocent colloquialism, Striker knew. The General simply had not known what to call her. Yet, Striker felt himself blush. He looked over at Ann, who was again looking at him. But Calder had not finished.

"It's a pretty foolproof plan. The instructions are clear and complete. There's just a little haziness around the drop, but that's deliberate, of course — so that we don't know exactly where it is. There are probably a number of tracks branching off that side road and they won't mark the route until just before midnight. They will almost certainly cover all the necessary radio wavebands as well, including VHF. And, of course, if we try anything, he has the ultimate form of retribution. I believe he'd do it too. The *Daily Express* won't publish yet, but you can bet your boots that the Editor has made a copy and will know exactly who to blame if things go wrong."

He looked directly at Stoddard, who was looking absently at the tape and sucking even more vigorously, if that were possible, on his pipe. Then, having created an almost impenetrable cloud around himself, he started to speak in a manner that left no doubt about what would happen to anyone who disagreed with him.

"What I shall recommend to the PM is that we comply totally. And there is little doubt," glancing at Calder, "from what he said to Matthew and myself yesterday, that he will agree. What is £25 million against hundreds of thousands of lives? It's a paltry sum. Brown could have asked for much more. I should think the Prime Minister will be immensely relieved."

Then he smiled broadly. They all felt the sense of relief and smiled too. All, except Calder. Striker wondered why.

Chapter 18

Friday, 23 May, p.m.

CALDER HAD NO trouble finding a space in the near-empty car park. The pub, on the bank of the Thames, was usually a very popular one at lunchtime. You could sit in the garden and watch the river traffic whilst eating good food. Above all, it was a "Freehouse", which had a selection of fine brews.

"Where is everyone?" asked Ann.

Calder set the handbrake and switched off the engine.

"I'm not sure," he answered, "but I suspect most people decided not to come into town today, because of the congestion on public transport, which cuts out a lot of commuters, and perhaps the locals have their property to protect."

"What do you mean?" she asked, getting out of the car.

He left it unlocked and walked round to her.

"I mean that a thorough search means just that. When the security forces come to an empty house, what do you think they do, leave a polite note saying they'll be back later?"

She looked at him, stunned.

"I never thought about it," she said, "but they can't just break in."

"Of course they can. The search has to be done systematically, in blocks of roads and buildings. They can't miss houses out everywhere. It would defeat the object."

She looked into his face.

"I can see the logic of that now, but it's monstrous."

He controlled his rising anger, lest she think it directed at her. But he was very bitter when he spoke.

"It's a frightening infringement of civil liberties. Perhaps some good will come of it. Perhaps people will begin to realize, now, precisely what a Plutonium Economy means, but I doubt it."

He put his arm round her and they began to walk towards the beer garden. He was still brooding.

"It means a police state, more or less," he said.

"Oh, surely not? That's being a bit melodramatic, isn't it?"

"Why?"

She hesitated.

"Well, for one thing, at least in this country people can sue, even the government, for compensation for damage done to their property. In Eastern Europe that would not be possible."

He couldn't help smiling at her traditional, blind-faith confidence in the infallibility of British liberal democracy. He shouldn't have smiled, because it wasn't funny.

"I'm sorry, Ann, but that's another thing. I don't think you realize, and neither do most people if it comes to that, exactly what an Emergency Powers Act means.

She looked at him. "No compensation?"

He shook his head.

"I'd better not spend too much time drinking then and get back to my flat," she said.

He looked down at her, knowing she was joking and glad she was with him.

"At least Peter's here," she said, looking up into the raised garden.

At the far side of the nearly deserted beer garden, Striker was sitting talking to a woman. Calder knew who she was, because Peter had said he would bring her along. They were holding hands. Then Peter noticed them and stood up clumsily, jogging the table and showing his magnificent teeth.

"Hi," he called, before they had really got within speaking distance.

"This is Judy," he said. "Ann and Matthew."

She got up and shook their hands nervously, looking a little longer at Calder. He surmised that she probably felt more confident in men's company.

"Peter has told me about you," she said.

"This is where I decide to go and get the drinks," said Calder.

The sun felt warm on his shirt-covered shoulders as he carried the tray of drinks to the table. Why couldn't he believe it was all over? There was nothing now that he could do. Everyone else had accepted it. But he felt uneasy. Nothing he could put his finger on; just a feeling deep in his guts. Perhaps it was the security measures he was worried about and the increased militarism within London, or perhaps it was the "them and us" syndrome that he felt would inevitably develop between the security forces and the citizenry. Or perhaps it was simply that he was a born worrier, and now that the major worry had been removed from his sphere of responsibility, he had to create another. Or perhaps, again, he was simply suffering from a sense of anti-climax. He smiled as he approached the table, to hide his thoughts. Ann was holding forth.

"...and I simply had no idea that that's what it meant — breaking into people's property and so on."

Judy looked down at the table.

"I'm afraid I've caused you a lot of trouble," she said.

"No way," said Striker, rather too forcefully. "From what you've told me, all that happened would have taken place whether you were there or not."

There was an awkward silence while Calder distributed the drinks and sat down.

"That's true," he said. "You mustn't blame yourself."

He held up his glass. Anyone who had befriended Peter Striker was good enough for him. Well, almost.

Just then, a military column rounded the bend and clattered past the pub. Apart from a few buses, and the very occasional car, it was the first traffic for some time. They looked on in silence.

"I never thought I'd see tanks controlling the streets of London," said Ann. "And it's going on in eight other cities in the country," she added as an afterthought.

Then she winced.

"Sorry," she said, smiling at Judy. "There I go again, opening my big mouth."

"No, please," said Judy, "I want to talk about it — to get it out of my system. You and Matthew must be very wary of me. I would be in your place. You must ask me any question you like."

The slight, probably Lancashire, accent was now unmistakable when pronouncing the letter "u". The rest she had mostly lost. Calder looked at her sitting up proudly. He lifted his beer and grinned.

"I never buy drinks for people I'm suspicious of," he said.

They all laughed, including Judy.

"But," continued Calder, "there is one question that does intrigue me. At the risk of incurring Peter's wrath...."

"Go on," interrupted Judy forcefully.

Calder looked at his friend, who was pretending to be unconcerned.

"Who made it — the bomb?"

"A man named Vaisey," she answered immediately. "I've never known anyone work so hard. He'd often been up all night when we got down to breakfast. We all ate at set times or it would have been impossible to organize meals. He used to look like death in the mornings. Actually, that's not very funny because, well, for one thing he nearly did die once, in a place crash. I don't know where. He never talked about it. One of the others told me. His face is a terrible sight. I couldn't begin to describe it to you. He was mutilated in the crash, you see, and of course he's got no legs — just metal ones that he gets round on."

She paused briefly from the stream of words. Calder had wanted to interrupt a few times but had decided against it.

"When I heard that tape this morning," she continued, "I thought of poor Vaisey. He used to talk to me quite a lot and I didn't mind. I suppose he wasn't afraid of me and I certainly had nothing to fear from him."

She looked down nervously.

"He was gay, you see, and the others stayed away from him. I felt sorry for him. He was a nice man really, but very bitter about the world and how it had treated him. He...He...."

She lapsed into silence and stared at the wooden table. The others stayed quiet, looking at her. Ann thought she had gone into some sort of *post factum* trance — delayed shock or something. She looked to Matthew for his reaction. He was gazing at Judy rather intently and she felt a momentary pang of jealousy. She looked at her watch extravagantly.

"I'm famished," she said brightly. "Isn't it about time we ordered some food?"

No one moved — not a muscle. Judy uttered something incomprehensible, then turned to Striker, her eyes stricken.

"He's going to do it!" she breathed. "Vaisey — he's going to do it!"

She put her head on Striker's shoulder and began to shiver.

Calder, too, felt suddenly chill, as if a dark cloud had covered the sun. He looked over at the Thames, dull and deep on the ebb. On the far bank, sunlight reflected off a roof window. Why was it only now that he noticed there was no traffic on the river?

"She remembered something Vaisey had said to her in a private conversation once," said Calder.

"Don't you think this is rather far-fetched — the mad scientist bit?" growled Stoddard.

The General was glaring at him under low brows, the pipe pointing like a gun. It made Calder feel as if he were confessing to raping his daughter. The birds continued to sing around him, though. They were walking on the grass to avoid being overhead and had just marched through some early sun-bathers. The fine weather had made the grass grow and it was long underfoot. Away to their right the normal traffic roar of the Mall was silent. It brought a strange solitude to the park, despite the fact that more people than usual were taking advantage of it. Stoddard started to walk again.

"He used to confide in her about many things apparently," continued Calder. "His homosexuality, his past life and recriminations. Anyway, they were talking about Brown at the time and Vaisey had had a few drinks. She said to him and I quote, 'He won't set the bomb off, will he?' According to Judy, his mood completely changed and then he became, and again I quote, 'sort of relaxed'. Then he said, quote, 'It doesn't matter whether he does or he doesn't. Things have a habit of happening, whoever is pulling the strings.' Apparently he was always saying things like that and she didn't think anything of it at the time. Incidentally, she replied, 'Of course it matters,' and he said, quote, 'You have a very naive view of life, young lady. What does it matter if a few of so-called mankind die?' He became rather angry then and the conversation ended by him walking away."

Calder paused.

"As I said, she didn't think anything of it at the time. But she suddenly saw it, where we were, at the pub. Seen in a new context it had a completely new meaning to her."

Stoddard stopped again and removed his pipe ominously.

"Is that all you've got to go on?" he shouted, as if Calder were a junior officer bothering him with trivia before he'd finished his dinner.

"It's enough, if you make the connections," answered Calder calmly.

"Do you believe her?" demanded Stoddard loudly.

A strolling couple looked over.

"That she's telling the truth?" asked Calder. "Yes. The situation, the conversation, her reaction, were not things she could have manufactured or acted. And anyway, why should she lie? What has she, or Brown, got to gain?"

He paused.

"I know you thought she might be a plant. That's why you invited Peter to hear the tape and our reaction to it — so that Brown would know we were playing the game. I thought she was too. That's why I sent Peter up to Stoke instead of going myself. I'm now convinced she's not."

The General was silent for a few seconds, still glaring at Calder, his pipe held low in his hand. Then a string of obscenities came out of his mouth. Having got it off his chest he seemed to calm down a little. He ran his free hand through his hair and stretched his eyes.

"OK," he said tiredly, beginning to walk. "Tell me why you believe it."

Calder got into the military step beside him and gathered his thoughts. They were heading for the bridge over the Serpentine.

"It all fits. An embittered man — a cripped homosexual, shunned by the scientific community. He would have something to prove. No, more than that. He would need to get back at them and the cruel society that rejected him as a leper."

"Since when did you become the psychologist?" interrupted Stoddard, but he was noticeably less hostile.

"Then he gets the chance," continued Calder, "in one fell swoop, to prove to the scientific world his true talents and also get his own back, not just on them, but also on the world in general. Brown is something predictable. He's after one thing — money — and if everyone plays according to the rules, no one else is likely to get hurt. But Vaisley is different; he's a psychopath, which means that he's unpredictable and unreliable."

Stoddard stopped again and both men looked at each other for some time. Eventually it was the General who spoke.

200

"All right. Let's suppose that you might, just possibly, be right. Would Brown necessarily be sorry about it?"

Calder fingered his beard.

"Difficult to say, but I think he would. It sounds strange, but I think he's a man of his word. Oh, I think he'll explode it himself all right, if we don't meet his demands. That's something that he could justify to himself — we didn't play the game and so on. But he might not be willing to explode it if we *do* go along with him. Also, I don't think he'd appreciate Vaisey going behind his back and doing the dirty without his permission. Anyone as brilliant and egotistical as Brown must take a tremendous pride in what he does — doing things correctly and being in control of events. He wouldn't like it if one of his subordinates upped and performed the *coup de grace*, unnecessarily and without his OK."

Stoddard was walking again, staring into space. Calder was looking past him at a girl, sunbathing topless — propped up on elbows and lying on her stomach, reading a book. The General appeared not to have noticed.

"Yes, I can see that," he said dreamily, then stopped and looked at Calder.

"But how could Vaisey do it, without Brown's permission?"

"Piece of cake," answered Calder. "Whatever method of detonation they're employing, it was almost certainly fitted by Vaisey. He'd be just as capable of setting it off as Brown. If we assume, for the moment, that it would be by radio signal, Vaisey could quite easily have made a duplicate tuner."

Stoddard ran hand through hair again.

"And no doubt," he said, "you've already thought of how we can stop him when we haven't a clue where he is. We can't even contact Brown for the same reason."

"I must admit," answered Calder, "that did require a little thinking, but really there is only one way."

Stoddard rolled his eyes at the sky.

"Frighten me again," he said heavily.

"It is a risky plan," said Calder seriously. "I thought at first that we could try sending a broadcast, over the TV and radio waves, but dismissed that idea fairly quickly. To begin with there's no guarantee that Brown would hear it and, even if he did, we could hardly just say that Vaisey has a duplicate. Our mad scientist may be listening as well. And if we merely asked for a meeting, to discuss something of 'compelling importance', Brown would simply ignore it, thinking we were trying to be tricky. No, the only way is to try and contact him at the drop. It's the only place we know he'll be."

Stoddard was nodding.

"That's what I was afraid you were going to say. Rather risky, don't you think?"

"Yes."

"He could just press the button himself because his conditions had been violated," persisted Stoddard.

It occurred to Calder, then, that the General was going to arrive at the same conclusion as he. The older man was using him as a guide — a totem pole, which he danced around — striving for a less risky, more amenable alternative. But in the end he would return to the central point. It was a form of self-justification and it wasn't the first time he'd used it.

"Yes," repeated Calder, "but he might also be willing to talk. He'd have the diamonds. What would he have to lose?"

"Exactly. He might as well just shoot you before you can open your mouth."

Stoddard stopped on the bridge, leaned over and gazed into the murky water. Then he lifted his eyes to the heavens.

"Lord, Matthew. You do pursue me with problems."

"Your only problem," said Calder, "is pulling rank and getting Peter and me as the drivers of the delivery vehicle. When we get there, I shall have to play it by ear."

He paused. Stoddard was still looking at the sky over the ministries.

"There is one thing I may be able to use to my advantage. Judy confirms that they've all grown beards. It's a perfectly natural disguise that helps to explain why none of them have been spotted. Brown thinks of everything — everything that is except Vaisey."

Stoddard swung round on him.

"Perhaps he has thought of Vaisey," he suggested.

Calder looked back.

"Perhaps," he admitted. "But do you want to take the chance?"

Stoddard looked down at the water again without saying anything. Calder let him think. There was nothing more he could say. Some fat ducks were converging on them, making arrowheads in the pool. A particularly noisy white one was creating figures of eight below Stoddard, who was now looking at it. The similarity between his behaviour and that of the duck was not lost on Calder. If it didn't shut up, it might cease to exist in a few days time, he thought callously. Eventually, the General spoke without turning.

"There is another problem."

He grimaced.

"The PM. He won't agree. To begin with, he won't see your story the way I do. I believe you because I know you. I have a certain trust in your powers of reasoning and," he turned slightly, a thin smile on his face, "your intuition. Past experience tells me that and that tips the balance. For the PM it will be different. He's the one who has to make the decision, and there is, inevitably, a tendency towards conservatism with a small 'c'. Also, he knows that if anything goes wrong, it's he who takes the can back. At least if he does nothing, he can claim that he abided by the terms of the agreement."

Calder thought that that didn't sound like a description of the man he had met the previous morning, but he didn't argue — Stoddard knew him far better. The General looked him full in the face as he spoke, a very faint smile on his lips.

"He might agree. But can we afford to take the chance of him refusing? The answer is clearly, no. So, I simply don't tell him. He need never know. Neither must anyone else. To everyone else — that is everyone except you and me, Bill and Peter, and I think, Ann — everything is proceeding normally. Meantime, I'll wangle it so that you and Peter are the drivers. It's a perfectly natural request."

Stoddard never ceased to amaze Calder. He knew him to be a man with a deep sense of morality, yet, here he was, talking of deception of the utmost gravity. He hadn't thought it possible that his admiration for the General was capable of going up any more notches. He didn't know whether to thank the duck or not.

"You know, Matthew, I thought that the decision I came to in Number 10 yesterday would be the most difficult I ever made. I was wrong."

With that he inserted his pipe and strode off again in true Army style. Calder smiled at the broad back. He'd already decided what he was going to do, whether the General had agreed or not.

"What did he say?" asked Ann.

She was sitting rather stiffly on the couch in her living-room, an untouched sherry in her glass.

"He's in a difficult position," answered Calder. "He feels that the PM won't give permission, so he's not going to tell him, just in case he refuses."

"So he agrees with you," she said unbelievingly.

"He came round to it in the end."

"But it's madness."

Calder could sense the strain and desperation in her voice as she went on. It wasn't difficult.

"He'll probably just kill you and set the bomb off anyway, and you'll have gained nothing."

Her voice trembled. He smiled.

"I don't think he'll kill me."

"Why not?" she shouted. "He killed the two security guards and that pilot."

He drained his Scotch, then walked over and knelt down in front of her.

"It's got to be done, Ann. It's the only chance we've got."

"But you could even be wrong about Vaisey. He could be perfectly innocent. You could be causing more problems that you're attempting to solve."

"Do you really believe that?" he asked quietly.

"Yes, I do," she shouted angrily.

There was a small silence.

"You can help," he said patronizingly.

To her credit she didn't throw the sherry over him. Instead, she drank it in one gulp and hurled the empty glass across the room to shatter against the far wall. Then she crossed her arms, pursed her lips and glared at him. His eyes didn't leave her the whole time.

"So that we don't compromise the General — he's needed in his job — we devise a plan of which we think he would approve, but which he doesn't know about. Besides, if he knows, he might get pangs of guilt and tell someone and that could be dangerous."

She remained immobile, still glaring down at him defiantly.

"I'm going to need a back-up team — just in case. I might need to move quickly, or Vaisey might not even be there. It can't be Striker, because he's got to drive the truck back to London, and since the only other person who's supposed to know, apart from Jensen, is you, you're it."

He didn't really think he'd need her, but he might and it should make her feel better. Besides, it would get her out of London. She wasn't glaring now, just staring.

"Newbury seems to be the nearest big town and I shouldn't think they'd be holed up too far from the drop. So, we pick up the phone and book you into an hotel in Newbury. Then, early tomorrow morning, you take my car and drive up, settle yourself in and wait for my call. You'd better phone me when you get there and give me a number where you can be reached at all times of the day and night."

She seemed to realize then that there was nothing she could do that would stop him and he could see a tear creeping out of the corner of one eye. He reached out to wipe it, but she pushed him away angrily. She was beginning to sob.

"Make love to me," she said.

He parted her legs and inserted his hand between them, feeling her body move towards it.

In the centre of London, within the rectangle bordered on three sides by Green Park, Piccadilly and Pall Mall, are some very fashionable and extremely expensive dwellings. The maze of streets has names like Crown Place, Apple Tree Yard and the Duke of York.

Near the end of one of these places stood a tall, elegant house. From the outside it looked smart and on the inside it was fit for a king. In fact, it was owned by someone connected with royalty, but he didn't live there now. Instead he had left it in the hands of a rental agency, who charged a large commission for managing the property. The substantial rent was, at that moment, fully paid up till the end of the month. An American millionaire, who found hotels too public, was using it as a temporary home during his month's stay in England.

For a couple of weeks, a North American visitor had indeed been resident there — or rather an actor pretending to be an American millionaire. But since the night of Wednesday 21st the house had been empty. The only sound now, in the whole building, was the intermittent whirr of the deep freeze in the kitchen and the steady drip of water in the large, deep water tank in the loft.

If anyone were so inclined as to lift the lid of this tank, he would have seen nothing within but dark water. But if, for some obscure reason, he were to have inserted a long stick, he would have found that the water level stopped about two and a half feet from the base of the tank. After some time, he might be able to work out that the water was, in fact, in a tank within a tank, and that the inner skin was only half as deep as the outer one. If he were even more inquisitive and scrutinized the base of the green metal, he might be able to find the wire that snaked under the felt insulation and up through one of the rafters, under the TV aerial.

But it's unlikely that he would have done all these things. Even a man conducting a search would see a perfectly ordinary water tank in a far from ordinary house. Why should it be anything else? How was he to know that death lurked in the centre of London, a third of a mile from 10 Downing Street?

Chapter 19
Saturday, 24 May

GEOFFREY TORRINGTON, a director in the oil business, was steering his new motor-cruiser down the Thames towards Putney Bridge. It was about five to eight in the morning.

The boat had been moored outside his house near Windsor all winter and he had spent every available minute preparing her for this, her maiden voyage. He planned on mooring the coming night in the Thames Estuary and then cruising round the South Coast harbours for a fortnight.

He was going a fair lick because he had just realized that he had made his first mistake. He was moving against the tide and he knew it would get worse. He'd already decided that he would try and moor until the ebb tide, just after midday, but he wanted to make as much progress as possible now, while the current wasn't too strong.

The Army had set up the westerly edge of their security ring on Putney Bridge, and river traffic was just as much subject to scrutiny as road vehicles. There were only two routes through that were not cordoned off — the second arch in on each side of the bridge — the right arch for down river traffic and the opposite arch if you were going up river. Engineers had erected stout, floating jetties leading from the bridge stanchions, pointing up and down river, on which boats could moor while being searched. A makeshift plastic boom, that parted in the middle, spanned the stretch of water under the two arches as a warning that boats must stop.

Torrington and his wife Gillian had been so busy in the last few days, provisioning their craft, that they hadn't heard anything of the "security exercise" that was taking place throughout the country. Their eldest daughter, Miranda, had mentioned something about it, but she didn't really understand and they hadn't really listened to her. She was only seven and always repeating what she saw on TV.

As he approached the bridge, Torrington noticed a large arrow directing him to the right passage, so he got himself into position for a straight run through. He noticed the jetty, completely bare of boats, and also a large, white on red "Stop" sign. This was puzzling, but didn't worry him unduly. He thought vaguely that it was probably the legacy of some sort of regatta that someone had forgotten to take down.

Then, at about seventy-five yards out, his stomach turned over as he saw the boom. He hadn't noticed it before because it was under the shadow of the bridge. It was then that it happened.

Before his hand could reach the throttle lever, he caught sight, out of the corner of his eye, of his twenty-month-old daughter Stephanie, climbing over the steering-well gunwale. He knew, in an instant, that it was a position from which she could not possibly recover and that she would be over the side in a second.

It was one of those moments when you don't decide on your priorities — they are decided for you. The decision has to be made faster than the rate at which the human brain normally works. It's almost as if it realizes that and allows something else to cut in — an emotion or feeling. The mind, rid of the normal societal encumbrances, is so minutely focused that in that flash of a second it becomes crystal-clear.

Without thinking, Geoffrey Torrington left the wheel and ran for his daughter. Before he could reach her, her hand slipped and she toppled back towards the water. Again, the man did not hesitate. Without checking, he dived over after her, shouted for his wife, grabbed the child's sweater as they disappeared below the surface and kicked out to avoid being dragged towards the thrashing twin propellers. As the boat was new, the rudder was a little stiff and the

206

craft ploughed on, at twelve knots, straight towards the boom.

Gillian Torrington, meanwhile, was making breakfast in the galley. She hadn't heard her husband's cry, but Miranda suddenly screamed down from above.

"Mummy! Mummy! Daddy's just dived overboard!"

Miranda was prone to playing practical jokes, but there was something in her voice. Gillian sprang up the steps and, looking back at their wake, she saw a man in the water, holding up Stephanie. She knew it was her because of the red, white and blue, striped sweater that they had bought her especially for the trip, to keep her warm. Instantly, she knew what must have happened and, her heart thumping against her ribs, she turned to the boat and saw the bridge.

If she had been a lesser woman she would have panicked then and swung the steering-wheel. But it was already too late for that. Instead she steered the craft straight for the centre of the gap. She didn't see the boom, now hidden by the rising foredeck and pushpit, but it wouldn't have mattered if she had, because her husband hadn't had time to show her how to work the controls.

"Mummy, what about Daddy?!" shouted Miranda.

"He can swim like a fish," said her mother breathlessly. "We'll get under the bridge first, then go back."

She looked down at the mass of dials and levers.

"When I've worked out how this thing works," she added.

Ned Sheen was busy conversing with his relief guard as the latter descended the ladder. It had been a long, cold night, perched above the river under the bridge arch. Although he'd noticed the craft when it was some way off, he didn't want to have to deal with the first boat of the day before he'd even had his breakfast. The lazy sod on the opposite arch had already ascended his ladder, without waiting to be relieved. That left muggins Ned holding the fort. Anxiously, he watched the corporal descend, in the hope that he wouldn't notice the boat before he officially relieved him.

Then, through his numbed and far from large brain, something struck him as odd about the boat's engine note. It wasn't slowing. He swung round and it was fully three seconds before he realised that it wasn't going to stop. Stunned, he watched it pass through the floating boom, its engines loud under the bridge. Then it was through and speeding away.

Ned raised his automatic rifle and set it to fire. He had direct orders to stop anyone who tried to run the boom, but he'd never shot anyone in his life. He hesitated.

"What the hell are you playing at, Sheen?" cried Corporal Bellows from behind him and fear of recrimination for not stopping the boat almost made him pull the trigger. But still, something stopped him.

Then the engine note deepened and the craft rose up in the water, accelerating away.

On getting under the bridge, Gillian decided she'd have to experiment with the levers. She pushed one down and the craft speeded up. It was the last thing she ever did.

The soldier fired a burst that cut the woman down. Too late he saw the child and too late he heard Bellows's further anguished cry.

"What the...."

Then one of the bullets punctured a petrol tank and the boat disintegrated in a mammoth explosion. No one stood a change — not even poor Ned Sheed and Corporal Bellows.

The Prime Minister heard about the Putney incident too late to keep it out of the midday news, but it was doubtful whether he would have been successful anyway. A frustrated mass-media jumped on it, like dogs at a bone. Up and down the country the populace were told about it on their radios and watched it on their television screens, and their mood became more hostile.

Wilf and Joan Painter heard of it on the TV in the bedroom of their St John's Wood house. Joan had been ill for some weeks with her back and, since she was seventy-three she took longer to recover than she used to. Wilf had insisted that she stay in bed as long as she liked. They'd just eaten a sardine lunch that he'd prepared as they listened to an interview with the tear-stained Torrington.

"Bastards!" said Wilf suddenly.

"Wilf!" reprimanded his wife, but he would not be placated.

"A man jumps overboard to save his daughter from drowning and sees his wife and daughter get blown to bits for his pains. Anyone'd think we were at war. For Christ's sake, what's it all about? None of the bastards had better knock at my door, that's all."

Joan knew that there was nothing she could say or do when he was in this mood.

"To think I was in the Navy during the war, fighting with bastards like that."

She let him mumble on. Eventually, he picked up the lunch things and walked downstairs. She heard him washing up and, soon after, the back door slammed as he went out to do some gardening. Then she heard the key turn in the lock. That was something he'd never done before. He was not only angry at those soldiers, he was worried as well. He was probably going down to the vegetable patch. It was at the bottom of their long garden and screened by trees, and he clearly didn't want any soldiers walking in while he wasn't around. She smiled to herself and let her neck relax on the pillow. Soon she was asleep.

When the first of the five soldiers knocked on the door, he received no reply. Joan woke on the second knock, but by that time there was so much noise going on that her feeble cries couldn't be heard. A soldier returned.

"All locked up round the back, Sarge," he said.

"Very well," said the sergeant. "Stand back."

He fired a small number of bullets into the lock of the thick wooden door.

On hearing the automatic rifle fire, Wilf, who had in fact been a Chief Petty Officer in the Navy, knew exactly what it was. He grabbed a nearby shovel and ran for the house, as fast as his seventy-one-year-old legs could carry him. He paused, frustratingly, to unlock the back door and entered the house just as a young soldier stepped into the kitchen.

"You Nazi bastards!" shouted Wilf and hefted his shovel.

The young man fell heavily, a gaping wound in his neck. Wilf charged on into the hall, laying about with the shovel and shouting. Caught completely by surprise, two more had fallen before their sergeant, leaving the living room, put out the raging man with the butt of his rifle.

Another young soldier came rushing down the stairs, from the room where he had discovered the nervous old lady in bed. He stopped and stared in stupefaction at the blood and devastation.

"Christ, Sarge," he said. "I don't understand."

The sergeant was very angry.

"Neither do I, lad. Called us Nazis. But I got the bastard," he said, holding up his rifle proudly. "Bloody Commie. Now, get on that phone and get an ambulance here. Our boys are hurt."

Judy felt the tension fall from her body. She kept hold of the man though, because she didn't want to break the tie just yet and also because she wanted to give him some security. She always felt that men were more vulnerable in these post-coital moments than women. She didn't know why, but there was definitely something ungainly about them — like seals out of water.

She held on for another reason too: because she knew what she was going to do. It had been taking shape at the back of her mind ever since the pub, but now she was clear about it. She stroked his hair and he stirred.

"Sorry, am I too heavy?" he said, lifting his weight off her and on to his arms.

She felt tears welling up at the back of her eyes and pulled him back down so that he wouldn't see.

"No, you're fine," she said, stroking his hair again.

She waited a while, until she had controlled her emotions.

"What happens when you get there tonight?" she asked.

"I'm not sure. All I know is that Matthew wants me to drive our vehicle away and leave him there — after delivering the diamonds, of course — so that he can tell Brown about Vaisey."

His voice told her that he was not confident of success.

"What do you think will happen?" she asked, trying to keep her tone matter-of-fact.

He got up and rolled on to his side. When he spoke, his voice was empty of expression.

"I think they'll either shoot him on the spot before he can get a word out, or they'll explode the bomb — perhaps both."

"So do I," said Judy, still lying on her back and looking at the ceiling.

Then she rolled off the bed and searched for his bath robe. Striker examined the perfection of her body in the afternoon light. Her modesty restored, she turned and looked at him, and he realized, in that moment, what she was going to do.

"Don't do it," he said desperately.

"I must, Peter."

"Why?" It was a cry from the depths.

She sat down beside him and held his hand. The words were surprisingly easy.

"Because they will recognize me and they won't shoot. Perhaps that will give me just enough time to talk to them and perhaps John will believe me. After all, why else would I go back to him if I weren't telling the truth?"

She paused.

"Because Matthew's life and thousands of others depend on it, and because I love you. I'm not a brave woman and I can't explain it very well, but I want to live with you for the rest of my life and I couldn't do that if I didn't go with you tonight."

He made to speak, but she covered his mouth with her hand and smiled.

"For years I've been searching for a purpose in my life," she said. "Now I've found it. It's funny, but I wouldn't have done this two days ago. I'd be with you under false pretences, don't you see?"

She continued to look at him and saw that he did understand, but that he wasn't going to admit it. It occurred to her that it was odd how two people so closely attuned could almost read each other's thoughts.

"You know what they might do?" he said. "You deserted them, don't forget."

"Yes, but I don't think so. I don't think John is a vindictive person."

"You couldn't have known him very well if you're not sure about that."

"I didn't," she said without hesitation. "I thought I did, but I didn't."

210

He stood up and put his pants and trousers on. She felt a sense of hostility in him.

"You're not going to give me any trouble, are you, Peter?"

He shook his head. "I don't know," he answered.

Then he turned and looked down at her still kneeling by the bed. She stood up and threw herself into his arms, the tears coming uncontrollably now.

"Come back, Judy," he said urgently.

She smiled to herself. How contradictory love was. You wanted to be with a man forever, yet you'd also be willing to die for him. For the only time in her life, the first love-making had been a bond. She hoped it wasn't a farewell as well.

"I promise," she said.

Chapter 20
Sunday, 25 May, a.m.

CALDER LOOKED at his watch for the fifth time in that many minutes. Midnight.

They had reached the turn-off without any trouble about forty-five minutes earlier and had been stationary ever since, just as Brown had said they should be. It had been the hardest and most uncomfortable forty-five minutes Calder had ever spent.

The worst thing had been the silence in the cab of the small one-and-a-half tonner. They had driven in silence and waited in silence, until, half an hour earlier, he had got out of the vehicle and left them alone. He had walked round the back of the lorry, leant against it and waited. He'd watched the cars moving past on the main road — moving as quickly up the hill as down — and was glad that the predicted rain had not come from the dark sky.

He had been amazed when Judy had offered her services. For one, brief moment he had considered refusing, but had realized immediately that there was too much at stake. So had Stoddard. Calder had pointed out the dangers, but she had been adamant.

No, the problem was Striker. Calder had been surprised too about the way in which she had explained her relationship with the blond man. She had told him, as well, that Striker had argued against her going and of the feeling she had that he might try to prevent her. Calder had interrupted then and said that it was too much of a risk for him to come along. She had smiled and explained, as if he were a child, that he didn't quite understand — that replacing Peter would not be an answer, because she would simply refuse to go. Her feeling for Peter, she said, was just as important as her motivation to help Calder. Indeed, it was the very reason she was doing it at all. It was imperative that he come along and make the decision for himself. He might try to prevent her from leaving the vehicle, but that was one of the chances Calder had to take, if he wanted her along. And, anyway, wouldn't he prefer Peter to be where he could see him?

When he had returned to the cab at 11.55, they were both still staring out of the windscreen into the blackness, in precisely the same poses as when he had left them.

Midnight. They must be going. He sensed Striker turn his head towards him and Calder looked in his direction. But Judy was squeezed in between them and he could not see his face.

"Let's go," said Calder.

Striker started the engine, put it into gear, released the handbrake and they started off down the country lane. Calder put his hands in the pockets of his anorak, sat back in his seat and tried to relax. It didn't work. He still felt tense, as he watched himself descending into the tunnel of their headlamps.

They followed the road faithfully. It was pretty well deserted, with just the odd house. The occasional rabbit faltered in their glare but, apart from that, nothing disturbed their passage, not even another vehicle.

After about four or five minutes there appeared to be a thick, unbordered wood to their right and then they came to the orange arrow. They could see it clearly from a distance, caught in their lights, pointing straight into the wood. When they got closer they saw that it was perched on a long stake and that what had seemed like impenetrable foilage was, in fact, a sort of track through the trees.

Calder noted that Striker turned the wheel without hesitation and they travelled down a green tunnel. They heard the sound of the undergrowth brushing the sides and the occasional low branch touching the roof. The track had clearly not been used regularly for some time, as the grass was thick under the wheels. But, from its flattened appearance, a vehicle had been down the path recently.

Then, no more than fifteen seconds after they had turned, they rounded a bend and saw the rear lights of what had to be Brown's lorry. As they closed, Calder saw that it was parked just the other side of where another path crossed their own, almost at right-angles. Brown had made sure that they could turn round after unloading without too much difficulty. Reversing back the way they had come would have been almost impossible in the dark.

"Pull over into there," said Calder, indicating the right branch of the intersecting path.

He jumped out and walked round to the back of the vehicle. The engine died, and he stood and looked and listened. There wasn't a sound — not even a breeze to rustle the branches. It was also nearly pitch dark, the roof of trees blanketing out any light. It was only the

212

red glow from the tail-lights of both vehicles which allowed Calder to see at all. It would have been useful, for the transfer of the diamonds, to back the vehicle up and shine the headlamps on the scene, but he wasn't going to do that. The darkness suited his purpose perfectly.

He flicked a torch as Striker trudged round to join him. Together they unlocked the rear door and transferred ten twenty-kilo bags. It only took a few minutes. That left one bag which was heavier than the rest. The plan was that Calder would take it over with Judy and they would both stay there while Striker drove off.

Calder felt a grip on his arm.

"You drive, Matthew. Let me go?" whispered Striker.

Calder held the other's arm in turn. He'd known it was coming and knew also that he couldn't comply with the request. The American was too emotionally involved. Besides, the blond man had been right about one thing: he, Calder, did make important, moral decisions for other people and Striker couldn't. The Englishman didn't care whether that was arrogant or not. It was simply something that had to be done.

"Sorry, Peter," he said and prayed that the friendship between them would be enough. He was heavier, but the American was quicker, fitter and more skilled, and, frankly, he didn't fancy his chances. He held on to the arm, waiting for the tightening of the muscles that would signal a blow. But to his immense relief the grip on his own arm was released and Striker walked back to the cab. Calder was glad he had not been able to see the face and wondered whether his friend had registered that he had not promised to take care of the girl.

He waited again, not sure what he would do if Striker tried to restrain her.

She appeared suddenly at his elbow from the other side of the vehicle. He tossed the torch in the back, hefted the remaining bag of diamonds, in itself worth about £3,000,000, and closed the rear doors. Then, together, they walked across to the other lorry.

They waited for Striker to start his engine and then Calder lifted the bag and Judy into the truck in the same movement. He got up too, being as quiet as he possibly could. Striker ran the engine for a further twenty seconds, opened and slammed his passenger door, then backed up and drove away. Within half a minute Calder could hear the vehicle accelerating up the road into the distance and, soon, silence again descended upon the wood. The only sound was the thump of his heart in his ear drums.

It was the moment, he knew, that was crucial. If Brown shot them on sight, that would be that. It occurred to him that if he had been a historian it would have made him realize how inadequate his usual long-term analyses were. That, ultimately, momentous events were determined by brief moments in time and space that tended to be ignored, but which were in themselves of overwhelming importance.

He reached for Judy's hand. It was steady but cold. Together they waited in the dark.

A minute stretched to five and then ten. He could no longer hear the beat in his chest. Still nothing happened. A pheasant called in alarm, very close by and his pulse began to race again, all his senses straining. He bent down to where he thought Judy's head would be and whispered, as softly as he could:

"Whatever you do, don't move a muscle."

Without a doubt, Brown himself was out there — had been since their arrival — and was now making sure that no one had been left behind. The pheasant shouted his alarm again and then the stillness was back — a silence so deep that a rustle of clothing or the creak of a bone would have sounded loud in the clearing. That would tell Brown what he wanted to know and he would shoot them before they had opened their mouths. At the same time he had to admire the man's coolness. There was £25,000,000 worth of diamonds in the lorry, but he was content to wait.

Calder's finely tuned senses picked up a car a long way off. Eventually it went by on the nearby road and so did another five minutes.

Then someone spoke right beside the vehicle and he heard someone else approach the rear of the lorry. Suddenly they were dazzled by a powerful torch beam and a man shouted. Calder put up his hands. There wasn't time to be afraid.

"Don't shoot!" shouted his companion. "It's me, Judy!"

"Hey! It *is* Judy. John...."

"Yes, I can see."

The voice was unmistakable.

"The diamonds are here, John," said Judy breathlessly, "just as you asked, and everything will be done as you instructed. But there is something you don't know about, about the bomb, that we must tell you."

Calder could see nothing through the blinding light, so he averted his eyes and looked at Judy. Her face, in the harsh glare, looked stricken as she waited for a reply. She waited for some time and Calder suddenly realized how brave she really was. He'd been thinking of her as a means to an end and not as a person. He'd committed the same appalling sin that he had accused the nuclear power lobby of many times.

"For God's sake, John," she cried. "Would we risk our lives and those of other people of it wasn't important?"

She turned to Calder.

"This man knows all about it."

214

Brown hesitated a few moments more before Calder heard whispering. Then he heard Brown say:

"Let's get moving. We've been here long enough."

Calder felt relief flood through him. The suspension creaked as men jumped inside. The light never left his face, though.

"Who are you?" he heard Brown say from close by.

"My name is Calder."

"And why shouldn't I shoot you right now, Mr Calder?"

"Hey! Will you look at these diamonds," someone interrupted excitedly, but he was quickly hushed.

"Because you're curious," replied Calder. "Curious to know what the message is that's important enough to risk nuclear devastation and because you're also curious to know where I fit in."

He heard the sound of a rope fall near him.

"Tie him up — by his hands," said Brown and Calder heard him moving off to the back. He also heard the tailgate being fixed up and then the engine started. The light left his face and centred on his hands, as he was roughly turned round and the knot tied behind his back. The vehicle was already moving. The light returned to his face again momentarily and then it was extinguished.

For at least a minute, Calder could see absolutely nothing as his retina retained the image of the glare. Even when his vision began to return and adjust to the darkness he could still see virtually nothing. The lorry bounced along the track for about ten minutes in second gear and all he saw were indistinct shapes. Then it met a road and speeded up. He was able to see a little more then, but only the hazy silhouette of men in the back of the truck. It turned numerous corners and negotiated scores of bends, and it was impossible for him to memorize the route in the gloom. He thought they were heading in a general south-westerly direction, but he couldn't be sure. No one spoke. After about half an hour, they pulled off the road on to a gravel drive and stopped.

Calder was pushed out and, when he looked up, saw an ordinary-looking gabled, country house, with fields beyond. No attempt was made to blindfold him as he was shoved through the front door into a bare hallway and then into a room on the left.

A light came on and two men came in, stationing themselves on either side of the door. One was tall and well-muscled, and the other was small, but looked equally fit. Their size was the only difference between them, though. They were both bearded, dressed in full combat gear and they both held machine carbines that were pointing straight at his stomach. He didn't know what the weapons were, but he had no doubt that they could both use them. The way they stood, with a wide stance, connected with the seemingly casual way in which they grasped the weapons and the expressionless, yet watchful faces, gave off a general air of competence that he didn't doubt. Not that he'd expected anything else.

While he examined them they looked at each other. The bigger man shifted his position. The smaller merely grinned. Calder walked over to the far wall, where the brown paper was peeling off with the damp, and used it to prop himself up. He waited — for fifteen minutes or more. Then Brown walked in.

The two guards didn't exactly jump to attention, but they did involuntarily stiffen. Brown moved away from the door so as not to interfere with the field of fire. Calder pushed himself off the wall and both men stood examining each other.

What Calder saw was a man about two inches taller than himself and darker, in full, unmarked combat gear, no different from that which the others were wearing. It occurred to him that photographs could indeed be deceptive. The resemblance to the snap was there, but only just. If he hadn't known he was looking at Brown he wouldn't have recognized him. The beard and receding hairline made him look a completely different person. No wonder there hadn't been a positive indentification. There was also something else that photographs couldn't portray. Calder felt an inner dynamism in the man that didn't have to be expressed in action. He stood perfectly still, hands in pockets, in the middle of the room, the brown eyes examining Calder's face.

"Judy has been telling me a great deal," said Brown. "Apparently you think Vaisey is going to explode the bomb without my permission."

It seemed, to Calder, to be said with gentle inquisitiveness.

"Yes."

"Persuade me."

Calder shook his head. "I don't have to. Judy must have told you." He paused. "Besides, you believe it yourself — now."

The eyes never left him.

"Then why you?" asked Brown.

"I was going to come on my own. Judy only joined later."

Calder shrugged his shoulders before continuing.

"I suppose I'm here to tell you that for the time being we're on your side. We violated your conditions because, unlike you, we value human lives and there was no other way of getting in touch with you. That bomb must not explode. You've got your diamonds and you have your forty-eight hours. Just give us Vaisey. We won't enquire of him where the bomb is until the forty-eight hours are up. You have my word."

Brown looked back at him calmly. Calder had expected him to smile at the last sentence. Yes, there was definitely a gentleness there.

"You haven't answered my question. Why you?"

216

Calder understood then and, in so doing, understood a great deal about why Brown was so successful at what he did.

"Because I happen to have been involved in trying to catch you from the beginning. I was the natural person to come."

"Again, why? Judy tells me that you are not permanently employed by MI5, or whatever they call themselves — that you are, how shall I put it, temporarily co-opted."

Calder looked straight back into the other's eyes. The dark man didn't flinch. There was no harm in telling the truth.

"Because I have a special interest and special knowledge in your particular activity: plutonium hijacking and the manufacture of home-made atom bombs."

Brown nodded for the first time and the traces of a smile could be detected at the corners of his mouth. He walked towards Calder and stopped about a yard from him, his hands now at his sides. The two men examined each other in silence for a second time. Calder decided that he had been mistaken. It wasn't dynamism that lurked beneath the surface, but a calmness — a satisfaction, a competence, an awareness, a total confidence in how to solve problems.

"You're my opposite number," said Brown suddenly.

"I am part of a team that...."

"No," said Brown emphatically. "You're the one. I feel it. Just as I have felt you breathing down my neck from time to time, Calder, I don't mind telling you. I think it is that which has allowed me to stay one jump ahead of you."

Calder held his gaze before speaking.

"It must have been pure luck in Norfolk rather than second-sight. I missed you by six hours."

Brown flicked his eyes away and then back again. He nodded.

"What put you on to Norfolk?" he asked.

"Your pick-up boy at Powne's shop bought an Ordnance Survey of the area."

"Did he, by God?!" laughed Brown.

He didn't seem at all concerned.

"And what put you on to Powne?"

Calder shrugged his shoulders again.

"A number of things. The Windscale security officer's wife overheard one of your men talking about getting something off to Paddington and one of your ex-fellow officers remembered that you were always going to Paddington straight from the barracks. We put two and two together and figured that an accommodation address would be useful to you. The rest was just legwork."

Brown was smiling fully now.

"That was very good," he said. "It seems to me, though, that you made five, not four."

He turned his head away before continuing, then walked back to his previous position, putting his hands back in his pockets.

"Isn't it interesting," he said, "the way in which seemingly innocuous pieces of information can be put together to provide a clue? The permutations are endless."

Brown was clearly enjoying himself.

"But that doesn't explain how you knew it was that particular house. It was searched in the morning. I was sure we fooled those sappers and that idiot officer."

Calder hesitated. He didn't want to implicate Judy any more than he had to.

"Oh, you did," he said. "I overhead a conversation of a description of the search. I was suspicious and we checked again."

Brown was looking at him intently.

"And just to put your mind at rest," said Calder, "because I can see that you're worried, I didn't trip your crude little explosive device."

Brown laughed fully this time.

"A worthy opponent," he said. "But it seems to me that you had your own little piece of luck there."

Calder said nothing.

"You're quite wrong though," continued Brown, "about my luck, that is. You make your own. I have made numerous mistakes, but then I recognized in advance that I would, or that those who work for me would. Therefore I planned for that contingency. The secret is to stay one jump ahead — to keep moving, so to speak — so that your mistakes don't catch up with you. I knew you'd work out who I was eventually."

He paused and looked up.

"How did you, by the way?"

"You can't expect me to give away all my secrets," answered Calder.

Brown nodded unconcernedly.

"It doesn't matter. I know I would have worked it out if I'd been in your shoes and, although I'm arrogant, I'm not so egotistical that I don't recognize that there are others who can think like me."

Calder let that one go. He thought he had better get back to the reason he was there.

"Your biggest mistake was in choice of personnel," he said.

Brown raised his eyebrows.

"Judy you mean?" he asked absentmindedly. "Yes, you're quite right there. But she didn't do any harm and, in the end, she's proved to be an advantage, hasn't she? She's told us about my other failure in personnel — our mad scientist."

He gazed abstractly at the wall behind Calder.

"A bit of an unfair accusation of myself, though. Vaisey is quite

218

brilliant, make no mistake, and he did the job I asked of him in double-quick time. What's more, I think you will appreciate that my field of choice was rather limited. Nuclear physicists with enough brains and no scruples don't exactly advertise in the *New Scientist*."

He looked at Calder consideringly.

"But you're right. He will explode it. I can see that now. What's more, I should have seen it before. I should have known that that combination would not just be interested in money."

He paused.

"You see, Vaisey isn't here. He went to a little hideaway he's got, after we set the bomb, asking me to send his share on. I should have wondered why he should trust me so much. Then I would have seen that the bomb itself had become more important than the two million I promised him."

Calder continued to say nothing as Brown looked at him.

"As you have no doubt surmised, it does bother me that one of my team should act in such a manner." He didn't look bothered at all. "I have given my word and, strange as it may seem, my word I keep."

He paused again. Then his eyes flickered and a faint smile appeared.

"The problem is that, as again I'm sure you can appreciate, I cannot spare the time to go looking for him myself and I can't exactly deactivate the bomb, because *my* legs would be knocked from under me."

He stared at Calder.

"It must remain where it is for forty-eight hours, while we make our escape, and it will. Vaisey won't explode it before then. He has some loyalty to me and the boys. Besides, he knows that I'd kill him if he did set if off before the two days had elapsed. But," he shrugged very slightly, "after forty-eight hours, he might think he can escape my wrath."

He was looking keenly and amusedly at Calder.

"It will be interesting to see if *you* can stop him. I think you could. Indeed, I think the personal approach will be the only way and I would seriously advise you not to inform your superiors. Send in the troops and he'll explode it immediately and then neither of us wins. He's afraid of me, but not that afraid."

Brown removed a small black box from his trouser pocket. It was no bigger than a matchbox. He held it up so that Calder could see. It had two buttons on the face: a red and a green.

"This is what you'll be looking for. He's no doubt made a duplicate. The buttons must both be fully depressed, three times, in sequence, to avoid the bomb being exploded by accident. A radio signal goes to a transmitter nearby, which sends a signal to the bomb and explodes it. He will almost certainly have one in his house, but it could be anywhere. He is very shrewd." He hesitated and smiled thinly. "Mine, by the way, will travel with me."

He looked Calder up and down.

"I'll leave his address somewhere prominent, but I can't have you rushing up to Scotland just yet. So you'll be unconscious for about twelve hours. It will take you several more hours to get organized, get up there and talk him out of it. But I don't think you'll manage to get him to tell you where it is. Why should he? Physical torture won't work on Vaisey. Oh, you might get it out of him, eventually, using drugs, but by that time I think my forty-eight hours will be up and you'll still have to work out how to deactivate the thing."

He walked toward the door. The two guards were like statues, but Calder had been too absorbed by Brown to have noticed whether they had been like that thoughout their conversation.

"What about Judy?" he asked.

Brown was looking at the door.

"Like I said, Calder, I always keep my word."

His voice was expressionless. He opened the door and looked back. The calmness was still there, like a sleeping man awake. After some time he said:.

"You know, I think there is only one major difference between us two."

With that he closed the door behind him. Calder reflected on the conversation. The most puzzling thing was what he had said about Judy. The Vaisey think might work. And Brown was right; he had to do it alone. Provided he was left enough time.

He turned away from his two guards and surreptitiously examined the windows. There were two and they were both covered with a thick blanket. He walked slowly over to one and tried to peer round the edge of the material without appearing to do so. With both hands tied behind his back it wasn't easy. He couldn't see a thing.

"Get away from there," said the bigger guard.

Then the door opened and a man with red hair and a moustache entered. Unlike the others he was wearing civilian clothes, dominated by a large overcoat. He seemed slightly older. He was also carrying a syringe. He placed this in his pocket, walked round Calder and began to untie his hands. They were both facing the guards, who seemed particularly alert. Calder decided that to try anything would be suicide and, anyway, stupid.

The prisoner's hands untied, the newcomer stepped to one side.

"Take off your anorak and pull up your sleeve," he said.

The rrrs were rolled in a Scottish accent. Calder obeyed.

"How long will it put me out for?" he asked.

He felt fairly sure that it would not be fatal, but he didn't trust Brown too much.

"Aboat twelve hours, give or take an hour or two," said the Scot, grinning. "And ye'll wake up with a wee man in your head, laying aboat with a sledgehammer."

"Thanks a lot," said Calder as he felt the crude insertion of the needle and the pain as the drug was forced into the vein. The syringe fully depressed, the needle was removed and the man walked to the door.

"Whatever happened to cotton wool and TCP?" asked Calder.

The man turned and grinned again. "Sorry," he said, "we ran out." After a pause, he added:

"If I were you I'd put that thing back on," pointing to Calder's anorak. "You haven't much consciousness left and it's going to get a wee bit cold in here."

Then he turned to the two guards, who had been watching this interplay with interest.

"He should be on the floor soon. Give it five minutes to be sure, then you can leave him."

They both nodded and smiled. Calder reckoned that they'd be glad to finish what must be a rather boring duty. The bigger one called out of the door.

"Hey, Mac! You don't need whisky when you've got that stuff," and he laughed at his own joke.

Calder heard the words, "Sassenach ignoramus," but that was all. The smaller of the two had not taken his eyes off him.

He was grateful to the Scotsman for his advice and reached down for his anorak. At least it indicated that he hadn't been given a fatal dose. The Scot wouldn't be worried about him getting cold if it had been and he didn't believe it had been double-bluff.

Already he was beginning to feel weak and groggy and, suddenly, dizzy. He zipped up his anorak and decided to sit down before he fell. But he couldn't reach the wooden floor. He kept bending down, but his hands wouldn't touch. He fell, consciously, with his hands out in front, but he still didn't reach the wood, just kept falling. Then he disappeared into a black hole. He was falling down it and at the bottom he could see Judy's face, but she never seemed to get any closer.

In another part of the house, Brown was watching Max Liden examining the diamonds. He was taking about ten from each bag at random and so far he had checked eight bags. After each one he exclaimed their authenticity with a certain mad glee and dipped his hand into the next bag so that the stones ran over it and through his fingers. Then he would extract one and examine it with his eyeglass. Strange animal sounds kept coming from his throat and his eyes sparkled like the gems the now dull diamonds would later become. Brown could understand Max's emotion. He supposed it was rather like a sex maniac waking up in a harem.

Brown turned and absentmindedly examined the Schmeisser, cradled in his hand. They would be genuine. The government wouldn't take the chance of throwing in some duds. What would be the point? He had never had any doubt that they would be prepared to give away a measly £25 million for the safety of London. It would cost the country a lot more, just in terms of money, to rebuild the place. Nor would they have planted a listening device in any of the bags or on Calder. The risk was too great to them.

He also felt that Calder might do it. He had made a mistake with Vaisey; not in employing him in the first place — that had been inspired — but in not seeing his real motivation and taking care of it. It was poetic justice to let Calder try to stop him. He was sure he would come close — probably succeed. He may not be able to understand men like Vaisey very much, but he knew men like Calder. They were more dangerous than a dozen heavies. Those eyes.

He looked across the room at where Judy was huddled in the corner. She was being ignored by the men, as if somehow they knew her fate and didn't want to be tainted by her. They were all watching Max. Occasionally, the door would open as men came down from changing into civvies.

Within the hour they would all be gone, with their share. The operation was finally over. He had made mistakes, but it had worked, just as, lying in that cold hangar at Carlisle, he had known it would. And he had enjoyed every minute of it. Indeed, he regretted that it was now over. He felt a deep sense of satisfaction and pride as he looked at his men. He wondered how many of them would be caught. Most. But *he* would survive. He had made arrangements.

It was then he noticed that Wilson was looking at him and not at the diamonds.

Chapter 21
Sunday, 25 May, p.m.

THE FACE AT the end of the tunnel opened its mouth for the first time. Calder strained to hear the jumbled whisper of words. That was odd. The face was relaxed and beautiful, but the words were hissed, as if she were out of breath or in pain. The voice seemed to be coming from beside him, not from the face at all. He felt a weight on his back and consciousness returned. He involuntarily opened his eyes. Then he remembered.

He remembered because of the pain. The Scotsman's description has been spot on. He saw the note, about two feet from his head, pinned to the floor with a bayonet. Then he tried to push himself up, but the heaviness of his back held him to the floor. He pushed more strongly and wriggled to escape. The weight slipped off him and there was a dull thud. Turning on to his side, he saw Judy beside him, face down, seemingly unconscious and completely naked.

His head reeled as he saw the blood on the floor and knew that he had to roll her over. He got into a kneeling position and turned her, as gently as he could. The handle of a knife protruded from her belly, in the centre of a crimson stain. The rest of her body was covered in abrasions. His head was forgotten as he sat back on his haunches and took it in.

He knew nothing of medicine, but he knew that the wound must be terrible. It also occurred to him that Brown was the most vindictive bastard he'd ever come across, to stab this innocent girl so that she died slowly. He also knew, in that instant, without a shadow of doubt, that if he ever came across him again, he would kill him with his bare hands and feel the better for doing it.

He felt for her pulse. His senses weren't too good, but he felt it — weak, but there. The red stain stretched to the door. She had obviously been stabbed some time before, in another room, and had dragged herself in here to find him. He didn't wish to think how long it had taken her. He lifted his hand and looked at his watch. 1.30!

Unzipping his anorak he shrugged out of it. His limbs felt very heavy. Leaving the knife where it was, he placed the anorak over her, as much to cover her nakedness as to keep her warm. The blue material was smeared in blood from where she had lain on him. He knew that he had to get an ambulance quickly if there was to be any chance at all of saving her life. Then he thought of Peter.

He stumbled to his feet and nearly fell over as the pain flooded through his head again and life came back to his stiff limbs. He remembered the note and lowered himself carefully to his knees so that he could keep his head upright. He removed the bayonet and slid the note from its blade. It was an address in the Trossachs, Scotland. He pushed it into his trouser pocket and rose to his feet. It was slightly less painful this time. Then he negotiated the door and lurched out of the room to look for a telephone, still clutching the bayonet.

There was nothing in the hall so he searched the other ground-floor rooms. A trail of blood led from almost every one. It *had* taken her a long time to find him. All the rooms were as bare as the one he'd been in for over twelve hours. Blankets covered all the windows, but there was enough light to see by.

He was just leaving one room when he noticed an odd-looking bundle in a corner. On drawing closer he saw that it was a man, in army combat gear, with a small, red circle in his back. It looked like Brown, but he knew it couldn't be. He bent down tentatively — more out of deference for his head than from fear of attack — and turned the man over. He had a crimson circle in the front too, but there was hardly any blood and this hole was directly over the heart. The bullet, Calder surmised, had passed right through and he had died instantly. Not exactly a brilliant deduction, but then he wasn't feeling all that bright.

The face was vaguely familiar. He searched his memory. It was difficult, but he came up with an image from the small gallery of snapshots they had sent over the air on the evening they had found Powne. The fellow's name was Wilson and by all accounts he was a pretty big fish in Brown's set-up. Well, now he was dead. There was no remorse.

He thought of Judy and decided that he would have to speculate later. He rose to his feet again, feeling steadier this time. But now a queasy stomach had joined his head and he was glad he hadn't eaten for nearly twenty hours. He walked to the front door. It opened immediately and he ran out into the bright sunshine. He squinted up at the house and, after about half a minute of adjusting his eyes and scanning the wall, decided that there was no telephone wire. That meant a run to a public telephone, or a nearby house. It would be a risk, knocking at someone's door, but Judy was the immediate problem. Well, at least his brain was working again. There was no point in going back inside to search the upper rooms, so he turned to the road. He hesitated, deciding which way the nearest village would be, chose and began to run, slowly; it could be a long way.

After some time and a number of bends and turns, but no houses with phones, he found himself running down a long, steep hill. The view to his left, down into the valley, was breathtaking and at any other time he might have stopped to admire it. The descent seemed endless and more punishing on his legs than running on the flat. He realized at one point that he was going too fast and slowed, getting into a rhythm. It was a long time since he had done this sort of exercise and a stabbing pain rode in his side with every breath. It was some compensation that it took attention away from the ache inside his skull. But he was fit and he knew he could keep up the same pace for miles.

Finally, he reached the bottom and a junction. A sign read: Vernham Dean $1/2$. There were some cottages on the corner, but since he was so close to the village, where there would almost certainly be a public phone, he turned and kept running.

He was soon entering the cluster of houses and slowed to a walking pace so that he wouldn't call attention to himself. In the centre, he spotted the telephone box, opposite the pub. He walked a small way past it and examined a large signpost, getting some breath back.

Then he entered the still empty phone box and looked at his watch. It was nearly 2 p.m. He picked up the receiver and began to dial 999.

It was only then that he noticed his hands were covered in dried blood. Well, that would have to wait till later too.

He asked for an ambulance and was immediately asked for his name and phone number. He refused to give them, but instead, described the route from the village back to the house.

"There is a woman there who has been stabbed in the stomach," he finished. "I would recommend that a doctor travels with the ambulance. Have you got all that?"

"Yes, but what is your name and number?" came the reply.

He replaced the receiver and dialled the Department. The phone was answered after three rings.

"This is Matthew Calder. I want to speak to the General immediately."

"I'll switch you through, sir."

Stoddard answered within a few seconds. "Hello?"

"This is Matthew. I...."

"Mathew! What's happened?" came the urgent voice.

"I'm afraid Judy's been stabbed. She's still alive, but barely. I've called an ambulance. Tell Peter, would you?"

"I take it he listened to you?" said Stoddard.

Calder could almost feel the tension at the other end of the line, but he kept the General waiting as he gave him the same directions as he had given to the 999 call.

"Did he listen to you?" repeated Stoddard.

Then the pips went. He fumbled in his pocket for another 10 pence coin and managed to insert it before the line went dead.

"Yes," he answered finally. "I'm sorry I haven't been on before now, but Brown put me out for twelve hours."

He hesitated.

"Vaisey wasn't there. But I have an address. I'm going after him."

He was about to replace the receiver.

"Matthew! You're not going alone?"

"No. Your secretary is coming with me. I'm sorry, General, but it's the only way."

This time he did replace the receiver, lifted it again immediately and dialled a Newbury number that he had committed to memory. It rang fourteen times. He counted.

"May I speak to Miss Ann Stuart, please? She is staying with you."

"Just a moment," said an officious female voice.

Ann would know it was him. No one else knew she was there. He wouldn't tell her about Judy, yet.

There was a two-minute delay. He began to imagine ambulances and police cars zooming through the village any minute. He felt in his pocket for another 10 pence piece, but there wasn't one. He'd forgotten how long you got for local calls at weekends.

"I'm putting you through now," said the voice.

"Matthew! I've been frantic. Are you all right?"

He hadn't heard the click.

"I'm fine, but I wish busybodies wouldn't listen in on private conversations."

There was an audible click this time as the telephonist went off the line.

"She's gone," said Ann.

"Yes. Listen. Take down this number in case my money runs out." He gave it. "I'm at a village called Vernham Dean. I've no idea how far it is from Newbury, but there's a signpost here which says: Hungerford, 10 miles, to the west; Upton, $1^3/_4$ miles, to the east; and Linkenholt, $2^1/_4$ miles, to the north."

"Hang on while I write that down," she said.

He repeated it.

"It can't be too far from Newbury," he continued. "If I had to make a guess, I'd say south-west, but I can't be sure. I'm not hanging about here. It's too public. So I'll walk along the road that leads to Linkenholt. And I hope your sense of direction is better than that of other women I've known."

He regretted saying it, instantly. You can't soften seemingly harsh words on the telephone by facial expression. There was a small silence.

"I'll be there as soon as I can," she said. "Anything else?"

He sensed a certain reticence.

"Yes," he answered. "First, don't check out of your hotel, secondly, don't contact the Department or Stoddard, and thirdly, I don't know what I'd do without you."

"This is no time for light-hearted banter, Matthew Calder," she scolded.

"I've never been more serious in my life," he said.

She paused. "I'll be there even sooner."

Then the phone went dead.

He replaced the receiver and left the phone booth, looking around. A couple of people were leaving the pub rather noisily, but no one else was about. It *was* Sunday lunchtime after all, to people who live normally, that is.

He crossed the wide street and began to walk, slowly, up the road that led north to Linkenholt. A picture of Judy flashed across his mind and he forced it away. Dwelling on her wouldn't do any good at all. As he paced, some of the tension left him and he focused on his head once more. The pain had become a dull ache centred over his left eye, but it was getting better. He had to make plans.

If a vehicle came he would get off the road quickly. It could be from the Department. The General might have had vehicles stationed in Newbury for just such a contingency, although he would almost certainly have mentioned it in the planning stage. More likely, he would have sent cars to Newbury on receiving no word from Calder.

He didn't like crossing Stoddard, but it had to be done. He had finally found something that was more important to him. Calder believed he could do better with Vaisey than a posse from the Department. He knew that he might be gambling with countless lives, but he believed he could succeed, whereas he wasn't sure about anyone else. It was as simple as that. It was supremely arrogant, but necessary. It never occurred to him to doubt his own ability, or to wonder whether he could cope with the terrible responsibility and guilt if he failed. As far as he was concerned, what he was doing was the logical and correct thing to do in the circumstances. But failure was, anyway, unthinkable.

When he found a suitable spot along the road, where he could see in both directions, without being seen himself, he would stop and wait. He estimated that Ann would be there within the hour. That would be about 3 p.m. or so.

When she arrived, they would go straight back to her hotel, and he could get cleaned up and changed. Then they would eat. Food was the last thing he felt like at the moment, but he might later. If he didn't, he would force himself to eat it. Then he would phone through and book them into an hotel in Carlisle for the night — ironically, where it had all begun. The route was through Oxford and Banbury, joining the M6 just east of Birmingham. Then it was motorway all the way to the border. If they left straight after the meal, he was sure they could reach Carlisle before midnight, providing there weren't too many lanes closed on the M6.

It was important that they get a good night's sleep. After a hearty breakfast they would buy hiking gear. The address in Scotland sounded very countryfied and hiking would be a good cover. They should be in the Trossachs by early afternoon.

There was no real hurry. As Brown had said, Vaisey wouldn't push the buttons until midnight the next day. The image of Brown made him think of Judy, but fortunately he couldn't dwell on it, as he heard a car approaching. He swivelled round, couldn't see it and jumped behind a nearby tree. His head caught a low branch and he decided then that his priorities had been all wrong; the first thing he was going to do was buy some aspirin.

Chapter 22
Monday, 26 May

ANN FELT THE butterflies start up in her chest as Calder turned the

Volkswagen off the A821 and on to the B829. She looked down at the Ordnance Survey on her lap. Matthew had marked the spot where he thought Vaisey's house would be. They needed to follow this road for a number of miles and then turn off right, on to what seemed like some sort of track. It was well past midday but she wasn't hungry. She turned to Calder.

"Sandwich?" she ventured.

"No, thanks."

Her mind returned to Judy again and what must be going through Peter Striker's mind. She also couldn't help thinking that Matthew shouldn't have let Judy go with him. God, they didn't even know whether she was alive or dead. Matthew had refused to phone Newbury hospital. It was that really which had made her phone Stoddard again, at least that's what she kept telling herself. She had done it after breakfast that morning, while Matthew was settling the bill. To her huge relief the General had approved of Matthew's plan and told her to play along. It didn't make her feel that it was any less of a betrayal, though. She would tell him, but not yet — not until after Vaisey.

He sensed her looking at him and flashed a smile.

"I wouldn't mind some of that coffee, though," he said.

She half-filled the lid of the flask with the still steaming black liquid and handed it over. She had filled the thermos that morning at the hotel. She didn't like black coffee but had suggested to him that she could always add milk. He had agreed that that was the best way to do it, but his mind had been on something else. Besides, she knew it wasn't quite as simple as that. He took sugar and she didn't. To pour milk into one mug and sugar into another, in a moving car, was no joke and, quite frankly, she couldn't be bothered. She had made black coffee with sugar, just as he liked it. This was his second cup and he hadn't noticed. Her butterflies had stopped flapping.

"Are *you* hungry?" he asked suddenly.

"No."

"Have some coffee anyway," he said, handing over the now empty lid.

She bit her lip. "I'm all right," she said.

Well, *he* was driving.

They sat in further silence for a mile or two. Something had occurred to her in the night, while she was lying awake. She was sure there had to be a good argument against it and had said nothing. But now they were nearly there....

"Matthew?"

"Ya?"

"Can't we just jam the radio waves or something, so that the signal can't be sent to trigger the thing?"

228

"Yes, the Department could probably do that. But I'm afraid it's not a very safe proposition."

"Why?"

"Well, to begin with, Vaisey might have a back-up trigger system."

"That's unlikely, surely?" she exclaimed, thinking he was creating difficulties.

"It's not a chance I'd like to take. Besides, there's another major problem. Since we don't know where the bomb is we can't jam the radio waves. It's not logistically possible to do it for every major city in England and, even then, it might be elsewhere. Also, Vaisey's transmitter may be mobile, or it may not be where we think it is at all. We just don't know. We think it's going to be down the road, but do you realize that Brown could be wrong? Vaisey may not be there either."

Well, she'd known there had to be a reason.

"I wouldn't like to play chess with Brown," he said suddenly.

"Why not?"

"Because I'd probably lose."

She decided there was no answer to that and they travelled on in heavy silence. She was torn between leaving him alone with his thoughts, so that he could plan his strategy, and her desire to hug him — to feel a part of him. Most of the feeling of guilt had gone now. The rising fear had pushed it out and she felt the butterflies again.

In a short while, Calder swung off the road on to a mud track, which fortunately was fairly dry. The names of the residences were listed. This was the way, he confirmed. The fine weather had followed them north and the sun shone from a blue and white sky. Calder had been thinking about the information that Crawford had sent him on the added problems of atomic explosions in fine weather. There was clear space to the left so he pulled on to the grass.

"It can't be far up here," he said, "so we'll get out and walk. We don't want to drive up to his front door."

It wasn't as hot outside the car, but it was still shirt-sleeve weather. He opened the hatchback and fitted the rucksacks on their backs. Then he picked up the map, locked the car, walked over to Ann and kissed her full on the lips.

"You choose the most awkward moments to give me the first real kiss of the day," she said.

"When we get this little problem over I'll kiss you all the time," he enjoined confidently.

"Not with that beard you won't," she answered and pulled his hand, adding: "Come on. As you said, it can't be far."

But they were both wrong. They had been walking for over an hour and the sweat was pouring down Calder's back. They had already investigated two lodges and now there was another, showing yellow through the trees. It was an ordinary-looking wooden, hunting lodge, with one floor and rather cramped conditions. The garden, if that is what it was, was overgrown and looked more unkempt than the hillside beyond. By high summer it would be a jungle. He could see no aerials, but thought that they would be at the back of the house, if anywhere at all, and that was screened by trees. A battered Landrover stood to one side. The embossed, faded name on the gate thrust out at him like a challenge. "The Grecian Urn".

Ann grasped his arm.

"Are you sure this is the place?" she whispered.

"Yes," he said, but he could see what she meant. A blackbird was chirping in a nearby bush and the soothing hum of bees could be heard. Shadows on the hill sketched buttercups against deep green. The path that led to the house was covered in splashes of sunlight as the glare penetrated the shade of the silver birches that filled the garden in apparently haphazard fashion.

The scene was so peaceful that for a moment he himself began to doubt that a man in that picturesque little house could destroy Central Manchester in a few seconds.

He unclipped the gate and paint flaked off in his hand.

"Don't forget," he said, "at the appropriate moment, look ill."

They walked towards the lodge. It was strange how, in moments like these, he could make himself feel relaxed. His heart was beating a little faster and the adrenalin was probably beginning to flow, but that was all to the good. His mind felt content. Ann still held his arm, but more tightly now. He looked down at her and smiled.

"There's nothing to worry about," he said.

There was no bell or knocker on the door, so he rapped with his knuckles on the wood. He felt the skin cut on some flaky paint. Nothing happened. He knocked again and waited. He didn't think it was possible for Ann to grip his arm more tightly, but suddenly she did.

"The curtain twitched," she hissed.

They heard a strange, shuffling sound through the thin walls and he sensed there was someone behind the door. Then it opened, quickly.

Neither had seen Vaisey before — not even a photograph — but Judy had described him and his appearance was not something you were likely to forget. It was Vaisey.

Calder's first feeling was one of relief that the man was here. Then it seemed to him that he had been standing, staring, for a number of seconds, which was probably not true. Anyway, it flashed through his mind that Vaisey must have got used to people staring at him a long time ago.

"Hello," said Calder, smiling. "Look, I'm terribly sorry to bother

230

you, but we're, well, we're lost. I wonder whether you can help us? Yours is the first house we've come to for ages."

He held out the map and looked into the thick lenses. It was impossible to see behind them and the man's expression said nothing. It was almost as if he hadn't heard and it occurred to Calder that he could try grabbing him now.

Suddenly, without warning, the scientist threw the door closed with such force that the whole front of the building shook. Calder didn't hesitate. He threw his shoulder against the door. The lock tore away from the rotting wood and he jumped through.

At first he couldn't see Vaisey, because he was looking at the wrong level and it took a few moments for his eyes to adjust to the comparative dark. Then he saw him, moving with incredible speed along the floor, using his arms as legs, the latter dragging behind like useless baggage.

Calder jumped after him, but the crippled scientist was too fast. He was through the door at the far side of the room and had reached up to a kitchen worktop before Calder was across the room. He stopped immediately as he saw what Vaisey was holding. It was a duplicate of the buttoned panel which Brown had shown him. The lips of the man on the floor were drawn back in a snarl and he was panting heavily.

"I knew I was right," he gasped. "You know exactly what this is, don't you?"

As he looked down at Vaisey, it came to Calder how slim the margins of history could be between totally different events. If a speck of dust had caused the gun to misfire at Sarajevo, would the First World War have started at all? Possibly. If the weather and an error of judgement had not caused the German pilot to lose his way, so that he released his bombs over London instead of over open fields, as he had intended, would the bombing of German cities in retaliation and hence British cities as well have occurred during the Second World War? Possibly. If he had grabbed Vaisey at the door, when he was within feet of him, if he had been a little quicker across the room, if he had not been hampered by the rucksack, if he had made different decisions earlier, would he have saved countless lives and the total destruction of Central London, or Birmingham, or Bristol?

"Matthew?" came the tentative call from the door.

Another man in the circumstances might have given up. He would certainly have allowed himself an inward groan of anguish. But Calder was already adjusting his method. So plan "A" had failed. He would just have to try another. He turned to see Ann framed in the doorway.

"Come in, darling," he said. "It seems that Mr Vaisey has us by the short-and-curlies."

He made to move.

"Stay where you are," said Vaisey.

The scientist had recovered a little and his voice was now firm.

"Tell the young lady to come in here and sit in that corner," he said, pointing, his eyes apparently not leaving Calder's face. "You too," he added.

Ann was already by Calder's side.

"May we remove our packs first?" he asked.

"Be very careful," said Vaisey.

They helped each other.

"Just let hers slip off on to the floor," said the scientist. "Don't make any attempt to grasp it."

Calder did as he was told.

"Fine," continued Vaisey. "Now kick them to the side of the room so that they are resting against the wall."

It occurred to Calder that Vaisey must have watched some good thriller movies, as he negotiated the packs to the side of the room. Then he and Ann sat down on the two pink, cane chairs indicated.

Calder forced himself to relax again by examining the inside of the house. In complete contrast to the outside, it was neat and tidy. There was an old-fashioned fireplace in the central wall, with logs stacked alongside. The oak table beside Ann was polished bright and the Persian-looking carpet was spotless. Light shone in columns through the two small front windows and the open door. It was light without being bright in the room. Vaisey was still lying on the floor in the kitchen.

"Who are you?" he asked.

"My name is Calder. This is Miss Stuart. We both work for MI5. Judy told us that you were going to explode the bomb and...."

"*The* bomb? *My* bomb!" interrupted Vaisey fiercely. "And you were going to stop me."

A strange wheezing sound came from his throat, as if he were choking and fighting for breath. Ann and Calder looked at each other. The latter decided that he was laughing. He stopped suddenly.

"How did you know where to find me?"

"With great difficulty, but once we found out who you were, things got easier. A nationwide checking system connected you with this place. You're not exactly Mr Average. People remember you."

The last thing he wanted to do was tell Vaisey that Brown had told him. The scientist was looking at him, considering. He found it disconcerting that the lenses of the man's spectacles made it impossible for him to see the eyes. It was his tuning stick as well as his weapon. Vaisey was not the one who was virtually blind.

"Please do not move, Mr Calder. One press of these buttons and you know what will happen."

He put the little box down on the worktop and proceeded to lever himself up. He was about fifteen feet from Calder. Three presses, Brown had said, in sequence. Could he reach him in time? After all, Vaisey had now to pick it up first before he could press it three times. Surely he could cover the distance before that happened? But, as he thought it, he knew that he couldn't. He had already seen how quickly the man could move when he wanted to. It just wasn't worth the risk.

Vaisey picked up the buttoned box and moved over to the door. He glanced outside and back again at Calder. This he did very swiftly a number of times. Then he closed the door as best he could and moved to the centre of the room. Calder spoke.

"I see your incapacity doesn't hinder your mobility a great deal."

Vaisey wheezed again before answering.

"Flattery will get you nowhere."

"How did you know," asked Calder, changing tack, "when we were at the door?"

The scientist sighed.

"You people. I didn't for certain, but you gave yourself away. You see, when people see me for the first time they behave oddly. I'm such a ghastly sight that they usually do one of three things: give a terrified grin and turn away; smile patronizingly; or they stare, as you did, wondering how to talk to me. I've got used to it now and I don't notice it. What I do notice is when someone reacts differently, however minutely. You didn't show enough surprised horror and you didn't stare for quite long enough. You knew what to expect. I also saw something in your eyes. I sensed something."

He seemed quite pleased with himself, but Calder couldn't tell from his countenance, just his voice.

"Your arriving is a nuisance though. I shall have to explode it earlier now. Unless I can keep you like that for nine hours. Actually, why can't I do just that? You'll wait, thinking that my concentration might slip at some stage and fancying that you can take this off me."

Calder saw the teeth again, paradoxically perfect, and thought he caught a gleam behind the lenses. The scientist seemed to have made an error of judgement. As far as he knew, if Calder and Ann didn't show, a back-up team would come in. Vaisey wasn't to know that no one else knew of the place.

"But why?" asked Calder, to occupy the man's mind with something else. "Why kill hundreds of thousands of innocent people? Is that so corny that —"

"Innocent!?" The word was almost screamed. "If you had looked like me from your early teens, Calder, with a reasonably intelligent brain on your shoulders, you would not ask such an absurd question. People treat me like dirt. The only parts of me that are not scarred in some way are my hair — that grew again — and my testes. I have feelings like everyone else. I can even reproduce the species."

He laughed for a long time before continuing.

"However, women do not interest me. Instead, I have to...."

He broke off and snarled, then quietened down. When he began again he was calm.

"Only two people have shown me any respect recently. One is Judy and the other is John Brown, who, I take it, you know about. Oh, yes, Brown used me, but not like the others. He respected my work."

Ann couldn't remain quiet any longer.

"But you can't blame everyone," she said. "Those who die will not have known you. Surely *they* are innocent?"

Vaisey seemed to look at her for the first time.

"I don't think you understand," he said. "Everyone is the same. The fact that they have not met me is irrelevant. They would react the same way if they ever did. They are part of the same shameful, corrupt system. Why should I not destroy it?"

He lifted his head and appeared to be looking above Ann as he continued.

"The race needs a shock to the system. Only good can come of it in the end."

Ann was silent.

"And what about Judy?" asked Calder.

The scientist was slow to react, as if coming out of some sort of daydream.

"What about her?" he asked eventually.

"Brown has stabbed her."

"I don't believe it," said Vaisey.

"She escaped and came to us. She told us that you would explode the bomb and came with me to see Brown, to find out where you were. She did it because she cared about people. She risked her life to save those lives that you are dismissing as so much rubbish. And Brown stabbed her in the stomach."

Vaisey was silent for a while.

"Is this true?" he asked shortly.

It was impossible to see exactly where he was looking and Ann didn't realize for a few moments that the question was directed at her.

"Yes," came the eventual reply.

Calder reasoned that Vaisey would be used to that sort of delay and would not read anything more into Ann's hesitation. The cripple lifted his head and appeared to gaze over her head again.

Calder realized then that he had made an unforgivable, fatal error. What felt like a black crow flapped its wings in his chest.

"Is she dead?" asked Vaisey.

"I don't know," answered Calder carefully.

"Where is she now?" persisted the scientist.

"Newbury General, I expect."

"I believe you," said Vaisey. "And in that case I have no need to wait until midnight. If I am going to get caught, then so can Brown."

Calder felt Ann look at him. He knew exactly what she was thinking. The bird felt as if it was about to take off.

"What *do* you believe in, Vaisey?" he asked desperately.

"Myself," came the immediate reply. "And very soon, so will those ignorant pigs who spurned my brilliance because they couldn't bear to look at me."

For the first time for as long as Calder could remember, he felt totally lost. He'd known before he came why Vaisey was doing it, but now he was here he couldn't stop him. The crow had apparently changed its mind and was now just flapping its wings slowly.

"You know they'll probably kill you," said Calder absently.

The wheezing started up again.

"You really don't understand, do you Calder? Don't you see? I don't care. It sounds pathetic, but I really do have nothing to live for. If I didn't press these buttons I would not be being fair to myself."

Ann made to speak.

"And please, young lady," said Vaisey, "spare me your sympathetic platitudes. I don't need them."

He looked at the deadly, black box in his right palm. Then he looked up and spoke.

"If there is a real sinner in all this, it's not me. Nor is it Brown. He was merely showing an entrepreneurial spirit that has been lacking in this country for many years. Perhaps it is your fault for not stopping me," he said unforgivably. "After all, that is your job."

He looked at the little box again and so did Calder. There was no outward manifestation that the decision had been made, but Calder leapt off his seat in the same instant that Vaisey's left hand began to move.

The next few moments appeared to occur in slow motion. He seemed to float through the air as he watched the index finger travel across the tiny box — one green, one red, one green. Then things speeded up as he cannoned into Vaisey, knocking him down and sending his spectacles flying.

He knew he was too late. He knew it by the sublime look on the scientist's face. The now completely blind man began to laugh.

Calder levered himself up into a sitting position and looked at Ann. Her mouth was open and she was staring at the cripple. The fireball was reaching its limit now and the blast wave was following. Soon, most people within that three-and-a-half-mile circle would be either crushed or destroyed by burns, if not already. More would die or suffer, terrifyingly, from radiation. How many tens of thousands had already died because he had not covered that short distance across the room more quickly; because he had been so arrogant as to believe that he could sort out everything on his own; because he had been so moronically stupid? He didn't even know what city he had destroyed, but was in no hurry to ask.

He became conscious of the absolute silence. Vaisey had ceased to laugh and even the birds seemed to have stopped singing. The crow had died. Ann was staring at *him* now.

Then a shadow appeared in the room and he looked up to see Peter Striker standing in the kitchen doorway, his face like death. Calder, already numb, failed to react — just gazed at his friend. Striker was looking at Vaisey, but the scientist couldn't see him. The blond man said:

"She told me where to find you. Before she died."

Vaisley stirred and looked in the direction of the voice.

"I decided to come up and give you a hand," said Striker hollowly.

Still no one else spoke. Striker was looking at Calder now.

"Don't worry, pardner," he said, his face still empty of expression. "I disabled his transmitter a couple of minutes ago. It's in a shed with a generator out in the field. Everything's OK now."

With that he turned and walked out the way he had come. Calder and Ann watched him go. They still said nothing. There was nothing to say.